CW00553351

The Hole Opportunity

Book I of the Hole Trilogy

Revised Edition

James Minter

MINTER PUBLISHING LIMITED

MINTER PUBLISHING LIMITED

Minter Publishing Limited (MPL)
Cheltenham, UK

Copyright © James Minter 2011 - 2023

James Minter has asserted his rights under the Copyright,
Design and Patents Act, 1988 to be the author of this work
Edition 1 – ISBN-13: 978-1-466375-18-5
Revised Edition – ISBN-13: 978-1-910727-51-5

Cover Illustrations copyright © Paul Shinn

Printed and bound in Great Britain by Amazon

What people are saying about
The Hole Opportunity:

Minter manages to do it again, blending simple everyday life with the most extreme and incredulous events, all combined to produce another piece of humoristic brilliance.
J.J Collins

Whimsical entertainment EVERY adult should read! I wasn't expecting such an entertaining story. Loved every minute! This is the kind of humour we stressed-out adults need in our lives!
Maureen

I liked the plot and found the last few chapters held my attention and at this stage there was pace and plenty of action and it was a page turner for me.
Mim Gamble

…a rollicking tale of colourful characters and humorous happenings. Sprinkled liberally with British witticism and flavourful turn of phrase…
J.C. Wing

Rough and ready romp - a fab celebration of English humour. Cheering. Kind. Fun.
Cherry Coombe

The story is unconventionally crafted introducing unlikely scenarios, consequences and events combined with some extremely amusing tongue-in-cheek moments.
Welly Jen

I like the way you write, and the start of the book gripped me and I couldn't put it down until I knew what happened to Jimmy.
Max Field

…vintage Minter in the combination of the catastrophic with the everyday. The humour of the characters and the situations keeps the whole thing frothing. **Tony Sims**

DEDICATION

To everyone who lets their inner child out to play

CONTENTS

Acknowledgments

1	We Need Money	1
2	Rabbodig Machine	18
3	Bank Loan	33
4	Planning and Preparation	44
5	Stockings and Traps	51
6	Pass Muster	63
7	Colin's Fame Spreads	76
8	Do rabbits have watches?	91
9	Golf Buggy	102
10	Resolute Rabbits	120
11	An Uncertain Future	141
12	Suspected of Murder	158
13	Fake News	176
14	Flanagan Fails To Impress	184
15	For My Eyes Only	202
16	Linda Comes Up Trumps	217

17 Griggs' Saves the Day   234

18 Account Review   244

19 Lady Wills' Arrival   262

20 Social Climbing   281

21 Party Animal   300

22 Everything's in the Detail   326

23 A kiss from Henry   341

24 Reach for the Sky   357

25 Intensive Care Unit   394

    Extract of Book II of the Hole Trilogy   431

    About the Author   443

    Other Works by James Minter   444

ACKNOWLEDGMENTS

A heartfelt shoutout to my wife, Maggie! She's the unsung hero behind my caffeination, the most patient listener to my wild ideas, and an expert toast-with-Marmite maker. (Also, let's not forget those bacon and egg sandwiches).

Big love to Louise, my daughter, who added her sprinkle of magic with her thoughts on the story and cover artwork. And to my son Paul - always keeping it real with his feedback, no sugar-coating involved.

Tip of the hat to Harmony Kent, our wizard of words! She not only worked her copy-editing and proofing magic but did so without making me feel like I'd stepped out wearing two different shoes.

Last, but not at all least, kudos to Paul Shinn for the cover illustration. You know they say, "Never judge a book by its cover"? Well, I think our cover begs to differ. Every time I glance at it, I'm convinced Paul just 'got' the vibe of the story. Perfectly. www.paulshinndraws.com

CHAPTER 1

WE NEED MONEY

'We need money!' Colin couldn't be any clearer. 'Did you hear me, Izzy?' The sound of the postman distracted him. He glared toward the front door. 'All the post we ever get are great tomes; directives, forms, surveys and statistics. You'd think the Ministry of Ag and Fish—'

'You mean DEFRA.' Izzy interrupted him.

'What?'

'It's DEFRA now, not Ag and Fish. They changed their name in 2002. You need to keep up Colin.'

'Okay DEFRA, but you'd think they'd have something better to do. I'm fed up with it. I'm not a bleeding pen pusher. All I want to do is farm.' He held his head in his hands.

She tried to make herself invisible clearing away the breakfast dishes.

'We'll get by somehow; we always do. You wait and see, something will come along.' Izzy's optimism felt out of place, even to her.

'Come along! What do you mean, come along? I just want to do what I know, what I'm good at. I'm a fourth-generation Griggs. Dad farmed here 60 years, like his father and his father before him.' Colin's voice trailed away; his head dropped further.

'Things are different now Colin; we can't live in the

past; we've got to look forward, keep up with the times. You like watching Formula 1 on TV.' Izzy sounded cheery.

'What's that got to do with the price of eggs?'

'Without progress, new ideas, new ways of doing things, we couldn't enjoy the benefits.'

'It doesn't alter the fact that to grow cereals I have to plant the seed, nurture it, wait for it to ripen and harvest it. That's what farming is. I'm a farmer and have been all my life.' Standing purposefully, Colin pushed his chair back; it hit against the fridge. Heading for the front door, he was met by an assortment of manila envelopes scattered on the hall floor like flotsam on a desolate beach.

'Look at this bloody post.' He kicked at it, trying to find something other than bills and official bumph. He failed. The front door slammed. Through the kitchen window, Izzy watched him mooch about the farmyard.

She wanted to be supportive but knew he'd have to arrive at some sort of plan himself. *If nothing else*, she thought, *the least I could do is read the post before he does.* One by one, she picked them up; bill, bill, junk, DEFRA, junk, and one C5-sized envelope which seemed empty. She held it up to the light; she could see the outline of a small square of paper. With the post collected on the kitchen table, she took up the paring knife and slit open each envelope. The junk was relegated to recycling, while she extracted the contents of the rest into separate piles. Finally, using two fingers, she reached into the C5 envelope and fished around to retrieve the folded sheet. She read it. It didn't take long; it only contained a few dozen words, none of which were challenging.

'We don't need this..., not now.' She stuffed the

letter into her pocket before Colin saw it.

He reappeared in the kitchen. Pushing at the piles of correspondence, he muttered incoherently before raising his arm high into the air as if he was on the verge of taking a sweeping swing.

'No! Izzy screeched. 'It won't help. We need a plan. We must look for our strengths; the positives. See what we're good at, so we can take control of our future life direction and fulfil our potential.'

Yeah right, thought Colin; he wasn't sure she knew how to achieve her full potential, let alone his.

'Let's face it, Izzy, we're sunk unless we can come up with another way of earning money, and quickly' His body language spoke volumes.

There'll never be a right time, she thought 'Here.' Izzy withdrew the letter from her pocket and passed it to him.

'What's this?' Dismissive, he rolled the paper into a ball. Like a dart-thrower, he aimed his focus on the recycling box. 'We need to concentrate on our future, what we're going to do next.' He followed through; it bounced off the side onto the floor. He kicked at it.

She reached down to pick it up. 'You really do need to read it.' Izzy turned away, knowing he'd overreact. All she heard was a mighty thump as his fist hit the wood of the table.

'Izzy,' his voice was muted. The lump in his throat made speaking difficult. He tried again. 'Izzy, what on earth are we going to do?' She didn't answer. In the silence, he reread the curt note. 'For goodness sake, when did we get this? How long have you known?' He scratched his head.

'Just now, it was in the morning post.' She kept

her distance. Everyone has their breaking point and she feared this was his.

'What does it mean?' He read aloud. 'Applications for subsidy payments are only accepted via the DEFRA website.' He stabbed at the text with his finger. 'What's wrong with a bloody pen and paper?' He continued his outburst; she retreated to the far side of the kitchen. Looking at him, she noticed the blood had drained from his face, his ruddy complexion replaced by a pale, haunting look.

'Are you okay, Colin?' He'd slumped back in a chair. 'Speak to me.' She was across the room in an instant. 'What is it?' His eyes were glazed and breathing shallow, but at least he was quiet now. She placed her hand on his forehead. 'You're cold. Colin, what's wrong?'

After what seemed an age, he let out a long sigh. He took deep breaths, and the colour started returning to his cheeks as he shook himself like a wet dog.

'I dunno, I felt all light-headed, as if I was going to faint.' His voice sounded more normal, calm and controlled. 'What are we going to do? We have no money, and by the time we reapply, it'll be next year.'

Not to be defeated, Izzy responded in a typically English manner and set off to put the kettle on.

'Tea?' The normality of the question and the comfort in her voice brought him back to the here and now and away from the Armageddon his thoughts had taken him to.

'What are we going to do, Izzy? We've no time to lose. What were you saying about strengths, achieving our potential and making plans? How do we start?' Colin grasped at straws.

She wasn't prepared for the tirade and was still pouring milk. 'Umm, well, you know,' she stirred his mug, trying to buy herself some time.

'Pen and paper, we need a pen and paper.' He said.

'Look in the printer; there's loads of paper.'

Snatching up a sheet, Colin opened the draw in the table and rummaged; triumphant, he held up a pen. Across the top of the sheet, he wrote 'Plan for the Future'. Surveying what he'd written, he crossed out the 'the' and substituted 'Our' instead. Colin clicked the ballpoint pen once, paused, and then clicked it again before placing its tip on the paper. Curious to see what would come next, Izzy looked over his shoulder. He curled his arm around, much like a shy schoolboy obscuring his jottings.

'Give me a break.'

She turned away and sat at the far end of the table. The silence hung heavy, broken only by the repeated clicks of the pen.

'Is that really necessary?' She said.

'It helps me think.' He kept clicking.

She reached into the drawer, pulled out a biro and threw it in his direction. It hit his hand. Snatching it up, he did a test scribble. The imprint was clear, but the ink wasn't. He resumed clicking his ballpoint.

'Colin, for goodness sake.'

'Right; Strengths,' he had written it before he had finished saying it. 'So, what are our strengths?'

'Retracting a ballpoint.'

'That's not helpful Izzy.' However, the corners of his mouth curled. He couldn't help smiling. 'Yes, it's our future; yes, it's vitally important; yes, we need to do this together. Sorry but—'

She cut him off. 'Together,' she emphasised, 'is the key to our future success.' She smiled back at him. 'We have 180 acres of arable land. That's got to be a strength.'

'And a farming history of over 100 years. So how did we get here?' Colin dropped his pen and flopped back into the chair.

'Box.' She wouldn't let the moment pass. 'That's what they're always saying.'

'What on earth do you mean? Box!' Colin's brow furrowed.

'You know, we've got to think outside the box, think beyond arable farming, expand our horizons, be creative.'

'That's easy to say, but I'm just a farmer!'

'Don't go huffy on me. That's exactly how we got here. Farming has changed beyond all recognition, but we haven't. It's time for some blue-sky thinking. We need to re-evaluate our options, take stock of our resources, and examine our achievements.'

'What have you been reading, Izzy? Blue-sky thinking, struth! All I want to do is grow cereal.'

'Then you need to become friends with DEFRA and computers instead of—'

'Instead of what?' He stared hard at her.

'Instead of floundering around like you're doing now. Do you really want to continue farming?'

'Of course.'

'But you don't like DEFRA.'

'Give me the Ministry of Ag and Fish any day!'

'Nor computers.'

'I just don't understand them.'

'Do you mind what you farm?'

Colin rolled his eyes up and to the left. 'Not really.'

'Okay then, outside the box. What about—,' Izzy held her finger on her lips, 'trout farming?'

'Are you serious?'

'Well, fish is a major source of protein. Fish farms are the future, the new cash crop.'

'That sounds to me like out of the frying pan into the fire!'

'Only if you want to barbeque the fish!' She smiled.

'Well, outside the box, I don't rate your chances as a stand-up comedian. Another thing, fish require water and lots of it which we don't have; any more ideas?'

'Hydroponics.'

'Water.'

'Yes, but not as much. Have you any ideas?' She pushed back.

'Coal farming.'

'Colin, at times you make me so angry—'

'I know, I know, I didn't mean to say that. I was just sort of thinking out loud.'

'So what other ideas do you have? Now think before you speak.'

'Okay, outside the box… umm; ant farming.'

Izzy had just taken a swig of tea. It was now dispersed over the kitchen table.

'Ant farming! Did I hear you right? Did you say ant farming?' She wiped her mouth. 'Right Colin Griggs, let's try another approach. What does everyone use every day?' She spoke slowly. 'What's in short supply? What'll will be in greater demand in the future, and how can we satisfy that demand with our land, skills and resources?' She waited for his reaction. 'If you can answer these questions, then we're onto a winner.'

She busied herself with chores. Colin sat, staring at the sheet of paper, and doodled.

He repeated her list in his head. *What does everyone use every day? Water.* He wrote it with a flurry. *Wash, soap, take a pee, toilet paper, razor blades, towels, shaving foam, aftershave!*

'This is more like a bloody shopping list for a chemist.' Colin crossed through the lot, screwed up the paper, and took another clean sheet.

Izzy'd been watching him out of the corner of her eye. 'Are you there yet?'

He said nothing, only stared at the blank sheet. 'This is hurting my head.' Colin massaged his temples.

She came across from the other side of the room and switched on the computer.

'That's it!' He jumped up and flung his arms around her. 'That's it! Don't you see? You said it yourself. What does everyone use every day? You're a genius.'

'What? Computers? You want to farm computers? You've really lost it this time.'

'No, I'm not a complete idiot. Don't you see? What makes computers work? Or the toaster, or the washing machine, or the kettle or food mixer.' He pointed at each device with a look on his face saying, for goodness sake, woman, don't you get what I mean.

'Well, in this house Colin Griggs, what makes all those things work is me. I'm the one who uses the computer, makes toast, loads the washing machine and cooks the meals.'

'No, no, no Izzy.'

'Yes, yes, yes, Colin. They don't work themselves, and it's not the fairies.'

'No, I don't mean you don't work them. What I mean is, what do they all need to make them work?' He was across the kitchen to the light switch, turning it on and off repeatedly. Staring at the bulb as if seeing it for the first time, his face lit up emotionally and literally.

'Stop that now, or you'll blow it. Anyway Edison, how is that going to help us?'

'Wind farming! Don't you see? We have acres of land. There's a 'green revolution'. I'm sure this is the answer to our problems. Think about it. In the lower field, we could site half a dozen windmills.'

'Wind turbines.'

'Yeah, okay, wind turbines, and hey presto, we're in the money.'

'If it's so easy, why doesn't everyone do it?' She waited for an answer, but none was forthcoming. He was back at the table, scribbling away.

'You might be onto something but —' she said.

'Yeah, I know your buts. That's what I'm doing now, or trying to if you'll let me get on with it.' Colin busied.

She left him to it.

After several minutes, he emerged waving a handful of paper. Izzy was in the utility room unloading the washing machine.

'Here, Izzy.' He thrust the papers toward her. 'Look at the calculations. Based on the current kilowatt-hour rate, if we had six wind turbines, we'd be better off by some £90,000 per year. I don't know why we didn't think of this years ago?' At that, he grabbed the washing basket from her, before sweeping her into his arms and waltzing back into the kitchen. All she could do was hang on and let herself be led around, and around, the table until she was quite dizzy.

'Stop, Colin, please stop!'

He made no change to his pace.

'I'm going to be sick.'

He relented. They came to a halt, although for Izzy the room was still spinning.

'I've got to sit down.' She collapsed into the nearest chair. Holding an imaginary partner, Colin was off again.

'For Pete's sake, stop! Yes, it looks like a good idea on paper, but there's a long way to go. What do we need to do to get this thing off the ground?'

Without notice, he stopped and faced her. 'Can't I just enjoy my idea for a bit longer?'

'You can celebrate till the cows come home once we've got payment for our electricity, but until then, no more. Now the tricky part begins. Investment needs, planning, contracts, satisfying local opposition. Wind direction and velocity evaluation. This is big Colin, massive!'

'Do you really think the locals will oppose the turbines?' He hadn't been listening. 'How could they? It's our land. Anyway, we've got no close neighbours.' He started dancing again.

'Do your sums, think it through and come back to me with facts and figures.'

Over the next few hours, she saw little of him as he beavered away on his plans. Occasionally he asked her to look up something on the internet.

'Right, my love, this is it.' Colin held a triumphant smile like he'd got a winning lottery ticket. After a paper shuffle and some final edits, he was ready to reveal his findings. The build-up was longer than the presentation.

'Half a million for the site preparation, ancillary buildings and turbines!'

Izzy's voice shot up an octave as she repeated him. 'Colin, what planet are you on? I can't believe you've taken, I don't know how long, faffing around with this.' Her hand swept across his papers scattered over the table. 'How could we raise half a million?'

'Hey, not so quick. We could sell off most of the land. That should do it.' He beamed at her.

'Why not go the whole hog and sell off the farm and buildings as well? That way, we could retire to a little place in the village. This sounds less risky to me.'

'That's blasphemy! We're fourth generation Griggs. This is our farm, our home, our past and our future.' Colin beat his fists in time with his words. 'We can't sell it; any of it.' His passion brought a red glow to his face until it looked like a Chinese lantern.

'Sounds to me like that's the end of the wind turbine project.' Izzy headed for the kettle. Tea is always good for shock.

Her words cut deep into his psyche. As he

realised the truth, his demeanour changed. He dropped his head, his energy ebbed, and clouds of gloom gathered. Pessimism reigned once again.

The next day, to cheer him up, Izzy bought Colin a doughnut. It didn't; instead, he pushed it half-heartedly around the plate while he slipped further into the depths of despair. Its bright pink icing, littered with hundreds and thousands, taunted him. Jolly, vibrant, and beckoning, its appearance was in dark contrast to how he was feeling. He turned it over to expose its brown underside. Forlorn and dejected, that side better reflected his mood. He considered it long and hard. It was then he noticed the hole.

'Izzy!' He had to tell her as his new business idea grabbed him. 'Remember at school how I wasn't good at the academic stuff.'

She nodded, wondering what was coming next.

'Well, I remember one thing.'

'What's that?' Izzy took a sip of her coffee.

'That quote by that Ozzie Wilde fellow. You know, we did it in English.'

'Oscar, I think you mean.'

'Whatever, but he said the difference between an optimist and a pessimist is the optimist sees the doughnut while the pessimist sees the hole.' Colin rubbed at his chin.

'What are you prattling on about?' Lines formed on Izzy's forehead.

'Look here, my doughnut—' He pushed the plate toward her.

She peered at it. 'And?'

'He was so wrong.' Colin's demeanour changed; he pulled himself up in his seat at the same time his facial expression turned into an ear to ear grin.

'What do you mean?'

'Our future's in holes!' He jumped up and skipped around the kitchen, peering at all the electrical sockets and pointing.

'For goodness sake, Colin, I've better things to do. Now get out of my way until you've come to your senses.' She continued busying herself. 'And please, no more of these hare-brained schemes.' She threw her arms up.

He took himself off to the sitting room and his favourite chair. From there, he could see four electrical sockets, each with three holes making twelve straight off. He resisted rushing out to tell her the great news; he wanted to be sure of the facts. *No, I must finish counting up the whole hole opportunity*, he thought, *so where am I? Eighteen in the bedrooms, two in the bathroom and six on the landing: that makes thirty-six in our home alone.*

With twenty-eight million homes in England, she can't fail to see the opportunity; the number's enormous!

'Izzy, where are you?' Colin darted from room to room until he found her in the yard, throwing poultry feed for the chickens.

Over the din, he shouted, 'No more chicken feeding for you my love.' Holding up his scrap of paper, 'Just look at these numbers. Holes for sockets alone run into millions and millions. Our farm is saved; we are saved!' His elation was reflected his in an impromptu dance.

She neither heard him nor saw the numbers, but only this demented figure leaping around and mouthing something about how electrical sockets in every home would save her and the farm.

'Stop Colin; I'll be finished in a minute. Tell me then.' She waved a dismissive hand.

When she arrived back in the kitchen.

He was waiting by the back door. 'Quick, look here.' He said.

Izzy glanced at his workings. 'That's all well and good, and there are probably 2.5 billion sockets, but they already exist. So there's no need for your "hole" business.'

'I know that, this is just to show you how necessary holes are and used by all of us every day. Holes are everywhere and needed by everyone all the time. Just look around you.' He spun on his heels. 'Here, on the back of the chair, the crocheted antimacassar. It has at least 200 holes, and someone had to make them. And see here,' he went on. 'Just take that drawer out of the sideboard, and what do you find? The hole it slides into. Or here,' pointing at the door, 'every time you walk from room to room, what do you go through? A hole! The doorway is just another hole. And here,' he felt in his pocket and pulled out a tube of mints, 'even here.'

His big round face transformed with a broad smile and wide eyes. And what Izzy thought was most amusing was how his nose holes seemed larger than ever as he breathed in his new idea, his newfound fortune, and solution to their money problems.

'You might be right, but we're farmers, not builders, nor furniture makers or even sweet makers. How is this whole hole business thingy, going to work for us?'

He thought for a while. 'Okay, for starters we have that area of rough pasture where we can dig holes and sell them to whomever.'

'Rabbits,' chipped in Izzy, getting into the spirit of things. 'They need holes, and moles and foxes and badgers—'

'No, no, no.'

'Yes, they do. They all live in holes. Over the last goodness knows how many years, all you've ever done is complain about the holes of rabbits, badgers—'

'I know that, but they won't buy my holes, will they? Anyway, they're more than capable of making their own. Actually, now you come to mention it, you may be on to something.' He looked guarded. 'Not selling holes to rabbits or badgers or foxes, but getting them to dig holes for us. What a splendid idea! A whole army, or should it be a 'hole' army, of diggers, waiting and ready!' He rubbed at his moustache as he considered the option.

'Okay, so how can we get them to work for us?' Izzy needed convincing.

They both fell silent. Colin kicked off his boots to reveal a large hole in the big toe of his sock. She noticed but thought to say nothing, just in case he wanted to sell that hole too!

'Well,' she said, 'moles dig long slim holes ideal for someone wanting to lay a water pipe. Foxes, on the other hand, dig wide, deep sets, ideal for someone wanting a...?' She paused and thought for a while.

'For someone wanting a wide, deep-set?'

'Come on, Colin. I'm only trying to be helpful.' The clock on the sideboard struck six. 'You set the table, and I'll finish cooking supper.'

The needs of his stomach replaced all thoughts of holes.

'What are we having, my love?'

'Rabbit stew,' she said it without thinking.

'No, Izzy. No more rabbit stew or we'll have no workers left!'

'Lucky cows don't dig holes then.'

Confronted by his rabbit stew, his appetite had gone. Ordinarily, he'd ask for seconds, if not thirds, but the thought of eating his workers made it taste distinctly different. *After all, no matter what type of boss you are, everyone draws the line at eating their workers.* Remembering they breed like rabbits so that it wouldn't be long before the couple in the stew would be replaced, he sheepishly ate his food and asked for seconds.

After dinner, the clearing was accompanied by incessant chatter, with Izzy asking many troublesome questions about the new hole business and Colin having to give convincing answers. She wouldn't be fobbed off.

Bedtime came, and Colin headed off upstairs to ready himself. Undoing his belt, he noticed a hole in the free end held the buckle in place. *Another example of a hole in use,* he thought. Dropping his trousers, he removed his left leg and then his right from the two holes that formed the pair of trousers. Unbuttoning his shirt, there were more holes, one for each button, before removing both arms from the holes forming the sleeves. All the time, he was thinking, holes, *we can't live without them. They're everywhere!*

Soon Izzy joined him in bed. It wasn't long before they both drifted off into a deep sleep. Within minutes, he was making strange noises followed by sweeping movements of his arms.

'No, you silly rabbit, I want the hole over here. No, don't hop off; you're at work now. Come back.' Arm thrashing accompanied the talking in his dream as he lunged out to restrain the disappearing workers. Grabbing a large handful of Izzy's hair, he lifted her head clear off the pillow.

She woke. 'Colin put me down!'

Startled, he let go. Izzy fell back. He was now fully awake and apologising profusely, trying to explain how rabbits weren't good at taking orders, but instead, they kept hopping off or wandering around or just eating carrots; and how they had no sense of urgency or commitment.

She listened to his woeful chatter about his dream and the realisation that rabbits weren't the answer to his workforce of diggers. His 'hole' business was slowly fading.

A sly look came over his face. 'That's it,' he said, 'rabbits free to roam are useless. What's needed are cages! We place a rabbit in a cage with no floor, over the ground where we want the hole dug, and hey presto, a hole exactly where we want it.'

Bolstered by his revised idea, Colin settled; within seconds, his rhythmic breathing told Izzy he was asleep. Taking no chances, she sought safety by placing a pillow wall between them.

CHAPTER 2

RABBODIG MACHINE

At first light, with the urgency of an unwinding coiled spring, Colin leapt from the bed. In an instant, he was downstairs searching the kitchen drawers, the dining room cupboard, and shelves in the pantry. The first thing Izzy knew was him standing at the bedroom door quizzing her on if she had seen them.

'Slow down. Seen what?'

'My steel ruler, drawing pencils and that spare roll of wallpaper leftover from decorating the sitting room.'

'Well, the steel rule is wedged under the washing machine, your pencils went to the village hall for the Whist Drive, and the roll of paper's in the cupboard under the stairs.' She felt smug having remembered where all the items were. 'Why?'

'Plans; I've got to draw plans for the rabbit cages. Rather than a single cage, I could have, say, six, ten, twenty or more, side-by-side. Mass production. Think of it; we'll be rich!' He disappeared again.

He unrolled the wallpaper across the kitchen table. It curled back up. 'Blast. Come on, stay put.' He resorted to using the pepper and salt pots along with the mustard dish for weights to keep it in place. Rummaging in the kitchen drawer, he found a pencil stub, and from the bookshelf, he took a large world atlas to act as a straight edge. *Not ideal,* he thought, *but good enough.*

He was fortunate to have an entire roll of wallpaper, allowing him to restart his design several times to include various refinements. He added a way of linking cages together so he could form groups depending on the order size. *Ingenious,* he thought. *Don't forget they'll need water and food while digging, as a happy workforce is a productive workforce.* His design evolved. Soon he worked out how much timber, wire mesh, plastic tubing, trays, latches, and hinges he'd need. Brandishing a lengthy shopping list, he called upstairs.

'Izzy, I'm off to Hartwells.' He closed the kitchen door and headed across the yard toward Old Alfred Mac, his flatbed lorry; he heard her calling him back.

'You've had no breakfast, and it's only 7 o'clock. Hartwells won't be open for another two hours. And you're still in your pyjamas!' *That's typical of him,* she thought. *Once he has an idea in his head, everything else gets forgotten.*

'I've got my old coat on.' He left.

Some three hours later, Colin was back. On the spur of the moment, he decided not just to double or even triple his order, but to quadruple it to forty cages. Old Alfred Mac groaned under the weight. Colin popped into the kitchen to tell Izzy all about the thirty percent discount for buying in bulk, and how he was so confident his idea was going to work that he bought all the supplies there and then.

'One thing's occurred to me, Colin, how are we

going to pay for this lot? No doubt you'll need other bits and pieces, but where's the money coming from?' Standing with her hands on her hips, it said to him she wasn't in a mood for any more nonsense.

'Oh, I'm sure we'll find it.'

'By magic, from thin air? You'll need a loan.' Izzy said.

'I'm not good at that sort of thing. I wouldn't know what to do or say.'

'You can't be a businessman making holes alone. You've got to find people, customers, who want to buy them. They've got to know you sell holes. You'll need to become more business savvy, including talking to the Bank Manager. I'll make an appointment for you.' She was determined he'd realise his plan.

'Thanks, Izzy. With you behind me, I know the business will be a success; you wait and see.' At that, Colin vanished, this time into the barn where he had his workshop and tools.

For the next few hours, all she could hear were the sounds of sawing, drilling, hammering and the odd expletive as he hit either his thumb, cut his finger or mis-measured some length of timber, cut it, attached it and then realised it wasn't long enough. Although an excellent farmer, his woodworking skills were not at the top of his list. But what he lacked in skills, he made up for in enthusiasm. He hardly touched the Marmite sandwiches and tea Izzy had brought him.

Late afternoon, Izzy was chasing the geese away from the back door and off toward the pond. Honking and fluttering with her 'phhhhting' at the rear, they processed across the yard. As they neared the barn, the doors flung open; Colin came running out, arms in all directions, gesticulating for her to come and view his masterpiece.

'Now Izzy, come now,' raising his voice to be heard over the racket from the geese. 'I've finished the Rabbodig machine. Come, look, you'll be surprised!'

He wasn't wrong! Greeted by what can best be described as a set of miniature starting gates from a greyhound race track; were a row of ten linked 'traps'. A complex set of levers and cables controlled the door openings. Plus controls for the supply of drinking water and a chute to roll carrots, shaped with a melon ball maker, into feeding trays. Topping the whole contraption was a large wooden sign proclaiming 'Griggs Hole Farming – The Rabbodig Mark I'. She was speechless. The clicking of levers and the clunk of carrot balls hitting the feeding trays broke the silence. Colin was in his element.

'All we need to do now is test it,' he beamed like a child with a new toy. He puffed out his generous chest even further. He didn't say more for the sake of humility, but he knew in his heart of hearts he was on to a winner.

'Right, let's position the Rabbos, in the field just below the pond. The sign just lifts off, and the individual cages can be separated for ease of transportation.' *I like that phrase; sounds so professional and business-like*, he thought.

Each cage was unhooked and carried to the field beyond the pond. Soon all ten were in a nice neat row waiting to be tested.

'Look, my dear, aren't they just the business?'

Colin stood on a mound, arms folded across his chest to admire his hard work.

'No sign!' chirped up, Izzy.

'Oh quick, run and get it for me, we must have the sign.'

Being a dutiful wife, wanting to show support for his business, she collected the sign. While waiting he made final adjustments to the levers and cables and practised opening doors, flowing the water and, the bit he liked best, rolling carrot balls to see how many he could get in a single tray before knocking another one out.

'Thanks, my love.' He placed the sign in its rightful location.

'Right now for the test. We'll have ten holes dug simultaneously, and because of the cages—'

'Colin,' she sounded hesitant.

'Not now dearest—where was I? Because of the cages—'

'Colin.'

'Just a minute, my love. Because of the cages—'

'Colin.' She was more forceful.

'What!'

'This Rabbodig machine, what's it powered by exactly?'

'What do you mean? You know exactly what it's powered by! You're so silly at times.'

'Right, so we have this ummmm, interesting machine,' she thought this was a polite way of putting it, 'positioned where we want the holes—'

'Yes, for test purposes.'

'As you say, for test purposes. So what's missing?' After what seemed an age for a budding entrepreneur, the penny dropped.

'Rabbits!' he spun around, his hands clasping his head,

he looked in all directions. 'We need rabbits and quickly! It'll be dark soon.' He was now in a tizzy.

Izzy came to the rescue. 'You know the old warren in the top field near the woods. They'll be feeding now. If we're quick, we should be able to bag a few before it's too dark.'

'Ideally ten so we can put the Rabbodig to an actual test.'

'Well, let's get moving.'

They ran back to the house to find all the things needed, including several rabbit-sized containers to put their catch in. She found an old leather satchel with only one buckle, her gym kit bag, which was unceremoniously emptied, two 'save the planet' hessian shopping bags, and her largest Tupperware container. Colin diced up half a dozen carrots for bait and grabbed the fabric carrier bag tidy thingy from the kitchen—the one with a hole at each end used to store and dispense old plastic carrier bags—and a fishing net. They met at the back door before setting off across the yard toward the top field.

'Okay, this is what we'll do. First, keep quiet and stay downwind. Rabbits post sentries while eating and will raise the alarm if anyone or anything approaches. From the cover of the bank, you'll throw out handfuls of diced carrot, away from the warren and toward that large bush where I'll be hiding with the net. As each one comes hopping by, I'll slip out and scoop it up and hey presto.'

Hey, presto always makes things sound easy, she thought. *I bet it won't be!*

At the warren, loads of rabbits were enjoying their

evening feed, unaware of the two hunters. Positioned on the bank above the warren, Izzy could see Colin crouched in a large bush, fishing net poised. She threw out a handful of carrots. A few bits fell near a couple of rabbits. They looked up before continuing to eat.

'Come on little rabbits, try the lovely carrots,' she whispered, before tossing another handful, but this time more toward Colin. She watched and waited to see if they'd fall for her bait.

'Oh, come on…' No sooner had she said it when one rabbit picked up the trail and bounced from bit to bit, happily munching. Ever so slowly, it advanced toward her intrepid hunter.

Colin, wondering what was going on, and heaved himself up by a branch to get a better look. It didn't bear his weight; snapping, he hit the ground with sufficient force to wind himself. The cry of pain sent the rabbits scurrying for safety. He picked himself up, dusted himself off, and crept back into the bush. He waited. She raised her eyes to heaven and made a mental note to put him on a diet.

It was another 20 minutes until the rabbits felt safe enough to come out to graze. Slowly emerging from various holes along the bank, they stopped, sniffed the air, and then went about their business. Several found the carrot pieces and were soon on the trail heading in Colin's direction and capture! With one deft move, he'd scooped his first prey and plonked him into the 'save the planet' bag. Seconds later, the bag was hanging from an overhead branch with the rabbit happily chewing on its prize. Within a few more minutes, he had scooped a second and a third and deposited them into other containers. He was feeling pleased with himself.

Izzy, watching from the bank above, had to concede he was doing a great job after a somewhat shaky start.

He scooped up the next rabbit in full flight and plonked him into the linen bag dispenser, which still contained a few plastic bags. Having no time to think, he scooped up a second and third rabbit. These, too, were dropped into the dispenser; stunned by what had happened, their instinct was to remain still. With holes in each end, the long linen tube, an assortment of plastic bags, and captured rabbits inside lay motionless on the ground. Colin bagged one more rabbit and placed him into the large Tupperware container. He closed the lid on three sides, leaving just enough of a gap for it to breathe but not escape.

'Izzy, Izzy,' he hissed. 'Let's call it a day. All the containers are full. We have eight rabbits, and anyway, it's too dark to see. Be careful, my love, the bank's extremely steep.'

It wasn't long before she was by his side, laden with various wriggling bags from which an occasional head or ears appeared. She tried to calm them down using her best baby voice.

'Don't worry, little rabbits, nothing nasty's going to happen to you. You're just part of a testy westy, an experiment. You'll get more water and carrots, and you'll soon be set loose.'

Whether it was her soothing tones, the promise of food and drink, or the thought of being set free, the rabbits seemed less distressed and more resigned to their fate. She was now halfway across the field heading back to the farm, leaving Colin with the fishing net, Tupperware box, and the plastic bag dispenser.

Emerging from the bush with the net and box in one hand, he bent down and grabbed the tie on the linen bag dispenser. He lifted it quickly to shoulder height. There followed a series of thumps. All three occupants fell to the ground amidst a collection of plastic shopping bags. Each one tried to dart for freedom and safety. Surprised at their release, the darkness and through sheer fear, somehow each ended up inside a different plastic bag. Unperturbed, they ran and ran.

Izzy turned to see where Colin was. What greeted her was unexpected. He'd worn dark clothes to blend in with the bush; in the darkness, and was now invisible. All she could make out was a disembodied, angry voice, calling out, 'Back here rabbits, get back here now. I'll not hurt you.'

Lower down the slope, she could see three white ball-shaped objects tumbling, rolling, and swirling at high speed. The entire scene was being played out to the accompaniment of a drumbeat. The occupant of the now-abandoned Tupperware box did what frightened rabbits do best; repeatedly thump their foot to warn others of danger.

Appreciating something was amiss, Izzy set off in pursuit. Gravity brought the wayward rabbits toward her. Soon one startled, bemused and confused rabbit was in her grasp. Finding the bag handles, she turned it the right way up before heading off for another running plastic bag. For this rabbit, too, its ordeal was over. It's world was back up the right way, and it found comfort in the motherly tones of Izzy.

Colin made his way across the field towards her. 'Ringo' in his Tupperware box was still playing out his rhythms, but somewhat less forcefully now.

Colin puffed. 'Let's… get… this… lot… into the cages, and I'll go back for the remaining… bagged… rabbit in a minute.'

By now, the third bag had stopped moving. Colin took this as a sign the rabbit was resting. The truth was, it had long slipped its plastic prison, and under cover of darkness, was away up the hill to the safety of the warren.

The remaining captured rabbits were placed gently into their new temporary home. With great relief all round, the door latches snapped shut, water flowed, and carrots rolled into the feeding trays. Despite a few hiccups, the test had started. By the morning Colin expected a series of expertly dug, accurately placed, quality holes any self-respecting hole farmer would be proud of.

'I'll just get the last rabbit, it'll be exhausted after all the running.' Colin turned, heading for the gate, he made a mental note to mind the pond, as it would be difficult to see in the dark, 'I'll be back as soon as.'

Izzy finished collecting up all the bags, fishing net and other bits and pieces before heading off toward the house, a well-earned bath and bed. 'Oh, that sounds so good,' she mused.

The wind had picked up. Colin felt refreshed after all that chasing around. *Just one more little fella and that's it for tonight.* Close by the five-barred gate, he could see what he thought was the last bagged rabbit, white, like a beacon in the inky black night. Slowing his approach, he went up on tip-toe to reduce the noise of his footfall. Closing in, he grabbed at it. Before his fingers secured a grip, the bag was off running, as if it had the wind behind it. Rising over the gate, it headed across the yard in the pond's direction. In hot pursuit, Colin watched it slow before veering left, directly for the pond.

'No, rabbits can't swim.'

With a leap any Olympic long jumper would be proud of, Colin was airborne, grasping at the disappearing bag. This was immediately followed by an enormous splash, numerous indignant quacks and honks from the pond's natural inhabitants and a more muted 'I've got you' as Colin emerged triumphant with an empty bag and a mouthful of pondweed.

Izzy stepped into a warm, welcoming bath with a mug of tea and thoughts of peaceful bliss. As she did so, the bathroom door flung open. Filling the void was Colin. Not her usual Colin, but a Colin soaked from head to foot, decorated with pondweed, lily pads and a dead branch which happened to be floating in the water at the time. From his jacket pocket popped the head of a somewhat disgruntled frog who had been minding his own business before that.

'I've killed it; drowned it. It's all my fault; I did not mean it to die. No one was supposed to die or get hurt or anything.'

'What are you babbling on about?'

'The plastic bagged rabbit. I got to the gate, and

suddenly it was off again, heading in the direction of the pond. I had to do something quickly. Without thinking, I launched myself at the bag as it flew into the pond. I got a grip on it before going under and emerged still holding the bag, but it was —,' his voice trailed off.

'What? Tell me what.'

'It… it… it —'

'It what Colin?'

'It was empty! I've killed it, drowned it; a poor defenceless rabbit, which only a few minutes earlier had been enjoying its evening food. Now, through no fault of its own, it's dead. And I did it!'

'I know it's unfortunate, but you didn't set out to kill it. Look on the bright side. Maybe it didn't die. It could have swum to the edge and hopped off none the worse for wear. I bet it's back in the warren right now, relaying its adventures to the other rabbits who think how brave it is. Yes, you've probably done it a favour. It's now considered a hero and looked up to.'

Her consoling words helped somewhat. Colin unpeeled his wet clothes, and dropped them in a smelly heap on the bathroom floor.

'Colin, what do you think you're doing?' Her withering look told him she was none too pleased. She could see he was upset by the whole ordeal. 'Okay, just this once…, here.' Retrieving her towel, Izzy sacrificed her long-awaited bath, swapping places with her more deserving husband. And anyway, he smelt foul.

Shaking uncontrollably as the cold set in, he slipped into the warm embrace of the water. It wasn't long before he felt better, especially from the mug of tea so thoughtfully left by the bath. *She is so good to me.*

In another 20 minutes, they were both in bed, lights out and the house in darkness. Colin fell into a deep sleep. Izzy took a bit longer, as she had to listen to the incessant rumblings of his snoring. It reminded her of the old bull his dad used to keep penned up in the yard; grunting and snorting all the time, but she loved him. After all, he was her Colin.

At the test site, all was not quiet or still. Rabbits like to be free, amongst their own. As Colin set up the cages, he paid scant attention to how even the ground was. Independently, two of the rabbits discovered their cages were balanced on tufts of grass, leaving a gap under one corner. Before he'd even clicked the doors shut, they'd squeezed through and were off running. In the dark, he was oblivious.

Rabbits dig holes for the sake of necessity, and escaping is a necessity. Colin's whole design was based on this. True to form, three of the remaining captives dug at various sites within the confines of their respective cages. He would have been pleased if he'd stayed to see it. Scattering earth everywhere, the holes grew in size, and little by little less and less of each rabbit remained above ground while more and more disappeared under it. Soon they'd vanished into a subterranean world on their way to freedom.

What goes up must come down. Here, what went down came up. A metre or so beyond the cage perimeter, three sets of ears followed by three twitching noses emerged into the night air and freedom. Now only two were left. One lucky rabbit ended up in a cage with a host of carrot balls littering the floor—the drive to eat superseded the drive to escape. After gorging itself, it fell asleep dreaming of a rather unusual day and its good fortune.

The last rabbit was not so fortunate. Although the drive to escape was as high as any rabbit's and its ability to dig second to none, the simplest of things easily confused it. While exploring its cage, it found one side was suspended off the ground. Though not big enough to squeeze through, it was an excellent place to dig. The rabbit ripped at the soil before pushing its nose into the gap. It was still too small for the rest of the body. It dug some more. This time it squeezed both head and ears, too. Frustrated, it pulled back and burrowed again. With its nose, head, and ears through, the real test began. A single mighty heave of its powerful front paws hauled itself to freedom. It stopped, listened, and sniffed the black night air. No danger. With a mighty push of its hind legs, it launched itself homeward.

What the rabbit hadn't realised was its escape route led into an adjacent cage. In its leap to freedom, it crashed into one of the timbers Colin had so methodically measured, cut, planed, screwed, and glued in place. Dazed but not perturbed, the rabbit set about exploring its surroundings again. Within minutes, its luck was in. Halfway along one edge of the new cage, it came across a hole which, with a bit of effort, it could squeeze into. It pulled itself through the hole, sat up on its hind legs, and sniffed the air. With another enormous bound, it launched himself skyward. A split second later, the rabbit was lying back on the ground dazed with its head throbbing. It had crashed into another of the timbers Colin had so methodically measured, cut, planed, screwed, and glued in place. The rabbit had gone back through the hole it had dug in the first place and returned to where it had started.

Keeping this toing and froing going until daylight, exhausted, the rabbit crashed out to get some well-deserved sleep.

CHAPTER 3

BANK LOAN

The next morning the farmhouse was buzzing with activity. Colin, refreshed after his bath and deep sleep, was keen to find out how his Rabbodig test had gone. Its success would shape their future. Unable to contain himself, he was out of bed, grabbing for any item of clothing in a desperate rush to get dressed. Bleary-eyed, Izzy couldn't believe what she was seeing as he tried to force himself into her blouse, mistaking it for his white shirt.

'Stop. All your clothes are still in a heap in the bathroom. Remember how you got soaked fishing an empty plastic bag from the duck pond?'

'Oh, don't remind me. How could I forget?'

'You'll need clean everything. Now take my blouse off.'

In his birthday suit, Colin went delving through his drawers for socks, pants, shirt and the like.

'Don't forget,' said Izzy, 'you're seeing the Bank Manager at 11.'

'Bank Manager, I'm not ready. My business plan is a roll of wallpaper and the back of an envelope with calculations about 2.6 billion electrical plug sockets. Who, in their right mind, would give anyone a loan based on that?'

'Colinnn,' said Izzy, emphasising the 'n', to get her point over. She was none too happy with his lack of preparation.

'First things first, I need to see how the Rabbodig test went.' With that, he was out of the bedroom, down the stairs, and off across the yard at top speed.

Confident he would find seven neat holes in a straight line following the layout of the cages, his heart sank. Instead, he saw what looked like a scene from Thumper on the Run – The Story of the Maniac Rabbit. Not seven holes from seven rabbits, but three holes, two rabbits and eight empty cages. And the holes that had been dug looked like explosions rather than skilled burrowers had created them.

'Who'd pay money for them?' he thundered. 'It's over! My hole farming days are over even before they've begun.'

Turning, he hooked his foot under a cage and flipped the lot over, releasing the last two captives. Without further invitation, they were gone. Dejected, disappointed, and downhearted, he dragged himself back toward the farmhouse, trying to think about how he would break the news to Izzy.

He didn't need to; she'd seen the entire episode from the upstairs window and was now heading to the kitchen to meet and console him. By the time they had both reached the kitchen, her demeanour had changed. She didn't even give him a chance to open his mouth.

'Colin if you're about to tell me the whole hole thing is a nonstarter, that your Rabbodig thingy was a failure and that I'm going to have to spend the rest of my life feeding chickens and selling eggs you've got another think coming!' Her voice boomed around the kitchen.

He hadn't seen her so forceful before. *Where were*

her you poor thing, better luck next time, no matter what, I'll always be right behind you supportive tones?

'And another thing,' she continued. 'You've got three hours to tidy up your business plan, get your thoughts together, get changed into your suit and get into town—so get moving!' She placed a couple of slices of toast and Marmite in front of him, glared and left.

Although one of his favourites, he found his toast tasted different somehow. He couldn't believe how Isobel, his Isobel, his oh so sweet Izzy, had turned into a monster. Yes, nothing short of a monster! He popped the last crust into his mouth, took a swig of his tea at the same time as standing up. He was up the stairs in a blur.

He heard her calling him from deep within the wardrobe. Rummaging for his only suit, last worn at his uncle's funeral twelve years ago, she knew it was somewhere, but where? *How is it,* she thought, *if you're in a hurry, things that are usually to hand, easy to find, just where they should be, seem to disappear, hiding as if they know you want them?*

As he entered the bedroom, he could hear a disembodied voice and saw an arm frantically waving a dark blue jacket with inch-wide pinstripes from within the wardrobe. 'Here, take this. The trousers have fallen off the hanger and are on the floor somewhere. Quick, take it!'

He took the jacket and laid it on the bed. Seconds later, Izzy emerged with the trousers and his best white shirt.

'Get this lot on, and I'll give your shoes a quick polish. Oh… and here's a belt. You'll need that to pull in your stomach.'

No attempt to hide the truth, he thought. *She thinks*

I'm fat. Actually, it doesn't take a lot of thinking. I am.

He entered the kitchen, not sure how she was going to treat him. His impending meeting with Mr Pryor, their Bank Manager, didn't help his nerves.

'Okay,' she said, 'you've got to show belief in your idea, conviction, and, above all, determination. Put the failure of the Rabbodig test behind you. Any hint and Mr Pryor will sense a problem, and you can say goodbye to your loan. Be truthful, but not beyond necessity. Facts, numbers,' she went on, 'Bank Managers like numbers. Numbers have a habit of adding up: simplicity not found in words. No matter how you look at it, two plus two always equals four. Simplicity and elegance is what bankers enjoy.'

He was trying to take in what she was saying. *Okay, yes. Two plus two equals four. Got that,* he thought. *Bank Managers are simple, oh, and don't lie.* With her advice scurrying around his head, he went out to the barn to collect his roll of wallpaper, picking up his envelope of calculations on route.

'I think I'll go now, dearest,' he said. 'I'll take it steady—don't want to get caught in traffic. Anyway, it will give me a chance to think things through.'

She heard the back door go and a few minutes later saw Old Alfred Mac pass the window, heading for the lane, the town, and their future. *I guess I was hard on him;* she thought. *But tough love is needed now and then. I'm sure he'll be okay.*

Lloyds Bank came up on his left-hand side. Slowing,

Colin took the entrance to their customer parking. *Today, I can use it legitimately.* He swung the lorry in through the gates and stopped. Unaware he was taking up three bays and blocking in at least two other cars, he was pleased to see he was half an hour early. He rehearsed his story.

At his desk, Mr Pryor sat contemplating his 35 years of unswerving, dedicated and loyal service. Today he retired. In the staffroom, unbeknownst to him, preparations were underway for his leaving party. Colin didn't know, and as luck would have it, he would be Mr Pryor's last customer.

Head Office was introducing an array of new processes and procedures. *I can't be doing with them. You can't even sneeze unless you get permission in triplicate. Trust, a gentleman's agreement and a good old-fashioned handshake. That's the stuff of British banking,* thought Mr Pryor.

Colin waited in reception—a single chair, with a low table, last week's Financial Times and a copy of the Bank's in-house magazine, at least two years out of date. He was nervous, his leg trembled. It's felt like waiting to see the Head Teacher at school, and hoping he wouldn't give him detention.

A smartly dressed young lady appeared. 'Mr Griggs, Mr Pryor, will see you now.' She escorted him to the Manager's office.

'Please sit down, Mr Griggs.' Mr Pryor thrust his hand forward; Colin duly shook it. In his bank manager way, Steve was doing his best to put him at ease. 'I understand you're looking for a loan; well, you've come to the right place. If it had been a book, I'm afraid I couldn't have helped, the Library is down the street.' Mr Pryor laughed at his own joke. Goodness knows how many times he'd made it. *It's time I got some new material,* he mused. 'Actually, today is my last day.' As he spoke, he smiled a real deep Cheshire cat-like smile, which made him feel good.

'Err, yes, a loan,' stammered Colin. 'I've got a new business venture. I'm sure it's going to be a real winner.' *Izzy would be pleased: that sounded like belief and conviction in the idea,* he thought, recalling her advice.

'It's based on the need for holes.' Colin saw Mr Pryor's brow wrinkle. 'Every day all of us need to use holes in just about everything we do, from plugging in the kettle to walking from room to room, or to playing a round of golf,' Colin went on.

'Ahh golf,' said Mr Pryor, 'great game. I'm all for any business which helps golfers. It's my retirement's today; golf will become a significant part of my life. As it happens, the Harpsden Golf Club is going through a major refurbishment programme right now, with a redesign of the fairways and greens; all 18 holes. So tell me about your…,' he looked down at his notes, 'hole business. That sounds a bit odd. Anyway, nothing too technical mind, I'm a bank manager remember.'

'I have acres of land,' Colin started, 'with lots of rabbits.'

'Yes, okay,' said Mr Pryor, unsure of the connection.

'And rabbits dig holes.' Colin remembered what Izzy said about keeping it simple. He went on, 'I've invented the Rabbodig machine.' He didn't want to say too much in case Mr Pryor asked any awkward questions that he couldn't truthfully answer.

'Did I hear you right? A Legodig machine. Hasn't that been done already?' enquired Mr Pryor, wishing to demonstrate his knowledge and give Colin some encouragement but not to put him off, all at the same time.

'No, no, a Rabbodig—here, look.' Colin pulled out the wallpaper, unrolling it across his desk.

Under normal circumstances, such an action would have been frowned upon. Nobody touched anything on Mr Pryor's desk unless they had explicit permission. It's the way he maintained control of the bank's business. He was about to say something, but remembered today was his last day. *What the heck,* he thought.

Gleefully, Colin pointed out all the different levers, catches, feeding mechanisms, including the carrot ball rolling device. And how the cages could be joined for precision hole digging, for high productivity or separated, for ease of transportation. *Gosh,* he thought, *it sounds excellent. I'm sure he'll be impressed.*

'Oh, and finally—'

'I like and finally,' interrupted Mr Pryor.

'Two cages plus two cages equals four.' *That ought to clinch it,* thought Colin. *Izzy's such a whizz.*

'I see Colin you have a good grasp of maths and your Legodig—'

'Rabbodig,' Colin corrected.

'Err, yes, Rabbodig, has flexibility; both enormously helpful for any business in today's competitive climate. So how much do you want to borrow?'

Colin hadn't thought of an amount. Let me see, he said to himself, using his fingers to add up. I spent £50 on timber, £38 on wire mesh, and around £60 on latches, hinges, cables, and other bits. That's £150 or near enough. I now need to redesign and extend, so, say, by the same amount again—oh, and I'd like to buy Izzy a present for being so supportive.

'500,' he said. 'That should do it.'

'500… thousand,' Mr Pryor's incredulity was plain to hear. 'No, no, no, Colin, the bank cannot lend you £500,000.'

'No, Mr Pryor sir, I mean just £500.'

'Come now, Colin, the bank can do better than that. Will £2,000 be enough?'

'Err um?'

'Oh alright then, £4,000.'

'But…, but Mr Pryor.'

'You drive a hard bargain, Colin. I know, I know, let's make it easy. How about a nice round £10,000 and that's my… Errm… I mean the bank's final offer.'

Colin, stunned, couldn't believe his ears. '10,000, urr, yes, fine,' he said rather timidly.

'You must remember, I'm making this exceedingly generous offer because I knew your father; a decent chap who would let no one down. Strong moral fibre, salt of the earth and all that. I trust you'll be able to pay it back?'

Colin didn't hear the question as he was too busy thinking about Rabbodig Mark II, Izzy's new dress and their future as hole farmers. He said nothing.

'It's at this point Colin, you're supposed to say 'Yes',' interrupted Mr Pryor. 'I'll get the paperwork sorted right away and have it in the post tonight. Oh, and one last thing, Colin, the Golf Club refurbishment, why don't you see if they'll buy your holes? They could be your first customer. I'm a senior Committee Member, along with Graham Woods, sorry I mean Major Woods, who's Captain, and Mr Ballard, the Head Groundsman. I believe you know Mr Ballard. Weren't you at school together?'

'Err… yes, I do, we were.' The thought of £10,000 had put his mind elsewhere.

'Excellent, you'll have my vote and Mr Ballard's. The order is all but home and dry. Just Major Woods. Tell you what, his wife Margaret—lovely lady—is chairperson of the Harpsden Ladies' Guild. They do such sterling works; all those scones and teas. A donation to their funds of say £10 or £20 ought to do it. Look, get me your quote by Monday morning and I'll propose it to the Committee myself. We're having a meeting in the afternoon between lunch and tea. Give me a ring Monday evening to confirm the quote was accepted. Remember, they'll want to move quickly as the club's re-opening is planned for next Saturday. Do you think you can manage that?'

Colin mumbled something and nothing while Mr Pryor shook his hand and led him to the door.

'Give Mr Griggs my home address and telephone details please Linda,' Mr Pryor called to his PA. 'Nice doing business with you, Colin, looking forward to your quote. Good man.' The pat on his back all but knocked Colin off his feet.

'Yes, thank you.'

With that, Mr Pryor was gone. Colin had a sheet of paper thrust in his hand before being directed to the customer car park. He reached his lorry in a complete daze, so much so the protestations of the two drivers whom he'd blocked in went unnoticed. Colin climbed into the cab of Old Alfred Mac, fired up the engine and was away without a bye nor leave. *£10,000,* he thought to himself, *£10,000!*

❧   ❧   ❧

During Colin's absence, Izzy could hardly contain herself in anticipation of the outcome. Every few minutes, she ran upstairs to look out across the lower field toward Henslow for any signs of his lorry. Eventually, it came into view, slowly meandering down the lane. She rushed out to greet him, reaching the cab door as he turned off the engine.

'Well, is it good or bad news?' Without waiting for an answer, she continued, 'Oh Colin, I'm so sorry. I know how much all this meant to you. If you were supposed to be a hole farmer, then—'

He cut her commiserations short, '£10,000.'

'What? I mean, pardon?'

'£10,000,' he repeated.

'£10,000,' she said, checking she'd heard correctly.

'£10,000.'

'You mean the bank's agreed to a loan of—'

'£10,000.' Colin said it before she had a chance to. Actually, he said it again and again and again and would have continued saying it for a lot longer if she hadn't shouted at him to stop.

'Oh, Colin, you're so clever.'

'And there's more,' he continued, 'Harpsden Golf

Club is refurbishing the complete course and Mr Pryor, who's on the Committee, has asked me to submit a quote by Monday morning, and he'll push it through the vote. By Monday night, we'll know if we've got our first customer. He seems to think it's all done and dusted as long as we can deliver 18 precisely placed holes by Saturday ready for the Grand Opening.' He took a breath. 'We've got work to do and no time to spare. Lucky I bought all those extra materials. A bit of redesigning on the cages and, hey presto, we'll be in business!'

Hey, presto, he said it again, she thought, *that always means disaster.*

CHAPTER 4

PLANNING AND PREPARATION

'Harpsden Golf Club as your first customer? Are you ready for this? Anybody who's anybody is a member. If we do well, it almost guarantees our success. If we do badly—'

'Don't think like that, Izzy. Be positive. Believe in our business. As you told me, we just need commitment and determination.'

'Yes, and 18 rabbits who'll dig precisely located and sized holes. Look at the catastrophe following last night's test.' She couldn't help reminding him. He grimaced at her comment.

'All is not lost. I have a plan.'

Izzy looked sceptical.

'What went wrong last night was the cages were on uneven ground, giving the rabbits a chance to escape through the gaps. I need to add weights—you know, like divers wear on their belts to make them sink. If we had a few dozen, I could place them in each cage as necessary. That would keep the blighters from escaping.'

'And where are we going to find a few dozen diver's lead weights around here? Hartwell's?' She was becoming exasperated with him.

'They don't have to be diver's,' any lead will do.'

'So I suppose you want me to shin up the church

tower to rob the flashing.'

'Now Izzy, don't be like that. Think positive.'

'Okay, so we can get some weights. What about the precise location and hole size. How are you planning to fix that?'

Colin thought for a few minutes. She busied herself and tidied away the lunchtime dishes.

'Templates, they're the answer. We can get the precise dimensions needed for a golf green hole from that Intergoogly thing your nephew is always on about, and hey presto.'

Here we go again, she thought. She rolled her eyes.

'I can make wooden templates to place on the floor of each cage to ensure the rabbit digs only in that spot and to that diameter.' A self-satisfactory grin filled his face.

'Genius Colin; that's why this business is going to be successful. You find answers to any problem.'

He sketched out a diagram for her to see.

'Also,' he continued, 'a blanking plate will allow us to load each cage with a rabbit here at the farm and then transport them to a site, such as a golf course or wherever before releasing them to dig when it suits us.' Excited by his Rabbodig modifications, he jumped up from the kitchen table and headed for the barn workshop.

'Where do you think you're going?'

He stopped dead. 'What do you mean, my love?'

'Look at you. You've still got your best suit on.'

'My only suit,' he muttered.

'That makes it worse. Change Colin. Get changed first.'

He went upstairs into the bedroom. Several

minutes passed. In the kitchen, all Izzy could hear were drawers being yanked open, slamming doors and thumping footprints plodding across the floor as he moved from room to room.

'You alright, Colin?' she called up the stairs. She knew he wasn't. All his favourite clothes he'd been wearing when he dived into the pond were nowhere to be found. While he was with the bank manager, she'd taken the wet, smelly heap into the lower field and given scarecrow a complete make-over.

'Lost something?' she called again.

'Where's my farm clothes? What have you done with them?'

'I've done nothing. I'm not the one who went diving into the pond fully dressed in the middle of the night. Remember?'

'So where are they?'

'Gone to a good cause.'

'What good cause?'

'A certain gentleman with greater needs than yours. You may have noticed him in the lower field as you drove back from town.' Her voice trailed away.

'You mean the scarecrow!' He couldn't believe what he was hearing. His favourite clothes on the scarecrow! By now, he was down the stairs and looking her right in the eyes.

'Yes,' she said.

He took a deep breath. 'Well, that explains one thing.'

'What do you mean?'

'On the drive back from the bank—as you know, £10,000 better off…' He loved hearing those words. 'I noticed me standing in the field. I thought it most peculiar, as I was driving at the time. It occurred to me it might be one of those 'out-of-body experiences' you're always telling me about in your magazines.'

At that, Izzy stopped to look at him. He had found various garments, some of which hadn't seen the light of day for many years and would have been better off being left where they were. At least they had no holes, and they didn't smell of dank, putrid water.

'That's better. Off you go now to your workshop. Things to do and all that.' She sounded like his mother. He left.

Several hours passed before she saw him again.

'Nearly done. I just need you to get onto that Intergoogly thingy and find out the precise measurement of a golf green hole.'

'Done. It's 4¼ inches or 11 centimetres.'

'You're so smart, Izzy, a genuine treasure.' He disappeared again.

A little while later, she was aware of him calling her.

'Izzy, Izzy, quick, come here.'

As she approached the barn, she saw him signaling for her to hurry. She followed him through to the back, where a door led to his workshop. It wasn't often she went there; always a place of mystery. Not that he stopped her, but she felt it was his place—his 'man cave,' and not a place for her.

'Here, look!' He was holding up his template. It was just like the drawing but with the addition of large black lettering proclaiming, 'golf hole template, 4¼ inch/11 cm hole size'.

'You're my Mr Wonderful, and so clever.' Not wanting to over-inflate his ego, she reminded him, 'just another 17 templates and eight more cages to go and we'll be ready for the golf course job.' With plenty of work to do and time moving on, she thought she'd pre-empt the 'hey presto' and inject some reality into the situation.

'No, you're right Izzy. We must make a plan of all the tasks and materials, and a timetable if we're going to deliver on time and to requirements. Planning and preparation—the key to success,' he said, puffing out his chest and feeling he was becoming a proper businessman. 'Planning and preparation,' he repeated, just to emphasise the lessons learned.

છ   છ   છ

'Tea's nearly ready; enough out here for tonight. Come back into the house, Colin, we'll eat and make our plan.'

'Oh and Izzy, we mustn't forget the quote! If I don't get it to Mr Pryor by Monday morning, there'll be no job.'

Colin sat at the table, staring at a blank piece of paper. He'd never prepared a quote before. Not sure where to start or what was needed, he closed his eyes, trying to recall a quote his father received for the barn extension built in 1948. The answer wasn't long in coming—he couldn't! As gifted as he was in her eyes, even he wasn't capable of remembering a time before he was born, no matter how hard he tried.

'I'm stuck. What are we going to do now?'

'Colin, you're hopeless; join the modern world. It's all on Google.'

'What? You mean there's already a quote written for 18 holes at the Harpsden Golf Club using the Rabbodig Mark II. Gosh, I knew we are moving toward Big Brother, but that's impressive by anyone's standards.'

'No, no, silly. I mean, we can search for other quotes and adopt and adapt as necessary. Here, look at these examples.' She'd found some quotes used in a business course run by an American college.

'They want the price in dollars?! I know Mr Pryor is on the Committee and a bank manager—'

'Ex-bank manager now,' she interrupted.

'But I'm surprised they want the price in dollars.'

'Now you're just larking around. Stop it! We haven't time.'

Between them, they soon drafted a quote and Izzy typed it up on the computer.

'That looks so professional. Now print out two copies, no three, no four. Yes, one for each Committee Member and one for our records. Hey, this business stuff is actually quite easy, you know.' Colin reread the computer screen.

'Well, don't count your chickens—'

'What have chickens got to do with hole farming?'

'I can't print. The ink ran out three weeks ago. I've been meaning to buy some, but keep forgetting to put it on the list.'

'Well, tomorrow. Put it on the To-Do list and mark it as a top priority.' *Gosh,* he thought. *I do sound business-like. Another crisis sorted.*

They spent the rest of the evening arranging, prioritising, and deciding who'd handled each task. They drew up a list of materials and created a budget, all cross-checked with the quote to cover their costs.

'All we need to do now is a price for the job.' Izzy looked at Colin.

'That's easy,' he said. 'The cost of the materials for the cages and say 15% on top for profit. I spent around £150 on materials plus 15%. Err, what's that?' He scratched his head as he pondered the mental arithmetic. '£15 I think. Oh well, that'll do, so £165. Add that to the quote Izzy. Lucky we haven't printed it yet.'

'What about VAT?' she asked.

'What about VAT?'

'Do we need to add VAT to the price?'

'Not sure. Just add 'plus VAT' to the bottom of the quote to be on the safe side.'

Izzy duly typed away, saving her document as she went.

'All done.' She powered off the computer. 'I think it's time we went to bed. Catching 18 rabbits is my responsibility. I need to think about it.'

CHAPTER 5

STOCKINGS AND TRAPS

Saturday morning saw Izzy up bright and early. Colin was still fast asleep dreaming, and judging by how his legs kept moving, he was chasing rabbits.

'Colin,' Izzy whispered, 'Colin.' She said it more forcefully, 'Colin, wake up! Here's a cup of tea.' She waited for him to grunt before going downstairs.

Busying herself, she couldn't hear any sounds and called up to him, 'Are you awake yet? Come on. Rise and shine, sleepyhead. Remember our plans, our tasks, our responsibilities, well it might not be on the list, but one of yours is to get up in the morning. Now do it!'

He heard that.

Slowly, he realised what she was on about. 'I'm coming!' He threw back the covers and was up, searching for his clothes. Soon he was downstairs.

'Right,' she started, 'as agreed, you're going to town for your timber and here's a list of other items I need.'

He surveyed the list while eating his toast and Marmite. Today it tasted a lot better. 'Izzy,' he mumbled through half-closed teeth and spitting crumbs everywhere, 'what are you going to do with nine pairs of support stockings? You can't ask me to buy those.'

'Oh, go on, they're only support stockings. They won't bite.'

'What about size and colour? Oh, and denner?'

'Denier,' she corrected him. 'Doesn't matter, any will do. What's more important is the ink cartridge. We need an HP56 black; no other will do.'

He finished his toast and lukewarm tea. Collecting up his bits, he set off for town in Old Alfred Mac. As he drove down the lane, passing the lower field, he saw himself standing there.

'Alright Colin?' he shouted at the scarecrow. 'Want to change places? I'm not sure about buying these stockings.' He wound up the window and drove on.

After turning into the High Street, Colin pulled into the service road running behind the shops where he knew he'd find a parking place. *Let's get it over with,* he thought, and wandered toward Bates the Chemist. Reaching the door, he hesitated before pushing on the handle. The tinkle of a brass bell hailed his arrival.

As he stepped over the threshold, a gloom reminiscent of the interior of an extensive old wooden cupboard replaced the light from the street. Struck by the odours of carbolic soap, lavender and a musty smell he remembered from childhood when visiting an aged aunt, he expected Charles Dickens to appear. Instead, he could only see Miss Bates sitting on a stool behind a heavy wooden counter. At 75 if she was a day, her head was hardly visible, hidden by the displays. The place was crammed with every conceivable thing—women's things—preparations, remedies, soaps, shampoos and stuff he did not know about.

He mooched around, hoping above all hopes that the support stockings would somehow jump into his hands so he wouldn't have to ask for them; and, more importantly, Miss Bates wouldn't ask him questions. He was sure he wouldn't know the answers and only embarrass himself. Turning a corner at the end of one display cabinet, he heard a voice.

'Can I help you, sir?'

He nearly jumped out of his skin.

The voice belonged to a rather attractive young girl who popped up from behind a stack of boxes she was busy emptying.

'Err no, I mean yes, err no… no.' Surprised, he stammered.

'Which is it sir, yes or no?' She moved fully into view.

'No,' he said. 'I mean, yes. You rather took me off guard.' Beads of sweat appeared on his forehead.

'So, do you need help or not, sir?' The shop assistant persisted.

Be a man, he thought, *Izzy's right, they're only stockings.* He wiped his hand across his brow.

'Yes, please. I want nine pairs of support stockings.'

'Brown, flesh, black or beige?'

'I'm not sure. Does it matter?'

The sweat was back.

'Not to me sir, but it might to whoever's wearing them. Who are they for?'

'My wife, Isobel.'

'Does she have a preference, sir?'

'I don't think so.'

'Does she usually wear brown or black or some other colour?'

'Oh, she's not going to wear them...' he let out a little chuckle.

'Not going to wear them?' inquired the girl. 'Then what's she going to do with them? Make jam?'

'Jam!' he repeated her.

'Yes sir, make jam?'

'Well, call me old-fashioned, but we normally have strawberry jam, sometimes blackcurrant, and once she made apricot. It was extremely nice, but apricots aren't easy to get in Harpsden. She hasn't made it since and I don't recall her ever making 'stocking jam.''

'No sir, you don't make jam from stockings. You use them to sieve the fruit.'

'Oh, I see,' he didn't, but wondered why anybody in their right mind would sieve strawberries through stockings. 'Sounds unhygienic to me.'

'So sir, if your wife will not wear them or make jam, can I ask what she is going to do with them?'

He was hoping the encounter would draw to a close. Instead of telling the assistant their real purpose, which he knew would lead to a whole raft of questions, he said, 'Well,' he hesitated, 'they're not for her but me.'

Before the words had left his mouth, he realised that was so the wrong thing to say.

'For you, sir!' She couldn't hide her surprise. *You just can't tell by looking at someone what sort of person they are.* She kept that to herself.

'Well, no, yes, no, not sure.' He shifted uncomfortably, moving his weight from foot to foot. 'They're not really for me,' he paused while he thought of a convincing excuse. He didn't manage it.

'Brown, flesh, black or beige, sir?' The assistant repeated her original question to cover the awkward silence.

He thought it better to say nothing and just answer the questions, pay and leave.

'Black.'

'Extra-large?'

'Yes, I think so.'

'You say nine pairs?'

'Yes, nine, please.'

The ordeal was close to the end; Colin's blushes were subsiding.

'Well, I'm pleased to tell you sir that we've got a promotion on support stockings and I'm able to offer you either a leg hair wax removal kit, a bikini line trimmer or a foot balm massage cream. Which of those would you like?' The shop assistant smiled up at him.

'No, none, nothing,' he sounded flustered. 'Can't I just pay and go?'

'Well, actually, with nine pairs of stockings, you qualify for three gifts.'

'Oh, for pity's sake, I don't want any gifts! Can I just pay and go?'

'Yes, but you see sir, the gifts were delivered with the consignment of stockings: one per three pairs. If you don't take your gifts, we'll have three extra left over, and the stocking company's sales rep won't be pleased. Basically, you need to choose three gifts.'

'Okay, okay.' He could feel his temperature rising. 'Three hair wax removal kits.'

'That's an awful lot of hair removal cream. Do

you have a problem in that area?'

'No, of course not!'

'I could have a look for you if you want, sir?'

He glared at her.

Probably not a good idea, she concluded, sensing he was about to explode.

Removing the stockings from the display stand, she realised there were only eight black pairs in extra-large. Colin was looking around the shop to see if anyone else had seen what was going on.

'Morning Colin,' a voice called from the far side. It was Mrs Bishop. She headed his way. 'Didn't know you were coming into town today. Izzy didn't mention it; otherwise, you could have given me a lift.'

The shop assistant tapped him on the arm.

'Excuse me, sir. We only have eight pairs of extra-large black stockings. Which other colour would you like?'

'I don't know. Any colour will do.' Colin was trying to distance himself from the transaction.

'But you're going to be wearing them, sir. What colour, brown, flesh or beige?'

'Oh Colin, I think you'd look nice in chocolate brown,' piped up Mrs Bishop.

That's all I need. It's going to be all around Henslow and Harpsden, no doubt, that Colin Griggs, farmer and son of Stanley Griggs, wears stockings.

'Thanks, Mrs Bishop,' he said under his breath. He collected up his stockings and gifts, paid cash, and left.

As he passed through the door, he heard Mrs Bishop say. 'My Jim always wears tights in the winter riding his motorbike; he says it keeps him warm.'

Convinced everyone knew his secret, Colin walked down the High Street looking straight ahead, not wanting to catch anyone's eye. He bought his ink cartridge and got back to the safety of his lorry. His last shop was Hartwells, where he purchased the plywood for the templates, and then home.

Nearing the farm in the lane that ran past the lower field, he could have sworn he heard the scarecrow say, 'Have you got a pair of stockings for me? It gets bitterly cold standing here all the time!'

As the lorry pulled into the yard, Colin could see Izzy busy feeding the chickens. He headed for the kitchen; she joined him.

Izzy spoke as she filled the kettle, 'Successful?'

'Don't be surprised if you hear I'm a stocking wearing weirdo. It'll be all around the village, if not the town, by this evening. 'Colin Griggs, son of Stanley Griggs, wears women's black stockings' will be on everybody's lips. Tights wouldn't have been so bad, but stockings!!'

'What happened? What are you talking about?'

'Here's the worse bit, Colin Griggs waxes his legs!'

'Tell me. What's happened?' Izzy couldn't hide her amusement.

'And the assistant in the chemist—'

'Yes, that's Bob's daughter Lucy.'

'What? Bob from the Lamb Inn? That's all I need. Mrs Bishop, who talks for England, and Bob Critchley, landlord of the only pub in Henslow, we might as well take out an ad in the Harpsden Chronicle. In fact, no, why not go the whole hog and tell the Sunday Mirror!

I'm going to be a laughing stock. Everyone will know I wear stockings and wax my legs and what's worse—I don't!'

'Nobody cares what you do.' She couldn't help smiling to herself.

'But I don't! I know I told Louise I did.'

'Lucy.'

'Louise, Lucy, what does it matter? But I only said I did so I could get out of the shop quicker.'

'And what's this bit about waxing your legs?'

'Well, look here.' He pointed to three leg waxing kits sat on the kitchen table.

'Why did you buy these? They aren't on the list?'

'I didn't buy them!'

'You mean you stole them?'

'No, of course not. They were gifts for buying nine pairs of stockings. I had a choice of three gifts: waxing kit, bikini line trimmer things or foot massaging cream.'

'Then why did you choose three waxing kits? I would have loved the foot massage cream, or are you trying to say my legs are hairy!' Izzy's nostrils flared.

'Izzy, I want to start this day again.'

'Well?'

'Well, what?'

'Have I got hairy legs? The truth now; do you think my legs are hairy? I want a straight answer, yes or no?'

'No, of course not. What are you talking about?'

'Then why did you choose three leg waxing kits? You must have thought subconsciously 'She has hairy legs,' to have picked the leg waxing kits over the other gifts. I'll have you know my legs are not hairy, well no more than anyone else's. And I keep them spotless — look.' At that, she lifted her skirt just above her knee. 'Go on feel, have a feel, slide your hand down my leg. Not a hair in sight.'

'Stop it, Izzy! I've not said or thought, consciously or unconsciously, that you have hairy legs. Please let the whole thing drop!' He was exasperated. 'And I never want to hear the words 'stockings' or 'leg waxing' ever again.'

Lunch came as a welcome relief. Neither spoke. The loud banging of knives and forks broke the silence.

He couldn't stand it anymore. 'Izzy, you've lovely legs. I've always thought they were one of your best features, along with your pretty feet.'

'That's good, Colin, and what else?'

'What do you mean, what else?'

'What else do you like about me? We've been together 40 years near-on. I can't believe it's just my legs and feet that have kept us together all this time, so what else?'

'Izzy, drop it! Now's neither the time nor place. We have work to do, tasks to complete, lists to check off, our first and most prestigious hole farming job to complete. We need to stay focussed and work together.'

He cleared away the plates before leaving for the sanctuary of his man-shed while Izzy disappeared upstairs.

&ou; &ou; &ou;

'Oxfam, Humana, keep. Oxfam, Oxfam, keep, Humana, keep, keep.' *Oh, this is so great*, Izzy thought as she cleared her way through Colin's half of the wardrobe. I need just thirteen more wire coat hangers. Keep, Humana, Oxfam, Oxfam. Keep, Humana. Within 10 minutes, Colin had received a total sort out of his clothes and the best part of it was he knew nothing about it. *He can use the payment from the golf holes job to buy himself a new wardrobe,* she thought. This shirt still has his name sewn into the collar, and he left school in 1968. 'Humana, keep, Oxfam.' She was enjoying herself.

With her eighteen wire coat hangers and her two bulging black plastic sacks, she made her way to the kitchen and out into the yard. *I'll show him; hairy legs indeed!* With that, she hoisted the sacks onto the back of Old Alfred Mac, ready to go to their new homes.

Right now focus, rabbit catching's my responsibility. Izzy had a new sense of purpose. So where are these stockings? She opened a packet. Ah good, they have strong elasticised tops. Now the tricky part; I need to bend the wire coat hangers into a circle about six inches across, just big enough for a rabbit to hop into. She looked around to find something suitable. Delving into the cupboard, she retrieved the stainless steel milk pan.

She'd just about finished as Colin came marching in through the back door.

'Those black bin sacks in the back of the lorry. What are they?'

'Oh, nothing.' She quickly changed the subject. 'How are the templates and the extra cages going?'

'Yeah, fine, and your rabbit traps?'

'Glad you asked. I was just about to come and find you. I need a big strong man with heavy-duty pliers. Know anyone who might fit the bill?'

'Sure, I'll just pop back and get a pair. What did you say was in those bags?'

'Nothing.'

'Well, it can't be nothing, otherwise they'd be lying flat, and they're not! In fact, they look bulging to me.'

'I didn't say there was nothing in the bags, but in answer to your original question, I said nothing.'

He looked confused as he headed back to the workshop, returning a few minutes later via the lorry.

'Nothing, nothing. How can you say nothing? First, all my favourite clothes end up on the scarecrow and now what he's not wearing is jammed into two black sacks on the lorry.'

'Now, don't take it like that. As a successful businessman, I just thought mixing with the Golf Club members' you might feel your old school shirt, maybe a teensy bit out of place. Don't you think?'

'Well, yes, a little, I guess, but it had memories.'

'You mean the collar had lipstick on from Josephine Wixen, more like? I used to watch you and her; disgusting, downright disgusting!'

'I must protest, my love. We did nothing to be ashamed of. I only had eyes for you, and that's always been the case.'

'For my legs, you mean?'

'Izzy!'

He finished twisting the coat hangers into circles while she turned over the elasticated tops of each stocking, fixing it in place with a running stitch. Each completed trap was hooked to the clothes airer suspended from the kitchen ceiling. By the time all eighteen traps were done, it looked like a bedroom scene from the Arabian Nights and the Dance of the Seven Veils'.

'Truce, Izzy.'

'Truce, Colin. I love you.'

'And I love you too.'

'It's been a long day. Bed my love?'

'Bed.'

The lights were out and calm returned to the Griggs household for a few seconds. Colin sat bolt upright. 'The quote. We've not printed the quote.'

'Sunday tomorrow. We'll do it then.'

'Yes, of course, you're right. Goodnight.'

'Night.'

Calm prevailed; seconds later, Colin sat bolt upright again.

'What now?' she mumbled through the duvet.

'Cups for the putting green holes. We need eighteen. Where are we going to get them from by Friday?' He was panicking.

'You know that Intergoogly thingy, Colin? Well, there's also the Inter-eBay thingy. It's like a giant car boot sale in the sky,' she was trying to keep it simple for him. 'We'll order them tomorrow, and they'll be here by Tuesday. Now go to sleep.'

He lay back down and turned over. Calm resumed. 'Izzzzy.'

'Colin,' she spoke through tight lips.

'You know, without you, I'd be useless.'

She considered his statement. 'Not useless, just less useful.' She always saw the best in people.

CHAPTER 6

PASS MUSTER

Sunday saw both Izzy and Colin up bright and early, with lists in hand checking off what still needed to be done, identifying new priorities and refining their plan.

'I'm certain we can pull it off. Right, number one task, check and print off the quote.' He said.

'Hold it right there.' Izzy raised her hand. 'The putting green cups aren't in the quote.'

'See Izzy, again, you've saved my bacon. We could have made a loss on our first job. Now you come to mention it, thinking of bacon—'

'Five minutes and the bacon and egg sarnies will be ready.'

'Toasted?'

'But of course. I don't forget things, Colin. Not like you.'

'I'll turn the computer on while we wait; let it warm up.'

'Colin, no! Don't you dare touch it; you know what happened last time.'

'In fairness, Izzy, it was the overhead power lines crashing together in the storm that caused it to explode. I just happened to be bending down, turning it on at the time.'

'Go on then.'

The screen came to life, lights on the big box flickered, and the sound of the computer's cooling fan filled the kitchen.

'Come and have your sarnie before it gets cold.'

Breakfast over; they set about finding putting green cups on eBay. While she busied, he just watched and made uninformed comments.

'Who's Knottyboy Izzy?'

'He's the seller.'

'Unusual name. Not sure I'd buy anything from someone with a name like Knottyboy.'

'It's not his real name. It's his trading name; a handle.'

'Why doesn't he use his real name?'

'He wants to be anonymous; everyone using eBay has one.'

'What's yours, then?'

'littlemissmuffet.'

'Little Miss Muffet!'

'Yes, littlemissmuffet, all lowercase, no spaces.'

'Why on earth did you call yourself Little Miss Muffet?'

'It just sounded nice and was available.'

'Available. I'm not surprised; you could have been izzygriggs or isobelgriggs, all lowercase and no spaces.'

'Well, actually, I couldn't. Both had already gone.'

'You mean there's more than one of you?'

'Yes, loads; eBay suggested izzygriggs519, so I guess there are many others and possibly another 518.'

'Well, I'll be blowed! And I thought you were unique.'

The UK stockists for Chinese-made putting green cups offered a 'Buy it Now' option. She purchased eighteen, including delivery within 24 hours, for £160.

'Right, tick them off the list. They'll be here Tuesday.'

'Lucky we hadn't printed the quote yet, or we'd be totally out of pocket.'

She was fiddling around with the printer, installing the new cartridge. 'There.'

'Okay, Izzy. Get the quote on the screen and add the extra putting green hole cups at £160.'

'Pass that scrap of paper; I need to work out the new total.'

'Well, it's just the old total of £165 plus the extra cost £160, isn't it?' he asked.

'I can see why you're not an accountant. For goodness sakes.' She raised her eyes to heaven. 'What about the cost of the rabbit traps and the profit percentage applied to the extra cost? Oh, and the stockings.'

'If you think I'm going to put nine pairs of black stockings at £4 per pair on a quote for the Golf Club, you must be joking! How would that look?'

'I agree, but we need to add in their cost. We'll just call it 'out-of-pocket expenses'. That way, they'll never know. So what have we now?'

'£150 for the original cages, £160 for the golf putting green hole liners, and £36 out-of-pocket expenses.'

'So that's...?'

'And the extra plywood I bought yesterday? That was £27.'

'So the total cost is £373 plus a mark-up of 15%.'

'I make that £388 all told, Izzy. At this rate, we'll be rich in no time.'

'Not with you doing the maths, we won't! Our margin is 15%, not £15.'

'Aren't they the same thing?'

'I tell you what, Colin, you just stick to the big ideas and I'll do the detail.'

She completed the quote and printed off the four copies. Finding an envelope, she addressed it, placed the contents inside, then sealed it with a flurry. She held it up for Colin to see.

'Our first quote.' He puffed out his chest again. 'We're truly in the hole farming business now.'

'Fingers crossed.'

'It's not down to luck Izzy; it's all down to—'

'Planning and preparation,' they said together and laughed.

He propped up the envelope on the shelf in full view, along with the one containing the donation to the Harpsden Ladies' Guild.

'Mustn't forget to deliver these first thing tomorrow.'

'Look, Colin. We're both ahead with our tasks why wait? Let's do it now. Come on.'

'Together?'

'Yes, together. We can go via the recycling place in town, drop off the Salvation Army bag, and leave the other one at the Oxfam collection point. Oh, and post the donation to the Ladies' Guild.'

'I'll drive, you navigate.'

He scooped up the envelopes and keys. They left.

Off down the lane and past the lower field; at seeing the scarecrow, he mused. *I bet you're cold standing there. The way my clothes are disappearing, I'll soon be running around naked. Not a pretty sight, you might say!*

'The recycle place is on the service road running behind the High Street shops, and Oxfam's collection point is just at the far end of the High Street,' Izzy was being efficient.

'What about Mr Pryor? Where does he live?'

'I think it's off the Reading Road across town. I'm just looking it up. Hang on.' She flicked through the map book. 'Page 26, B7. Yes, here it is.' Her focus was on the route. 'Oh, and guess what? We have to pass Elliott's. It's ages since I've been to the old school.'

'Good thing, I say.'

'Don't be like that. If it hadn't been for Elliott's, we might never have met. Don't you remember all those times behind the bike shed? You were so passionate. It makes me go all funny just thinking about it.'

'Passionate, me, bike shed? Izzy, I don't believe so.' He shook his head. 'Are you sure you're not confusing me with someone else?' He stared at her.

She shifted in her seat.

'Er, yes, maybe. It's been over 40 years; the old memory plays tricks.' Her brain raced. 'You know, you're quite right, it wasn't us.' Trying to make light of his remark. 'I'm confusing you with one of those stories I read in True Life magazines, or whatever it's called.' She chuckled, hoping to sound more convincing.

She didn't say it wasn't her and Colin, but her and her first love, Stewart. *I wonder where he is now?* They travelled in silence. She sat dreamy-eyed, thinking about her 'true life' story.

'… yes, you're right, I'm confusing it with one of my magazine stories.' She didn't want to disillusion him. A smile followed as she relived the memories.

Colin slowed; the gates to Elliot's were locked. They both peered at the buildings. The bike sheds weren't visible from the road, but Izzy could see them clearly in her mind's eye. He drove on.

'Where now? Come on, you're navigating.' His words snapped her out of her dream.

'Um, er, left, no right, I mean left. I don't know. Where are we, Colin?'

'We're on the Reading Road, just passing the Catholic Church.'

'Okay, I've got it: second left and first right. Granby Avenue—it's a long road. You're looking for number 26, Dunroamin.'

With envelopes and charity bags delivered, all they could do now was to go home and wait.

❧ ❧ ❧

Mr Pryor, Steve, was pleased with his decision to loan Colin Griggs £10,000. *He won't let me down*, he contemplated. *His quote's in early, a sign of efficiency; it's typed on a computer—you need to keep up with the times to be successful these days—and three copies. Excellent; a great start. Apart from a little cajoling of Major Woods, I think this should pass Committee with no problem.*

Over lunch in the clubhouse, the conversation turned to the golf course's refurbishment and the Grand Opening on Saturday.

'My experience of these sorts of things,' said Major Woods, 'is that they require being a stickler for detail. Nothing left to chance. No 'I' un-dotted or 't' uncrossed. Success is in minutia. When I was in the army,' he went on, 'it was details, details, details. No campaign ever advanced until everything was checked, cross-referenced, and rechecked again.'

'Well, how long have we got to the Grand Opening!?' interrupted Stewart, the Head Groundsman.

'This is neither the time nor the place for sarcasm—especially not from you.' The Major twisted his moustache.

'Gentlemen, gentlemen. This is lunch, remember? The Committee Meeting is afterwards. Let's keep it amiable.'

'No, you're right Steve.' The Major turned toward Stewart. 'Pass the sugar, oh and the cigars, be a good chap.' Stewart obliged but less than graciously. At times, he felt like the Major's skivvy.

Major Woods puffed on his Havana, his mind drifting back to the Officers' mess. 'Those were the days, no shilly-shallying then. Men were men, and women knew it. Straight posture, shoulders pulled back, chest out and stiff upper lip. That's what the British Army was made of. None of this 'Police, Camera, Action' loutish behaviour, binge drinking, hoodies, and boys with earrings. Everyone knew their place and a place for everyone.' His rant ceased. He held a satisfied look, the sort that comes after an ample meal, copious drink and agreeable company.

I think he's going to require a bit more cajoling in

committee than I thought, reflected Steve. 'Another brandy, Major?' *That'll do the trick.*

'Don't mind if I do. You're a good man Steve.'

Stewart realised the ploy and poured him a generous helping, the sort you get on holiday in one of those Greek taverns where a sixth of a gill never found its way. Calm was restored. The table cleared and the three diners moved to the Committee Room where only the select few ever enter, apart from Mary, the Club Secretary to take the Minutes.

The Agenda and copies of the previous Minutes were distributed, along with other items for the meeting.

'We don't want to make a meal out of this. As Club Captain and Chairman—'

'Person,' Stewart said, under his breath.

'… I think we should cut to the chase. We have six items on the Agenda; five are the usual topics, Apologies for Absence—we're all here; Questions arising from the last Minutes—I take it there's none; Rota for Changing the Flowers in Reception. What on earth is this doing on the agenda? Whoever is doing it now, tell them to keep doing it. For goodness' sake, I have better things to do with my time.'

Mary made it clear. 'Actually, Major, it was you who specifically asked for it to be added to the Agenda. You said, I quote, 'your goodly wife is no longer available to do it.'

'Ah yes, well maybe, possibly, at the time I was under pressure. She started her new Digital Image Manipulation course, whatever that is, and says she no longer has time to do it. So who are we going to volunteer?' He looked at each. 'What about your wife, Stewart? Now the boys have left home she must have time on her hands.'

Stewart had no time to reply.

'Good. Now Mary, let the Minutes show that Pauline, wife of our Head Groundsman Mr Stewart Ballard, duly volunteered to take over the duties of Mrs Margaret Woods, wife of Major Woods, Club Captain and Chairman, I mean Chairperson, to manage the rota dadedadeda. Fill in the rest as appropriate, please Mary.' He reviewed the Agenda. 'Right, next item—'

Stewart bent forward, turning toward the Major. 'Whoa, hold on, you can't do that. That's my wife you're volunteering. She needs to be asked, spoken to, treated civilly, not just volunteered in her absence.'

'Too late. I'm sorry, the records clearly state that your wife will take over from mine forthwith. Next item.'

Stewart was beside himself, but kept quiet for now. You wait, he thought, I'll show you.

'Item six—The Contract for Creating the Putting Green Holes,' stated Mary. 'We have a quote from Griggs Hole Farmers of Henslow. You all have a copy for perusal. Any questions?'

'Looks fine to me.' Mr Pryor felt it prudent to keep any thoughts to himself.

'And me too,' said Stewart.

'Looks fine! Is that all you can say?' Major Woods had different ideas. 'Ultimately, golf is all about the holes. Looks fine isn't enough. What do we know about...' He inspected the page before him, 'Griggs Hole Farmers? Who are they? Are they dependable? What experience do they have in this area?' He read on. 'And what's this Rabbodig machine they're proposing? I need answers. Do you know?'

'Actually, provided the hole is 4 ¼ inches—'

'Or 11 centimetres,' interrupted Stewart.

'Or 11 centimetres, are deep enough to take the cup and placed in the correct area on the green—'

'Which is decided by us,' interjected Stewart again.

'Yes, and only one per green.'

'Yes, that's important.'

'Then what else do we need to consider?' Mr Pryor looked at both of them. 'Personally, I've known the Griggs and Colin—'

'Oh, Colin Griggs. It's him, is it?' said Stewart. 'I went to Elliott's with him. So now he's in hole farming. He married to what's her name, let me think. I know, Little Miss Muffet.' In his mind, he was back behind the bike sheds.

'Who?' asked the Major.

'Isobel Mumford. Little Miss Muffet. Gosh, I remember her, all that cuddling and canoodling around the back of the bike shed. Splendid girl, and great legs too.'

'Yes, well, enough of that; back to business. So Colin Griggs is a good chap?'

'Major, I interviewed him just the other day for a loan. Sharp as a knife. His mathematical skills alone are outstanding. Good for precision work like hole creation and placement. And as for his business plan; it's fair to say in my 35 years of banking, I've never come across one quite like it. He has my vote.'

'Stewart?' Asked the Major.

'Well, at school, Colin turned up every day and on time, from what I remember. The only class we shared was woodwork. I recall him having an innovative approach to problem-solving.' He smiled. 'And of course, Isobel, his wife now, excellent girl—came across like any chap would wish. With her behind him, he certainly gets my vote too.'

'And this machine—the Rabbodig—he's proposing to use. Any ideas on that?' continued the Major.

'As part of his business plan, I saw his drawings. It's something he designed and built himself. He seemed proud of it and got extremely animated explaining all the levers, catches, cables and other controls for providing drinking water and food.' Steve took another sip of brandy.

'Drinking water and food for a machine? What sort of machine requires drinking water and food? Any particular type of food, or isn't it fussy?' Stewart was alarmed by a machine which needed feeding.

'Balls.'

'Mr Pryor,' the Major looked aghast, 'you of all people know the club rules on swearing. Mary, let the records show that Mr Pryor, Senior Club and Committee Member used a profanity unacceptable to Committee and contravening rule 31 of the Harpsden Golf Club Rule Book, Edition 3, as revised in 1991.'

'No, no, no. I'm not swearing. Colin feeds his machine balls, you know, carrot balls.

'I'm afraid I don't.' The Major looked to Stewart for his reaction.

'Their favourite food, apparently; they'll do anything for carrot balls.'

'Mr Pryor, are you quite well? They, favourite, anything, balls—what are you talking about?'

'Rabbits power the Rabbodig machine, hence the name.'

'What! Rabbits!' The Major and Stewart exclaimed together.

'You can't introduce rabbits onto a golf course. They're the bane of my life. As Head Groundsman, I must object in the strongest terms.'

'Hear, hear,' chipped in the Major. 'I knew we'd have problems with a quote so cheap.'

'Gentlemen, gentlemen. Let me assure you, having seen the drawings and listened at length to the way the machine works, and having known the family for more years than I care to remember, I have every confidence in Colin and his Rabbodig machine. My vote stands.' Steve picked up the quote and reread it.

'Mr Ballard?'

'Okay, I guess so. If you're happy, Mr Pryor, and provided, I do my inspection Friday morning.'

'Of course.'

'Then my vote still stands.' *Anyway, if he gets the contract, I get to see Little Miss Muffet again.* He was back behind the bike sheds.

'All well and good,' said the Major. 'Two votes, but I still have my doubts. I mean, hole farming, with rabbits. What sort of business is that?'

'Look, gentlemen,' Steve felt he needed to add some perspective, 'we want to create a dozen and a half holes. What could be simpler? What on earth could go wrong? And the price quoted, nearly £1,000 less than the budget, you can't fault it. He has my vote.'

'Stewart, have you anything to add?' asked the Major.

'Obviously, I won't get involved with any of the digging, but I'll be inspecting the greens Friday morning, and as long as they pass muster, they'll get the thumbs up.'

'Pass muster! Thumbs up! What's wrong with you, man?' The Major was vexed at the way Stewart sullied a treasured military phrase. 'Yes, well, I see what you mean, but please don't use these phrases in the same sentence again. Well, not in my company at least. There's a good chap. So the Griggs Hole Farming quote's been passed by the Committee. Mary, let the records show...'

'Already done, sir.'

'Who will inform Mr Griggs that he has the contract?'

'All in hand, Major. Because of the short timescale, I've told him to telephone me this evening.'

Well done, Mr Pryor.' The Major looked at his watch. 'That concludes business today. As Chair... person—I'll never get used to this Nancy-boy chairman person stuff—the meeting is closed. The good news is gentleman, ... and lady, the bar is open. Let's adjourn.'

CHAPTER 7

COLIN'S FAME SPREADS

'Colin, you'll wear a hole in the carpet. You've done nothing but pace all day.'

'I'm nervous. Our whole future—'

'Hole that's funny!'

'Be serious Izzy; our whole future hangs in the balance.'

'Don't you think you're a bit dramatic? Anyway, I'm confident it'll be a 'yes'. Mr Pryor all but said so, didn't he?'

'Well, he did, but you should never count your chickens—'

'Or rabbits.' She couldn't help herself. 'You wait, it'll be fine.'

'What time is it now?'

'Watch, Colin. You've got one, remember!'

He glanced at his wrist. '7 o'clock. Do you think I should ring him?'

'Go on, do it.'

His hand was shaking as he picked up the phone. Then, as if demented, Colin thumped his chest and pocket area of his trousers.

'I can't find the paper with the number.' The more he searched, the more frantic he became. 'Quick, get the telephone directory.'

'I'm sure he'll be ex-directory,' Izzy said, unhelpfully.

In his panic, he now had his back to her as he jigged around, thumping himself.

'Colin, mind the phone.'

'But you don't seem to understand. No number, no phone call, no phone call, no contract, no contract, no business. What am I going to do?'

'Colin,' she called again. 'What's this I'm holding?'

'Not now; this is a crisis. No time for playing guessing games.'

'Turn around. Look!' She was insistent. He saw she was holding the note Mr Pryor's assistant had thrust into his hand.

'You had it all the time. Why didn't you say something?'

'If you had been listening rather than doing some crazy dance, you might have seen it sooner.'

'So read me the number.'

'824175'

'It's ringing. Once... twice... see, he's not in.'

'Give the man a chance.'

'Shush, hello, hello. Mr Pryor? Sorry, you say it's his wife, Julia. No, I don't mean you're sorry for being his wife, I meant sorry... Oh, can I speak to him? It's Colin Griggs, he's expecting my call. Okay, I'll try in about an hour.' He put the phone down.

'His wife Julia says...'

'Yes, I heard. All we can do is wait. Fancy something to eat?'

'Eat, eat! I can't eat. Not in my condition.'

Thank goodness men don't have babies, thought Izzy.

Of course, the hour was only an hour, but to Colin, every one of the 60 minutes felt like an hour.

'Don't get so worked up. Try eating something. You'll be hungry later.'

'If we don't get this contract, we won't have a later. It's important.'

'I know that, but there's nothing we can do. If the man's not in then, he's not in.'

At that precise moment, and with still five minutes of the hour to go, the telephone started ringing. As Izzy was close by, she leant over to pick it up.

In a bid to answer it before her Colin flung himself across the kitchen like a man possessed 'No, Izzy!' In the ensuing mayhem, no one answered the call. He's grabbing for the handset, knocked it clear out of her hand, sending it across the room and under the Welsh Dresser.

From within the dark recess where the cat had lost its Ping-pong ball, where fluff the thickness of a child's duvet lay, and where cobwebs hung, that would make any self-respecting spider proud, the handset glowed as it rang.

'Izzy, now what!'

'Get the broom. We can use the handle to scoop it out.'

'Great idea.' Colin's fishing produced an array of detritus. Embarrassed, Izzy made a mental note to clean under there more often.

'Got it!'

'Here, let me give it a wipe.'

'So who rang? I bet it was Mr Pryor. We've missed it. What will he think? I bet he'll change his mind as we didn't answer. Not efficient or committed enough.' His mood spiralled downwards.

'Calm down. Just ring 1571 to check the messages.'

Colin did as he was told. 'She says press 1 to listen or 3 to delete, or hash to hear the choices again.'

'Well, press 1 silly!'

'This could be it.' His finger hovered over the 1 button.

'Go on. Press it!'

'I can't. What if he says no?'

'Press it!' she was getting exasperated. 'And?'

'Just a burring sound.'

'You've waited too long. Here, let me.' she snatched the phone from his hand and pressed redial, followed by 1.

'And what? Come on, tell me...'

'We've been chosen to have a 20% special introductory discount off the price of double glazing, provided—'

He had heard enough. 'I'm going to ring him. What's the number?'

'824175'

It answered straight away.

'Evening Mr Pryor. You said to call.' After a brief pause, his face lit up like a cat with cream.

'Well?' Izzy bounced from foot to foot. 'Tell me.'

'Shh,' he covered the mouthpiece. 'Yes, we've got it,' he mouthed.

'Great Mr Pryor. So I'll liaise with your Head Groundsman, Stewart Ballard. Oh… Stewart! I know him. We went to the same school.'

On hearing that name, Izzy went weak at the knees. She had to sit down.

'Goodnight Mr Pryor, and thanks again.' He put the handset down. 'Are you alright, Izzy? You look quite flushed.'

His concerns didn't last long. 'We've got the business! We've got the business! Smile Izzy! Look excited!' He punched the air several times.

'I am, I truly am. I'm just a bit surprised.' She didn't want to say it was about Stewart. 'I know, how about walking to The Lamb for a drink to celebrate?'

Scooping her into his arms, he landed her a kiss on the mouth. 'Great idea, let's go.'

❧   ❧   ❧

As Colin closed the backdoor to the farmhouse, the security lights came on. The brightness was short-lived. As soon as they moved out of the range of the sensor, the night was ink black. Their farm track had no street lights, and the only illumination came from the Lamb Inn far in the distance. It was too faint to be of any help. Izzy hung on to Colin's arm for fear of tripping or falling. They slowly progressed down the lane that ran past their lower field—the place where their scarecrow stood. As they drew near, a voice called out.

'Hello, Colin. Not seen you for a while.'

Colin's response was an involuntary jump.

'Gordon Bennett,' he puffed, trying to get his breath

back, 'the scarecrow's alive! You heard it didn't you?'

They both turned to see the dim light of PC Wright's bike approaching.

'Evening, you two. Lovely night for a walk.' He rode on without stopping and was gone as quickly and quietly as he'd arrived.

'That gave me a real turn.' Colin's voice quivered. 'I'm still shaking now.'

'Nothing that a glass of champagne won't settle.'

'Champagne?' It's only a small contract. You'll have spent all the profits.'

'It's our first, though. Anyway, don't be such a skinflint.'

Reaching the pub, they could hear the sounds of a piano accompanying a singsong. Everyone seemed in good voice. Colin led the way, clicking the latch and pushing open the door. All heads turned. Everyone fell silent. Then to a man, they all joined in, 'Colin, Colin, show us your leg, show us your leg, show us your leg. Colin, Colin show us your leg, a yard above your knee,' followed by peals of laughter, wolf whistles and cries of 'Where's your black stockings. Come on, Colin, don't be shy!'

'I told you, I knew I'd be the laughingstock of the village and no doubt the town.'

'Oh, come on now, where's your sense of fun? Two glasses of champagne, Lucy.'

'Celebrating are we?'

Before Colin had time to answer, Clive, who was propping up the bar, chipped in.

'I guess you're here to celebrate Griggs Hole Farmers winning a contract for Harpsden Golf Club? Part of their major refurbishment programme.' Clive winked at Colin. Colin's mouth hung open.

'How did you hear that? We've known ourselves for less than an hour. You can't do anything in this place without everyone knowing your business.' Izzy stood nodding beside him, 'anyway, what are you doing here? Last I heard, you were a guest of Her Majesty at Martlesham Open Prison, wasn't it?'

'All a complete misunderstanding. I'd only been running my new business for about a year. I was sure that kiddie's entertainment was zero-rated for VAT, you know, like their clothes and shoes. Well, it turns out that bouncy castles aren't.'

'But how did you end up in prison for non-payment of VAT? It's surely not a prisonable offence, is it?'

Colin whispered to Izzy, 'I'm so glad we added VAT to our quote.'

Ann Bishop joined them at the bar, on her break from playing the piano.

'No, it wasn't the lack of VAT payments that sent him to prison; it's what he did to the unfortunate VAT inspector's car. Didn't you hear?' she asked Colin out of earshot of Clive.

'No, can't say I did.'

'Poor chap. The inspector was with his wife at the Raj Tandoori in Harpsden High Street—the Indian right next to the shopping centre entrance. It was late on a quiet Wednesday, and the inspector was celebrating his promotion to Regional level. Clive was driving past and spotted his car outside. Well Clive, always a prankster, pulled alongside and took one of his bouncy castles from his van, and laid it in the road right next to the shopping centre entrance, the one with a large flat awning where everyone shelters if it's raining.'

'Yeah, I know it.'

'He rolled the inspector's car onto the deflated castle, fired up his compressor in the back of his van and in no time at all, lifted the car 15 feet in the air.'

'Oh, my gosh. And then?'

'Well, he wasn't going to leave it like that. He shimmied up the castle and manoeuvred it onto the flat awning. At that point, I came along to see him deflating the castle before packing it back into his van. As I watched, calm as you like, he just drove off.'

'So what did you do?'

'I finished walking the dog, before I passed back about 20 minutes later. Couldn't believe my eyes. Three police cars, a fire engine and ambulance, plus a reporter from the Harpsden Chronicle were all milling about. The VAT inspector looked lost, as if he was missing something. Of course he was, it was his car. We get little crime in Harpsden. All the services had turned out hoping to get some extra money, overtime, I guess. It was all too much for the inspector's wife. She broke down in tears. Inconsolable, she was. A sizeable crowd gathered, all laughing and pointing, while the Police and Fire Brigade ran around like headless chickens. It was like Christmas, with the pantomime season come early.'

'So how did he get caught?'

'Well, it wasn't me. I think as he pulled the bouncy castle out of his van, one of his business cards fell out. The police found it lying on the road for all to see.

'Beer's Inflatable Fun'. It clearly stated 'Proprietor Clive Beer' with his full name, address and telephone number. For Clive, it could have been the best thing ever to have happened to him. The Press, complete with pictures, covered the entire story. Front-page and centre spread. Unluckily for him, the inspector in his new Regional position got him put away for 18 months. Though he was out in six for good behaviour, he could not take advantage of all that free publicity.'

'The old rogue.' Colin turned back to Clive.

'So how'd you know I won a contract with the Golf Club?'

'Well, I'm part of the Grand Opening on Saturday also, providing inflatable fun rides for the children. I called Steve Pryor about the arrangements, and he told me.'

'Sounds like that compressor of yours is pretty powerful to lift a car!'

'That's nothing. It turns out hundreds of PSI. You know pounds per square inch, enough to blow the top off a hill I shouldn't wonder.'

Colin and Izzy finished their second and third glasses of champagne before leaving everyone to it and wandering back home. In the frosty night air, the champagne's effects meant Colin had problems telling the road from the path and the path from the ditch. For every step Izzy took forward, he took at least three or four sideways, backwards, in fact anyway, except the way she wanted him to go. Slowly, they made their way back to the farm.

As they rounded the corner in the lane that runs past the lower field, he told the scarecrow how handsome he looked in his fine apparel and how he had once owned a similar coat, jacket, shirt and trousers and quite by coincidence, they too had a tear in the knee right where his did.

For Izzy, her bed couldn't come soon enough. Though she didn't mind him telling her how much he loved her, after twenty-six, or thirty-six, or was it forty-six times, she'd run out of ways of sounding grateful, appreciative or flattered.

For Izzy, Tuesday started typically; for Colin, Tuesday didn't start until lunchtime.

'Why didn't you stop me? You know I hardly ever drink.' He swigged at a large glass of water.

'Hardly, plus one, now!'

He thought she was too cheerful. 'Izzy my love.'

'Don't start that again. I need you up, shaved, and showered. Lunch will be in 10 minutes. We've got things to do. Get a move on.'

He grunted as he turned over; with that, she pulled back the covers.

'Remember, we're in business and have a contract to fulfil. Mr Pryor, or Major Woods or Stewart wouldn't be—'

'Mr Ballard, Izzy.'

'I know, you don't need to remind me.' A dreamy intonation coloured her voice.

'Wouldn't be what?'

'Wouldn't be impressed with you lying around in bed nursing a sore head. First thing, after lunch we'll run over our plan and see what's been done and what's still outstanding. You've now 5 minutes.'

❧   ❧   ❧

The paper rustled as Izzy spread out their 'To Do' list on the table,

'Not so loud, love,' Colin rubbed his forehead, 'it really hurts.'

'Cages?' She was determined to press on.

'Fourteen done, four to go.'

'Templates?'

'Ten completed.'

'Rabbit traps all done. Just need to get a big bag of carrots from the shed and turn them into balls.'

'I've been thinking,' Izzy spoke up, 'you won't need balls for the traps. Only for Thursday when we load the Rabbodig. Chunks will be fine for the traps.'

'That'll save a bit of time,' Colin said. 'What about the green hole cups?'

'What about them?'

'Aren't they due today?'

'They'll be here.' Izzy sounded confident.

'Did you give the postcode on the address?'

'Of course I did.'

'If the driver's using one of the satellite pointing global navigators, he'll end up in the village and nowhere near here. I bet that's it.'

'What's it?' Izzy crunched her forehead.

'Why he's not here yet? Why they've not been delivered? You said Tuesday, and it is. I bet the poor driver's aimlessly wandering around the streets of Henslow looking for us right now.'

'No, don't worry, Colin. If he's that lost, he's just needs to ask. Griggs have lived in this house for over 100 years. Everyone knows that. Anyway, I filled in the details on the computer, and the form had an option for further information; you know notes to help the driver, like directions or a neighbour where you could leave the package if no one was home.'

'That's handy. So what did you put?'

'Nothing really. Just a little extra detail. He might find useful when looking for us.' Izzy turned away so as not to look him directly in the eye.

'Such as?'

'Oh, nothing.'

'Izzy, it's not nothing, or you'd tell me. What did you say?'

'I suggested the driver stop and ask anyone if they knew where the man who wears black stockings lives. Some people may not know Griggs Farm, but everyone knows where you live.'

'How could you! Now, not only does the village and Harpsden know, but the DHL driver and all his driver colleagues and the control staff. And they're an international business. It will be all around the world—Colin Griggs of Griggs Farm, Henslow, Oxdenshire, England wears black stockings. Well, you've certainly put us on the map.'

      ℒ   ℒ   ℒ

In the Pryor household, the phone rang.

'Mr Pryor, Major Woods here. Good morning.'

'Morning Major.'

'I thought I'd ring to let you know I've just had that Clive Beer chappie on the phone, the one with the inflatable rides.'

'Is there more than one?'

'More than one what?'

'Clive Beer.'

'Well, I guess so, but only one with inflatable rides, as far as I know. Why do you ask?'

'I didn't, but you seemed to intimate there are more.'

'Mr Pryor, now listen. Colin Griggs—'

'What about Colin Griggs? I thought we were talking about Clive Beer?'

'We are, I mean, we were, but now we're not.'

'We're not? I'm confused.'

'Look Mr Pryor' Major Woods was becoming exasperated. 'Why I rang you is that it's been brought to my attention that Colin Griggs—'

'Are you sure you mean Colin Griggs?'

'Let me finish, man. As I was saying, it's been brought to my attention that he wears women's black stockings.'

'And does Clive Beer also?'

'I don't know, and I don't care! The fact is Griggs does.'

'So it's alright for Mr Beer to wear stockings, but not for Mr Griggs. Is that what you're saying?'

'No!'

'Do you think this will impair his ability to provide us with the 18 putting green holes we need?'

'Well, I guess not.'

'Then what he does or doesn't do behind closed doors is his affair and his affair only, don't you think?'

'I suppose so.'

'So no more needs be said on the issue, Major.'

'No.' The Major held the telephone receiver away

from his head and looked at it.

'Well, bye for now.' Steve put the phone down. 'I guess he doesn't know what 15 denier feels like against the skin. Silly old duffer!'

❧   ❧   ❧

It was late afternoon; Colin was busy in his workshop surrounded by an ever-growing number of cages piled higgledy-piggledy. He heard a van pull into the yard, followed by the muted sounds of conversation. Too distant to make out what was being said, he realised his name was being called. The call got louder as Izzy made her way into the barn and workshop.

'Can you come out here, Colin? The DHL driver wants a word.'

He opened the workshop door to be greeted by an outstretched hand.

'Put it there, cobber. I'm Bruce, and I'm on the UK leg of my walkabout. I'm just earning a bit of extra cash driving for DHL, and had to stop by and say hi and shake your hand. Well done you. Who'd have thought it? Brave man to come out like that and publicly tell, not only friends and family I guess, but the entire world. Gotta hand it to you Poms. You've got balls.'

'Gotta…, got to hand what to us?'

'Coming out like that. Now don't go all shy on me. You're an inspiration. A couple of guys in the Sydney office and Jack in Perth asked me to thank you on their behalf. On reading the driver's notes, he felt so inspired he phoned his missus straight away and told her outright—just like that!'

'Like what? What have I done?'

'You're a hero, mate. Give me your hand again.'

'What on earth are you talking about?' Colin felt like he stepped into a parallel universe

'Just check stockingwearers.com. You're famous Colin. Can I call you Colin? I feel we're brothers in this repressive world. We need more Colins.' He checked his watch. 'On a tight schedule; I've gotta go. Oh, here's your package. Sign, please. Get blogging, mate. See ya.'

With that, the DHL van pulled out of the yard and off down the lane toward Henslow. Drifting across the field, you could hear Bruce shouting at the scarecrow, 'Do you wear stockings too, boy? Should do! I bet it's cold out here at night,.'

'Izzy I don't. I never have and never will.'

'You don't need to convince me, just the rest of the world, it seems.'

'Anyway, what's blogging?' The deep lines on Colin's brow said it all.

The rest of the evening, he worked away, still confused about Bruce and what had happened. Izzy was entertaining doubts. Everyone else seemed to think he does, and he told Lucy he did. *I wonder,* she thought. *I just wonder.*

CHAPTER 8

DO RABBITS HAVE WATCHES?

Wednesday started much as any other day did. Both Colin and Izzy were up at their usual time, around 7 o'clock. Over breakfast, they discussed the plans, completed their tick list and revised their priorities.

'Actually, we need to spend the morning catching up on the usual farm stuff. Then this afternoon you can finish your cages and templates ready for the workers, who'll becoming later this evening.'

'If the traps work,' Colin added.

'No negativity! Businesses don't succeed by being negative. Think positive Colin. Positive.'

Izzy went to the storeroom and got a bag of carrots. In the kitchen, she got her chopping board and knife, recently sharpened, her peeler, a colander and a five-litre bottle of Highland Springwater. Finally, she fished around in one of her cupboards for her two Lakeland containers to keep vegetables fresher longer. Right, all set, she thought. She was poised with a carrot in one hand and knife in the other when Colin walked in.

'What on earth are you doing?' He said.

'Preparing the trap bait—carrot chunks, remember—for tonight.'

'These are wild animals. Rabbits eat anything tasty. You're not preparing a gourmet meal; peeling, slicing and dicing, washing in spring water and storing for freshness. It's rabbit bait!'

'They're our workers, and our workers deserve the best. As you know, a happy worker is a productive worker!'

'Yes, so you keep telling me, but...' He left, she continued.

Her stack of neatly peeled sliced and diced carrots soon grew into a substantial pile. 'So, eighteen rabbits and say two chunks each to entice them to the trap mouth, one to induce them inside and two in the stocking foot to keep them happy. And one more for good measure. That's, err... two, three, four, five, six chunks per rabbit. So all told 108 chunks.' Planning and preparation, she thought. And it helps to control waste and keep the costs down. She felt pleased with herself. 'A good job well done,' she mused, as she snapped the lid closed on the second Lakeland container.

'Colin,' she called across the yard in the barn's direction. 'It's 5.30, and we need to set off in an hour.' There was no response. 'Colin, Colin, can you hear me?!'

'Yes, my love.'

'Kettle's on. We'll grab something to eat before setting out. Beans on toast with an egg on top?'

'What? I mean, pardon?'

'I said beans on toast with an egg on top,' raising her voice. At that moment, he walked into the back door.

'Alright, no need to shout, not lost my hearing yet.'

'You could have fooled me; deaf old bugger,' she said under her breath.

'I heard that and I'm not a deaf old bugger!'

'I never said you were. Beans and egg, okay?'

'Two please.'

'What beans! That'll never fill you up.'

'Yeah, yeah, hilarious.'

'Right, carrot chunks are here—two containers, one each. The eighteen traps are in my two 'save the planet' hessian shopping bags, nine in each. Now, all we need is the wheelbarrow—the one with the pneumatic tyre. It gives a less bumpy ride.'

'What, you want me to push you up the hill to the warren?'

'No, silly, it's for bringing back the full traps. How else were you proposing to carry hoard of disgruntled rabbits? Ask them to follow behind you in a crocodile?'

'Yeah, I suppose you're right.'

'And don't you forget it.' She busied, putting on her coat and boots. 'What are we going to do back in the farmyard?'

'It'll be just about time for News at 10—haven't seen it for a few days. I've no idea what's going on in the world.'

'You've no idea what's going on in your head, Colin, never mind the world.'

'What do you mean?'

'I suppose you think the rabbits will appreciate catching up with current affairs, seeing what's going on in politics, or if the FTSE has rallied. What I meant was, where will the cages be so we can deposit our now angry rabbits—especially as they'll miss News at 10!'

'Oh, I see. I've lined them all up in the barn with water and food. They should be safe until we move them tomorrow afternoon.'

They set off across the yard through the five-barred gate with the wheelbarrow loaded with traps and carrot chunks. From there, they headed for the warren in the bank of the top field.

At the warren, they placed all the traps in a line about two feet apart, with the entrances facing the burrows and the stockings unrolled down the hill. Each trap had the allotted carrot chunks placed, ready and waiting. Coli and Izzy retired to the bush he fell out of previously and waited.

'Planning and preparation,' they whispered to each other.

Almost on cue, the first rabbits appeared. 'Do rabbits have watches?' Colin asked.

'Shhh, you'll scare them.'

After a lot of random hopping around, sniffing the air and general play, the rabbits picked up the smell of the finely peeled, chopped and washed in Highland Spring water carrots; the bait had the desired effect.

Soon, they were hovering around the entrance to the traps. First one, and then a second, took the plunge and ventured in. The steep slope, combined with the sheerness of the stocking material, soon had the rabbits sliding into the foot. After the initial surprise, accompanied by a flurry of activity, each foot soon fell quiet. A combination of the carrot snacks and a dark tunnel making the rabbits feel at home—all warm, comfortable, and fed.

'You're a genius,' he whispered. 'We must have ten at least all snuggled up and not a complaint amongst them. What do we do now?'

'Wait for the last few to take the bait. If we break

cover and scare them, I doubt if any more will come out tonight.'

'Look, that's it, Izzy. The last one is just slid down the hill. Guess we've done it!'

Izzy took charge, 'Right, so working across the hill, pull the wire stays from the ground and tie a single knot in each leg, not tight but just enough to stop the little fellas making a break for it. Place each one in the wheelbarrow. Gently does it, not too rough. We don't want to cause panic. Go, go, Colin, quick. I'm right behind you.'

'That was easy. Eighteen little workers sorted.'

'Actually, I think we may have nineteen. I'm sure I saw two slide into one stocking. You see what planning and preparation can do?' Izzy smiled up at him. He returned her gaze.

Rather too confidently, Colin wheeled the barrow down the hill and across the yard toward the open barn door and the line of waiting cages. Dusk was turning to night. The movement operated security lighting, all 5000 watts, flicked on with the ferocity of a lightning strike, illuminating the total scene. Blinded, he couldn't see where he was going and steered the barrow, and himself, headlong into the slurry trench running across the yard. The rabbits didn't need an invitation. In an instant, eighteen black stocking balls took flight, darting for cover whilst still imprisoned.

Izzy sprang into action to shouts of 'Come here! No, you don't; come back!' together with an assortment of more dubious expletives. She rounded up the errant prisoners and cage them before they did any serious damage. He dragged himself from the slurry, covered from head to toe.

'What is it about this farmyard and your clothes? First the duck pond and now the slurry trench. You're not coming into the house like that! I know dung is part and parcel of farming, but I draw the line at having it walked around the house. Get everything off out here, now.'

'Izzy please, no!'

'Everything. I want you in your birthday suit. No one's around for miles to see you. Go on, get on with it.'

'It's really not necessary.'

'Not necessary! The bathroom carpet still stinks of pond water. New carpets throughout or off with the lot. Your choice!'

'That's not fair. It's cold out here.'

'Your choice. I'm not letting you in the house like that unless you promise new carpets throughout.'

He slowly removed his jacket and threw it against the barn door.

'Now your shirt, come on, Colin.' He peeled off the sticky garment. 'What's wrong with you? I've seen you naked on numerous occasions. Don't go all shy now and don't tell me it's because the rabbits are looking. Get on with it.'

Both parties were stationary in a stale-mate; the movement-activated security lights switched off. *Now's my chance,* he thought as he dropped his trousers in an attempt to hide under cover of darkness. His action had quite the opposite effect. He was caught, like a frightened rabbit in car headlights, with his trousers around his ankles. Illuminated for everyone to see, he stood as bold as brass, dressed in a pair of black stockings with suspenders.

'I knew it, Colin! I just knew it. How long has this been going on? All those jokes weren't jokes at all; they were the truth! You…,' she could hardly bring herself to say it; 'you wear women's stockings. How could you?'

'Izzy, Izzy, please. It's not what it seems.'

'It seems blatantly obvious to me! You wear women's stockings; I can see them as bright as day, and I wish I couldn't. So don't say to me 'it's not what it seems'. It's exactly what it seems.'

She welled up; not a sob or a trickle, but floods, buckets, uncontrollable.

'Come on, Izzy. It's still me, the same old Colin.' He shuffled over to her and went to put his arm around her to console her.

'Don't you touch me, Colin Griggs, ever again.'

'Listen to me; let me explain.'

'Explain! Explain what? How your mother didn't love you; how you were bullied at school or how I've been a terrible wife. Go on, which of those excuses had you in mind, or is it all three of them?'

'None!'

'None? So what is it?'

'Cold.'

'Cold, cold? You mean it's the cold? Pull the other one; it's got bells on.'

'No, really. In the chemist shop the other day, Ann Bishop said her Jim frequently wears tights on his motorbike. Keeps him warm. She was very matter of fact.'

'But you're not wearing tights, and you're not riding a motorcycle.'

'No, I know but—'

'But… I knew there'd be a but. Go on.'

'Well, Lucy—'

'Don't bring her into it.'

'She is partly to blame.'

'Oh, I should have guessed. She's only 20 something and youngsters these days have some strange ideas about what's acceptable behaviour or not. I suppose she suggested you wear them. Or are they hers!? Colin, how could you? You're old enough to be her father.'

Izzy was in floods of tears again.

'For goodness sake, woman, listen.'

'What!' Izzy blow her nose into a bedraggled tissue.

'As I was buying the nine pairs of stockings, Lucy counted them out and said she only had eight pairs in black, so I had to choose another colour. That's when Ann Bishop joined in and said I'd look good in chocolate brown, and she told me about Jim.'

'So?'

'So back here I checked the packets to find Lucy had miscounted, and I had ten packets, nine black and one chocolate brown.'

'Why didn't you say anything?'

'Well, if you remember, you were preoccupied with the three leg waxing kits and why I hadn't chosen the foot massage balm instead.'

'And.'

'So I put the extra pair back in the bag to return it. I left it by my bedside to remind me when I next go to town.'

'Well.'

'I haven't been. Then tonight as we were getting

ready to go trapping I remembered how cold I got last time so I thought if it's alright for Jim Bishop and Ann seemed fine with it, then why not?'

'And the suspender belt?' She was glaring at him.

'Well, I guess women who normally wear support stockings have fatter thighs than me. They kept rolling down, so I rummaged through your underwear drawer for yours.'

'It has some plausibility, but Colin Griggs, I've not done with you yet!'

'It's the truth. Please believe me!'

&- &- &-

Colin woke on Thursday morning to find himself alone in bed. Bleary-eyed, he stretched out his hand feeling for his watch; instead, his hand fell across a small pile of nylon with a note attached. It simply read, "get rid of these!" In an instant, the memory of the whole ghastly episode came rushing back, followed by the realisation it was the day his Rabbodig machine was going to be put to a proper test—to create eighteen holes at the Harpsden Golf Club. All thoughts of stockings were erased and replaced with sheer panic.

'Izzy, Izzy, today's the day!' He threw back the covers and sprinted to the bathroom, flinging on anything to hand before rushing headlong downstairs.

'Izzy, Izzy.' He called again. Still no answer; she was nowhere to be found. He dashed into the yard but still no sign, and then into the barn. Passing eighteen, or maybe nineteen, bemused rabbits, he headed toward his workshop. *She'll be somewhere,* he thought, *must get the lorry loaded ready for the off.*

Reaching for the door handle, he noticed it was ajar. He could hear drawers being opened and cupboards being rifled. He stopped dead. *Izzy! She doesn't believe me. Do I confront her now, or…?* It was 'or'. He backed away, careful not to make a sound, returning to the kitchen.

He had just taken a mouthful of cereal as she walked in.

'Morning darling.'

'Don't "morning darling" me Colin Griggs, as if everything is okay?'

'It's the truth, I promise. I'll never do it again.'

'Did you see my note?'

'Yes.'

'And?'

He hesitated. 'It's in hand.'

'What does that mean?'

'No, I haven't got rid of them yet, but I will as soon as I finish breakfast.' He looked sheepish. 'Anyway, that's all by the by. It's our big day today.'

'You're telling me. While you snored your head off, I've been out freshening up the rabbit's drinking water, topping up the carrot balls, creating a whole lot more and set the extra rabbit free. I've been working hard on your business.' She folded her arms across her chest.

'Our business, it's for both of us; our future together.' He reminded her.

'Mmmmm we'll see. You've got some thinking to do first, and changes to make.'

The phone rang. Izzy was close by and picked it up. 'Griggs Farm.' There was no hint of angst in her voice. 'Yes, he's here; I'll just get him for you. Who shall I say is calling?' At the response, she sat down, fearing her knees would weaken. The words stuck in her throat, 'it's Stewart Ballard.' She passed the handset to Colin.

'Stewart, good morning.' What followed were a few minutes of conversation, checking the details about what was required, equipment, timings and the like. 'Okay, see you in the Clubhouse car park around 6 o'clock this evening.' He cleared down the phone.

'We're on Izzy; it's all coming together.'

CHAPTER 9

GOLF BUGGY

All previous thoughts were pushed aside; Colin and Izzy sprang into action. Well, nearly all thoughts. Izzy realised she would see Stewart for the first time for many, many years and was feeling both excitement and trepidation.

With her task list in hand, she set about ensuring all was ready for that evening, and nothing would be forgotten or left to chance.

'We'll wait until much nearer the time before loading Old Alfred so as not to disturb the rabbits until we have to.'

'Fine by me,' said Colin, and they set about their respective tasks. The day passed without incident and little conversation.

'Colin,' Izzy ventured into the barn; he was just clearing up. 'I think it's time to load the lorry. Let's get moving; we don't want to be late.'

Colin appeared dressed, ready for an evening on the golf course with a thick jumper, jacket, jeans and waterproof leggings. 'These should keep me warm and dry, just in case I get too near one of the water obstacles on the course.'

'Sensible, extremely sensible, and no stockings.' She kept all conversation to a minimum.

He backed Old Alfred Mac toward the barn. Izzy

bent down and grasped a cage handle, one in each hand, ready to lift. She straightened her knees. Nothing happened; she froze stock-still. Even with a mighty heave, nothing happened. The cages stayed as they were, not moving, stationary.

'Mind yourself, love,' he shouted from the cab, 'remember the problem with the cages not being level and rabbits burrowing under the sides? Well, I fixed it.'

'Fixed it! You nearly fixed me! Why didn't you warn me?' Izzy did a gorilla imitation around the yard.

'I found a roll of lead left over from the barn repairs and lined the roof of each cage to give it extra weight.'

'Well, it worked! How the heck am I going to shift these onto the greens?'

'Just lift one at a time. You'll soon manage.'

'Okay Colossus, you can load them onto the lorry; I'm going to save my strength.'

They busied sorting and loading.

Colin stood back to admire the laden lorry. 'I think we're done.'

'Signs Colin, what about the signs? Each cage must advertise 'Griggs Hole Farming' to get our name known.'

Slowly but surely, a fully loaded vintage flat-bed lorry wound its way across town and out to the golf course. The clock on the tower of the clubhouse showed 6 o'clock as they pulled into the car park. In the far corner, a figure waved them over.

There he is, she thought, *after all these years.* Her tummy turned. *No, it's all in the past. Colin's your man and anyway, no doubt Stewart's happily married.*

As they got closer, the boy she remembered, the rebel with long hair, slim with an athletic build, was now a man with little hair and a small paunch where his abs had been. But his eyes, his dark brown pools, his oh so sexy eyes, were still present. From working outdoors he was tanned and his face craggy with laughter lines, which showed off those dreamy eyes, as she'd never seen them before.

'Evening Stewart. We're here on time. Always a good start if you wish to impress your customer.' Colin sounded nervous. 'And this is—'

'I know Colin—Isobel.' He put out his hand to shake hers. They touched, their fingers closed together, not too tight but a little too long for a typical handshake. Nothing was said, but she saw a smile creep into the corner of his eyes; coy, she responded in kind.

Colin didn't see any of this as he was busy at the rear of the lorry unleashing the stay ropes and getting ready to offload.

'Wow, slow down, Colin. We can't drive the lorry onto the fairway or the greens. It's too heavy and would leave tracks worse than bunkers; there'd be a members riot. I suggest we use electric golf buggies to transport your equipment around. They're designed to leave no marks.'

'Okay, fine by me, whatever you say.'

'So what have we got here?' Stewart peered at the lorry load.

'We have eighteen specially designed cages, each containing one rabbit.'

On hearing the "R" word, an icy shiver ran down Stewart's spine. 'These cages, are they secure? The last thing I want, or need, is to introduce a whole family of eighteen, eighteen…,' he said a second time just to make sure Colin fully appreciated the enormity of the situation, '… rabbits onto this fine and hugely expensive golf course.'

'Unless their father was Houdini, I'm confident they won't escape.' Colin was trying to make light of the concerns.

'Yeah, well maybe, but before we load anything, let's have a practice with a buggy. I assume you're not golfers.'

'No, neither of us.' Colin and Izzy exchanged glances.

'They're simple: one pedal to go, one to stop, and a steering wheel to change direction. But they need a key to start. Here; have a go.' Stewart handed them both a key.

Izzy and Colin jumped into one each and spent a couple of minutes driving around the car park.

'Simple ay?'

'Yes, simple, Stewart.' She said it; she said his name and now was on cloud nine.

'Right, time's moving on; let's get this show on the road. Colin, each buggy will take two cages. Why don't you start on the 18th and work your way back? While Izzy starts at the first and works her way up. You'll meet somewhere in the middle. All the fairways are well signposted, and on the greens, I've marked the position for the new holes with a chalk paint cross. You can't miss them.'

Colin had already loaded two cages on his buggy

and was ready for the off. 'See you later.' With that, he was gone.

Before Colin was even out of sight, Stewart took advantage of his absence. 'Isobel, my Little Miss Muffet, my —'

'Stewart no, not now; we've things to do.'

'Is that 'no not now' or 'no never'?'

She didn't answer, as she was struggling to offload a cage.

'Here, let me.' He quickly lifted two off the lorry and placed them onto the buggy.

'I think I might need you to come with me,' she said, trying to avoid eye-contact.

'My pleasure Little Miss Muffet.'

She couldn't help notice the twinkle in his eye.

Things progressed well, with many buggy trips toing and froing across the course. Several hours passed. Dusk had turned to night by the time Colin returned from the ninth. All the cages had gone. *I guess Izzy has the last two and will be back soon.* He parked his buggy and climbed into the lorry cab to wait.

❧ ❧ ❧

Out on the fairway, Izzy behaved professionally, resisting Stewart's advances and fighting her feelings.

'Hole eight, right, that's the last one. Just rotate the blanking plate to give our little furry friend access to the green and let him dig. Farewell, little rabbit, dig hard.' Izzy waved to the rabbit.

Both she and Stewart jumped into the buggy and headed off in the clubhouse's direction. Hole eight was on the far side of the hill and out of sight of the car park.

Now's my chance, thought Stewart, but fate overtook them. The little light on the front of the buggy grew dim, the speed slowed, and within a couple of yards, they'd stopped dead. Izzy was worried she done something wrong.

'Battery,' said Stewart, 'flat as a pancake. There's no point turning the key; it's dead. We'll just have to abandon it here and walk back.'

'How long's that going to take?' Her voice showed a hint of panicky.

'Isobel, it's not a big deal. Yes, it's dark—'

'Pitch black, if you ask me.' She clung onto his arm. He smiled; in the dark, she didn't see.

'Okay, it's pitch black, but this is where I work and walk every day. I know this place like the back of my hand. We'll be fine. I'll have you back in the clubhouse within a few minutes.' They set off in a straight line heading toward the 18th.

All was going well until Izzy missed her footing and stumbled into a bunker. As she fell, she grabbed at the nearest thing—Stewart—bringing him down on top of her.

'Oh, Isobel, I knew you still had feelings. I saw them in your eyes in the car park. I hadn't appreciated they were so strong.' To anyone else, his sincerity was wafer-thin; to her, she was smitten.

'Oh, shut up you! I tripped.' Moving to get up, his proximity, the warmth of his body, the smell of his aftershave, got the better of her. Feeling like a schoolgirl again, the intervening years slipped her mind; she kissed him long and passionately. 'I've not forgotten you.' She brushed sand from his cheek. Her light touch sent a shiver down his back. He responded by kissing her back.

'No, stop… Stewart, we can't, we mustn't.'

❧   ❧   ❧

It had been half an hour since Colin climbed into the lorry's cab and there was still no sign of Izzy. The thought crossed his mind he should look for Stewart to see if he knew where she was. *I guess he went home hours ago—no point looking for him.* With that, he jumped out of the lorry and back into his buggy. He set off toward the seventh hole. They'd been doing pairs of holes at a time and, since his last was the ninth, he figured Izzy's last would be the eighth. Just to make sure, he decided to check the seventh first.

At the seventh, a cage was there, right in the middle of the green. With no time to lose, he swung the buggy in the direction of the eighth. Here, too, a cage was neatly placed. *So she's finished. But where was she?* He jumped from the buggy and switched off the lights. Standing stock still, he listened, scanning the surrounding scene. A rustle of the wind in the trees was all he could hear, but against the darkness, he spotted the white of the fibreglass body of another buggy a short way down the fairway.

'Izzy, Izzy, I'm coming.' He fired up his buggy, his white charger, and set off at full speed, at all of four miles per hour, to rescue his damsel in distress.

Approaching, he called her name again.

'Izzy, it's me, I'm coming. Don't be frightened.' His heart sank. No Izzy; just an abandoned buggy. He tried the key; nothing.

'I guess she's walking back. Out here all alone, she could be anywhere. Okay, think,' he said, talking to himself. 'If I was her, what would I do? Well for a start I wouldn't treat Colin so harshly. I'd tell him it's okay about the stocking thing and I fully understand how he came to be wearing them. An easy mistake anyone could make.'

'Colin.'

'What?'

'Stop talking to yourself.'

'I'm not.'

'You are. Listen right now, that noise you can hear, it's you, talking to yourself.'

'But doesn't everyone?'

'Colin, get a grip. Izzy, we—'

'What do you mean, we?'

'Shut up. I need to find her! A straight line in the direction of the clubhouse.'

Silence returned. Colin, on foot, torch in hand, set off with new determination and purpose.

He reached the 18th green where he'd placed his first cage several hours earlier. Some 20 feet away, in the rough, his torch picked out the eyes of a rabbit frozen on the spot. 'Rabbit, green, damn.' With that, Stewart's words came back to him. 'I haven't time. I must find Izzy,' He called out her name.

'Did you hear that? It's Colin looking for me.'

'Shhh, he'll hear you.'

Izzy peeked over the side of the bunker. She saw the flash of Colin's torch as he swung it around searching for her.

JAMES MINTER

'Look there.' Izzy tried to stand up. Stewart pulled her back.

'No, don't. He can't find us together. Think about it. How will you explain?' Stewart held her arm tight.

'No, you're right. Anyway, he's heading toward the clubhouse.'

'I know,' now Stewart peeked over the bunker rim, 'if we're quick, we'll beat him back. He'll never suspect a thing.'

The pair scurried off. They stuck to the edges of the fairway so as not to be seen and to avoid any bunkers, trees, bushes or other objects that have the habit of jumping out at you when you least expect or want them.

Safely sat at the bar, they were in time for last orders. She and Stewart drank a celebratory glass of champagne for an excellent job well done and a new business partnership.

'To Griggs Hole Farmers and the Harpsden Golf Club.'

'My pockets are full of sand,' she whispered.

'Occupational hazard.' Stewart smiled, looking around to see if anyone had heard.

'This can't happen again. You know that!' Izzy tried to look serious.

Before he had time to answer, the bar doors flung wide open, Colin loomed large.

He bellowed, 'I need volunteers for a search party. Please, anyone, now!'

Izzy flashed Stewart a look. Her eyes showed panic.

'Stay calm; we're doing nothing wrong. Just call him.'

Over the din, she called, 'Here Colin. I'm over

110

here. All's well. Stewart, Mr Ballard, that is, came to my rescue.' A rose blush moved up her neck till her face turned the distinctive red of guilt.

By the time she'd finished speaking, Colin was alongside her, breathless but happy to have found her.

'Oh, my Izzy, my love, are you okay? I thought.' He paused. Standing back, he looked her up and down. 'I didn't know what to think. Anyway, you're safe, but sandy? And your face, it's bright red.' His voice became rather quizzical.

'Oh, it's hot in here, and I tripped in the dark and fell into a bunker. No bones were broken.' She made light of her plight. 'Mr Ballard, was doing his rounds, found me and brought me back here.' She looked toward Stewart.

'We thought you'd been rather a long time.'

'Thanks, Stewart. Glad to know my wife was in safe hands.' He patted him on the back.

'It was nothing. Drink Colin? My round. We were just celebrating a good job well done.'

'Okay, just one, and I mean only one. This stuff has a habit of sneaking up on me. Anyway, we've got to drive back.'

'So tomorrow morning you'll come to collect your Rabbodig thingies, insert the putting green cups and have a final inspection. I have the say-so with the Committee. They'll want to know all is well.' Stewart finished his glass of bubbly.

'Understandable.'

'Right Colin, see you at nine in the car park.'

'Fine, right. Goodnight Stewart.

'And to you Isobel. Goodnight.' As he turned

away, he left her with a knowing smile.

'Goodnight Stewart and thanks for rescuing me.'

'The pleasure was all mine.'

Colin appeared not to notice the exchange.

'Home Izzy; another busy day tomorrow.'

❧   ❧   ❧

Back at the farm, with lights out, they both snuggled down to a well-deserved sleep.

'Izzy?'

'Colin.'

'Just one thing's bothering me.'

'What's that?' She feared the worst.

'You know tonight, out near the 18th.'

'Yeeesss,' she was hesitant, quickly trying to think of a cover story.

'As I looked for you, I flashed my torch around and saw—'

'Saw what?' *Please don't say what I think you're going to say.*

'A rabbit sitting in the rough, alongside the green.'

'Is that all?' She sounded relieved.

'Well, that's enough. Remember how Stewart looked, after he discovered the Rabbodig was powered by rabbits? If he sees any at tomorrow's inspection, it will be all over for us.'

'Not to worry.'

'What do you mean, not to worry? It's our business, our future.'

'No, I mean about rabbits. I'm sure they've a good homing instinct and will be back in the warren before you can count your chickens.'

'Let's hope so. Night, my love.'

'Night, Colin.' She slept easily, if not a little excitedly. *After all those years, who would have thought it? Izzy, no more. I mean it.*

Over breakfast, they discussed the events of the night before. Well, most of them—how Colin found the abandoned buggy, how he'd tried to think like her, dependable Izzy, reliable Izzy, the person to be with in a crisis. How she tripped and fell into the bunker and was rescued, and how he nearly made a fool of himself by calling out to everyone to form a search party.

'No, Colin, don't be silly. I love that. To think my man was raising a rescue party for me. Just a pity you didn't see me sitting at the bar before you shouted out quite so loudly and in such a booming voice.'

Colin swung a look at his watch. 'Look at the time; I need to be away.'

'Do you need me? I'm sure you can handle Stewart, I mean Mr Ballard, by yourself, can't you?'

'Don't forget, I was at school at the same time as you both. I know you and he had a thing going. You can call him Stewart.'

He knows about last night. I bet he knows, flashed across her mind, followed by a guilty expression across her face. Luckily, Colin was half out the door.

'Good luck; I love you,' she called after him.

Going down the lane, past the lower field, Colin noticed the scarecrow had lost his trousers and gained a pair of stockings. *Blighters,* he thought, *little buggers.*

He pulled into the Club car park at 9 o'clock sharp. Stewart was waiting; he was smiling. *That's a good sign.*

'No, Isobel?'

'Morning Stewart. No, she's busy feeding chickens. The farm won't run itself.'

'I thought hole farming was your business now.'

'It will be, but we need to build our reputation and get more customers.'

'Well, if the inspection goes well today, and the Grand Opening tomorrow, I think there's every chance you'll get more customers. Following how I saw you two working last night, your punctuality, efficiency and coping with the switch from the lorry to the buggies to distribute the Rabbodig machines, I've already written a personal recommendation you can use with other customers. I won't give it to you just yet. Let's complete the inspection first.' Stewart wafted an envelope in front of him.

On hearing this, Colin was overly excited. *A personal written recommendation from the Head Groundsman of the county's biggest Golf Club. Don't let it go to your head. We've an inspection to go yet.* He puffed out his chest.

'Okay, how do you suggest we do this?'

'If we take a buggy each and do as last night, you start with the eighteenth, and I'll start with the first. Take half the putting green cups and the hole pins. Collect up the machines, drop in the cup, followed by the pin—'

'And hey presto,' Colin finished his sentence. *Good job Izzy didn't hear.*

'And you can buy me a drink in the bar after we've finished.' Stewart climbed into another buggy.

'Let's go.' They left in different directions.

On approaching the eighteenth green, Colin caught sight of a white tail disappearing into a hole. He turned quickly, but it had vanished from view. Jumping from the buggy, he ran to the edge of the green. In the rough, he found an entrance to a burrow with signs of fresh digging. He bent down to inspect it.

'I thought you guys had a strong homing instinct. Get out of here. Scram!' He kicked soil down the opening while pulling up great tufts of grass to hide the offending hole.

'You're talking to yourself again.'

'Don't be silly; I'm not.'

'Then who are you talking to?'

'The rabbits.'

Colin's monologue was interrupted.

'I do that sometimes; the only way to get a sensible answer now my wife's dead.'

Colin spun around. 'For goodness' sakes.' He clasped his hand to his chest to help himself breathe. 'You made me jump.' He saw an elderly chap walking his dog.

'Talk to myself, or the dog, much the same thing. Do it all the time. I thought I was going quite mad, but obviously, I'm not alone. Actually, you're never alone if you talk to yourself. That's why I do it. Is your wife dead?' inquired the stranger in a matter-of-fact way. 'Nasty thing, death; not for everyone. Don't be silly, not for everyone. We all die in the end!' His voice drifted off as he and his dog made their way across the links.

Oh gosh, now I'm worried, thought Colin as he watched the chap disappear down the fairway. I must remember, no talking to myself.

'Okay,' he said out loud and laughed. He looked around to see if anyone else was listening. Once again, he saw the back end of a rabbit disappearing into the same burrow. He went back over to the entrance, bent down and cupped his hand to his mouth.

'Now keep out of sight, there's a splendid chap. I need this personal reference.'

He loaded the Rabbodig on to the buggy and slipped in the cup. It fitted like a glove, and then the pin. The 18 proudly hung over the hole.

'Planning and preparation. It's paid off.'

'Colin, stop it!' He was back to speaking to himself.

'What?'

'You know what? Now just stop it.'

'You first.' He looked at his watch.

'You're going to make me late.'

'It's not me.'

'Right together, on the count of three; three, two, one.' Silence reigned. He was on his way to the seventeenth.

Stewart was going great guns and feeling extremely pleased he had given his vote at the Committee to Little Miss Muffet. 'I knew she wouldn't let me down.' He was approaching the seventh and saw Colin leaving the ninth.

'See you in the bar in about 20 minutes,' he shouted across the fairway.

'Yes, fine.'

116

Colin stood the first round and ordered a ploughman's.

'Good work this morning. All looks 'A' okay.'

Lucky you weren't at the eighteenth, thought Colin, hoping above all hopes that the rabbit would soon make its way back to the top field warren.

All rabbits look pretty much the same; what Colin hadn't realised was that it wasn't just one lone rabbit.

'Here. I've signed and dated it; your written recommendation. Now don't forget when you're rich and famous, it was me that gave you a bit of a helping hand.' *More truthfully,* Stewart mused, *it was Isobel in the bunker which swung it for me!*

'Cheers, Stewart.'

'Cheers Colin.'

'And cheers to both of you.' Clive Beer had arrived at the bar. 'I saw the lorry in the car park. You can't miss Old Alfred Mac. I guess with this success, you'll be trading it in for the Porsche version.'

'I don't think so. My father bought him from the wife of Alfred MacPherson, painter and decorator after he died in 1948. He's a part of the family.'

'Go on, get me a pint in.' Clive licked his lips.

Colin obliged. 'Why are you here?'

'Setting up for the Grand Opening. Stewart's given over a corner of the car park to Beers Inflatable Fun. I have several inflatables lined up to keep the youngsters occupied while the parents play golf.'

'Okay, so what's planned for tomorrow, Stewart?'

'The first tees are at 8 o'clock. All the pros and the better players want to be first to use the new course. Since it would take too long for all of them to leave from the first, we've decided to have a 'shotgun start', a mass tee off simultaneously. The top 72 players have been split into eighteen groups of four. Each four will make their way to their designated first tee, and on the stroke of 8 o'clock by the clubhouse tower, eighteen players will tee off concurrently, followed by their three teammates. All teams will play all eighteen holes, but if your first tee was say the twelfth, then your game will be complete after you finish the eleven.'

'Bit of a logistical nightmare. I think I'll stick to inflatables.' Clive sank a large part of his pint.

'All you need is good planning and preparation and expect the unexpected.' Colin voiced his advice, feeling smug with himself. *I'm getting the hang of this business malarkey.*

'Another drink Colin, Clive?'

'Oh, that's kind, but no thanks; driving.'

'Wise man; you Clive?'

'I've got three inflatables to get up and anchor down.'

'Well, I hope your lungs are in good order.'

'Yeah, ha-ha. I tell you what, though; this new mobile compressor can't half push out the old PSIs. A marvellous piece of Japanese kit.' Said Clive.

'Okay, gentlemen, must go.' Colin slipped down from his barstool and headed for the door.

'Regards to Isobel. Is she coming tomorrow?' Stewart didn't want to seem too eager.

'Wouldn't miss it. Till tomorrow.' Colin waved as he passed out the door.

'Izzy, Izzy, look at this.' Colin couldn't get out of the lorry quick enough. He ran across the yard waving the typed sheet of headed paper. 'Our first written recommendation. Dated and signed and everything.'

'Here, let me see. Signed by Stewart Ballard, Head Groundsman.' *Good old Stew*, she thought, smiling. *Now don't go there!* 'Here, put it back in the envelope. We'll need to keep it safe.'

Given their hectic week, they gave themselves the evening off. Colin just about stayed awake for "News at 10" before retiring. Izzy had gone up ages before and was asleep. Tip-toeing around the room readying for bed, he noticed the packet of stockings was missing from his bedside table. *It wasn't kids after all! I guess she put them on the scarecrow. She must have forgiven me by now.*

CHAPTER 10

RESOLUTE RABBITS

That might have been the end of the day for the Griggs, but by no means was it the end of the day for the new warren being dug under the hill around which Harpsden Golf Course lay.

Placing caged rabbits on all eighteen holes and releasing them to dig at pretty much the same time caused a seismic wave in rabbit terms. The frantic sound of digging travelled far underground in all directions. Each rabbit could hear the others and was drawn to the sound. They dug the holes for the putting green cups to the correct diameter and in the right place, but nobody told them to stop at that point. They created, and were still forming, an enormous maze of tunnels, crisscrossing beneath the hill—a veritable Pan's Labyrinth—the main entrance to which was in the rough just off the eighteenth.

In his farmhouse, Colin switched off the "News at 10" early and missed the weather forecasting a significant storm overnight. Around midnight, the winds picked up from the south-west and, with them, hours of continuous rain; some six centimetres fell overnight.

Amongst the worst affected were the rabbits of Harpsden Golf Club. The water ran down the hillside and found its way into the lower part of the new warren via the many greens which were temporarily flooded. Not only do the holes provide the golfer with a target and ultimately a well-loved game, but they also acted as drainage for the greens. Each putting green cup had a hole drilled in its domed shaped base too small for the ball to fit through but sufficient to accommodate the pin, with enough clearance for any accumulated water to pass through and soak away into the underlying subsoil. The heavy rains meant a temporary inconvenience for the digging rabbits, causing them to move uphill into the warren's upper chambers.

™ ™ ™

'Did you hear that rain last night? It sounded like it was going to come bursting through the windows.' Colin asked.

'I heard nothing. I was out for the count. Never even heard you come to bed.' Izzy rubbed at her eyes. 'Any damage done?'

'Not that I can see; hope all's well at Harpsden. It's the Grand Opening today. Today!' He realised what he'd said. 'Izzy, what time is it? Quick, we'll be late.' He sat bolt upright in a state of acute anxiety.

'Hey, it's okay. It's only 6.30.'

Stewart, meanwhile, had been up since the early hours, woken by the lashing rain. He donned his waterproofs and set off to inspect his new, prized, beloved, and expensive course. He'd done a tour of all eighteen holes and was just returning toward the Clubhouse as the Major's car pulled into the car park.

'Status report, Mr Ballard, if you please.'

'Morning to you, Major. What a storm.'

'Yes, I know that. Kept my Margaret awake most of the night. Gave the old Teasmade a run for its money. And the course, any damage?'

'I've inspected all eighteen holes. The design and drainage seem to have worked as planned, apart from a few soggy areas on fairways four, seven and eleven. All the greens are clear. I don't foresee any problem with the mass tee off at 8 o'clock.'

'All tickety boo and shipshape. Good man. They're doing breakfast in the Clubhouse. Let's grab ourselves one before the onslaught.'

'I'm with you Major.'

They joined a table where Mr Pryor and Clive Beer were sitting.

'Morning Mr Pryor.'

'Morning Major.'

'Ah Clive, Mr Beer. Are we going to have some inflatable fun today?'

'Apart from one guide rope that came adrift, everything is as it should be. Just need to inflate all the rides to their full pressure, and then let the fun commence!'

'That's good to hear. Got to keep the kiddies amused. Don't want them to get in the way of the real reason we're here. Golf—God's own.' The Major pulled back his shoulders and lifted his head high. 'I feel it's going to be an exceptional day in the Club's history.'

The Clubhouse was busy and alive with chatter about the storm and whether the course would be alright to play. General excitement and anticipation filled the room.

The Major got to his feet. Striking his cup with his knife, all went quiet, apart from the sounds of cutlery on crockery. 'Can I have your attention, please?'

'I say, Major, this is a fine breakfast you've laid on. Can't I finish it in peace?'

'Thanks, Mr Waghorn. I won't take up much of your valuable time. First let me say good morning to you all, a splendid turnout given last night's rain.' The murmuring started again. 'Gentlemen please; the good news is, over and above the quality of the breakfast—my thanks to the kitchen staff and Restaurant Manager—that Mr Ballard has done a complete course inspection and has given us the okay for play today.' A ripple of applause went through the assembled. 'It's 7.10 now,' he continued. 'You all have your allotted team and start tees. If you're unsure, they're on the notice board. I'm assured all the buggies are fully charged, but you will need to double up with so many going out at once.'

'As you go round, please note any problems you may come across. This has been a major and expensive revamp. I expect a few teething problems, but please bear with us. Before I let you go, there's just one more thing. I will be in my buggy travelling around observing, so I'll have my mobile phone on if you've an urgent need to get hold of me. Oh, and finally, just to say the BBC is sending a news crew down, so let's be on our best behaviour. Good luck, and have a great game of golf, and may the best man, sorry person win.' He returned to his breakfast.

The room emptied, and the noise abated.

'That seemed to go, alright. Mr Pryor, are you playing?'

'Yes, I need to get going. See you later.'

'Just keep an eye out for me. As a committee member, I trust you have the club's interest at heart.'

'Of course, Major. You have my full support.'

'Mr Ballard, will you travel with me in my buggy in case we have to deal with a crisis.'

'Sure, fine but I can't think what might go wrong. I've done extensive checks, and everything's in place.'

'Oh, have you seen that Griggs chappie? I assumed he'd be here today.' The Major asked.

'Just noticed his lorry pulling into the car park. I'll go and have a quick word.'

'We need to be off in five minutes. I'll meet you by the Captain's buggy then.'

❧   ❧   ❧

'Colin, Isobel, good morning.' As Stewart spoke, he turned to Izzy, 'you're looking radiant may I say.' A mischievous grin took over from his concerned groundsman expression. She looked away to hide a blush. 'All's okay on the greens. I checked them myself.' Colin visibly sighed. 'Any problems on the farm?'

Colin shrugged. 'Not seen anything yet. Actually, I haven't bothered to look. I wanted to be here for the tee off. Oh, I noticed we had one casualty. As we drove past the lower field, our scarecrow was leaning at a precarious angle.'

Clive appeared alongside. He was touting for business and handing out his card to anyone he could find.

'You never know when you might need an inflatable ride.' With that, he pressed his card into Colin's hand and was gone. 'See you later,' he called over his shoulder.

'He's a bit of a character, our Clive. I guess he needs to build his business back up after his umm—'

Colin finished Stewart's sentence. 'Extended holiday?'

'Yes, that's the polite way of saying it. Colin, have you had your business cards done? Excellent opportunity today to get yourself known.'

'Izzy's been busy with the computer and has made us some.' Colin handed Stewart one and watched while he read it. He felt so pleased. *A business card,* he thought and puffed out his chest.

'I see you've got a mobile phone. Essential these days. And an email address—that's so high tech.'

'Well actually, I'm not good with mobiles—'

'He's never used one in his life. I carry it,' Izzy chipped in. 'I manage the emails, too. Colin's not a computer sort of person. With fingers the size of bananas from all that farm work, he keeps hitting the delete key every time he wants to press "enter".'

Stewart noted those two facts with interest. 'So you're in charge of communication, so to speak, Isobel?'

She saw that twinkle creep into the corner of his eyes. *No Izzy, no,* she thought.

'Oh, but I tell Colin about everyone who rings or emails. Mustn't keep him in the dark.'

'Mr Ballard, we need to get going.' The Major's unforgiving tones reached their ears.

'As you heard, the Major's after me. I must be off. See you later.' Stewart turned to leave. 'Are you planning to stay for lunch? I would if I were you. Get to meet the members, never know who may need your hole services.'

With that, Stewart was across the car park and away off into the distance with the Major.

The 8 o'clock chimes rang out from the Clubhouse tower clock. The air was filled with the sounds of 'swish', followed almost immediately by the satisfying 'thwack' as the wood connected with the balls, driving them high and forward toward their target. Then followed a silence only broken by the occasional and distant shouts of 'fore', where intention was thwarted by physics.

Those who were first to tee off were joined by the rest of their group, and soon the sky and fairways were filled with some seventy-two balls, all heading for their chosen green, pin and hole.

'Look at that,' said the Major, turning to Stewart, 'all those months of planning and preparation, the attention to detail, the cross-checking, amending and correcting have all paid off. Our brand new leading-edge golf club. Makes you proud to be involved, nay proud to be British. We are the masters of organisation, of detail, of getting things done.' He surveyed the fairways like a military man preparing for battle.

'Major, Major, it's a golf course.'

'Stewart, Mr Ballard. Fancy hearing that from you, of all people, after the work and dedication you've shown. Yes, it is a golf course, but it's the County's finest. It'll put us on the map, on the circuit for the foremost championships, sponsorship, TV rights; just think of it.'

From deep within a pocket, the unmistakable sound of a mobile phone ring was clear to hear. Stewart checked his.

'Major, I think your phone's ringing.'

'Not now, Stewart, let me enjoy this moment.'

'Listen… Now mine's ringing. Hello, Head Groundsman.' The tinny sound of an irate voice projected at speed vied for attention. 'Slowly, slowly, can you repeat that? Your ball? What about your ball? Gone! Are you sure? What green are you on? Seventh. We're not far away. We'll be with you in a couple of minutes.'

'What was that about?' The Major eyed Stewart with suspicion.

'That was Matt Childs.'

'The club pro? I don't like the sound of that.'

'Yes, says his ball's disappeared. Birdie three, great shot; went to recover his ball and nothing.'

'What does he mean nothing? His ball can't have gone.' The Major shifted in his seat. 'Can't you get this thing to go any faster? We can't have him upset.'

'Look there, at the seventh. Everyone's standing around the hole, staring. And there goes my phone again, and yours, Major. You'd better answer it this time.'

'Major Woods... No, please don't shout… Say again. Your ball vanished? Balls don't just vanish. Okay, this one has. What hole are you on?… Sixteenth? I'm just arriving at the seventh. We seem to have a minor issue here. I'll deal with it and be with you as soon as I can.'

'My call was from the fourteenth. Same problem. Phone, Major.'

'Woods, can I help?'

Within the space of five minutes, players from all eighteen holes reported missing or vanished balls. 'Mr Ballard, we need to sort this out without delay.' A distinct edge had crept into the Major's voice.

❧   ❧   ❧

'Stand aside, please. Matt, what's happened?' The Major was impatient, 'come on, man.' He wanted to resolve the problem sooner rather than later.

'Great birdie shot, followed by a single bounce on the green and in she went. Before Paul took his shot, I went to recover my ball, and it was gone. I know it went in; we all saw it. Alex even congratulated me, and you know what he's like with compliments!'

'Thanks Matt. Now Michael, did you see it?'

'Sure, it was a real sweet shot. If I hadn't been playing against him, I would have congratulated him too.'

'So there's no doubt it went down.' The Major bent down to retrieve the putting green cup. Scrutinising it as it came into full view, he passed it to Stewart.

'Anything?' said the Major, before turning away to answer his phone again.

'Nothing obvious; can anyone lend me a ball for a second?' With that, Stewart dropped the ball into the mouth of the cup. After a momentary struggle, it worked its way through the drain hole in the bottom and dropped onto the green.

'See, if you look closely, the drainage hole in this cup was drilled from the outside in, giving a counter-sunk profile to the hole so the ball can drop through the bottom. That's the answer. The balls haven't vanished or disappeared. They're in the bottom of the green's hole.' Stewart felt pleased he'd identified the problem so quickly.

'So where's mine?' Matt was peering into an

empty hole. 'That's a competition ball: a Titleist Pro V1. I want it back, or the club will have to pay for a replacement.'

The Major was in command mode—no please or thankyous, just orders. 'Yes, yes, Matt. We'll worry about balls in a minute. Mr Ballard, what are you going to do? Griggs supplied all these cups, and they're all giving the same problem. Get him on the phone.'

'Hello, Griggs Hole Farmers. How can I help?'

'Isobel it's Stewart. We're on the seventh. We've got a problem with the hole cups Colin supplied.'

'What sort of problem?' She placed her hand over the phone's microphone. 'There's a problem on the seventh.' she whispered to Colin.

Colin raised his eyes skyward and grimaced.

'The balls drop through the bottom and—' Izzy relayed her conversation.

'And what Stewart?'

'And disappear.'

'What do you mean, disappear? Aren't they just in the bottom of the holes?'

'That's the even stranger part. They're nowhere to be found.'

'Colin, Stewart says he's got disappearing balls.'

'It's rather an odd time to be telling you about his medical problems. Just how well do you two know each other?'

'No, not him. If a player gets a ball into the hole, it drops through the cup and disappears. There are a lot of balls involved. And of course, because it's the Grand Opening, the players have all splashed out on

129

competition ones. Stewart and the Major are looking to us to do something, and quick!'

Colin paced, beads of sweat appeared on his brow. 'I bet it's those darn rabbits. After they dug their hole, they didn't stop digging. They haven't gone home, but have created a massive new warren under the entire golf course. The entrance will be on the eighteenth. Remember, I told you I'd seen one there in the rough. I thought it was just one lone rabbit that hadn't made it home, but now I'm not so sure.'

'So what can we do? How are we going to get their balls back? Think, Colin, think, this is serious. The future of our business is at stake.' The enormity of the problem dawned on Izzy.

'I know; just give me some time.'

'Time is something we don't have. They're looking for action, and now.'

'So, if the balls have dropped through the bottom of the cups, they've rolled into the warren tunnels. What we need is a way of fishing them out; a stick with a hook of some sorts on the end.'

'Keep talking.' Izzy gave him her full attention.

'Well, something like a… I don't know… a stick with a hook.'

'That's not at all helpful, Colin. Come on, think harder.'

'Clive!' Colin looked excited. 'He's the answer.'

'What about Clive?'

'Clive and his inflatable fun. He's got a compressor. Always on about how powerful it is. Remember how he lifted the VAT inspector's car?'

'And?' Izzy hadn't made a connection.

'Well, maybe, just maybe, he could blow the balls out from the warren.'

'Colin, keep it sensible. How on earth is he going to do that?'

'I don't know. What about if he hooked up the compressor to one of the holes—'

'Or the entrance to the warren,' she added.

'And applied some pressure—'

'Like blowing up an inflatable ride.'

'The balls will be pushed back up onto the greens and hey presto, problem solved.' He rubbed his hands in glee. 'Come on, no time to lose.'

It was all going so well, she thought, *until the hey presto.* 'I guess we've no other option but to try it. I'll get Clive on the phone. Where's the card he gave you?'

'Here.'

'Clive, Isobel Griggs, Colin's wife. He needs to speak to you rather urgently. I'll put him on.'

'Clive, Colin. I don't know if you've heard. Okay, you have. Well, I just thought we'd get the balls back by blowing up the greens... No, not dynamite—this isn't The Alamo! Compressed air. I'm sure the rabbits have created a warren under the course, and the entrance is in the rough by the eighteenth. I saw one there yesterday morning. Can you meet me with your van and compressor as soon as. Just drive close to the edge of the fairway, you'll be okay. We're near the seventeenth now. See you soon. And hurry!'

Colin and Izzy made their way on foot to the eighteenth.

Izzy looked at her phone. 'I ought to ring Stewart to tell him what's happening.'

'Not sure that's a good idea. You know what he thinks about rabbits.'

'I'm not sure we've got a choice.' She dialled as she spoke. 'Stewart? Colin thinks it's…' she hesitated, 'rabbits.' She held the phone away from her ear. 'Stewart, Stewart, calm down. Let's deal with the issue of the balls first. He's got a plan. He suspects the rabbits have been tunnelling and the balls are in the tunnels. He's asked Clive Beer to take his compressor up to the eighteenth where he believes the warren entrance is. The plan is to feed compressed air into the tunnels and pop the balls back up the holes and onto the greens. Can you tell the Major please?' She didn't let him interrupt in case he asked too many questions.

'Major, the Griggs's and Clive Beer are on the case. Colin thinks its rabbits.' Stewart caught the look of hostility in the Major's eyes. 'They have a plan to blow them up onto the green.'

'Too good for the pesky little blighters. Dynamite might be the best solution. I remember being held up by some fuzzy wuzzies in North Africa; a stick of dynamite soon sorted them out. Great stuff. A bit overkill, but it'll show those furry buggers whose boss.'

'No, no, Major, with compressed air. Clive Beer will feed his compressor into the tunnels, and the balls will pop up onto the greens.'

'It brings tears to my eyes thinking of it! I know they breed like rabbits but having their balls blown off!'

'Major, you're not listening. Just watch, it shouldn't be long now.'

❧   ❧   ❧

The rough near the eighteenth was a hive of activity. Clive had arrived with his van and compressor and was busy feeding a large diameter tube into the warren entrance. Colin had inspected the cup Izzy bought from eBay and pushed it back into the hole.

'Ready?' Clive held his finger on the start button.

'Ready. Let's try say, 10 PSI to begin with.' The motor roared into action and forced the air into the warren.

'Can you see anything, Colin?'

'No, not yet, Clive. Give it a minute or two.'

'I'll up the pressure a tad—right 20 PSI. That should do it.'

Colin listened intently. 'Still nothing.'

'Okay, 40 PSI.' Clive increased the pressure.

The pump whirred away, the sound of rushing air into the warren could be heard, but no balls popped up.

'Crank it up, Clive.'

'80, here we come!'

'Now I can hear something, but no signs of any balls.'

'150.'

'Clive, steady on.'

'It's only compressed air. Anything?'

'Yes, yes, I can see a ball through the bottom of the cup.'

'Has it popped up onto the green yet?'

'No, in fact, I think it's acting as a valve and blocking off the hole.'

'Well, 200 PSI should shift it.'

'Clive, are you sure?'

'Well, okay, let's go for it; 300 it is.'

'I didn't mean more pressure.'

The words were no sooner out of Colin's mouth when the tranquil scene of lush green parkland, of an immaculately manicured golf course, was turned into something more reminiscent of Beirut at the height of their troubles.

The warren connected all the greens from the first to the eighteenth. None were spared, including where the Major and Mr Ballard found themselves, with the course professional Matt Childs and the rest of his team. Matt had a good following in the Club, in the County and around the professional circuit. Typically, it would cost spectators a considerable sum to watch him play, but today—Grand Opening day—the course was open to anyone who wanted to attend. A sizeable crowd had gathered around the seventh green. All whispering to themselves, they tried to make some sense of what was happening. Matt was protesting vociferously to the Major, while he was trying to keep himself up to date on the situation by listening to the phone conversations Mr Ballard was having.

Matt's team members tried to calm the situation, and several of Stewart's groundsmen were wandering aimlessly, thinking they ought to do something, but not sure what that something was. To cap it all, the BBC News crew, interested in the local celebrity, Matt Childs, were hanging on his every word, waiting for the all-important sound-bite, to make sure their efforts made it to the 6 o'clock newsroom and not the cutting room floor.

With the crowd's noise increasing in sympathy with the more irate language and gestures of Matt, the faint hissing sound emanating from the hole on the seventh went un-noticed. However, as the flag attached to its pin started rising from the ground with increasing speed to a height of eight, nine and then ten-foot, the crowd, camera crew, players, groundsmen and Mr Ballard soon realised something was definitely afoot.

The flag, with pin, now fifty feet or more above the green, settled into a comfortable trajectory following the line of the fairway and in an arc any golfer would be proud of. The crowd was now offering their opinions.

'I reckon that'll reach 300 yards.'

'No, that's more a 380 yarder at least. Look how steady and straight she's flying and no crosswinds.'

The observant soon noticed that accompanying the flag pin was the putting green cup and a row of four, brand new, hardly played, top of the range, hugely expensive Titleist golf balls. They were evenly spaced about one yard apart, but with their superior aerodynamics, were making up ground and would, it was estimated, overtake the flag pin before it reached the half-way point along the fairway.

The crowd was enthusiastically pointing and shouting. The usual etiquette shown by such a gathering of this type had gone. Everyone wanted to see the outcome; after all, money was now riding on it. A few fans set off down the fairway, trying to keep up with the spectacle.

These were the lucky few since, with no obstruction in the hole, all manner of things were unimpaired to follow suit. Copious amounts of rain from the previous night's storm had found its way into the tunnels. The BBC news report estimated a small river. In truth, no one could be certain. Water doesn't like pressure, and these rainwaters were no exception. With the immense force, the water, understandably, sought relief by going somewhere else. It had a choice of eighteen potential exits from its underground prison but being undiscerning, the waters took all eighteen at once.

The water, on route to its chosen exits, the rivulets picked up the spoil from the rabbits' digging and mixed it into fine, not too odorous, but extremely clingy slurry. Like the blending's of a fine parfumier, this water-soil concoction was launched as a fine mist onto the amassed crowds attending Harpsden Golf Club on its Grand Opening.

The thing about gravity, as discovered by Newton, was that what goes up must come down; the water-soil mixture was also subject to this law. As all ladies know, a pump-action aspirator turns a small stream of perfume or cologne into a scented mist, providing an alluring fragrance to attract the opposite sex. The aspirated slurry, reaching a height of 70 feet, formed a cloud some 100 yards across before obeying Newton and behaving in the way any object falling back to earth would behave. As the upward thrust of the escaping air was replaced by the downward force of gravity, the momentary pause gave the crowd a sense of impending doom, but no time to consider their options. Not even the world's top sprinter would have much chance to escape something travelling at 30 feet per second per second.

The vibrant colours of the lush new greens and

fairways, the multitude of colours of the coats, jackets and suits worn by the crowd, and the rather dubious colours and patterns which make up the usual attire of the golfer, were soon to be replaced by a monotone brown; a delightful shade of brown, the sort chosen to redecorate external windows and doors in some Cotswold village, but not usually a hue associated with anything else. The slurry descended with such velocity and in a great volume that none but the few, including anyone who had the foresight to wear a wetsuit to a golf match, were spared a torrential soaking that went right through to their undergarments.

In the moments following, the crowd, who had turned out so enthusiastically to support Matt Childs and the other golfers, saw a side to Matt they weren't expecting. The rugged, tanned features, the dark blond-styled hair, the designer clothes and the suave laid-back, devil-may-care attitude evaporated within seconds. What appeared was a figure more reminiscent of a David Attenborough character caught on film in some remote jungle preparing to wage war on a neighbouring tribe. Demented, waving his golf club like a spear, and lashing out with his arms and legs as if performing a tribal ritual dance, Matt was enraged. He took no consolation from the fact his teammates, especially Michael, who had been standing right next to the hole as it blew, received a double dousing, once on the way up, and once on the way down.

The BBC crew, who had the prudence to weatherproof their outside broadcast cameras, caught all the action live and with surprisingly good sound quality.

However, much of what followed had to be bleeped out for the sake of decency.

As for the Major, he was convinced he was back fighting in the Falkland's, and took cover in a nearby bunker. Unlike more traditional conflicts where the enemy came at you on foot or in tanks, this one was solely airborne and soon found him in the bunker, before exerting its full force.

Clive and Colin were now troubled men, desperate to quell the enthusiastic compressor which was doing such a fantastic job—Hammer Koshi, the Japanese manufacturers, would have been delighted.

'Clive, turn that bloody thing off.' Colin struggled to make himself heard over the din of the engine.

The complete course looked like Yellowstone National Park, geysers going off everywhere, people running for cover in every direction, only to run into others doing the same thing. Eighteen holes issuing forth simultaneously left little room for escape.

'Where's the kill switch or whatever?' Colin shouted again. It was another five minutes of mayhem before calm was restored.

Still lying face down, now half-submerged in a sandy, muddy pool, the Major checked himself over before raising himself on his arms. He could just see over the bunker's rim, enabling him to survey the devastation. He felt for his inside jacket pocket where he'd left his mobile phone. Although the glass screen was cracked, it was dry and still showed signs of life. *This can't happen again to anyone,* he thought, *and certainly not at the Harpsden Golf Club. I knew that Griggs was trouble.*

'Mary, is that you? I need you to take a letter urgently and deliver it right now. It's to that Griggs chappie, the hole farmer fellow—he's here somewhere with his wife. Oh, and don't leave the Clubhouse without your wellies and umbrella.'

As she was told, Mary eventually tracked Izzy down to a densely wooded part of the course where she had taken shelter. From the dappled colouring of her clothes, hair, face and, in fact, all over, it was apparent she hadn't escaped the onslaught but, compared to others, had got off lightly. Mary handed her the sealed envelope and left without a word.

Hesitantly, Izzy wiped her hands, opened the envelope and removed the letter.

Dear Mr Griggs,

It is with great regret I must inform you of your contract to supply holes for the Harpsden Golf Club has been terminated with immediate effect. Considering the circumstances surrounding the new greens' opening, I must insist that this is non-negotiable.

Yours sincerely,

Major G J Woods
Club Captain

P.S. If you were expecting payment for works rendered, I'm afraid none will be forthcoming.

'I guess it could have been worse,' said Colin, 'back to the drawing board.' He wouldn't admit defeat. 'The principle's sound, just the rabbits were over-enthusiastic.'

'You're not going to continue with this hole farming business?' Izzy sounded dubious.

'Oh yes, my dear; this was a blip…'

Colin and Izzy continued walking arm in arm along the fairway, surveying the scene.

'Colin.'

'Yes, my love.'

'Can rabbits climb trees?'

'You're so silly at times, of course not.'

'Then why are two sitting on the branch of that oak tree?'

'Fallout I guess, just fallout.'

CHAPTER 11

AN UNCERTAIN FUTURE

'Hello, Griggs Hole Farming. How can I help you?'

'Izzy,' Colin called for her. He sat re-reading the story in the local paper. It was over three weeks old.

'Shush Colin, I'm on the phone.' She listened intently while he mulled over the details. After a couple of minutes, she placed the phone back in its cradle.

Without looking up, he asked, 'Who's that?'

She didn't answer. He wasn't paying much attention and just kept reading. After a few more moments, he asked her again, but still no reply. Confused, Colin lowered the paper and looked across the kitchen in Izzy's direction. She was standing ramrod straight, staring into the distance, expressionless, dumbfounded and barely breathing.

Colin tried again. 'Looks like you've seen a ghost. What's happened?' Still nothing, no response, not even a twitch. 'My love, what is it? Who was that? Is it your Mum? Is she alright?' He was becoming quite concerned.

'Colin hush, no not Mum, she's fine, I think. That was Sarah Weaver.'

'Who the heck is she when she's at home?'

'That SHE Colin, that SHE is the woman who has our future in the palm of her hands. Her decision will mean whether we have to sell the farm, leave here, sign on the dole, move into a council house, go begging in the street, or rummage through the bins. SHE—' Izzy's almost hysterical voice tailed off as she broke into uncontrollable tears. With that, her legs softened, and her knees buckled.

Thankfully, Colin's lightning-fast reactions saved her from any serious injury as she collapsed under the weight of the news. But Izzy wasn't Twiggy, and he had a job to hold her up. With one foot firmly planted, he used the other to hoik out a chair from the table, turning it so he could manoeuvre her onto it. She slumped down, stopping herself from slipping off with her right arm acting as a stay against the table top.

He did not know what was going on and felt now wasn't a good time to ask. *Just wait and be patient. Water,* he thought, *get her a drink of water.* Uncertain of letting her go in case she fell on the floor, he was stuck as to know what to do for the best. While contemplating, he felt her stir.

'What are we going to do, Colin?' This moment of consciousness allowed him to turn her in toward the table whereon she collapsed again. Better supported, he could let go without fear of her falling. He fetched a glass of water and used a few drops to sprinkle on her face.

'Tell me who was on the phone? This Susan Weaver, who is she? What did she say? How can she make us sell the farm? Izzy, what's going on?' Silence, nothing now except the sound of deep breathing—she had slipped into semi-consciousness again.

While she was out, he tried to recall what she'd said, attempting to unravel the phone conversation. *She needs to calm down and sit here to help her,* he thought, *but while she's out cold, I'm getting more stressed by not knowing.* Once again, he was in a quandary, and once again, she resolved the situation by regaining consciousness.

She lifted her head. 'Oh, Colin, what are we going to do?'

'About what? I've no idea what's going on!'

'Haven't you been listening? Haven't you heard a word I've said?' She was now fully with it and getting quite agitated again.

'Of course I have. This Susan Weaver—'

'See, I told you, you weren't listening! It's Sarah Weaver'

'Okay, Sarah Weaver is going to sell the farm, and we will move into a council house. Is she an estate agent?'

'Give me strength! Sometimes I wonder what planet you're on! Of course, she's not an estate agent! She's our new Business Banking Manager,' she said in slow, deliberate tones. 'Remember Mr Pryor, who opted for early retirement before the banking world went pear-shaped? The Manager who so generously loaned us the £10,000; the Manager who realised that banking in the 21st century wasn't something he wanted to be part of with shareholders, stakeholders, account holders, hedge funds and triple-A ratings; the nice Mr Pryor who worked on a handshake, who had provided banking services to you and your Father for over 35 years, well it's his replacement. For Ms Weaver, it's all targets, margins, security, limited exposure, base rates and LIBOR. She is after blood, our blood. You are famous, or more likely infamous, after the golf course fiasco. It was on the national TV news; you cannot get more coverage than that! I wouldn't be surprised if 'Hello' magazine doesn't want to do a double-page spread right now.' Izzy took a large gasp of air.

'I still don't understand?' He sounded rather sheepish.

'Okay, in black and white, SHE is to decide whether or not to call in our business loan—all £10,000 of it, plus interest, plus set-up fees, plus no doubt anything else she can think of. And if she does, we are, to use the vernacular—stuffed! Well, and truly stuffed! Banks don't take prisoners, they take assets and since we have no money over and above the loan, and with pending claims from over 500 spectators and players from the Golf Club debacle, never mind the Golf Club's claim for damages, I think us having to sell the farm, our home and everything else, is pretty much a foregone conclusion.' The colour was returning to her cheeks.

As the full enormity of their situation dawned on Colin, the blood drained from his head. He now felt his legs soften, and his knees starting to buckle. Izzy had no chance of catching him; he collapsed like a sack of potatoes—all eighteen stone. As he went down, his spread-eagled arms caught the piles of crockery and saucepans stacked on the draining board, along with the cutlery-holder full of drying knives, forks and assorted spoons. Besides the noise, a lethal combination of shards from breaking china and untethered blades flying across the kitchen that was uppermost in Izzy's mind.

Colin was out cold, face down on the kitchen floor and she was under the table waiting for the noise to abate and all the currently gravity defying objects to be pulled back into order and take up their new homes scattered here and there around the kitchen.

The hand of fate hadn't finished yet. From under the table, she heard a moan, slight but perceptible. *At least he's still alive,* she thought. Gingerly, she rose from her crouching position to look across in Colin's direction, expecting, hoping to see him looking back at her. Instead, nothing. His eyes were still shut but worse, much worse, from under his head she could make out blood amassing.

'Oh my God Colin. Speak to me!' She straightened up fast. In doing so, the kitchen table, with all its contents, was sent on a mystery journey to the far side of the room. Oblivious to the noise and the new commotion, she rushed to his side.

'Colin, are you alright' she was frantic; the pool of blood was growing. 'Doctor, A&E, ambulance, phone, where's the bloody phone?' In the mayhem, the phone had taken a direct hit from one of the flying knives and was now lying useless on the kitchen floor, blinking as if it was drawing its last breath.

'Quick, front room, the other phone.'

Sirens blared, and paramedics scurried. Colin hadn't stirred, and Izzy thought it best not to move him. The blood pool was more extensive, but much to her relief, his breathing seemed regular. He had been unconscious for some while now. Like her, the paramedics too were drawn to the red pool. Slowly, they turned him over; he coughed.

'He's coming round. We're going to take him to

A&E for an x-ray and observe him for few hours to make sure he's okay.'

Now the immediate panic was over, the paramedics looked around the room.

'What the hell went on here, missus? You two had a domestic?'

She thought of trying to explain about the Business Bank Manager, the Golf Club disaster and all that, but decided not to say anything. It was easier that way.

'You could say that,' she said.

'Not sure we shouldn't call the police! It looks like you gave him a real good whack on the head. What was it, rolling pin or saucepan?'

'No, no, nothing like that. He fainted, collapsed, after some bad news.'

'Bad news. Bad news! What sort of bad news could bring a big guy like him crashing to the floor?' The paramedics didn't sound convinced. 'This room looks more like a tsunami passed through it. I'd say you two had a right ding dong. It would be more than our job's worth not to report this. I reckon you're looking at a GBH charge or worse. It's always us men who are seen as the villains, but in this case, we clearly aren't! We'll call it in as we drive to the hospital.'

'I'm coming with you,' Izzy protested and grabbed her purse.

'You travel in the back with her?' The driver suggested to his mate, 'we can't leave her in the back alone with him; we've no way of telling what she'll do next!'

The ambulance pulled out of the farm and off

down the lane, passing the scarecrow in the field. They had made him temporarily redundant as the blaring sirens frightened away every living creature from miles around. The villagers of Henslow, too, were shaken from their otherwise tranquil state. As the ambulance sped, people looked quizzical, speculating about who was in the vehicle and wondering what had happened.

Soon the ambulance arrived at Harpsden General, A&E Department where Colin, now on a stretcher, by-passed the normal triage procedure to be whisked into an observation suite under the watchful eye and tender care of Nurse Dee. Izzy, on the other hand, was met by brother's PCs John and Billy Field, who escorted her to a small side office for an interview.

Colin woke confused and in pain, with a throbbing in his right temple and blackening around his right eye.

'You're in the hospital, you had an accident and hit your head,' said Nurse Dee, trying to reassure him. 'It looks worse than it is. I'm going to clean it up.' She had a moist wipe in her hand, and lent in to clean his wounds.

'What looks worse?' He pulled back to avoid her advancing hand.

'The cut, your ear. The paramedics found you in a pool of blood.' She put a hand on his neck to hold his head still. 'Steady, this won't hurt.' *Me*, she thought.

'Found me? Ouch,' Colin flinched, 'what do you mean found me? I have been nowhere.' He flopped back; out for the count.

The paramedics came into the observation room. They shared the entire story with Nurse Dee, or at least their version of it.

147

'I reckon she hit him with a rolling pin, or worse, maybe it was a hammer. Anyway, he was spark out cold on the kitchen floor, table overturned, crockery, pans and everything everywhere. I've never seen a domestic like it. Of course, as usual, she denies everything, saying he fell after hearing some bad news. What twaddle! Bad news eh—'

'So you're saying she—'

'Yes, his missis. Well, we assume it's his wife, as she was in the kitchen when we arrived.'

'She hit him with a hammer?' continued Nurse Dee, 'lucky she didn't kill him.'

'That's what we told the two coppers. They're with her now in the interview room.'

❧   ❧   ❧

Izzy was alone with her thoughts. The PCs had left her to discuss the situation and decide what to do next. *Oh my poor Colin,* she thought, *first, the bank business, then the fall and now this. Can it get any worse?* The interview room door opened.

'Considering what we have found out and, from the statement of the two paramedics, we believe we are dealing with a serious case here. We think it would be in all our best interests to take you in for questioning. Please come with us.' PC John Field took Izzy by the arm.

'What serious case? It's just an accident. My husband, Colin, fell, he fainted, that's all!' She was outraged.

'That's all well and good, madam, if you'd just like to come with us.' PC Billy Field was getting quite insistent.

'But my husband, who's going to look after him?'

'This is a hospital, madam; they are used to looking after people—that's what they do.'

PC Field sounded quite exasperated. Now let's go, madam, or we'll have to arrest you.'

'Arrest! Arrest..., for what?' Her outrage was now turning to outright anger. She seethed. Her blood was at boiling point; she banged her fist on the table.

'No madam, we've had enough violence for one day; we don't want to handcuff you as well.'

If PC Billy Field had been any other person, he would have wished he hadn't been standing so close to her as he said that. Without hesitation, this usually reserved farmer's wife spun around and let fly at him. Unbeknownst to her, Billy was a Taekwondo black belt, and in the blink of an eye, and with no harm done to him, she had both hands behind her back with her wrists secure in a pair of police regulation handcuffs.

'Now madam, if you'll come quietly, we'll continue this interview down the Station.'

❧ ❧ ❧

As every young reporter knows, an excellent place to get a story is at the local hospital. Jimmy Flanagan, of the Harpsden Chronicle, was often to be found at the hospital's Maternity Unit. Births, marriages and deaths were his brief, but he wanted to be a real reporter. He felt he had a good eye for a story and was observant, tenacious, and discrete. He had ambition. Contacts were essential, and he knew all the nurses, porters, receptionists, in fact, anyone who would talk to him.

Getting people to talk wasn't a problem for Jimmy. This day was no different.

He'd strolled over to A&E and was hanging around the vending machine—his favourite haunt. *It always surprises me how much information can be exchanged for a coffee, tea or coke,* he thought. The two paramedics turned up.

'Here, let me.' Jimmy, as quick as a flash, popped in a couple of fifty pence pieces. 'What will it be today, lads?' he said cheerily. In no time at all, Jimmy had copious notes on the Griggs household's apparent goings-on and how his missis had beaten him within an inch of his life with a 7lb club hammer. Blood everywhere, up the walls, pools on the floor, just everywhere—he wrote furiously, with some creativity.

Out of the corner of his eye, he spotted the two PCs escorting a handcuffed Izzy through reception toward the front door.

'Is that her, lads?' Jimmy was getting excited, believing he was on to a major crime scoop.

'Yes, that's her. They must have arrested her. See Jimmy, what we said was all true! Believe us now?'

'Of course; must go.' Jimmy grabbed his laptop, notebook, and coat before rushing for the door, his car, and the local Police Station.

      ✀   ✀   ✀

Colin's constant state of semi-consciousness was as much a result of his fall as of a way of not having to deal with the news that had caused him to collapse in the first place. Nurse Dee, or Tanya, from her name badge, was caring and comforting. He thought he'd stay put a bit longer. She had several other patients and kept flitting between rooms and cubicles, doing her job. One of these flits took her to reception, where she saw the two PCs escorting a woman from the building. *Gosh, it must be true. He was attacked with a hammer. Poor chap; I better tell him the police have arrested his wife.*

The large cotton pad held in place over his right ear with a bandage more akin to a turban didn't make hearing easy. The mild sedative he'd been given, his drowsy state and the bandage all conspired to complicate further what was already a confusing situation.

'What do you mean, arrested? For attempted murder!!' He couldn't believe what nurse Dee was saying. 'She's the sweetest, kindest, gentlest person you could meet.' He was fully alert and sat bolt upright. 'I've got to get out of here. She needs me. They can't lock her up; she's not done anything. It was the Bank Manager woman; it's all her fault.'

Through his bandages, he was indistinct.

'What are you saying, Mr Griggs? The Bank Manager attacked you?' Tanya thought this unlikely. 'You sure you're not hallucinating? Bank Managers have done and been called many things, but I've never heard of one attempting to murder a customer.'

'I've got to go, to leave now and save Izzy.' He started pulling at the attached saline drip. 'Where are my clothes, nurse? I need them now.' At that point, he swung his legs out of bed, catching his foot on the saline drip stand. The force sent it flying across the room toward a stack of glass-fronted shelves. Off-balance, he continued south toward the floor, cracking the left side of his head on the visitor's chair next to his bed.

The stand hit the shelves. The impact caused the glass doors to explode, whilst their contents were hurled in all directions. Nurse Dee ducked for cover. The ensuing sounds were heard loud and clear in reception. Within seconds, the two paramedics who had brought Colin in were at the Observation Suite doors.

'I've heard of Deja Vue, but this is ridiculous.'

Colin was out cold on the floor, Nurse Dee was crouched under his bed, and the entire room was littered with assorted medical debris in various states of disrepair.

'Nurse, what happened?'

'You wouldn't believe me if I told you. Is he okay?' She was concerned.

'Out cold again. We need to get him moved. What about you?'

'Yeah, I'm fine. But what he said before knocking himself out was that Izzy, that's his wife, didn't try to kill him. Rather, it was the Bank Manager.' Nurse Dee crawled her way out from under the bed.

'Are you sure? I know Bank Managers are having a bad time but... Anyway, we didn't see anyone else at the house as we collected him. Maybe he's imagined it. Concussion, you know.'

❧   ❧   ❧

'Now, Mrs Griggs, this is not a joking matter. Your husband is lying in a hospital in a life-threatening condition, and a charge of attempted murder is before you. My advice is that you fully co-operate with the investigation.' Inspector Adams sounded serious.

The front Desk Sergeant was adamant. Jimmy, you know the rules. I cannot tell you anything about an ongoing investigation. If it comes to trial, the Jury won't be impartial, and the case will be dismissed.'

He wasn't about to give up easily. 'Okay, I appreciate that, but you can say yes or no.'

'What do you mean?'

'I ask the questions, you just answer yes or no; that way you're not actually telling me anything.'

'Like what?'

'Is the lady you're holding, Mrs Isobel Griggs of Griggs Farm, Henslow?'

The Desk Sergeant said nothing.

'Since you didn't say 'no', I'll take your silence as a 'yes'. Now we're getting somewhere.'

At that moment, Jimmy's mobile phone rang. The Desk Sergeant threw him a rather disdainful look and pointed to the sign on the wall. Jimmy got the hint and went outside to answer it.

'Are you sure it's the Bank Manager? Did you see anyone else at the farm? Well, thanks for the tip. I owe you one.'

Jimmy went back inside the police station. 'Here, Serg—'

'Desk Sergeant Walker to you.'

'You've got the wrong person. It was the bank manager.'

'What, Mr Pryor? I rather doubt that. Anyway, why would Mr Pryor want to kill Colin Griggs?'

'You read the papers and saw it on the National

153

News. Griggs caused a right kerfuffle at the Golf Club's re-launch, and Mr Pryor is on the Committee.'

'Hardly grounds for a murder.'

This story just keeps getting better, Jimmy thought. He was beaming. 'Right Serg... err sorry, Desk Sergeant Walker, I'll get out of your way. You don't happen to know if Griggs Farm is well signposted from Henslow, do you?'

The Sargent's look told him not to pursue the point.

As Jimmy left the Walker went to the interview room to inform Inspector Adams of this development. Adams was just as sceptical of any involvement by Mr Pryor. 'I'll keep an open mind, but we need more evidence. Has anyone spoken to Mr Griggs yet?'

'I sent the Field brothers back to the hospital, but as yet, I've heard nothing.'

'Well, give it a chase up, Sergeant, please.' Adams just wanted a quiet life, and this whole Griggs thing was spoiling it for him.

As the Sergeant returned to his desk, the two PCs were coming through the front door.

'Well,' said the Desk Sergeant.

'You're never going to believe this!'

'Try me.'

'Griggs' is only unconscious again. We haven't been able to speak to him yet. We went to the Observation Suite, where they're caring for him. The whole room looks like a disaster zone. Broken glass, kidney bowls, bandages, bedpans, anything and everything all over the place. A total wreck.'

'And,' interrupted the Sergeant.

'Well, it transpires Griggs was trying to make a

run for it and you know Nurse Tanya, the pretty one with the great ass… etc.' The two PCs looked knowingly at each other. 'Well, she tried to stop him and did a bit of a too good a job. Left him spark out cold again.'

'Where is he now?'

'In a secure side room under sedation. We won't be able to talk to him until the morning at best!'

'Thanks, Billy. So we are no further forward. I'd better tell Adams. I've heard talk that the Bank Manager, Pryor, might be involved. Some sort of revenge attack. Can you two go over to his house, cautious mind, he may be dangerous, and see what you can find. Bring him in if you need to. You know the drill.'

The two PCs turned to go.

'Actually,' continued the Sergeant, 'go out to the Griggs' farmhouse first. Here's the address. And see what evidence can be gathered from the crime scene. Seal off the place for the present. We may need to get forensics at some point, and I'm sure Adams will want to see it for himself.'

As they were halfway through the front door, the Desk Sergeant called them back again. 'Oi, Tweedledum, Tweedledee, that damned reporter chappie Finnigan, I'm sure he's off there as well. You better make it pronto before he gets his great clodhoppers all over the place.' The Desk Sergeant shook his head in disbelief.

The sound of the siren reverberated around the building; they were gone. Adams took this as an indicator of some sort of development and came to the Front Desk for an update.

'Has she admitted it yet?' enquired the Sergeant

on seeing Adams.

'What's all the commotion? Has something happened?' Adams didn't like being left in the dark.

'I was just about to update you, Sir. Griggs is still unconscious and now in a secure room at the hospital. Seemingly he was trying to make a run for it when one nurse, Nurse Dee, I think. You know the pretty one with the big—'

'Alright Sergeant, enough. What happened?'

'Well, she was a tad overzealous and took him down. The upshot is that he's still unconscious and won't be available for questioning until the morning.'

'I'm getting nowhere. Mrs Griggs is adamant that it's all a misunderstanding, an accident which, until we can speak to Griggs himself, we cannot corroborate. I cannot let her go, just in case. All she's talking about is her poor Colin and geese.'

'Geese?'

'Apparently, they have a flock on the farm and other livestock which need feeding, and there's no one to do it. What am I Walker, an Inspector or a Nursemaid? Give me strength.'

'We'll try this for size.'

'What now, sergeant?'

'According to that journalist bloke, Finnigan.'

'Flanagan. What's he got to say?'

'He had a tip-off that it wasn't her but their Bank Manager.'

'What Pryor? He wouldn't hurt a fly! Why would he go round attacking his customers? Anyway, I thought he'd retired. I saw him the other day at the Golf Club, and he was telling me how he was looking forward to... Golf Club, Sergeant, that's it!'

'What do you mean, Sir?'

'You remember the re-launch day? As Bank Manager, Pryor loaned Griggs £10K and as a committee member, had put him forward for the hole contract. I guess after the disaster he's flipped and wants revenge.'

'Well, I never. Okay, Sergeant, give Mrs Griggs a cupper. I'm off to see Pryor. We'll hold her until I get back.' With that, Adams was gone.

CHAPTER 12

SUSPECTED OF MURDER

Jimmy Flanagan could see the farmhouse across the field. Ahead, the road turned through a long left-hand bend. 'Okay, slow down, Jimmy. Who's that?' He noticed a man standing in the field unmoving, staring ahead. He pulled over into a gateway and stopped for a better look. *Get a grip*, he thought. *It's a scarecrow*. He felt such a fool. *Hey no, look, just beyond there's a car parked out front of the farm. Right Jimmy lad, this is your big chance, don't blow it. Camera, yes, smartphone recording app, yes, wellies, yes.* He was all set to go. *No more flower shows or christenings for you, my boy, you're about to become a real crime reporter. The Harpsden Chronicle won't know what's hit it.*

With these thoughts racing through his mind, Jimmy got out of his car and closed the door, mindful not to slam it. He didn't want to give his presences away. He got into the lee of the hedge, running around the field all the way up to the house. Well hidden, he could see without being seen and hear without being heard. His heart was pounding. Slowly, he progressed down the lane; the house was clearly in view. *I'm sure that's a figure.* He stopped and peered hard in the farm's direction. *What now? What if that's the murderer returning to the scene of the crime? Wait, observe, record. Record! I need pictures.* He got his camera out and lifted it to his eye. He saw the figure moving around the outside of the house. The figure peered through windows as he worked his way toward the back door. Click, click, click. Jimmy repeatedly pressed the shutter, zooming in all the while. *This is real journalism;* the nervous excitement caused him swallow hard.

Engrossed in his 'covert' operation, Jimmy failed to notice PCs John and Billy Field draw up alongside him. They had the car window down.

'Ah Inspector Clouseau, what have we here then?' Billy enjoyed Micky taking.

Jimmy nearly dropped dead with fright. 'What the hell did you do that for?' he said in a loud whisper. 'Quick, stop, pull over. Out front of the farm is a car, and some guy peering in the window. Maybe it's him, the attacker, returning to the scene of the crime.' Jimmy pointed vaguely at the farm.

'Look, Jimmy, you're a reporter, well of sorts,' Billy turned to John and smiled, 'we do the crime investigation. Now get back in your car, and get out of here or we'll have you for loitering if you're not careful.'

'Billy, call yourself a policeman? How come you've only just got here now?' Jimmy's smug smile didn't go down well with Billy. 'Look, we can do both ourselves a favour. You do the police work, I'll report it. You'll look good arresting a murderer, and I'll get my scoop.' *Smart move Jimmy.* He smiled again at Billy.

Before Billy had time to answer, events had taken over. Having found no one at home, and with Izzy's girls—a gaggle of geese—in hot pursuit, the intruder raced back to his car before heading off down the lane at a rate of knots.

PC John Field spotted the fast-approaching car, and without hesitation, leapt from his driver's seat and stood in the centre of the road. Arms raised, palms forward, and shouting at the top of his voice. 'Stop, stop!'

Jimmy took a double-take; he switched on his recording app and raised his camera to his eye.

The driver didn't stand a chance of stopping in time. Both the recorded sound of tyres screeching and the frame by frame time-lapse photography clearly showed how he tried. An audible screech, followed by the heavy thud with piercing scream, matched John being lifted high into the air, bouncing off the windscreen, and slowly descending the car's bonnet to the waiting road below.

Everything came to a stop; silence followed and time appeared to stand still.

Jimmy could only stare before stating the obvious, 'Did you see that? It lifted him clear off his feet.'

'Don't stand like a statue gawking, quick get around here and help.' Billy took command. 'Look after him,' he pointed at driver, 'and here, cuff him.' He passed Jimmy his handcuffs. 'I need to get help for my brother.'

The driver, pale, shocked and on the verge of passing out, struggled from his car.

'What did he do that for? I could have killed him.' The driver tottered across the road, unsteady on his feet.

'Oh no you don't,' Jimmy lead him to the grassy bank, 'sit down here.'

'Don't you understand? They're after me! We can't stay here.'

'Who's after you?' Jimmy looked back up the road.

'The Griggs—' Before he completed his sentence, the driver passed out.

'The Griggs? What on earth are you on about?' Jimmy was quizzical. 'Billy, did you hear that? He says they're after him.'

'Who's after him? More to the point, who is he?' Billy turned back to John. He was more interested in his welfare. 'I need your help here now. Poor John took one hell of a smack. Lucky that bloke didn't kill him.'

'He says the Griggs. I dunno, maybe there's a gang of them.' JImmy shrugged his shoulders, 'Best not take any chances.' He snapped the cuffs shut.

Billy got onto his radio pronto, requesting an ambulance and back-up. 'How many men? Not sure, but before the bloke passed out, he mentioned the Griggs were after him. I've no idea how many are at the farm. I only know we have Mr and Mrs at the hospital and down the Station. There's a gang, according to him. I'm not taking any chances. Call Special Ops. Oh, and let Inspector Adams know.' Billy hung up his radio.

'We can't move, John; we just need to make him comfortable and wait for the ambulance.' Billy pointed at the driver. 'Any sign of him coming to?'

Jimmy went over to check on him. As he bent down, from the corner of his eye, he noticed the first airborne attack coming straight for him. Instinctively, he raised his arms over his head while turning his back on the dive-bombing, enraged goose. Unperturbed, the goose jabbed at his neck whilst beating his wings and Jimmy in a frenzied attack.

Billy saw what was happening and glimpsed another three heading in his and his brother's direction. With no thought for his safety, Billy threw himself on top of John to protect him from these savage attackers.

The Special Ops, an airborne force, scrambled their helicopter of six highly trained and armed commandos. Arriving within minutes, they hovered overhead to watch the unfolding scene in utter amazement. Through the din of the rotor blades, you could hear the disappointment in their voices on realising the Griggs gang of armed murderers were nothing more than a gaggle of furious geese protecting their owner's property. The helicopter turned for home. As it did so, the downdraft scattered the attacking birds in all directions. Disgruntled, they reassembled before setting off waddling and honking back to the farm, secure in the knowledge they'd fought off any would-be intruders for the time being. The scarecrow too suffered, and was now dishevelled, and lying face down in the muddy field.

The ambulance soon arrived, and the paramedics stretchered PC Field into it, as Inspector Adams pulled up.

'I'll take over now,' he said assertively. 'What's been going on here?'

Billy filled him in. 'And finally, over here we have a gentleman who was seen loitering around the farmhouse before speeding off, being chased away by the geese and then slamming into John.'

At the side of the road, the driver lay slumped. Still, in the care of Jimmy Flanagan, Adams approached them.

'Now then, what's this? Good gracious, Steve Pryor, what on earth are you doing here? You're the last person I expected to see. I was just on my way to your house to eliminate you from our enquiries.'

Dazed, Mr Pryor looked up; he took a few seconds to realise who it was speaking. 'Ah, Bob, it's you, so nice to see a friendly face after all the mayhem.'

'Sorry Steve, we're not at the Golf Club now.' He caught sight of the handcuffs. 'I'm afraid I must caution you. It's alleged that you attacked one Colin Griggs of Griggs Farm, Henslow, sometime earlier today with a hammer, rendering the said Colin Griggs unconscious, and in which condition he remains. I must remind you that anything you say may be taken down and used in a Court of Law. You are—'

'Hold on, Bob, hold on! Are you arresting me? I thought you said you were going to eliminate me from your enquiries.'

'That was the case until I found you here.'

'But Bob, you know me. I'm a bank manager, I'm not the violent type, and certainly not capable of hitting anyone with a hammer. And definitely not someone the size of Colin Griggs. 'You certainly don't need handcuffs! I'll come peacefully, honest gov!' Steve rattled his pair under Adam's nose.

'I don't think now is the right time for sarcasm, Steve. You're in a difficult position. Now get into the back of my car, and I'll get PC Field to drive yours back to the station.'

Sat in the back, Steve Pryor refused to be drawn into conversation with Bob Adams. *Where are your friends when you really need them?* He thought.

In the commotion, Jimmy Flanagan believed he'd heard enough, and had all the facts, with pictures and sounds. *I need to get back to my laptop and get my fingers dancing across the keyboard.* Excited at the prospect of his first major scoop, his first real crime report, Jimmy let out a throaty laugh before shushing himself.

He slipped away from the arrest. Gently and quietly, he got back into his car. No one noticed. All he needed to do was turn the car around without drawing attention. Jimmy noticed Pryor, PC Field, and Inspector Adams all facing away from him. *This is my chance.* He turned the ignition key and slipped his Ford Focus into first. Letting the clutch up sufficiently for it to bite, the car moved forward momentarily. He was able to apply a hard lock. With one deft movement, he turned the car through 180 degree 'U' turn. Pressing the accelerator, he sped off down the road and out of sight before anyone realised.

The sound alerted Adams to the disappearing back-end. 'Curse that Flanagan, he'll have this story all over the Chronicle's front page before you can say, Jack Robinson.'

That's what Jimmy hoped would happen and would try his damnedest to achieve. In the car, his grin got wider and wider.

By now, Izzy was beside herself. She'd no news of Colin, and her animals and birds were unattended all day; she'd not eaten save a curly cheese sandwich, and to top it all, no one believed her about the accident. Over and above this, there was the small matter of losing their farm, their home, and their livelihood if Ms Weaver got her way. She paced the interview room; it seemed like they had held her for hours. The door opened. *What now* crossed her mind?

'Sorry for the delay,' Inspector Adams began, 'but we needed to check your story and since we cannot question Colin—'

'Can't question Colin! Here we go again. Why not?' She was most insistent.

'Err, well, don't you know?' Adams was taken off guard.

'Know what, exactly? I've been locked up here all bloody day.'

'Temper please, Mrs Griggs.'

'I'll give you temper, what's happened to my Colin, where is he, how is he? He's not...,' she hesitated, 'dead, is he?' She could hardly bring herself to say the word.

'Of course not, Mrs G,' Adams wanted to make light of the situation. 'He's just had a minor accident.'

'I know that, that's what I've been trying to tell you all day.'

'No, no, I appreciate that. No, this was another accident in the hospital.' His words trailed away.

'Look, Inspector Adams, I'm normally an easy-going, devil-may-care sort of person, but today is enough to drive even a Saint to do something they'd regret. Look, let me see Colin. Let me go; let this bloody day be over.'

'I understand your frustration, Mrs G.'

'Stop calling me Mrs G!' She was seething.

'Sorry Mrs Griggs, we had, have,' correcting himself, 'a difficult situation on our hands and we need to be sure of our facts before making any decisions.

Please, I ask you, just bear with me a short while longer.' With that, Adams turned on his heels and left the room.

'Inspector Adams,' she called after him. 'Inspector Adams, what about my Colin?' Her scream slammed into the closing door.

Adams kept walking; he headed straight for the Desk Sergeant. 'Can you get an update on Griggs and tell me, and Mrs Griggs, as soon as? No, no, thinking about it, just tell me, and I'll tell her.' *I'm sure this wasn't in my job description.*

Colin had regained consciousness. He'd had his second injury dressed as well. Large cotton pads over both ears were held in place by meters of bandages. Sporting double black eyes, he'd taken on the appearance of some alien creature out of a Dr Who episode. However, his sedation, combined with the attentive and caring labours of Nurse Tanya, meant he'd lost any desire to escape his hospital bed and was, in fact, resigned to staying put.

In Interview Room 2, Inspector Adams set about quizzing his friend, or soon to be ex-friend, over his alleged involvement with the Griggs, and in particular "Colin's accident".

'I need you to be straight with me, Steve. Just keep to the truth; plain and simple facts. It's been a long day, so I'll cut to the chase. Did you attempt to murder Colin Griggs by clubbing him around the head with a hammer? Now take your time.'

'Bob, I'd put you down as many things, but being an outright fool isn't one of them.'

'Steve, just stick to the question, yes or no?'

'No.'

'No, what?'

'No, I didn't try to murder Colin Griggs by battering him around the head with a hammer.'

'But you were there?'

'Where?'

'At the Griggs farm.'

'No.'

'How can you say no? That's where we arrested you.'

'Well, yes, I was then.'

'Then why did you say no?'

'Because I wasn't at the farm when Colin was hit around the head with a hammer.'

'So you admit, Colin was hit around the head with a hammer. Where were you at the time?'

'No, of course not. I was up at the Club House trying to sort out the mess created by Colin and his bloody rabbits.'

'So you are angry at him?'

'Of course, but not angry enough to club him with a hammer.'

'Did you get someone to do it for you? Maybe the whole committee is involved.'

'Don't be ridiculous, nobody at the Club wants any harm to come to him.'

'Are you sure? Talking to other members, me included, I'd like to wring his bloody neck. I'm sure our esteemed Captain's none too impressed either. He totally ruined an excellent golf course we have been waiting for over the previous twelve months.'

'So was it you, or one of your coppers who attacked him and now you're trying to blame it on some poor innocent victim, namely me?' Steve thought attack was a good defence.

'Steve, Steve, Steve. Just hold on, this is getting us nowhere. Tell me about today and why we found you skulking around Griggs Farm.'

'Okay. I took a phone call from Sarah Weaver.'

'Who in God's name is she?'

'Listen, after retiring, all things changed at the bank. No longer are friendly Bank Managers looking after their customers, now it's all specialists, call centres, stakeholders and goodness knows what. Sarah Weaver is Lloyds Bank's Business Manager in this area. She works out of the regional head office and visits branches every month. Anyway, she's going through all my business customers' files to get herself up to speed. Part of the process is to review existing arrangements. That's the banking euphemism for causing pain and misery to its borrowers. She sees the news like everyone else. It hadn't escaped her notice that Griggs Hole Farming has recently had a spot of bother. That's my euphemism for a right cock-up. I guess she wants to renegotiate, or more likely call in the £10K loan I sanctioned as a parting gesture on my retirement day. I've known the Griggs for years and anyway, the banks have loads of money, so I thought I'd help out a friend and give him a leg-up.' Steve wiped his brow.

'So why were you at the farm?'

'I'd gone to warn Colin and Izzy of the impending Sarah Weaver review. I knocked on the front door but got no reply, so I checked through the window to see if all was okay. It's unusual for no one to be in, as they have animals to look after and, in particular, some ferocious geese.'

'Your explanation corroborates with Mrs Griggs. In fact, you were too late with your warning about Sarah Weaver, or, as Mrs Griggs called to her, 'that bloody woman'. She phoned her this morning. It was this call and the potential for the Griggs to lose everything that caused Colin to pass out so injuring himself. The ensuing mayhem and his rather unfortunate second accident are consequences of poor communications and misunderstandings.'

Adams was feeling rather pleased with himself and the way things were turning out. 'Right Steve, you can go now. No hard feelings, old chap. Just doing one's job, you know, just doing one's job.'

'Well, it's easy for you to say, you've not been chased by demented geese, run over a policeman, collapsed at the side of the road, or been scared witless by a helicopter full of hooligans—'

'Highly trained officers, I think you'll find.'

'Handcuffed, bloody handcuffed, before being driven to the police station with sirens blaring and then subjected to an interrogation.'

'That's a bit harsh; I only asked you a few questions.'

'Even so,' continued Steve, 'it's not a day I'm going to forget easily, though I'd like to.'

'Will I see you later at the Golf Club for a pint?' Adams asked cheerily.

Steve stared straight at him in disbelief. Turning to the door, he said nothing and left.

In Interview Room 1, Izzy was desperate to be away. The door opened; as it did, she got a glimpse of the fast retreating Mr Pryor while Inspector Adams entered the room.

'Right Mrs Griggs. Izzy isn't it?' Her eyes bore into him. 'Right Mrs Griggs,' Adams started again, 'it seems you've no charges to answer and that the whole day has been a rather unfortunate set of events.' He sounded quite upbeat.

'What's Mr Pryor doing here?' She wasn't.

'Mr Pryor,' he answered inquiringly, trying to disarm her.

'Yes, Mr Pryor, our ex-bank manager. I saw him just now as you came into the room.'

'We needed to ask him a few questions; in fact, it was his statement which now allows me to let you go.' He patted her on the back.

She didn't need a second invitation. 'I've got to see my Colin.' She grabbed her purse and marched straight out to the front desk.

Desk Sergeant Walker was busy minding his own business as the tirade hit him.

'I need to get to the hospital, and I want you,' she wagged her finger at him, 'to provide a car right now!'

Engrossed in the evening paper, he didn't look, 'Excuse me Madam, but this is a police station and not a Mini Cab firm. There's a taxi rank about 100 yards down the road, left out of the building.' He gesticulated to emphasise the point.

On the desk lay Walker's truncheon. Within a split second, she had it in her hand and raised above her head.

'Mrs Griggs, that's enough,' bellowed Adams as he came marching down the corridor. 'Now put it down, and Desk Sergeant Walker will arrange for a patrol car to take you to the hospital.' By the time he had finished his sentence, he had reached the desk. He took the truncheon from her and passed it back to Walker. 'What were you thinking?' Don't leave it around in a public place again.'

Sheepishly Walker put it under the desk. 'I'll get a car sorted right away, Sir.'

'And Walker, how's Mr Griggs? You contacted the hospital, didn't you?'

'Yes. He's fine; conscious but being kept in overnight for observation.'

'There, there, Mrs Griggs, see, no need to worry. Sit yourself here until the patrol car is ready.' Adams was king of smarm when needed.

Jimmy Flanagan made the whole of the front page of the late edition. 'Local Bank Manager arrested for attempted murder' screamed the headline. The story was graphically illustrated with one picture of Mr Pryor peering in the farm's windows and another of him laying apparently concussed at the side of the road and a Police crack-squad, with their guns clearly visible, thundering overhead in a helicopter. Jimmy had gone to town in his first real crime report. Where he didn't have facts, he made them up, and where these facts lacked excitement, he'd given them plenty. The article read like a scene from a James Bond movie. Of course, as Jimmy had not only witnessed the whole thing first hand, but had taken part; he cast himself in the role of James Bond. *Well,* he thought, *at least I have the right first name.*

In the bottom half of the front page, smack bang in the centre, was a photograph of the victim in his hospital bed looking for all the world like an Egyptian mummy on steroids. A copy of the paper lay folded with Colin's picture uppermost on the hospital's reception. Izzy marched in and straight up to the desk.

'I've come to see Colin Griggs, which Ward is he... Oh, my word.' She caught sight of the paper. 'My Colin, what have you done to him?' She clasped her hand to her mouth to stop herself from bursting into tears. Lifting the paper and stabbing at the picture with her finger, she repeatedly cried, 'That's my husband; I want to see him now!' Despairing, the tears flooded down her cheeks. 'Colin, oh Colin, what have they done to you?'

'Sit here, Mrs Griggs,' the receptionist pointed to a nearby chair, 'just while you get your breath back. I'll ring the Ward to see if it's okay for you to see him.'

She slumped, muttering to herself. 'What have they done to him, my poor Colin?'

A couple of minutes passed before she felt a hand resting on her shoulder, accompanied by a comforting voice.

'Mrs Griggs, I'm Nurse Tanya. I've been looking after Colin since they brought him in this morning. Let me take you up to him. He's fine by the way,' she sounded reassuring, 'a little groggy but he's awake and asking for you.'

Izzy stood to follow Nurse Tanya. She was still holding the newspaper and staring at Colin's picture. 'What's happened, Nurse?'

'Tanya, call me Tanya.'

'This morning, I left him with a simple cut to his ear and now he looks like a victim of a major terrorist attack or something. I thought hospitals healed, not harmed.'

'Colin can be a little reckless at times, Mrs Griggs. He took it into his head to discharge himself, but in the process, he got rather caught up, so to speak.' Tanya was evasive. 'But he'll be alright once the swellings go down. The x-rays were all clear; we just want to keep him in overnight for observation. You know, to keep an eye on his vitals.'

'You want to keep an eye on his vitals; I thought it was his head he hurt!'

'Yes, blood pressure, heart and breathing rates, temperature, you know.'

'Oh, I see.'

'Ah, here he is,' raising her voice, 'look who's here to see you, Colin.' Nurse Tanya was almost shouting. 'You need to speak up, as he can't hear you through the bandages.'

'My Colin,' Izzy threw her arms around him. 'What have they done to you?'

He produced a stream of random noises in an effort to speak through his bandages.

'Never mind, it can wait until they're off. Are they looking after you? Have you had anything to eat? You must be starving.' He pointed toward a cup with a straw. 'I'm so glad to see you. You wouldn't believe what sort of day I've had! They're keeping you in overnight just for observation.'

❧   ❧   ❧

'That darn paperboy; I'll swing for him one day.' Steve was still in a bad mood after his day's ordeal. 'Why can't he get off his bike instead of riding over our lawn?'

'You stay put. I'll fetch the evening paper and get you a nice cup of tea.' With that, Julia, Mrs Pryor, went into the hall to retrieve the paper.

'Julia,' Steve called to her from the front room, 'why are people gathering around the front gate? They're all pointing and staring at our house. What's going on? Tell them to go away, confounded neighbours.'

She was silent.

'Julia.' He called again, but this time more insistently.

'Could it be something to do with this?' Julia was standing in the doorway, holding up the front page of the Chronicle.

'What the flipping heck—' he stopped himself.

'Steve, there's no need for language like that.'

'Quick, give it to me. What does it say?' The more he read, the more his jaw fell open.

In today's electronic world, newspapers publish in print and on-line simultaneously, and their customers are prone to use Facebook, Instagram, Twitter and the like. It's not every day a bank manager or even ex-bank manager gets accused of murdering their customers by clubbing them to death. Stories like these spread like wildfire. People are curious or morbid or just morbidly curious. The upshot was the road outside the Pryor's house was impassable as a large crowd of onlookers gathered. Crowds draw interest and interest draws the media.

'Quick, Julia, we need to shut all the curtains, front and back, upstairs and down. You do the front, and I'll do the back.' They sprang into action; the phone started ringing. Steve was right next to it; without thinking, picked it up.

'Pryor here.'

'Is it true you attempted to murder one of your customers?'

'Who is this?'

'I would just like to get the facts straight before going on air. Yes or no, Mr Pryor, that's all I want.'

'Air, going on air. What do you mean?'

'Sky News, you should make the nine-o'clock bulletin, if not sooner.'

Steve jabbed at the red button on his cordless handset. *I'll give him nine-o'clock news.* 'Whatever you do,' he said, calling up the stairs, 'don't pick up the phone, it's bound to be one of those reporter people.'

Julia ran around the house, closing curtains. She was now back in the kitchen, quite out of breath.

'What was that you said?'

'Never mind, just don't answer the phone.'

CHAPTER 13

FAKE NEWS

'I need to get back to the farm; the animals need feeding. I best make a move now but don't forget, as soon as they discharge you, I'll be back.' With that, Izzy gave Colin another hug and tried to find his mouth to kiss him. All she got were wet bandages. 'Here's the evening paper. I'll leave it for you. I've not really read it, but you're on the front page.'

She hurried out of the hospital and into a waiting taxi.

'Where to, love?'

'Griggs Farm, Henslow please.'

'I wouldn't if I was you.'

'Why not? That's where I live; and can you be quick about it?'

'Haven't you heard?' The taxi driver caught Izzy's stare in his rear-view mirror.

'Heard what?'

'About a police raid earlier on, helicopters, special operations with snipers, guns, stun grenades, the lot. It's been on the telly. A vicious murderer was on the loose. Some grudge killing. I'd keep away if I were you.'

Her only concern was getting back to the farm. 'I need to get home to feed my animals and geese.'

'Geese! Don't mention geese. Apparently, they

attacked the police and almost downed their helicopter. It's been a right to-do.'

The taxi reached Henslow and was just passing through the village.

'What's that, there,' the taxi drive pointed off in to the distance?'

'That's my farmhouse,' Izzy felt perturbed. 'Can you see what's going on?'

'Looks like loads of cars and vans with big sky dishes on. I reckon it's awful chocka. I don't think we'll get through.'

Izzy peered intently out the taxi's window. 'But look,' she stretched over the front seat to point, 'they're all heading back this way… and fast!'

Sure enough, those who could drove, and those who couldn't ran. Within seconds, the lane up to the farm was grid locked. Cars trying to reverse, others trying to 'U' turn, whilst others had wedged their wheels into the water ditches at the side of the road, were now stuck. All in all, no one was going anywhere. Flashing in their headlights, every now and then, large white birds could be seen diving and honking at anyone and everyone. The whole gaggle of Griggs Farm geese had taken up the fight to protect the farm from invasion.

Izzy slipped from the stationary taxi and went on foot, dodging all and sundry, trying to work her way back to the farm. Food, she thought, is the only way to get them back.

At her kitchen door was the old saucepan and heavy wooden stick used to alert the birds to feeding times. Even above the din of screams, shouts, car horns, and revving engines, the geese heard the familiar sounds of their dinner gong. Like Pavlov's dogs, they all took flight back to safety, to their sanctuary, to their pond. In the lull, the crowds of reporters, journalists, TV crews and technicians made hasty retreats to their vehicles and were soon glad to see the farm disappearing in their rear-view mirrors. And even more delighted to see the Lamb Inn, Henslow looming up in front of them.

Soon the pub was heaving with locals and media types, all talking ten to the dozen about the day's events. Lucy, the barmaid, caught the eye of one rather dishy young TV reporter. The truth is, Lucy caught every young man's eye; she was a bit of a stunner.

'You must know everyone around here.' The reporter inquired. 'I'm sure all the locals come in here, especially if you're behind the bar.' He was almost licking his lips.

'Oh yes, I know everyone hereabouts.'

'So...' he hesitated.

'Lucy—my name's Lucy Critchley.'

'Nice to meet you, Lucy. I'm David Ross, reporter for Sky news. So Lucy, what do you know about this...,' he stopped and referred to his notepad, 'this Griggs fellow.'

'Oh, Colin; yeah he's an okay sort of bloke. He's old enough to be my dad, polite, quite quiet though.'

'Anything else about him?'

Before she could answer she heard... 'Over here, Lucy. What does it take to get a drink?'

'Just a minute. I'll be back.' She left the reporter to serve another customer. 20 minutes passed before she could make it back to where David was stood. The din in the pub was deafening. 'You were asking about Colin.' Lucy saw this reporter as a way of making her TV debut.

'So what can you tell me?'

'What do you want to know? Ask away.' She said cheerily over the din.

'What about any gossip about him? Something to give my story an edge.'

'A what?' Lucy said shouting to be heard over the noise.

'You know an edge. Something a bit different; something to make the viewers take note of my story. Anything.' The conversations got louder and louder.

'Sorry, must go again; I've another customer waiting.' Off Lucy went down the bar. The reporter took another swig of his Becks. She was back 'You want some gossip on Colin?' she hollered. 'Try this for size.' Just as she was about to speak, her dad rang 'time' on the barbell, and the whole place fell silent. All except for Lucy, who, at the top of her voice, announced, 'Colin Griggs wears black stockings!'

Everyone turned and stared at her. The noise levels rose to a new fever pitch, as, to a man, they echoed her words just to make sure they'd heard her correctly.

'Sorry, looks like you've missed your scoop; seems like everyone knows now.'

David's interested was peaked. 'By the way, how do you know, did you see him?'

'No, I've not actually seen him, but I also work in the local chemist, and a few weeks back, he came in for nine pairs.'

'Nine pairs?' said the reporter. 'That's an awful lot of stockings?'

'I asked him if they were for his wife, but he said they were for him, just like that. Honest.' Lucy sounded convincing.

'No bother, Lucy, I'll make good use of that. I'm going to pop out to my OB van and upload my story before anyone else.' With that, the young TV reporter slipped away.

'Hey what about my interview, my TV appearance?' she called after him but to no avail. He was gone.

ও   ও   ও

Izzy finished with the animals, chickens and geese.

'That's my girls,' she said as she locked them up for the night. 'Time for a nice cup of tea and to put my feet up. What a day. I'm glad it's over,' she confided in them.

She came into the kitchen for the first time since the accident. 'Oh my word,' she gasped, 'look at this mess! And here's my Colin's blood.' A tear gathered in the corner of her eye. 'I can't tackle this now; I just want to sit with a cupper.' The sound of her voice reverberated around the room. She cautiously moved, picking up the odd item. Within a few minutes, she'd plonked herself in front of the telly. The late-night news was just starting. All the usual stuff, the pound's up, inflation down, the economy in crisis, bankers' bonuses. She felt her eyes getting heavy.

'Now over to what's happening where you are,' the news anchor person announced.

'An extraordinary revelation has just come to light regarding the attempted murder in Henslow today.' The mention of Henslow brought Izzy around straight away.

'Here is David Ross, our reporter, close to the scene.' The picture cut away to the car park at the Lamb Inn with a smartly dressed young man holding a microphone.

'It seems the earlier Police report on the events here today may have been incomplete or inaccurate and it did not make the motives clear for this appalling crime. It is public knowledge in these parts that local farmer, Colin Griggs, 58, the victim of the attack, regularly wore women's black stockings and may have even been a transvestite. The motive, rather than being a revenge attack as first reported in the local paper, could have been sexual with person or person's unknown wishing to stop such behaviour.'

Izzy was in a rage. 'Where do they get this stuff from' she screamed at the TV? Hitting the off button on the remote before she threw it across the room. 'Bed, sleep, I want this bloody day to end,' she shouted at the top of her lungs.

☙ ☙ ☙

Steve and Julia were prisoners in their own home. The journalists, TV crews, reporters and camera operators were camped front and back, watching for any and every movement. Shouts of 'Just give us a statement' or 'let's hear your side of the story' or 'the British Public have the right to know the truth' would ring out every few minutes. Neither Steve nor Julia responded; they tiptoed around the place, talking in whispers to avoid any chance of giving the press anything.

One thing the media has is a lot of communications equipment and many communication sources. One is used to scan the other continuously, so if something breaks anywhere, the information, or frequent misinformation, spreads rapidly. As news of the developments in Henslow reached the media-pack, within minutes, the whole circus had packed up shop and left.

Julia couldn't contain her curiosity. 'It's gone real quiet out front; shall I take a look?'

'No, I bet it's some ruse to lure us to the window.'

'Do you think so?'

'Well, I'm not an expert on media siege tactics, but they're sure up to something.'

'I know, if I go upstairs into the bathroom and stand on the side of the bath, I can peek out of the expel-air vents with no one seeing.'

'Good idea. Keep low, move slowly and don't put any lights on.' Steve said.

Julia was across the room, into the hall and up the stairs like a pro. The SAS Hereford Training School would have been glad for her services.

'Don't slip off the side of the...' Steve considered the heavy thud above him. 'Too late,' he said to himself, 'I guess that bath's got her.' He too was up the stairs and into the bathroom in no time at all. The only use the SAS would have for his services was as an example of how not to do it. In the bathroom, Julia greeted him, lying face down on the floor, swaddled in the shower curtain with the rail laying across her back.

She was muttering, 'If I've asked you once, I've asked you a dozen times to fix that damn rail. Now you're retired, you've no longer got any excuses.'

From this, he gathered she was not seriously hurt. 'What did you see?' he enquired rather gingerly.

'From here I can see we need a new loo brush holder, the skirting needs repainting, and there's loads of fluff stuck behind the radiator, but no journalists.'

'You're right on one thing, but I don't know quite how you saw from where you are. I can't see any journalists, vans, neighbours, or anything out of the bedroom window. Just the usual Granby Avenue.' The life of the Pryor's had returned to normal.

CHAPTER 14

FLANAGAN FAILS TO IMPRESS

The next morning, Izzy awoke to the sound of the paperboy ramming the newspaper through the letterbox in his usual 'I don't care' manner. Clad in her dressing gown, she went to collect it. *They won't let him out for hours. I want some me-time before the invalid returns; I think I deserve it.* The phone ringing interrupted her thoughts. *Well, that lasted all of 30 seconds.* 'Hello, Griggs Farm.'

'You poor thing having to put up with that sort of behaviour. These men, what makes them do it?'

Izzy held the receiver away from her ear. 'Hello, who is this?'

'They all seem so respectable on the outside, then next minute, they're wearing stockings and goodness knows what else.'

'Who is this? Please, tell me, or I'll hang up.'

The caller continued, 'It's nothing to be ashamed of, dear; we all have our crosses to bear.'

'Okay, I'm going to hang up.' With that, Izzy put the phone down. 'Bloody busy body do-gooders.'

The do-gooder had already seen today's newspaper; Izzy pulled hers through the letterbox. The headline jumped off the page: 'Britain's Morals in Decline – Transvestite Farmer Attacked.' *Take no notice,* she told herself. *Yes, Colin has worn stockings—I've seen him, but it*

THE HOLE OPPORTUNITY

was all entirely innocent. These journalists wouldn't know the truth if it bit them on the backside. She refused to read further and screwed the paper into a ball.

The phone started ringing again; she picked it up, and she spoke without listening, 'No, thank you,' and put it straight down. Immediately, it rang again. 'Can you please stop ringing me? I've nothing further to say, nor do I want your good wishes or anything else.' She rang off.

Again, the phone rang. She hesitated about picking it up; it got to four rings, then six, then eight. 'Yes,' she snapped.

'Mrs Griggs?' A rather timid voice enquired.

'Yes.' Izzy said with less force this time.

'It's Harpsden General Hospital here. I'm ringing to let you know you can collect your husband after the doctor's finished his rounds later this morning.'

'Oh, okay, thank you. Sorry for being a bit short; I've had rather a lot on my mind. What time did you say?'

'Around 11.'

'Thanks for letting me know.' Relieved, Izzy put down the receiver.

🙢 🙢 🙢

Jimmy Flanagan woke to the incessant ring of his smartphone. He reached out one hand and grovelled around until he found it. 'Yeah.'

'Where are you, Flanagan? Get your backside into my office, pronto.' It was his editor.

Blear-eyed, he looked around. 'I'm on a sofa.'

185

'Where?' his editor demanded.

'No idea; it's not mine, so I guess I'm not at home.'

'Just get yourself here right now; you've got some explaining to do.'

Jimmy continued to listen but heard nothing; he dropped the phone. *That doesn't sound like a man who's overly happy with his star reporter,* thought Jimmy. *He's always an awkward cuss, not good at showing his gratitude. Miserable git!* Forgetting where he was he, rolled over and ended up on the floor.

'Ouch, my head.' His pain was not from the fall. 'Please God, I promise never to touch another Tequila shot again if you make this headache go away.' He was well and truly hungover. The celebration of his new self-proclaimed status as ace crime reporter for the Harpsden Chronicle was short-lived.

He already had most of his clothes on except for one shoe, a sock, and his jacket. He scrabbled his stuff together, looked around, saw no one or anything he recognised and left. Hitting the street, it turned out he was a few hundred yards from the office. Within 10 minutes, he was standing in front of the Editor's desk, wishing he wasn't.

'Your scoop, your attempted murder, your revengeful bank manager was all hot air, a pack of lies, fiction, something Enid Blyton would be proud of. We want facts, well researched and corroborated facts, true stories, news. Am I making myself clear?' The Editor ranted.

'Yes, Sir. I know. I did all that, pictures, tape

recordings; it all good stuff. Okay, I may have embellished one or two facts—'

'What do you mean by one or two facts? The story has no facts to embellish; it all fiction.'

'But my pictures, the tape, I saw it all,' Jimmy protested.

'And what about the poor copper, mown down in the line of duty? Where was he in your news report? Not a mention.'

'Well, yeah, that happened.'

'I know, I'm not disputing that. It's the rest that didn't. Bob Adams, you know, Inspector Adams, has just been chewing my ear off. What am I to tell him? The Chronicle is branching out into fairy stories to improve circulation?'

'But, but, Sir.'

'Don't but me son. Now, get back to your desk. There's a christening this afternoon at St Anne's. That's your scoop. Let this be a lesson for you. Get tidied up and scram… and close the door on your way out.'

Flanagan left, confused, seething and extremely hungover.

❧ ❧ ❧

The morning after, The Lamb Inn looked like something more akin to backstage at a Glastonbury festival. Bodies, bottles, abandoned clothes, discarded food, dog-ends and upturned ashtrays; the smell of stale beer, unwashed bodies, and smoke hung thick in the air.

The evening before, the landlord saw an opportunity and took full advantage of the media circus.

Wine and beer flowed with food aplenty, accompanied by the unreserved merriment of the local Ann Bishop on the piano. It was not the sophisticated evening these media types were used to, but they and the villagers enjoyed it and would remember it for a long time to come. Gradually everyone cleaned themselves up and sorted themselves out, returning home or to their respective vehicles ready to invade the life of some other unsuspecting victim in the name of news reporting.

Lucy sauntered around, clearing up. She was still mad at not been interviewed. 'I was so close to getting on TV,' she kept repeating, 'so close.'

Her dad made useless parent-like conciliatory platitudes, 'You wait; your turn will come. What will be will be.'

She didn't know what was worse, her dad or the fact that she allowed herself to be used by the TV reporter, 'Damn Ross'. She felt guilty about letting Colin's secret out of the bag. *We probably won't see him in here for a while,* she thought. *I hope not; I'm not sure I could look him in the eye.*

Colin couldn't look anyone in the eye in his present condition. Swellings and bruising worsen before they get better, making his eyes invisible through his bandages. No one could see him, and he could hardly see out and certainly not sufficient to read the newspaper Izzy left, nor the Red Top brought by some chirpy hospital volunteer that morning.

Izzy arrived promptly at 11 o'clock with clean

clothes, notably a shirt. The shirt Colin had been wearing was heavily blood-stained and stored beside his bed in a plastic bag as the Police mentioned they might require it for evidence.

Over and above his head wounds, Colin had sustained extensive bruising to his chest and ribs, where he'd hit the ground twice. While his right arm had several small lacerations from the cutlery and crockery, he'd so gracefully scattered around the farmhouse kitchen. Though he was not in any real danger, Izzy knew he'd be walking wounded for several more days to come. She picked up his medication and collected a wheelchair to get him down to the car park.

As they passed through reception, she saw one of the PCs who'd arrested her the previous day. 'Not travelling in pairs then, today,' Izzy joked.

PC Billy Field looked stern and pointed to the wheelchair. 'What's wrong with him?'

Incoherent, Colin tried to answer, but he didn't know what happened, and even if he did, he couldn't make himself understood.

The next few days were going to be peaceful, but also difficult trying to understand what he wanted, Izzy reflected.

They journeyed home in silence as they both mulled over the past 24 hours and thought about their future. Actually, Colin fell asleep behind his bandages, but Izzy couldn't tell. At the farm, she stopped close to the front door to let him straight in and up the stairs—the quickest way to their bedroom, and by going in the front door meant he wouldn't be reminded of the devastation that still awaited her in the kitchen. *For the better*, she surmised.

The phone had constantly been ringing. Before setting off for the hospital, Izzy decided not to answer it but let them go to voice mail instead. That way, she could filter out the crank calls, nuisance calls, journalists or whomever. She let it ring. The answerphone cut in 'Griggs Hole Farm, we're unable to take your call right now. Please leave your number after the beeps.'

'This is Sarah Weaver. I left a message for you yesterday. Given what I've seen on the news and read in the papers, I think we need to meet to review your account as a matter of urgency. Please return my call as soon as you hear this.' She hung up. Izzy listened; she thought; she picked up the phone; she put it down again without dialling. 'I know what you want; I'm in no hurry. Anyway, Colin's in no fit state to see anyone.' She felt defiant. 'Just wait, you vulture, just wait!'

Whilst stood by the phone, she noticed ten other messages were waiting. It turned out six were from various journalists and reporters just wanting her side of the story or some such rubbish. One was from Kevin Glenn, a local villager who always relished a beer or two and who wanted to thank Colin for the great night at the Lamb, one of the best he'd ever had and what a pity he'd missed it, and hopes he gets better soon. Another two from various women's charities offering her refuge, counselling, support, and even setting up a fund-raising day for 'wives and partners of transvestites' and finally one from a chap who called himself Rita. He could give Colin the address of a clothes shop near Euston Station,

London, where they have outfits for all builds, shapes and sizes, including undergarments and stilettos for up to UK size 12. In particular, they were known for their extensive range of stockings. He also had details of a club not far away from where you can be whoever you want to be. Izzy deleted them all and turned her mobile back on after being at the hospital. Up popped a text message; You're a star, Colin. Seen it all on Sky News. Take a look at stockingwearers.com. It's all on there. Bruce, DHL Driver.

'Will this ever go away?' She sighed and deleted this text as well. Izzy busied cleaning up the kitchen and popped upstairs now and then to see if he wanted anything. All he seemed to do was sleep. She took the time to prepare one of his favourites, chicken soup, and even put it through the blender to make it easier to suck up a straw.

She spoke slow, deliberate and loud. 'Here you are, Colin,' she said, gently rocking him awake. 'Some nice chicken soup.' Puffing up his pillows and adding an extra two from her side of the bed, she helped him sit up. He took the mug plus straw and seemed okay sucking it up.

'I'll get you one of the baby feeding beakers tomorrow if you like.' *Is this what it's going to be like when he's old and infirm? Let's hope that's a few years away yet,* she pondered.

As he sucked up his soup, she sat on the bed and filled him in on the abbreviated version of yesterday's events. She decided he didn't need to know all the cock and bull stories floating around the press and TV news.

'They held me at the Police Station for over six hours,' she shouted. 'It was because of that nice Mr Pryor

191

that Inspector Adams believed my story and let me go. They were going to charge me with your attempted murder. Whatever's next? I'd never want to kill you.' She puckered up to kiss him again but thought better of it. Soupy wet bandages weren't appealing.

He drained his mug.

'More?' she shouted.

He shook his head; it was easier than trying to speak.

'I've got an old hand-bell here with a notepad and pen. I'll leave them next to the bed so you can call if you need me. Her voice was sounding hoarse after all the shouting. 'The nurse will call in tomorrow to re-dress your wounds.' *Maybe I won't need to shout so much then,* she hoped.

❧ ❧ ❧

It was late afternoon; Izzy was in the yard near the pond, tending to her birds. Hearing a car pull into their driveway, she looked up but didn't recognise the driver.

'Mrs Griggs', the young man shouted in her direction, not wanting to come much closer to the geese than was absolutely necessary. 'Hello Mrs Griggs, we haven't met before. Can you spare me a moment of your time?' He moved cautiously toward her.

'If you're a reporter, I've nothing further to say to you lot. Get off my property. You've caused enough damage already.' She stood to her full height, all five foot four inches, and pushed out her chest. She was going to stand her ground.

'Oh, Mrs Griggs, Isobel, isn't it? I just want five minutes, please.'

'Which bit of 'no' don't you understand? Now get away with you.'

'Look, I've made a bit of a mistake, and I need to put things right.' He was almost pleading.

'Are you that Jimmy Finnegan from the Chronicle?' She could feel her hackles rising.

'Flanagan,' he corrected her.

'I don't care who you are. You can't put things right. It's been all over the telly, the Nationals and the internet. How can you put things, right? My poor Colin's ruined because of you. Not only have you made him a laughing stock with that ridiculous picture, but his reputation is in tatters.'

'He's quite capable of doing that himself, from what I've heard.' Jimmy said under his breath.

Izzy was thinking the same thing, but she tried not to let it show. 'Go on, scram, or I'll get my girls onto you.' She turned toward the geese. Jimmy got the message loud and clear.

'Just in case you change your mind, here's my card. I won't come any closer if you don't mind. I'll just put it down here.' He placed his card on a nearby saddle stone and got back in his car. As he drove away, he saw her in the rear-view mirror pocket his card. *Well, at least there's some hope she may contact me,* he thought.

&ఐ &ఐ &ఐ

The following morning, Nurse Dee was doing her community nursing rounds. She arrived at Griggs farm to change Colin's dressing.

'How's our patient today, then?' She noticed the

swellings were reduced. 'I can see you now,' she shouted, 'are you feeling any better?' Directing the question at him, Izzy looked on and said nothing.

He picked up his pen and pad and wrote, 'Yes, but can you loosen these bloody bandages so I can speak?' Nurse Dee sensed his frustration.

'Yes, of course, now let me see.' Tanya busied about her duties and unravelled his turban to reveal blue, blackish, yellow bruising, pasty white skin, two day's growth of stubble and a smattering of congealed food around his mouth.

'Now that's a sight to behold. I wouldn't like to meet you in some dark alley in the dead of night!' Tanya smiled.

Izzy had to agree, but thought Tanya should have kept her opinion to herself.

'You'll be okay soon, Colin, don't listen to that nasty Nurse.'

Tanya looked surprised. *He's nearer to 70 than 6,* she thought, but said nothing.

'Now, these wounds. Your left ear is only a flesh wound and will heal much quicker left uncovered. And the right side.' She turned his head more abruptly than he had been expecting.

'Ouch, that hurt.' He spoke.

Maybe he's closer to 6 than 70, after all. 'You've plenty of bruising, but the X-rays show no broken bones. The cut above your right eye is deep and will need a new dressing in a day or two. I think we can dispense with the mummy look.' Within a few minutes, Nurse Tanya had completed her duties. 'Now, plenty of rest. You can bathe, but be sure to keep your head dry. Get up if you feel you want to but take it steady near stairs. If you have dizzy spells, let me know; otherwise, I'll be back in a couple of days.' She collected her stuff, bagged up the old dressing, and left in a flurry. 'Onto the next,' she said and disappeared out of the front door.

With the help of Nurse Tanya and Izzy's constant caring, Colin's health improved. Copious bowls of chicken soup and servings of Izzy's apple and rhubarb crumble with custard lifted his spirits. To keep himself entertained, Colin watched all manner of television regularly punctuated with adverts for this and that, most of which he had never heard of, nor likely to purchase. His normal TV diet was the 10 o'clock news, as their farm kept them too busy for anything else.

'Colin, I've not said anything about the phone calls.' Izzy emphasised her words.

'Sorry. What?' He was unsure of what she meant.

'You know, that call, the one we got earlier this week?'

He gave her a blank look and frowned.

'The one that started this total nightmare off. Stop being so silly. Sarah Weaver, you remember, that bloody bank woman who wants to put us out on the street.' Izzy promised herself she wouldn't get upset, but a wave of rage surged over her. 'She's rung three times chasing us to make an appointment for our account review. So far, I've dodged speaking to her, but we can't avoid her much longer. A letter came this morning from the bank asking us the same thing.'

Hospitalisation had blanked Colin's mind. Izzy

noticed his pallid complexion as the memories flooded back. The realisation washed over him he was in danger of losing the farm his family had occupied for over 100 years, and it was his fault. Shame and humiliation engulfed him. Never mind the practicalities of living on the street—everything was all too much. Luckily, he was sitting in an armchair, so there was no falling or breaking of anything and no more head injuries. Instead, he just slumped to one side as he passed out again.

'Colin, speak to me, Colin!' Izzy tapped his face before listening to his breathing; it sounded okay, not that she was medically trained. 'Quick, water,' she rushed off into the kitchen. Glass in hand, she returned. He groaned as he came around. 'Oh Colin, you scared me. Here, drink this.'

He managed a few sips. 'Thanks, my love, what are we going to do?' He sounded despairing.

The noise of the TV in the corner filtered through. 'We can't talk with that thing on.' She searched around for the remote before hitting the off button.

Just at that moment, Colin cried out. 'That's the answer!' pointing to the TV and a blank screen. 'Quick, quick, turn it on again.'

'Just ring this Freephone number. 0800 888 8881 and Injuries Claim4You will do the rest.' The advert finished and changed to one for Fairy Liquid.

'Did you see that? Our salvation, Izzy. We can claim for my accident and... hey presto, our financial worries will be over.'

She hadn't seen him so excited since his last great idea. *Yeah, hey presto, nothing's ever that easy.* 'So, what are you saying, Colin?'

'Let's put in a claim for damages against Harpsden General for my second accident—loss of earnings and all that stuff. Once we get the money, we'll be rich, and Ms Weaver can have her loan back.' He beamed.

'I'm not so sure. What do you know about claiming damages? I know, I know nothing! It doesn't sound right.'

'But what have we got to lose?'

'Well, everything you said so yourself.'

'No, I mean by contacting these Injury Claims people. We can at least ask them, and it's a Freephone number.'

'What was it then?'

'Umm 0800—I can't remember the rest.'

Izzy raised her eyebrows. 'Well, that's a lot of help; all Freephone numbers are 0800.'

'I know, Izzy, can you fetch that pen and pad you got me when I couldn't talk? Leave it with me, and I can get the number when the ad's on again.'

She disappeared to come back with it.

Colin sat glued to the TV. 'Right, Mr Injury Claims I'm ready for you. There'll be more ads in a few minutes; we just need to be patient.' He looked up at Izzy for her approval.

Izzy couldn't keep her eyes open any longer. 'Colin, it's after 11; I'm going up.'

'Yeah, yeah, you go, I'm fine. I'll just wait here for the ad break, get the number and be right up with you.'

She left, he watched. *Right this time,* he thought

optimistically. The adverts came, and the adverts went; more programmes, more ads, but none for Injury Claims. By 2 a.m., he was drifting in and out of sleep.

'Call 0800 888 8881' came from the TV.

'0800 8... what was that? Blast, I missed it.'

Izzy's disembodied voice floated down the stairs. 'Colin, come to bed; we'll get the number tomorrow off the internet. Come up here.'

'You could have told me earlier,' he grunted. 'I've wasted flipping hours watching loads of pointless rubbish.' He huffed.

ℕ ℕ ℕ

'Julia, you don't seem to realise what this could do to me. If Sarah Weaver looks into Griggs' file, she'll see I should have never loaned him £10K in the first place. Well, not without some collateral guarantee at least.' Steve brushed a bead of sweat from his forehead.

'What do you care? You're retired now; it's her problem, not yours.'

'Oh, if it were that easy.'

'Why? What can she do?'

'For starters, she could file a report for incompetency at best or fraud at worst.' Steve felt more beads of sweat pop out on his brow.

'Fraud!' Julia was astonished.

'Yes. These days, many consider banks as just serving their own interests, and much of the media and politicians are gunning for their blood. They'd like nothing more than seeing them getting their just dessert.'

'But what's that got to do with you and fraud?'

'Well, banks feel by taking a hard line they can somehow show how squeaky clean and upstanding they are, so deflecting their critics.'

'And you?' Julia was now quite concerned.

'I'm an easy target, and by making me an example, Lloyds could preserve or bolster their standing without it having any real impact at a local, regional or national level, as I've already left the company.'

'Was it fraud? Could they prove fraud?'

'No, of course it wasn't. It was a rather cavalier, devil-may-care gesture. I was retiring after 35 years, and Griggs were good, loyal customers. Colin was down on his luck and trying to do something about it by starting a new business. I was able to help, so I did.'

'Well, there you are, then. All's okay now.'

'No, Julia, it doesn't work like that. The bank wants forms filled, paper trails, security, offer letters, adherence to procedures—they want blood.' Steve got quite animated.

'What can you do? How can you stop this Sarah Weaver from taking it further?' Julia didn't relish the thought of weekly prison visits.

'I know what I should have done after Colin came to see me. I also knew the staff were organising a surprise party, and I knew the whole application rigmarole would have taken days, much longer than I had left at the bank. I started to complete the form and planned to slip it into his file at some other time. Regarding the letters, well, I have a mountain of blank letter headed paper in the study here; they're easy.'

'And where is this half-completed form now?'

'Probably in my briefcase. I've not opened it since the day I left.'

Julia was out to the hallway near the hat stand by the front door where Steve always left his briefcase. 'It's not here,' she sounded panicky, 'you always put it here. Where is it?'

'I don't know. Maybe you've tidied it away now I'm retired.'

'Don't blame me. I bet you've left it somewhere. Have a look in your study, or maybe it's in the car.'

Steve roamed around the house and out to the car, looking for it. 'It's no good, dear; I can't find it anywhere.'

'Well, the fairies haven't taken it. Think, man, where might you have left it? I don't want to be married to a fraudster. Come on, think,' she was sounding hysterical, 'think!'

'The office, I must have left it at the office. During my retirement party, I had several glasses of champagne. Linda said she'd look after it for me. After the party, they put me in a taxi. I collected my car the next day, a Saturday, so that I couldn't get into the bank. Actually, I've not thought about it till now.'

'Well, go now.' Julia pushed Steve on the shoulder toward the door.

'What happens if she's at the bank?'

'Who? Linda?'

'No, the Weaver woman.'

'Well, ring Linda and check.' I'm sure she'd love to hear from you.' There was venom in Julia's tone.

'Have you tried ringing the bank lately? I'll end

up in India or Cardiff or some other godforsaken place.'

'Email her,' Julia was trying to be helpful.

'You're not allowed private emails in the bank. All branch emails go to a central account for filtering.'

'Do you have her private email or mobile phone number?'

'Of course not, dear.' Steve didn't want to admit to knowing either, in case Julia started asking questions. 'I know she usually has lunch at 12.30. If it's fine weather, she sits in the park near the fountain. I'll pop up and see if I can collect it.'

'You seem to know a lot about her movements.' Julia folded her arms.

'I should do; she'd been my PA for the last fifteen years.' He was dismissive; Julia was suspicious: she always thought Linda was too helpful, above and beyond the call of duty.

'Well, it's 12.00 now, and it's not raining. Go on, get in your car.' Julia held the front door ajar.

'It's all a bit sudden. I've not had lunch yet. Hang on a minute.'

'I wonder what you'd get for lunch in Martalsham Open Prison.' Julia mused. Steve was out of the door before she finished her sentence.

CHAPTER 15

FOR MY EYES ONLY

'Ah, Billy, what news of your brother?' Inspector Adams sounded genuinely interested.

'Well, he's fully conscious, but both legs are in plaster, and he's in traction. His jaw's wired together, but they think he'll keep most of his teeth. Other than that—'

'I don't expect we'll see him back on duty for several months by the sound of it.'

'No, he took it full pelt; over and above the call of duty.'

'Dereliction of duty more like. What he did was extremely foolish.' Adams gave Billy a stern look.

Billy protested vehemently. 'But sir, that bank manager was driving recklessly. He was suspected of murder and he should face a charge, not John.'

'I've heard talk of him having to face a dangerous driving charge, but whatever, we need to measure up at the scene. You know, skid marks and the like, and examine his car. The trouble is, I know Pryor socially, so I cannot be the one to investigate.'

It didn't take long for Billy to realise if the bank manager gets off, then John will face a disciplinary charge. Billy was back at the hospital as soon as he came off duty. John was feeling better, but not great as he thought about not being at work, learning to walk again and only being able to have liquids. Things went downhill sharply after Billy told him about the possible disciplinary.

John, unable to talk scribbled on his pad. 'That's all I need right now. All I want to do is get back to work.' His frustration showed as he dug his pen hard into the paper, almost ripping it as he wrote.

'Brother, I'll be with you through this. We'll find a way. I'll be your eyes and ears.'

'And mouth.' He wrote.

'Well, at least you haven't lost your sense of humour. See you tomorrow. I'll see what I can find out. Cheers.' Billy left. He spent the car journey home thinking about the events that afternoon, trying to get a clear picture in his mind and find some way of getting John off the hook. His conclusions weren't helpful. His thought turned to Flanagan. *That bloody journalist witnessed the whole incident and had a camera and a tape recorder. I need to get hold of his pictures and listen to the recording, but how?*

At the station, Inspector Adams was contemplating the same situation. *Steve's a friend, golf companion, and on the Committee. I wrongfully arrested him and treated him heavy-handedly; now, he's potentially facing a dangerous driving charge or worse, which could lead to a prison term. However, John's a copper and a good one at that. He may face a dereliction of duty charge, which will stop his career dead in its tracks. I need Steve's friendship if I'm going to get on the Golf Club Committee, but I want nothing to happen to John.* He rose from his chair, flicked off the office light and left for the Golf Club to get a swift half on the way home. *What to do for the best?* He was troubled.

Jimmy Flanagan still wasn't sure why he received such a ticking off from his editor. *Okay, so I embellished the story somewhat, but that's what journalists do; poetic licence. Everyone does it all the time. Who wants to hear a straight reporting of facts? People would be bored with the news after two minutes. I might have been premature with my conclusions and rather selective with what I included and missed an excellent story with that copper being run over. Still, otherwise,* he told himself; *I did a pretty good job, even if I say so myself.*

Jimmy spent the next hour reviewing, editing, and cropping the pictures he'd uploaded from his camera onto his laptop. The audio files from the Dictaphone recordings were now on the laptop. He combined them all, synchronising the sound with the stills, before he played it back. The pictures and narrative were better complemented by the adjustments he made to the slide timings. He watched it again.

The look of sheer desperation on the face of the bank manager as he repeatedly tried to brake whilst avoiding a demented copper who seemed hell-bent on getting himself killed was there in glorious high definition colour and stereo sound for all to see. As the car swerved, so the policeman changed his direction to keep in the path of the approaching vehicle. *What was he trying to do?* Jimmy pondered; *he must have been mad.* The screeching tyre sounds were plain enough; *the driver was definitely braking.* Then the thump and groans as John hit the car, before being tossed like a rag doll onto the windscreen. *I'm surprised it didn't break.* Jimmy kept watching. Next were several shots as John slid down the bonnet before slumping to the ground in front of the nearside wheel.

The pictures paused on John all but under the front wheel; the audio was non-stop with Billy Field clearly taking charge and getting Pryor out of his car. Billy and Control's full conversation was clear to hear. The audio continued with the sounds of honking, flapping geese, the unmistakable clatter of the helicopter rotor blades, shouts from the Special Ops team, and later Inspector Adams arriving and charging Steve Pryor with attacking Colin Griggs.

Accompanying the audio were more images of frantic geese, guys with guns in the helicopter, the ambulance taking John Field away and, although taken much later, pictures of Colin Griggs in his hospital bed. *A complete audio-visual record,* thought Jimmy. *Who could argue with that?*

To make certain, he watched and listened to the whole lot again. *Too late now to use this in a story. Oh, what might have been? Pity. You might as well delete it.* With his finger poised over the 'delete' key his mobile phone burst into life.

'Hi, Jimmy Flanagan, how can I help?'

'Colin, I know you can hear me,' Izzy was calling up the stairs, 'it's eleven, what do you want on your toast?'

Silence. 'I thought you wanted to look up that phone number on Google; you know those Injury Claim people.' She tried again and then went back into the kitchen. After a few minutes, she could hear shuffling sounds in the hall, followed by the kitchen door opening. She looked up, expecting to see him walk through the door. Nothing. 'Where are you?' No response. 'Colin' she sounded more urgent. She went to see what was wrong and found him sat on the hall chair next to the kitchen door with his head in his hands; he was snoring.

'Colin, don't do that; you gave me a real turn. I thought something had happened to you. Are you alright?' Head wounds and a late-night had taken their toll.

He did one of those long, drawn-out yawns whilst speaking at the same time. She didn't understand a word but presumed it was something about 'I'll be fine soon.'

'Come on, get some breakfast inside you; you'll feel better then.' She sat him down and sorted him out. 'I've been thinking,' she continued, 'we need to decide what to do about this loan.'

He interrupted, 'Injury Claims that will sort it.'

'Well, I'm not so sure. To be on the safe side, we need a proper plan. As I see it, we have a couple of options. We can arrange an appointment with Sarah Weaver, well that will happen anyway, and see if we can get her not to call in the loan. You know, tell her the golf course contract was a learning experience for us; our first contract as a new business and how we'd taken on board loads so it wouldn't happen again. And how we have better procedures in place, reviewed our purchasing approach, developed our supplier relationships and improved our customer care strategy.' Izzy took a deep breath.

'What are you talking about?' He looked bemused.

'She's some high flying corporate businesswoman who expects her customers to be the same. She'll want business plans, projections, forecasts, P&L's, a balance sheet, ROI calculations—'

'What's ROI?'

'See, that's exactly what I mean. She'll think we're some small-town outfit from Henslow. Colin, you need to sharpen up, or she'll ship us out.' She folded her arms across her chest. 'You've got to take it seriously.' Her piercing glare told him she was serious.

'But I'm ill.'

'We haven't got time for that; we've got work to do.' A new determination came over her.

'Couldn't we just tell her I'm ill, you know? Go for the sympathy vote.'

'Straws, Colin, that's called grasping at straws.' Exasperated, Izzy kept the pressure up.

Colin smiled up at her. 'Yes, but, well, women are more understanding, you know, caring, soft. They appreciate the difficulties of juggling home and work life. I'm sure she'll understand.'

'Gordon Bennet! You men know nothing. That might well have been the case 10 or 20 years ago, but not now. It's tough in the workplace and even tougher for women. They've learned, responded by being the same. Tough is the new soft for them.'

'Izzy, that's not us. We're not a Corporate thingy.'

He paused. 'What did you say? Tough is the new soft; what the heck does that mean?'

'Not now, don't go off the point; this is what we're going to do. First—'

'First,' he interrupted, 'First, we're going to ask Steve Pryor what we're going to do. After all, he made us the loan initially.'

'Genius Colin, why didn't I think of that?'

'I think you were too caught up in your P&L and ROI's or whatever to see the wood for the trees.' He felt quite pleased with himself.

'Okay, the revised plan. First, we'll call Steve Pryor. We've got his home number; remember his PA woman, Linda gave it to us so we could follow up on the golf course quote.'

'Not sure where it is. I need to look for it.'

'Well, what are you waiting for? This is our future. Go, Colin, go.'

'Do you think he'll want to speak to us? He's retired now, and of course, the Golf Club incident. After that fiasco, he'll probably be glad to know that we're in financial trouble; a kind of retribution.'

'No, he's not like that. Come on; he wouldn't hold a grudge. Find that number.'

❧   ❧   ❧

'Linda, I thought I'd find you here.' Steve's approach was tentative.

'Steve, Mr Pryor, oh hi.' Her voice dropped a semitone, and the corners of her eyes showed her inner smile. 'What a pleasant surprise.' She turned to face him.

'Yes, I find this place a little haven; it helps with getting through the day, my oasis of calm.' She let out a little giggle, not wanting to appear too eager. 'We all miss you, you know. It's strange not having you around, our little chats and your Hobnobs with morning coffee. What about you? How's retirement? All lie-ins and long lunches, punctuated by rounds of golf, no doubt.' Her smile broadened. 'Come…,' she patted the bench, 'sit down here.'

'Well, not quite; I miss you too,' he paused, 'all of you,' he quickly added to deflect the moment. 'Look, I've got a little favour to ask you.' He sat beside her; she didn't make room. His leg pressed up against hers.

'Ask away; I'll do anything for you, you know that.' Her voice was now deep and throaty. She looked straight into his eyes.

'Well, it's slightly delicate,' he hesitated, 'at my leaving do I never really thanked you for that great bash.' He loosened his collar. 'it was a genuine surprise.'

'I know you knew, but thanks for pretending not to.' She looked for some sign of acknowledgement. 'Was that it?' She hadn't shifted her gaze.

'Was that what?'

'Why you've come here today to say thanks for the party?'

'Well, yes, I mean no…, partly.' Steve blustered.

'Which one, yes, no or partly?' She wondered if she'd overdone her response.

'None actually. I've something else I want to ask you.' He pulled his shoulders back to recover his position.

'Yes, and I've missed you too.' Linda swooned, her

heart fluttered. 'I truly have.' She didn't want to let the moment pass.

'Linda, please, not now. You misunderstand my intentions.' Steve felt awkward. 'Have you got it?'

'What?' Linda sounded disappointed.

'After the party, you got me a taxi and said you'd look after it.'

Linda tilted her head. It was clear she hadn't understood.

'My briefcase.'

'Oh, why didn't you say? Yes, of course, I've got it. I was wondering when you'd want it back. Why didn't you come to the bank and ask?'

'I didn't know who'd be there, whom I might bump into from Head Office.'

'Silly. You've still got an account; you've every reason to come in.'

'I didn't want to run into her,' he looked around to check no one was listening, 'you know, that Sarah Weaver woman.'

'So that's your real reason?'

'On my last day, I sort of didn't follow procedure and didn't want her to find out.'

'What, with the Griggs' loan?'

'How did you know?' He was wondering if it was too late.

'Oh, that's easy. Mr Griggs came and went in a few minutes and no paperwork. Not like you at all. I guessed you were excited about the surprise party and your retirement.' She slipped her arm into his, 'Well, your secret's safe with me.' Snuggling up, she leant her head on his shoulder.

'Linda,' Steve lowered his voice, 'I can't leave it like that. Once Sarah Weaver scrutinises the files, she'll find out, and I'll be for the high-jump or worse.'

'How bad's worse?' She feigned concern.

'Shhh, keep your voice down; prison for fraud.'

She trembled. 'No, no, they can't send you to prison, not my Steve.' Tears welled up in her eyes. 'I won't let her.' Overreacting, she feared she might alert him to her actual intentions. For good measure, she threw her arms around him.

'Linda, please. Someone will see us. Look, all is not lost here. I started to fill out the loan form for Griggs, but it's in my briefcase. I need to complete it, get him to sign it, and a letter of acceptance, and get the lot into his file before Ms Weaver finds out.'

Linda nodded, wiping away a tear.

'First, I need my briefcase. Can you meet me with it back here after work?'

'No.'

'Why on earth not?' Steve looked puzzled.

'I haven't got it.' *Ooo, my plan's coming together*. 'Well, not here,' she cast her eyes down.

'Then where is it?' Steve could feel his stress level rising.

'At my place; it's quite safe.' She sounded matter of fact. 'I took it home so no one else could get their hands on it. I knew eventually you'd want it. I was going to tell you; it's on the hall table. I see it every time I go or come back to the flat. A reminder of you; it's as if you're waiting for me like I've waited for you all these years.'

Linda couldn't help herself; she could no longer hold back her emotions.

Steve swallowed hard. 'Can you meet me here tomorrow at lunchtime?'

'I think it'd be safer if you collected it; she's due in tomorrow on one of her weekly visits.' It was only a little lie.

'Has she started on the customer files yet?' He sounded panicky.

'Oh yes…, just though. She took A–C last time and wants D–F tomorrow.'

'D–F! That means we have a week before she goes onto the Gs.'

'Come tonight then and collect it from my flat.' Her look was one of concern. 'I'm going to the gym on the way home. Obviously, afterwards, I'll need to shower and tidy myself up. So what about 8 o'clock? I'll fix us a bite if you like.' She didn't want to sound too pushy.

Steve was feeling flustered.

'Yes, okay, whatever.' He just wanted to leave. 'Fine, see you at eight.' He stood and left; she remained on the bench to plot the entrapment. *Tonight Steve Pryor, you're mine!* Her mind went into overdrive. *It has taken some doing,* she thought.

Steve wasn't aware that Linda, the efficient Linda, the loyal Linda, the caring Linda, had taken matters into her own hands regarding the loan. She knew no paperwork was unacceptable to any bank, however modern or traditional it might be. Handshakes had to be backed up by the necessary form filling and signature gaining activities. Immediately following the retirement party, she'd completed all the details and got Colin to sign both the form and acceptance letter as Steve had already signed and dated the half-completed form; no further work was needed. She had even filed it in the Griggs' customer file. More precisely, she started a new one as all the existing files were so old, worn and thick they were breaking their way out their binders.

Linda used the rest of her lunch-time for shopping for her sting. *Men are always partial to a little steak, especially rare. The blood brings out the animal in them. Something a little different, like Dauphinoise potatoes, Dwarf French beans and a nice full-bodied Saint Chinian red.* She was playing out her fantasy in her head. *I guess he's a white lace man, nothing too in-your-face. A thong and a little lift and separate with lace trim.* She went back to her office wearing a smile any Cheshire cat would be proud of.

Clock watching, her afternoon dragged. Fortunately, the bank did flex-time; by 4.30, she was gone. Come 7.45, and she was all set; she'd even showered to wet her hair so Steve would believe she'd just come back from the gym.

'PC Billy Field here.' Jimmy listened; he didn't say a word. After a brief pause, 'I know you're listening, Jimmy. I can hear you breathing,' continued Billy. 'I just need a quick word about the Griggs farm incident.'

'Look, Bill, I meant what I said about you and John doing the policing, and I would faithfully report it, making you two out to be heroes. How was I to know your brother would jump out in front of a fleeing car? Even you didn't expect him to do that.'

213

'No, you're right, I didn't. However, an investigation's underway to establish what really happened, and I know you have pictures and a tape recording of most of it.'

'Well, I'm a talented reporter and well prepared.'

'No one is disputing that. I just need…' Billy paused, 'sorry, we just need to see the material for ourselves. The originals mind. So if you could meet me —'

'At the Police Station', interrupted Jimmy.

'No, don't put yourself out. Look, I'll be visiting John tomorrow, and you're always toing and froing from the hospital. Why don't I meet you near the A&E vending machine at about 16.30 hours? I'm on earlies, so should've finished by then.'

'Right, fine, see you then.' Jimmy hung up his mobile and removed his finger from the laptop's delete' key without actually pressing it. *So what was that all about?* He smelt a rat. *Not the Police Station and the change from 'I' to 'we want to see the information. Just play along and see where it goes. There were no more hasty conclusions, but a police corruption story would definitely put me back in the good books with the Editor.*

Billy, too, was pleased with the outcome. Some good news for John, but not so good for Pryor. *I'm not sure Adams will be happy, but my brother's reputation is worth more than some old retired Bank Manager's.* Billy could hardly wait till tomorrow to tell John.

At 16:30, Jimmy arrived at A&E, bought himself a tea, and found a seat in a quiet corner of the waiting area.

With his overcoat collar turned up, he made furtive glances over his newspaper. Anyone watching would have thought he'd read too many spy thrillers. In his mind, he was Jimmy Cagney or James Bond. Either would do; after all, he had the right first name.

Billy Field appeared in his full uniform, complete with a peaked cap looking, for all the part, like a legitimate policeman; because he was.

'Jimmy,' Billy called to him.

Jimmy pretended not to hear; he was enjoying himself.

Billy picked up his cup from the tray of the hot water spout and walked over.

Billy lowered his voice. 'Jimmy,' he called again, 'what do you think this is? The Bourne Ultimatum? Look, I've asked you here for your convenience, nothing else.' Billy tried to sound convincing.

'Yes, of course,' Jimmy, too, replied in a low voice, 'then why are we whispering?'

'We aren't.' Billy spoke at his normal level. 'Have you got the evidence with you?' He sounded exasperated.

'Yes.' Before handing over anything, Jimmy took a good but apparent casual look around just in case. Taking his camera's SD card and micro-cassette from his jacket pocket, he held out his hand with a newspaper over the top to conceal his actions. 'Here.'

'Just give me the stuff.' Billy snatched it up before popping it into his tunic pocket. *Excellent,* he thought. *John'll be off the hook now.* 'Thanks... Oh, by the way, are these the originals?' he asked casually.

'Yes, of course.'

'Did you make any copies?'

'The stuff is no good to me nor have I had time. Anyway, why would I want copies? Is something wrong?' Jimmy was suspicious but trying not to sound it.

'No, no, all's fine. Thanks. I'll be in touch.' With his mission accomplished, Billy didn't hang around. 'Just off to see my brother, you know, visiting times and all that.' He left.

John looked a little better, but by the time Billy's visit was over, his spirits were lifted.

'Go home now,' John wrote, 'and review the stuff. I want to hear all about it tomorrow.' He was elated.

Uploading the SD card, Billy couldn't believe his eyes as picture after picture showed his brother hell-bent on stopping the car come what may. Nobody can see this stuff. From the look on Pryor's face, it's obvious he was doing his utmost to avoid hitting John. In the last couple of pictures of the John being struck sequence, distant geese were clearly visible. Billy was in no doubt that Pryor was escaping the soaring gaggle and not fleeing the scene. He would have played the tape but without a mini Dictaphone machine, he couldn't. He assumed its contents also put Pryor in good light, leaving John further in the quagmire.

Confining both the SD card and the mini cassettes to his desk's bottom drawer, Billy supposed John would want to see the materials after leaving the hospital. He closed the drawer tight. *For my eyes only!*

CHAPTER 16

LINDA COMES UP TRUMPS

Steve was hardly through the front door before Julia bombarded him with questions. 'Did you get it? Is everything okay? Are you in trouble? Come on; you've been gone ages. What happened?'

'Stop, just hold on. Let me get my breath back. Right. No. Not sure. She wanted to chat about old times. Nothing. Okay.'

'Is that it?' Julia wasn't satisfied.

'Look, let me have some lunch first, then I'll tell you all about it.'

'If you must—'

Steve tucked into cold meat and salad. Focused on satiating his hunger, he was oblivious to the letter in front of him. Ten minutes passed.

'Better darling?' Julia enquired rather sarcastically.

'Yes, fine.' He kept eating.

'You sure?'

'Yes, fine. Why shouldn't I be? Any more of that ham, it's excellent.' He sounded like his old self.

Julia cut two more slices. 'Here.' She slid them onto his plate. Unable to contain herself further, 'If everything's fine, what's this then?' She pointed at the letter with the carving knife.

'What do you mean?'

'Look, here,' she ran the knife over the franking and the crest.

'It looks official.' He took another mouthful.

'Well, open it then. I can't believe you've sat in front of it for the last 10 minutes and not noticed it.'

'Well, I was thinking about this morning, you know.'

'Linda?' There was a cutting edge to Julia's tone.

He ignored her remark and opened the letter. Reading, he paused. Julia saw the blood drain from his face. He dropped the letter, dropped his head, and said nothing.

She picked it up to read it. 'Tell me this is some sort of mistake. What a day this is turning out to be. First, I find out I'm married to a fraudster, and now he's facing a charge of attempted manslaughter of a policeman, heaven forbid. What else should I know about?' She sounded demanding, 'they say that bad news comes in three's; I guess we won't be winning the Lottery then!'

Steve hesitated, thought about his earlier assignation and decided better of it. *I guess now's not a good time to tell her about Linda flirting with me and the fact I'm seeing her again tonight.*

'Oh my God, Julia, this is serious. I know what this is; it's that blasted Adams. What's he playing at? First, he charged me with attempting to murder Colin Griggs and now this! What have I done to him?' Steve was seething.

'Well, you ran over one of his men, who is, by all accounts, seriously injured in hospital.' Her comment didn't help.

'Run him over, run him over.' The incredulity in his voice was obvious. 'I didn't run him over; the man behaved like a demented lunatic. The more I swerved, the more he jumped in front of me. I was breaking as hard as I could. The tyres were screeching and smoke and smell the burning rubber filled the air.' Steve went quiet.

'I know what his game is. Adams, so-called friend and golfing companion, is nothing more than a conniving so-and-so, who'll stop at nothing. He wants a seat on the Committee and will go to any length to get one.' The red mist of anger filled his eyes. Julia saw the look on his face.

'Quick, the phone, pass me the phone.' He spoke through gritted teeth. 'Where's the bloody phone?' He stomped out of the kitchen.

'Steve, no, do nothing while you feel like this.' Julia's concern was obvious. 'You'll regret it. Just breathe deeply and calm yourself down; now count slowly back from ten.'

He did as he was told.

'Nice and slow, nine, eight, seven…' she helped him out.

'I can't just do nothing.'

'Well, let's think. Take a few moments to compose yourself.'

From under a pile of paper, the phone rang. Steve was standing right next to it. 'Yes,' he was abrupt. 'Who?' He was on the verge of being rude. 'Yes, this is Pryor; who is this?' He listened, 'Ah, Mrs Griggs, so sorry, you caught me at a rather, how should I say, challenging moment.' He turned on the old bank manager's charm.

'Yes, for you, it's convenient to talk; how can I help?' In the excitement of the letter, Steve had totally forgotten about the other issue until Izzy mentioned her name. 'Ms Weaver,' a shudder went through him, 'how can I help?'

Izzy explained about the account review.

'Standard procedure' Steve was trying to sound reassuring. 'No, she won't call in the loan.' *Rather, she'll send me to prison,* he thought. 'No, I can't be a hundred percent sure; yes, I appreciate a lot hangs in the balance for you.' *It's only your home; it's my liberty that's at stake.* 'Look, Isobel, Mrs Griggs, I've just had some rather disturbing news. Can I call you back in a little while, and we can discuss the matter further?' Steve went to put the phone down. 'Oh, Mrs Griggs, are you still there? I haven't got your number.' Another shudder went through him. 'On file, yes, of course. But don't forget, I'm not in the bank now. Actually, it will be in my Filofax in my briefcase.' *It just goes from bad to worse.* 'I don't sound my usual self? Sorry, I don't feel it either. They have summoned me to appear in court for attempted manslaughter. You know the incident the other day outside your farm...' He put the phone down.

'Why on earth did you say that?' Julia's brow furrowed.

'Oh, I don't know, it just sort of came out; heat of the moment and all that.'

'Colin, come here, quick. I've just been speaking to Mr Pryor. You'll never believe what's happened to him.'

'What about Sarah Weaver? Can he help us?'

'Well, no, yes, we never had time to talk about it.'

'Why not?' Colin huffed.

'That's what I'm trying to tell you. They've charged him with attempted manslaughter. Can you believe it?'

'Of whom? It's not that stupid charge about trying to kill me, is it?'

'No, far worse.'

'What could be far worse than murdering me?'

'A policeman!'

'You're talking nonsense. Mr Pryor would never try to kill a policeman.' Colin was confused.

'It happened the day you had your accident, while I was being held at the police station and you were at the hospital. It was here in the lane, apparently. I don't know anymore.'

'We need to find out. Anything could happen to him. We need his help with the loan and that Weaver woman. Who can we ask?'

She thought, 'What about Kevin Glenn? He was around that day, I guess. He was at the lock-in in the evening; I bet he'll know more.'

'Given the number of pints of Old Tom he's shoved away, his brain's all mush by now. He's not reliable. Can't you think of someone else?'

She started hunting around the kitchen. 'Have you seen it?'

'What?'

'That business card, the one that reporter chap Flanagan gave me the other day.'

'Him! Given the rubbish he wrote, I wouldn't trust a word he said.'

'Well, it's worth a try. Who else is there? I'm going to ring him just to see what he has to say. He said whenever we needed help, just to call him. Most insistent he was.' Izzy picked up the phone and dialled.

It rang once, then a second time. 'Hi, Jimmy Flanagan, how can I help?'

'Hello, are you the reporter?'

'Yes, that's me. Who's this?'

'Izzy.'

Izzy, Izzy, I don't know any Izzy, thought Jimmy.

'Isobel Griggs.'

'Oh, Izzy, I hoped you'd ring. What can I do for you?'

'You did say ring if we needed any help.'

'Yes, sure, what can I do?' Jimmy picked up a pen.

'Well, it's not actually for us, me and Colin; it's more for a friend, well we like to think he is.'

'Okay, shoot.'

'You know the thing in the lane the other day with the police? Well, of course, we weren't there, and we're keen to know what happened. Can you help?'

'What, when the bank manager chap, Pryor, ran over the policeman? Yeah, no problem saw it all. In fact, I can do better than that; I've got a slide show on my laptop. I'll bring it over and show you in high definition with stereo sound a blow by blow, quite literarily, repeat of the entire event. Is later today, any good?'

'Yes, fine. How about six? See you then, and thanks.' She clicked off the phone.

'Colin, I don't believe it. He did it! He actually ran over a policeman. Mr Pryor, our friendly lifelong bank manager, tried to kill a policeman. I'm lost for words.'

'You don't sound it to me,' he said it under his breath.

'Anyway, Flanagan's coming here tonight.'

'Yes, I heard.'

'I better get a few sandwiches and some cakes sorted.'

'It's not a party Izzy.'

'I know, just being hospitable.'

Whilst she busied, Colin sat at the computer in the corner of the kitchen, searching away on Google.

'Here, found it; our Plan B. The telephone number for Injury Claims, you know the 0800 number.' He was feeling pleased with his surfing skills.

❧   ❧   ❧

Inspector Adams was getting more and more impatient.

'Ah, Billy, what news?'

'News?'

'You know, news.'

'Well, the 2.30 at Haydock was won by Golden Boy at 10:1.'

You know what I mean, your brother and the Steve Pryor investigation.'

Billy Smiled. 'Because they're connected, they've been taken over by the complaints lot. I did some legwork for them, measuring up the scene, but nothing else. I believe they have set a preliminary hearing date for Steve Pryor.'

'The IPCC? So they must have charged him. Can you find out more?'

'Yeah, will try to, Sir.'

223

'Sounds like John's off the hook, then. By the way, how is he?'

'Frustrated, he can't speak or move, but he's pretty resilient. I'm going to see him later.'

'It's not a foregone conclusion that John won't be disciplined. It depends on the evidence they have on Pryor and whether he gets off.'

Well, they'll have none if I have my way; Billy was thinking of his bottom drawer. 'Thanks for the heads-up.'

❧ ❧ ❧

The evening at Griggs farm proved eventful. Jimmy Flanagan ran through his PowerPoint slide show twice, stopping it at various points to pick up details or add a few comments of his own. A dumbfounded Colin and Izzy were totally unaware of the events that had taken place at their farm: special ops, gun-toting guys who were ready to use them, the mistaken understanding of the Griggs gang hiding out on their farm, and Mr Pryor, nice Mr Pryor, who had come around to warn them about Sarah Weaver, being chased off by some irate geese. Although Izzy was proud of her geese, it was just a shame they saw off Mr Pryor.

What Colin and Izzy couldn't get over were the actions of PC John Field. His actions were reckless, putting his own life and the lives of others in danger. The pictures showed, without a doubt, Mr Pryor was a victim of all this.

'This is just what we need to help him. If we give Mr Pryor this, he will put in a good word with Ms

Weaver.' Every time Izzy spoke her name, she could feel her hackles rising. 'Another sandwich Jimmy or how about some of my home-made apple cake?' She knew how to get her own way.

'Do you have a USB data stick?' Jimmy enquired between mouthfuls.

'A what?' Colin's eyebrows met as he tried to fathom out Jimmy's question.

'Oh, don't mind, Colin. Him and computers don't go back far; he's just about mastered Solitaire and how to get to the Google page, but little else.'

Colin, not wanting to sound too useless, piped up. 'I bought printer cartridges a few weeks back, remember? And I found the Injury Claim website.'

Izzy rummaged around in the drawer.

'Here, Jimmy.' In no time at all, they had a copy of the PowerPoint slideshow for themselves. 'You're a lifesaver, Jimmy; we're ever so grateful. More cake?'

'I won't, thanks. I must go. Things to do, people to see; you know the life of a reporter is never dull.'

'We truly appreciate what you've done. Let's hope it will get Mr Pryor off the hook. He's plainly innocent.' Izzy wrapped a slice of cake for Jimmy to take with him.

'Well, Mrs G, thanks again. See you.' With that, Jimmy shot out of the door and sped off down the lane. *That's my good turn done for the day;* he smiled to himself.

Steve wondered what to do. *How am I going to tell Julia he had to go around to Linda's flat tonight to collect the briefcase?*

She's bound to think I've an ulterior motive; she always thought Linda was more than my PA. He pondered. *It'll be quite reasonable for me to go to the Golf Club tonight to see Adams and ask him about this letter. That way, I don't need to mention Linda at all.* Seven-thirty chimed on their hall clock.

'You've been quiet this evening, are you alright?' Julia asked.

'Just thinking about recent events. I've decided to pop over to the club to see Adams. Catch him off-guard, unprepared to see if he can throw any light on this letter and summons. He owes me.' He rose out of his chair.

'Now? You're going now?'

'Strike whilst the iron's hot. There's never a right moment; might as well get it over and done with.' He pulled on his jacket.

'Look, I've not been out today; I'll come with you. A bit of moral support and all that.'

Steve winced at her words.

'Not sure that's wise, dear. This is man's stuff, not a social outing. You stay here and catch up with your Oprah Winfrey programmes. You know she's your favourite.' He hoped above all hope, and behind his back, he had his fingers crossed.

'Oh, good idea. Yes, you're right. Keep it civil; I don't want you on another charge.' She picked up the TV remote.

He headed to the hall.

'And don't drink too much', she called after him, 'that's the last thing we could do with now.' She heard the click of the front door, followed by the slam of the car door.

That was a bit of quick thinking; he thought as he

drove toward Linda's flat. Deception didn't sit easily with Steve, but needs must, and on this occasion, they did. He pulled up in a side street and parked out of sight. *Walls have ears, aren't a patch on the rumour-mongering in Harpsden. You only need to cough, and the universe knows about it.* He'd rather be safe than sorry. He wasn't sure why he was cautious. *This will be a quick in and out, collect the briefcase and away—nothing else. Though given how she behaved at the park, I'm not so sure!*

Leaving his car, he started walking the 100 yards to her flat. It was dusk. He looked at his watch; four minutes to eight. *Punctual as usual. Of course, Linda knows I'll be on time; she often commented on my qualities, especially my punctuality.* 'I bet you won't be late for your own funeral,' she'd say, then give a little giggle. He could feel his heart beating. *What's that all about? She's my PA of 15 years, not some floozy bit on the side. Calm down,* he told himself, *calm down.*

Tentatively, he reached out to press the buzzer on the entry phone. She didn't answer but he heard the electronic latch go on the door. He pushed and walked in. The sensors picked up his movement, and the lights turned on. Linda's flat was on the first floor. Up the stairs he turned to the left; in front of him, her door was wide open. Inviting, he hesitated, drinking in a banquet of smells wafting forth. Tantalising, it looked dark inside. Low lights, accompanied by dancing shadows, suggested candlelight. He stood, not sure if he should venture further. The sounds of soulful saxophone music added to the experience. Linda still hadn't appeared.

He'd stopped moving so the automatic sensors

extinguished the hallway lights. Only a glow came from the candles. His eyes needed to adjust. Crossing the threshold he saw it, there, right in front of him. Not ten feet away, his briefcase, sat where she'd described. *I could get it and be out of here in a few seconds.* The thought lingered in his mind. He took another step and stretched out his arm; still no Linda. *Here's my chance*—another step. Quietly, almost imperceptibly, he moved forward, his hand getting closer and closer to the goal. His fingers were slowly closing around the handle; then, he saw a glint of light reflecting off steel. His hand closed tight on the handle to the sound of a series of clicks—a ratcheting noise. A handcuff secured his wrist.

'Hey, big boy, so glad you could make it.' Linda sounded like she'd never sounded before. A deep guttural voice, smooth, melting, evocative, and sensual. Another click announced they were joined at the wrists as one.

Instinctively, he jerked his arm toward himself. He pulled her in close. An aroma, the floral notes of her perfume, so distinctive, filled his nostrils. He'd smelt it from afar for all those years; now, he could revel in it. Her face was only inches from his; the scent added to the uniqueness of the moment.

'I knew you wanted this as much as me. The quiet ones are all the same. Tigers, mad passionate tigers, waiting to be unleashed.' She hissed as she spoke.

He could feel the warmth of her body.

'Linda, stop this right now. Please. I'm a married, retired bank manager, not some gigolo, some sex-crazed monster.'

'Protest if you must, but it's only to salvage your

conscience. I've watched you for all those years, taking sly looks at me, my body, my breasts, my legs, smooth in black stockings. You would lick your lips.' She curled her tongue over hers.

'That was my Hobnobs. The crumbs, nothing more,' he paused, 'so they were stockings. I thought they were, but never asked for fear of sounding too forward.'

'I knew you liked them; that's why I'm wearing some right now, just for you.' She stood back and raised her hem high enough to glimpse a stocking top.

'Linda, stop! I may be 60 and retired, but I'm still a man.'

'I know, I'm banking on that.'

'Look, what will they say in the office? You can't behave like this; I'm your boss.'

'Not any more. Remember, you've retired?' She moved past him to shut the front door. 'Ummm, that's better; no one can see us now,' she purred.

Tugging on the handcuffs, she led him into the lounge. He noticed the set dining table in the corner with a single rose and a candle centrepiece.

'You've planned this down to every last detail.'

'Over and over in my head many times, but today, well, it's all fallen into place, and here we are... Now I'm going to undo the cuffs. I know you won't do anything silly, but maybe you'll do something naughty.' Her throaty chuckle underlined her hopes.

He blustered a few inaudible words before blushing. She saw nothing in the candlelight.

'Now sit here.' She pointed to the dining table. 'Help yourself to a glass of wine. I just need to finish in the kitchen.'

He sat, she left, he mused, she smiled, he drank, she reappeared.

'Here, tiger, I hope you like this.'

Leaning forward to place his plate, Steve got sight of her revealing neckline. In the heat of the moment, he spoke what he was thinking.

'Where did you get them from? I've never seen them before.' His jaw fell open. She placed her index finger on the underside of his chin and closed his mouth.

'I see you like what you saw.' He didn't know where to look. He was like a naughty schoolboy who'd been caught out.

'They're for you. I'm all for you. Consider it a...,' she placed her finger to her own lips and looked thoughtful, 'a retirement gift.' She smiled seductively as she sat down.

'Linda, please. I have weaknesses; there's only so much I can take before—' He stopped.

'Before what?'

'You know.'

'No, tell me.'

Trying to take control, Steve sat up straight and, in his best bank manager voice, spoke. 'As much as I appreciate what you've done, are doing, and I have to admit I find it,' he paused, 'alluring and flattering, and under different circumstances might have shown less self-control. But the truth is after I got home at lunchtime, I had a letter waiting for me, a summons for attempted manslaughter.'

'Steve, how could they? You wouldn't hurt a fly.'

Linda was outraged.

'That's all well and good, but nonetheless, I've been summonsed. With that and the possible fraud charge for the Griggs loan, never mind the media siege the other night, life is extremely stressful right now. I don't think, with the best will in the world, I could give you what you want.'

'My poor Steve. All the troubles of the world. I wasn't your PA all that time for nothing, you know. I'm sure I can release some of that stress right now.' She came over and stood beside him. Wiping his brow, she bent down to whisper in his ear, 'I've got just the thing for you. We'll make that nasty stress go away.' She lingered; he shuffled in his seat. 'Now, close your eyes.'

'What do you mean?'

'Shh, just relax. I'll be back in a moment, and no peeking.' She went to the briefcase to retrieve the new Griggs file. 'Hold out your arms... Here big boy and don't say I don't look after you.' She placed the file on his outstretched hands. 'Now, open your eyes.'

He held a quizzical frown. 'What's this?'

'Open it and see.' Linda fixed her gaze on his eyes.

His frown turned into a smile and then into ecstasy. Without hesitation, he jumped up, threw his arms around her, pulling her in tight. He kissed her fully on the lips. In response, she clasped her hands around the back of his neck and held him tight. It was a good minute before they broke apart.

'You are wonderful, my lifesaver, my guardian angel. What am I going to do without you?' He was over the moon. They were still in each other's arms. He looked back into her eyes; she smiled the happiest smile. He hesitated before gently releasing his grip. They shared a knowing look.

'Oh gosh, look at the time. Julia will wonder where I am.' The moment was over; they both knew it.

'What can I say, Linda? You are the greatest. I really enjoyed my retirement gift and this present.' He held up the Griggs file, 'And this is the best ever.' With that, he collected his briefcase and left, leaving the file for her to return. 'See you.' He disappeared through the front door without looking back.

She mouthed at the disappearing figure, 'I love you; I always have and always will.' Tears ran down her cheeks.

It was after ten when Steve arrived home. Julia was viewing yet another Oprah episode. She looked up. 'What did Adams have to say?'

'He wasn't there, so I had a couple of halves with the Major and discussed the Griggs thing—you know about cleaning up and compensation.' Steve was humming a tune.

'You sound pleased with yourself.'

'Oh, on the way, I popped into Linda's to collect my briefcase. She'd taken it home for safekeeping— remember, I told you at lunchtime. Well, anyway, she'd been up to her usual tricks. She always liked a little joke. Not only did she have my briefcase, but best of all—' Steve paused.

'Best of all, what? Come on, tell me.' She was trying to hurry him up.

'Sorry, yes I was thinking, best of all, she had completed the Griggs loan form and letter etc., all signed, sealed and in their customer file. Sarah Weaver won't find a thing out of place.'

Julia jumped up and kissed him on the lips. If she tasted Linda's lipstick or smelt her perfume, she didn't say a thing. 'So no fraud charge? Hey, that's great. I hope you thanked her. I know, why don't you send her some flowers or chocolates to show your appreciation? Get onto it tomorrow.'

'Apart from the small matter of attempted manslaughter, we're home and dry. That'll have to wait until the morning.'

Steve went to bed a happy man. Julia followed.

CHAPTER 17

GRIGGS' SAVES THE DAY

'Colin, the pressure's on to make an appointment with the bank. You're well enough now, but I don't want to see Ms Weaver until I know our options. We need to speak to Mr Pryor, pronto. There's no time like the present. Go on, give him a ring and ask him if we can go round to see him. Tell him we have something he'll be extremely interested in.' Izzy took a breather.

'Me?'

'Well, he's your bank manager.'

'Was.'

'Was your bank manager, and your name is on the loan agreement. Here.' She passed him the phone. 'And here's the number.'

Colin dialled. 'Is Mr Pryor in?' Julia had answered. 'Can you tell him it's Colin Griggs, and it's quite—'

'Very,' mouthed Izzy.

'Sorry, it's very urgent I speak to him.' He paused. 'Mrs P's just gone to fetch him.' Colin kept Izzy updated. 'Ah, Mr Pryor, Colin Griggs. I just want to say thanks for coming to the farm the other day to inform us about Sarah Weaver. We were so sorry to hear about all the commotion it caused, and especially you being chased by our geese. It's not their fault; it's what they do. Great guard dogs, but they get over-enthusiastic. Anyway,' he stopped to gather his thoughts. 'About Sarah Weaver; as you know, she wants this accounts review. We need help in preparing for it and wondered if you could be of service.' Colin waited for a response, but none was forthcoming. 'I know you're not happy with Griggs Hole Farming after the golf course re-launch day, so if you say no, we'd fully understand. However, I think we can be of service to you and get the attempted manslaughter charge dropped.'

Hearing the words charge dropped peaked Steve's interest. He gave Colin his undivided attention. 'How?'

'Certain evidence has come our way, which you'll find most useful.' Colin could hear muffled chatter on the other end of the phone, but couldn't make out what was being said. He held his hand over the mouthpiece. 'That's got him talking, Izzy.' He continued. 'We'll come to you if it's more convenient. I'm sure you won't want to see any geese for some while.'

'What's he saying?' Izzy couldn't contain herself. 'They're just talking amongst themselves... Oh yes, Steve, later today after lunch,' Colin echoed Steve's comments for her benefit. 'Yes, great, we'll see you about three at your place.' He hung up the phone. 'Great stuff Izzy; he seems more than happy to see us. He won't be disappointed, given what we've got for him.'

Next, Izzy rang the bank and left a message for Ms Weaver to the effect that they'd take the 10.00am appointment offered in the letter they had received earlier.

☙ ☙ ☙

At 3 o'clock sharp, the Griggs were on the Pryor's doorstep armed with copious amounts of paper — all things Izzy thought might be useful to present at an account review. Additionally, and most importantly, she had the PowerPoint slide show on the USB data stick. As she rang the doorbell, she turned to Colin and mused, 'I wonder if they have a computer; otherwise, we're going to be a bit stuck.'

The door opened, and pleasantries exchanged before they were shown into the lounge. Izzy's eyes perused to the décor.

'Oh, I do like sunburst yellow; it always brightens a room up. It makes one feel so cheery.'

Colin spotted a cabinet full of golf trophies. It made him shudder.

'Tea anyone?' Julia did the necessary, while they all helped themselves to milk and sugar.

'Right,' said Steve, taking control, 'where shall we start?'

Izzy launched the conversation by saying how worried they were about Ms Weaver calling in the loan and the impact on them, their business and their farm. She had made various notes, some handwritten, some typed and loads of calculations, plus an attempt at a cash flow forecast. She wanted to do a proper job.

'This is all good stuff, Mrs Griggs.'

'Izzy, call me Izzy; everybody does.'

'As I was saying, it's all good stuff, but from what I hear, Sarah, Ms Weaver, is a bit of a high flyer, fair but firm. She will work to the new guidelines on lending which the Government, via the Bank of England, has now imposed. It's kind of out of my hands. All I can say to you is your loan application form and letter of agreement are correct in every detail, signed and filed with the rest of your records. Honesty, above all, will be the best approach.' He paused, satisfied he had done enough making no commitments he couldn't fulfil.

'What about an up-to-date business plan? A P&L and Balance Sheet, an earnings forecast, and ROI calculations.' Izzy waved the papers in front of Steve.

'As I say, Izzy, that's all great but beyond me; that's why I retired.' He felt deflated.

'Well, I think we've got a good idea of what we need to do.' She paused and looked at Colin. He just looked back at her and shrugged his shoulders.

'Now, this is how we can help you.' Izzy fished in her handbag and pulled out a data stick. She popped it down on the table in front of them. Steve leant in and picked it up.

'And this is?'

'For goodness' sake, Steve, you know what that is, don't you?' Julia couldn't hide her amazement.

'Well, I had staff, lots of them. My PA—'

'Yes, I know, Linda, lovely woman. I met her when Colin signed the forms. She seemed extremely efficient.' Izzy went on. 'I bet you're lost without her.'

'He's got me, you know.' Julia bristled. 'I'm a dab hand with computers; I've even got my own laptop, Windows, the latest version. I'll just get it.' The others exchanged glances.

'Here.' Julia set it up on the table. 'Steve, move the tea things… please. Do I have to do everything?'

'Let me,' Izzy loaded the tray, 'there's plenty of room now.'

After a few minutes of fiddling, the PowerPoint slideshow burst into life. The laptop's volume was at maximum, and soon the sounds of screeching tyres, thuds and screams, helicopter rotor blades, shouts, honking geese and all manner of chaos reverberated around the room. All four sat mesmerised, with their eyes glued to the screen. Comments flowed: unbelievable, how stupid did you see that? Look guns! Everybody was in awe.

'You see, Mr Pryor.'

'Steve, please.'

'You see why we had to show you this, and soon.' Izzy waited for his reaction.

'Can we see it again, please Julia, but with less volume this time? I just want to be sure.' The PowerPoint slideshow started again. Steve grabbed a pen and paper in order to take notes.

'It's okay; you can have it and study it at your leisure.' Colin chirped up.

'I need to think about how best to use this.' Steve deliberated.

'Well, it seems like you've no case to answer, darling. Poor you. What you went through just doing a good turn.' Julia looked distinctly relieved.

Izzy exchanged glances with Colin. 'Right, we'll be off now. Thanks for the tea and reassurances.' She collected all her bits together.

'Before you go,' Steve spoke up, 'you say you've got an appointment with Sarah Weaver.'

'Yes, why?'

'Well, let me send her an email on your behalf.'

Julia looked sceptical.

Steve saw. 'Yes, I can do emails.' He turned back to Izzy. 'I'll just say what a long-term and fruitful relationship the bank's had with the Griggs family and how she, Ms Weaver, should look favourably on your needs. Not sure it'll do any good, but it's worth a try.'

'Oh, Steve, that would be so kind. Thanks again. Goodbye.' Izzy put her arm through Colin's and pivoted him down the drive.

'No, no, thank you.' Steve called after them. 'You don't know how much that has relieved the stress of the last few days.' Although he was physically present, Steve's mind was elsewhere.

Izzy drove, as Colin still wasn't a hundred per cent. They pulled out of the Pryor's drive and headed for home. 'We've got some work to do to make sure we're ready for that appointment.' The rest of the journey went in silence.

As they approached the lane up to the farm, Colin sat bolt upright.

'Where is he? What have you done with him?'

'What are you on about? Done what with whom?'

He was pointing forcefully. 'Where's the scarecrow?'

'Is that all? You had me going then. I thought something was wrong. Actually, it was the helicopter; you saw in the pictures and how close it came to the ground. Those rotor things—'

'No, they didn't chop off his head, did they?' He was panicking.

'Don't be silly. The wind, downdraft, or whatever

you call it, blew him face down in the mud. What with one thing and another, I've not stood him up. Tomorrow Colin, that'll be a good job for you.'

❧   ❧   ❧

Steve wasted no time in getting the charge dropped. 'Bob, it's me, Steve. Meet me at the club at eight in the Committee Room. We need some privacy.' He put the phone down. *A pity I wasn't able to speak to him in person, but my voice message should be enough to get him there,* he hoped.

'Julia, I'll need the laptop tonight. Can you set it, so all I have to do is play the slideshow? I don't want to have to faff around, and I doubt if Bob Adams is any better with this stuff than me.'

'Yes, Sir, anything else, Sir!'

'Remember, you said I had you now that Linda isn't around?' Said Steve.

'Oh, that reminds me, did you send her some flowers or chocolates?'

'No, I'll get round to it tomorrow.' He sounded flustered.

By 7.55 pm, Steve had pulled into the Golf Club car park. By eight, he was sitting in the Committee Room with the laptop ready to go. All he needed was Adams. By 8.30, there was still no sign of Bob. Steve looked at his watch again. It was two minutes later than the last time. *Come on, man, where are you?* He was becoming frustrated. There was a knock. 'Just come in, Bob, ' Steve shouted at the closed door. It opened cautiously. 'Come in, man, let's get on with it.'

Bob pulled up a chair so he could see the laptop

screen. 'Well, what's the emergency?'

'Just watch... carefully', Steve added. He used the mouse pointer pressed the play button. Bob watched the screen intently. Steve watched him, his face, his reactions—neither spoke.

A host of thoughts flowed through Bob's mind; *obviously, Steve wasn't trying to kill anyone, accidentally or on purpose. Now John's in a tough spot. He acted on instinct to stop what he thought was an attempted murderer fleeing the scene. But he should have known better. His training had taught him so. If I get Steve off, I'll be back in his good books and my seat on the Committee one step closer. Getting Steve off is leaving John open to a disciplinary. He's a good man, but he over-reacted on this occasion. However, his previous record is excellent, so the IPCC will consider that. I'll write him an outstanding reference. Okay, on balance, get Steve off and shop John and push for lenience. Now I can't be seen to be in Steve's camp by the IPCC.* The slideshow ended. Steve interrupted Bob's thoughts.

'So, what do you think?'

'Well, obviously you're not guilty, and you had to endure a lot of stress and emotional turmoil.' He didn't want to lay it on too thick in case Steve got it in his head to make some sort of compensation claim from the police. 'But from where PC John Field is sitting, you appear to be fleeing the scene,' he continued. 'Now strictly, I'm not involved with the case. It's with the IPCC, you know, an internal investigation people, because another policeman's involved. And as they know I know you, it's best if I wasn't seen to be helping you out, so to speak, by bringing this evidence forward.'

'What do we do, then?'

'Not sure right now. I'll need to think about it. One thing though, I'm glad it's come to light,' he was smarming up to Steve, 'I could never live with myself if I knew you were behind bars. Anyway, for now, I'll say goodnight; we'll speak soon.'

Bob hurried out to his car. He was on the phone in seconds. 'Did you know anything about this?' He hollered. 'He made me look like a right fool. What are we going to do now?'

'Hello, do I know you?' came a rather timid response. Bob stared at his phone.

'Who are you?' he yelled.

'I asked first,' came the reply.

Bob hit the 'end call' button. I hate these damn small buttons. He'd mis-dialled. He scrolled through his recent calls to find Billy Field's number.

'Ah, Billy, you're there. I hope it's not too late. Look, I've just been to the Golf Club with Steve Pryor.' He was interrupted and listened.

'What? No, it doesn't matter if we had a few beers. That's not the point. The point is that he had a load of pictures with sound, which shows him in the clear. Do you know anything about this?'

Billy listened, thought, weighed up the consequences and said, 'No, Sir.'

'Well, I don't know where Pryor got them from, but it shows in full colour with sound. He's the victim and John, I'm afraid to say, is the perpetrator.'

'Can't we just say nothing? Pretend they don't exist.' Billy said optimistically.

'Good grief, man, that's suppressing evidence. I'm not risking that; I'm too close to my retirement. No, we've just got to face up to it. Pryor goes free, and John's on a disciplinary. I'll write a reference for him, of course, but I'm not sure I can do much more.'

'Do you have a copy?' Billy was curious.

'No, I don't. Pryor had a laptop with this PowerPoint or some such thing.'

'We could always tell the IPCC he used Photoshop to create the whole thing just to make himself look innocent.'

'He's an ex-bank manager, not Steven Spielberg, and he certainly doesn't seem too knowledgeable about computers.' Adams was racking his brain. 'Let's sleep on it.' He hung up.

CHAPTER 18

ACCOUNT REVIEW

In the Griggs' household, Izzy was frantic. 'We have £10,000 of the bank's money.'

'Nearly; we spent some on the Rabbodig cages.' Colin reminded her.

'Okay, nearly, but we still don't have a plan to save the farm. If we don't, Ms Weaver won't hesitate to call in the loan. We need a watertight, well thought through, Business Plan to show her we are a viable low-risk business. Security; she'll want security.'

Colin rested his chin on his palm. 'What we need now is to forget about little holes but rather go for larger one-off holes. The sort needed for, say, ornate garden features or swimming pools. Griggs Hole Farming needs to become specialist hole farmers. What we need are holes with substance.'

'Colin, are you telling me that after the Harpsden Golf Club fiasco, you still want to pursue hole farming?'

'Of course, my love. Every new business has its problems and pitfalls. We learn from our mistakes. The whole hole idea is a good one. Where it went wrong was using rabbits. They've never been known for their dependency. Rabbits dig, granted, but that's the problem; they don't know when to stop. Some local chap estimated that the warren under the golf course was over three miles of tunnels. Now that's impressive if you want a hole three miles long and ten inches in diameter, and I'd be the first to get rabbit workers in if that's what was needed. With the golf course, for all 18 holes, the total length required was only 9 feet. You see the problem, overzealous not knowing when to stop. Uncontrollable, rabbits aren't reliable. But credit where credit's due. Take away the extra tunnelling, and they did a great job.'

'So what have you in mind?'

'You agree holes are essential for all of us all the time.'

'Well, of course.' Izzy wanted to see where he was going with this.

'And you agree that rabbits and I guess small rodents or other animals of any size aren't responsible enough to be left unsupervised to dig holes for us?'

'Well, yes, we've seen what a right mess that makes. Do you know since that day Stewart, I mean Mr Ballard, has spent the last month back-filling all the tunnels? He needs to be certain rabbits aren't inhabiting the warren before re-opening the course.'

'One thing he can be certain of is there's nothing in those tunnels now. Clive Beer's compressor made sure of that. Nothing was spared that morning. If you walk around the course even now, you can still see debris in the trees and scattered around the rough.' Colin admired the Hammer Koshi compressor.

'Since the Grand Opening, no one has played a round of golf.' Izzy continued. 'In fact, no one could play a round of golf as the tees, fairways and putting greens were covered in a layer of silt, finely aspirated mud up to an inch thick in places. Where silt had accumulated, they raked away it and carted off to be used in the flower beds around the Club House.

Apparently, the Major's hardly spoken as he's still in shock. As for Matt Childs, the golf pro, an uncut version of the BBC News footage, found its way to YouTube and has been viewed over a million times.'

'That only goes to show my decision not to use animals in the future business is well-founded.' Colin had a feeling of self-satisfaction.

'Understood, so now what?' Izzy was getting frustrated.

'Holes are what people want, but a hole doesn't remain a hole without a container of some sort.'

She looked quizzical. 'Okay,' she said, hesitantly.

Colin noticed, 'I see you don't understand. Remember, as I explained, holes are everywhere.'

'How can I forget!' She shot a glance skywards, suggesting she couldn't.

'Now think of an electrical socket. Right, what is it?'

'I'm not sure what you mean.'

'Describe what you see; look over here.' He pointed to the wall socket just above the kitchen worktop.

'Well, it's a square flat shape about three inches by three inches.'

'And—'

'It's white.'

'And—' He was getting exasperated.

'I know, don't tell me! It's got three holes in.'

'At last.'

'Oh, and one more thing, it has a switch on it.' Now she was feeling pleased with herself.

'Forget the switch for the minute; look at the socket again. What bit is the useful bit? The bit you and every other person really want to use.'

She said nothing; excitement had given way to puzzlement again.

'Right, tell me what you and everyone else does with sockets.'

'They.' She paused. 'I know they plug things in like phone chargers, blenders, toasters, kettles, reading lights… ummmmm.'

'Okay, okay, there's no need to list every electrical item you know. So of a socket, what's the only part that's used? Now think before you answer. It's the...' he made a HOLE sound shape with his mouth, trying to encourage her to give the correct answer.

'Hole' She jumped up and down, clapping herself much like an excited toddler who'd spelt their own name for the first time.

He sighed. 'That was reminiscent of pulling teeth. Izzy, that's not like you.'

'I just had a complete blank. So how does that help?'

He slapped his hand to his forehead in disbelief. 'Give me strength!'

'We've established that holes are what's needed and that a hole only exists if it's contained in something—'

'Like a socket.' She completed his sentence.

'Exactly. So take away the socket's flat plate, and

there'd be no holes and hence nowhere to plug into.'

'Progress.' She said optimistically.

'Of sorts, now for the big step.' He went quiet whilst he was thinking. 'Okay, here's a test. Why do people want doors?'

'So they can pass through from one room to another. Did I pass?'

'Pass what?'

'My test?'

'Only if you tell me the most important bit of the door.'

'The hole you pass through.'

'And the container?' He wasn't hopeful.

'The doorframe.'

'Correctomondo! No frame, no container for the hole, no hole, no way from one room to another. Easy. Now, do you see? We are in the hole business, which means we provide holes in containers for people to do things with.'

'My head hurts now, Colin. It's late; let's go to bed.'

From the Summons he received, Steve got contact details for the IPCC and the Officer in charge of the investigation. Wishing for his plight to cease, he was on the phone to him first thing in the morning. ' —my wife has put the slideshow on a CD-ROM. I'll put it in the post later this morning. First Class and mark it for your attention.' He put the phone down.

'Right, I'm off into town. Where's that CD? I'll get a jiffy bag from the Post Office. Just think, by tomorrow, I'll be a free man.' Steve rushed about the house, getting his jacket, wallet, shoes, car keys and CD. As he closed the front door, he heard her shouting.

'Linda, flowers. Don't forget.'

'I won't.' And he was gone.

❧   ❧   ❧

At the police station, things had taken a turn. 'Quick, into my office.' Adams gave a furtive look up and down the corridor before he grabbed PC Billy Field's arm. 'They know. I've just got off the phone with one of the investigation team. Pryor's contacted them.'

Billy was confused and wished he could re-run the conversation. 'Yes, and good morning to you, Sir.'

'We haven't got time for that; just keep up. The IPCC know about the slideshow,' Adams continued, 'I think you should tell John what's going on. Make sure all his reports are up to date with no outstanding paperwork. Check he's nothing untoward in his desk or locker. Once these guys dig around, all hell breaks loose. We don't want to make it any worse for him than it already is.'

'You're right, Sir. But I don't have a good feeling about this.'

'He doesn't have any skeletons I should know about, does he?'

'Not as far as I know, none that I'm aware of.' Billy racked his brain. 'No, he's a diligent cop. Oh, but he did once get a free cup of coffee from the vending machine after it spat his money back.'

'This is no time for jokes. The IPCC guys do a thorough job; no one is safe.'

'Something to hide, Sir?'

Adams gave Billy a dirty look. 'Off you go now.'

They walked together down the corridor toward the front desk.

'Anything for me, Bob?' Jimmy Flanagan was just in doing some schmoozing for a tit-bit or two.

'Inspector Adams to you. Nothing that concerns the Press. Anyway, I thought your editor had put you back on hatches, matches and dispatches, given your last crime report.'

'Yes'ish, but Jimmy Flanagan never gives up.'

'More's the pity,' Adams looked at Billy.

'How's your brother, Billy? Ready to take his place back in the Harpsden football team. I reckon John on crutches would improve their skill level by one hundred per cent.' Jimmy laughed at his own joke.

Billy sidled up to him. 'I thought we had a deal.' He spoke through his teeth.

'Deal, deal, what deal?'

'You know your pictures and tape recording.'

'Why? What about them?'

'The IPCC has them, and my brother's now for the high jump.'

'Not in his condition, he ain't.' Jimmy laughed again. 'High jump!'

'You watch your back from now on, Jimmy Flanagan.' Billy walked off in a huff.

❧   ❧   ❧

Files amassed on the computer hard drive, and the kitchen table was awash with print outs: spreadsheets with cash flow forecasts, word-processed drafts of the business plan, strategic and tactical objectives for the hole business, and sales and marketing plans. In short, a plethora of documentation representing days of work, their future and their success. If nothing else, Izzy and Colin deserved full marks for tenacity, preparation and, from looking at some of their numbers, inventiveness. The Chancellor himself would have been impressed.

'Tomorrow at ten is the most important day of our lives, and I think we're just about ready for anything Ms Weaver can throw at us.' Izzy felt satisfied with her efforts and pleased and relieved it was nearly all over. 'Of course, you realise after the meeting's finished, and we still have our £10K—'

'Don't be too confident! Pride before a fall.' Colin interjected.

'Colin, I want nothing other than a positive attitude. No negativity. As I was saying, the end of the meeting represents the beginning for us. We have to make the plan for this business to work. I never want to be in this situation again.' She sounded scary. He paid special attention.

❧ ❧ ❧

By 9.45, Colin and Izzy had pulled into the Bank's car park. Five minutes later, Linda had shown them into the meeting room and plied them with coffee. As a throwback to the days of Mr Pryor, the bank only ever served fresh Columbian Gold. Nothing else would do. Of course, under the new regime, it was impossible to know how long this would last.

'Tesco's Finest before long. You wait and see', Linda mused. She longed for the return of Mr Pryor, bank manager, and the foundation of all her dreams.

'Do you see Mr Pryor much, Linda?' Izzy made polite conversation.

'Only if he pops in to make a deposit or check his balance. Thoughtfully, he sent me a beautiful bunch of a dozen red roses for services rendered.'

'Oh, that was nice.' Izzy didn't feel it was her polite to enquire about the services rendered. 'Well, you worked for him for such a jolly long time.'

'Did you hear they dropped the charge of attempted manslaughter? Apparently, some fresh evidence came to light, which showed he wasn't at fault. I knew he couldn't hurt anybody.' Linda let a smile show.

'Well, that's great news, isn't it, Colin?' They smiled too.

Linda left the room; They looked at each other before she looked at her neat pile of documents laid out on the table in front of her. She felt proud. Her stomach churned, he coughed, just a dry tickle, the door opened, then nothing for several seconds. A trolley appeared stacked with files, folders, box files, and archive boxes, all in assorted colours and various degrees of wear and tear. Pushing the trolley came Ms Weaver. Surprise turned to fear. Colin and Izzy sat rigid, hands just resting on the table, silent and waiting.

'Well, at long last. Hello, I'm Sarah Weaver, but I guess you knew that. Please call me Sarah; we're all friends here.' She stretched out her hand.

Izzy was the first to take it. 'Morning, Isobel

Griggs, pleased to meet you.'

'Ah, and you must be the famed Colin Griggs. I've seen and read a lot about you.' Sarah shook his hand. 'Well, look at this lot.' Sarah pointed to the trolley. 'I'm doing account reviews to get to know my clients and how best to advise them. I've got my work cut out with you two. It'll take some time to wade through all these. As the bank's Business Manager, my job, amongst many, is to give you the wisdom of my extensive knowledge and business experience. I did my MBA at the LSE, you know. So feel free to ask for my help anytime.'

Colin and Izzy exchanged glances. 'This coffee's nice. Where did you get it from?' As soon as the words left her mouth, Izzy felt a fool.'

'Oh, I leave that sort of thing to Linda. Any other questions? No..., well, it was so nice to meet you both. What you say, we have another review in six months. Sounds okay? I'll get Linda to send you a letter nearer the date. Right, must dash.' She rose. 'Can you see yourselves out? Nice meeting you.'

Izzy's mouth moved as if she was going to say something. Sarah saw. 'Can I help you with anything else?' smiling all the time as she spoke.

'No..., no,' Izzy stammered, by which time Ms Weaver was nowhere to be seen.

'Can you believe that?' Izzy scooped up her papers. 'All that work, all those sleepless nights, all that worry, and for what? "I did my MBA at the LSE". I feel cheated.'

'Well, I thought it went rather well. We've still got our loan, our farm and our livelihood. It's not all wasted by any means. And we now have a plan.'

Linda came in to rescue the files and clear away the coffee. 'All okay with you?' she beamed.

'Yes, fine', Izzy paused, 'I think.'

'Nice, isn't she? You'll find her ever so helpful in the future. I'll write nearer the time. Oh, here, she left this for you.' Linda handed over Ms Weaver's business card. 'It's her direct number; call anytime, but try to keep it within business hours. And one other thing, I think you should know, Mr Pryor, sent her an email on your behalf just before the meeting.'

Colin and Izzy stood, looked at each other, smiled, and left. As they walked out of the bank, Linda noticed they held hands and had a spring in their step.

Izzy and Colin chatted ten to the dozen on the drive back, reliving the last few days and especially the strange meeting they'd just experienced.

'Well, he came up trumps that nice, Mr Pryor.' They were just approaching Henslow. 'I know, let's spend some of that money.' Colin said. Izzy looked quizzical. He pull into The Lamb car park. 'I think a celebration's called for.'

They passed through the door into the Saloon bar.

'This is a treat.'

'Nothing but the best for you, my love.' Colin squeezed Izzy's hand.

'Long time no see. What will it be today?' Bob Critchley was his usual avuncular self. 'I owe you one, Colin,' he went on. 'That bash a week back means we can have a three-week holiday in Menorca next year. A real treat. Booked it already. Fornells we're going to. Looks great on the Internet. I've heard excellent reports as well. I've got a couple of customers who go regularly; it seems they can't get enough of the place.'

'Are you doing lunch today, Bob?'

Izzy looked at Colin. 'Don't spend all our money straight off.'

'No worries, Izzy.' Bob looked to them both, 'Chicken Kiev okay, on the house, of course? It's the least I can do. Oh, and Lucy told me to tell you says she's really sorry.'

They both looked puzzled.

'It was her who told that Sky Reporter chap about... well, you know?' Bob didn't want to say anymore. 'You know, Colin, stop acting so dumb, or you'll make me say it.'

Izzy intervened. 'Colin suffered a serious head wound and cannot remember some recent events, Bob. Some things are best left unsaid.'

'Oh, okay, Mrs G, mum's the word. Anyway, Lucy says sorry.'

The two of them went and sat at the corner table while waiting for their lunch. Colin noticed an Evening Post nearby. He picked it up. 'Should we get an evening paper? We never know what's going on around here.' He wasn't reading it, just wafting it around.

One story caught Izzy's eye. 'Look here, Colin.'

'Where.'

'Here, on the front page at the bottom. It's about that policeman who got run over. The one they accused Mr Pryor of his attempted manslaughter. Well, he's got off.'

'We know. It was because of us he got off.'

'No, no, the policeman got off.'

'Well, of course, he got off; he could hardly run himself over!'

'Sometimes I think you'd try the patience of Job. He didn't try to run himself over. Because Mr Pryor was let off, it was possible that policeman would be charged with, as it says here, Dereliction of Duty. Doesn't sound good. Anyway, it appears, since he suffered such horrendous injuries, which in itself is an enormous price to pay, they dropped all charges.'

Their Chicken Kiev's arrived, conversation ceased.

'Why do things always seem to taste nicer if someone else cooks them?'

'That's not true, Izzy; you're a splendid cook; I always love what you cook.'

'See what I mean?'

He thought, but didn't see the irony.

'I know what I meant to ask you. What happened with the Injury Claims people?' Izzy said.

'As you know, I Googled the number.'

'Excellent; and?'

'I spoke to some woman who wanted me to run through the accident details. Date, time, place, cause, who was involved, where the blame lies, what was my part in all of it. You know all that sort of thing.'

'And?'

'Well, because of my first accident earlier that day and the medication I was on, my memory was hazy. I couldn't answer her questions about the second accident as I did not know about any of it.'

'Well?'

'She said something about stop being a time-waster, and there were plenty more people who needed their services. She mentioned another 20 in the call centre queue and for me to get off the line and not call again.'

'So no Plan B then?'

'Not sure I wanted to do it, anyway. It would have meant getting Nurse Tanya into trouble, and she certainly did a great job. Sometimes I can still feel her tender hands caring for me as I'm drifting off to sleep.' Colin held a wistful expression.

'Colin!' Izzy sounded firm. 'Right, eat up; we've got to get back to the farm. Lots to do; this is serious now.'

Izzy drove as they headed for home.

'As a Director of Griggs Hole Farming Limited, I call a Board Meeting for,' she paused and looked at her watch, '4 pm at the kitchen table. I know it's not quite a boardroom, but it's the best we can do. You will need your copy of the Business Plan and to have read it.'

'Is this what it's going to be like in the future?' Colin looked glum.

'You're worse than a goldfish.'

'A what?'

'Have you forgotten the last few weeks of worry and angst?' Putting on a mock Colin voice, 'Oh, I'm so humiliated, so ashamed of losing the family farm after 100 years.'

He recoiled.

'Yes, of course, this is serious. And yes, this is how it's going to be from now on. You'd better get used to it.' Izzy emphasised how serious she was by banging her fist on the dashboard.

With that, they turned into the lane leading up to the farm.

'Can you drop me here, please?'

Izzy looked surprised.

'I've got something I need to do.' He closed the car door and set off toward the gate to the lower field and the direction of the scarecrow.

'Well, old chap, you still look dishevelled after your brush with the Special Ops. I bet you could have given them a run for their money. A couple of barrels from Grandad's old 12 bore would have sent them packing.' He busied himself doing up the scarecrow's jacket, pulling the shoulders back into position, so it fitted better and brushing off the dirt that stuck to it after its face-down in the mud experience.

'We cannot have any old scarecrow in our fields. It's got to be one of distinction. Your future depends on ours. Any ideas for the hole business?' Colin waited, but no response. 'Take your time, old chap; it's difficult sometimes to come up with new ideas. Well, good ones, at least.' He paused. Colin was still brushing him down and tidying him up. 'Anything?'

'I see the Manor House up the hill has a new owner.'

Colin's mouth dropped open; he was agog. 'What did you say?' He peered at the scarecrow. 'Did you speak to me?' He waited and listened before moving his head closer to the scarecrow's mouth to see if that would help.

'What are you doing, Colin, you old fool? It's me, here by the wall. I've been here listening to you for the last 10 minutes.'

Colin spun round to see Kevin Glenn laughing at

him. 'You thought it was that old scarecrow talking to you? I might like a pint or two of Old Tom, but at least I don't hallucinate. I reckon that bang on the head did you more harm than you realised.'

'Kevin, you old rogue. So what's that you were saying?'

'Yep, it's true. You know the old manor. It's been empty for a couple of years now. Well, it's been bought by some la-de-da woman. Wills, I heard. Lady Wills. Oh, that's right, rumour has it she wants to bring it back to its former glory, gardens and all. You know fish ponds, swimming pool and all that sort of stuff. It sounds to me she'll need you, you know, your holes. What else is a fish pond or swimming pool but a hole with water in it? Right up your street.'

'Kevin, you don't know it, but you're a lifesaver. I've gotta tell Izzy. Thanks, you're a real pal; I owe you a pint or two, or three. See ya.' With that, Colin leapt the wall and was off up the lane at a rate of knots. Kevin was left bemused.

'Oh well, there's nowt so queer as folk,' he continued his walk back to Henslow.

Come 4 o'clock, and Colin was sitting at the kitchen table. It was spotless and free of clutter. Izzy had arranged two A4 paper pads with pens, one either end of the table, a jug of water with ice and a slice of lemon and two tumbler glasses. She sat at the far end.

'Have you read it?' She was pointing to her copy of the Business Plan.

'Sort of.' He sounded sheepish.

'What do you mean, sort of? Either you have, or

you haven't.'

He couldn't contain himself. 'I've got some exciting news.'

'Don't change the subject. Have you read the Business Plan?' She raised her voice enough for him to realise she wasn't joking.

'No.'

'Why on earth not? I told you specifically not to come to this Board Meeting ill-prepared. You're giving me no encouragement or sign that this venture will work. Writing a plan is not good enough; it must be checked out, digested, acted upon, maintained and changed as circumstances dictate. And you cannot even be bothered to read it.' Standing, her face reddened, her voice elevated, she turned to leave.

'Hey, hey, Izzy, calm down. It's not the end of the world.'

'Don't you dare tell me to calm down? Given what you've put me through over the last weeks, months! Colin, haven't you learnt anything?' She was on the verge of storming out.

'What if I was to tell you we have a great opportunity for at least two large holes, and maybe more? Would that help?'

'What are you talking about? How big is large? Who wants them, and when? How did you find out about this opportunity? I hope it's none of your we'll just, I don't know, put an ad in the Evening Post and hey presto, it will all be okay nonsense.'

'It was the scarecrow.' Even to him, it sounded farfetched.

'For pity's sake, Colin, are you totally crazy? I reckon that bang on the head did you more harm than you realised.'

'That's odd; you're the second person today to say that.'

'So stop talking riddles and tell me what you're on about.' Izzy rolled her eyes.

'Okay, after I got out of the car—' He then told her about hearing voices, Kevin Glenn and Lady Wills moving into the Manor. 'Now, do you see?'

'Never count your birds until—'

'Chickens, it's never count your chickens until they're hatched. I appreciate that, but we're a significant step closer to getting our first—'

'Second—' Izzy corrected him.

He flinched. 'Don't remind me!'

'Contract.' She finished his sentence. 'That's all well and good, but how do we go about getting the work? We can hardly march up to Lady Wills' front door and say gisserjob.'

'True, so let's use the rest of the Board Meeting to hatch a plan.'

CHAPTER 19

LADY WILLS ARRIVES IN HENSLOW

'What in Heaven's name have I done? Just look at this place. Davy, you should have warned me. I rely on your guidance. Poor Mummy has no one else to ask.' Davy licked her chin. 'Now you know Mummy doesn't like that. Here, you can lick my hand if you must lick something.' Lady Wills popped Davy down onto the hall floor. The dog ran off, exploring their new home.

'Come on, Davy, let's see what's through here.' She opened the double doors next to the magnificent staircase. With a large amount of fluttering from a trapped pigeon, screams from Lady Wills and scampering around from Davy attempting to catch the circling bird twenty-foot above him, they entered a rather splendid drawing-room. It had seen better days, but it had all the makings of an elegant living room. 'Just what I've always wanted: I think we'll be happy here, Davy.' She looked around. 'Davy, Davy, where are you now?'

Pekes are so inquisitive. Note to oneself; remind me not to get another one.

Lady Wills and Davy spent the next hour exploring the Manor room by room before venturing outside to see the extensive outbuildings and gardens. With a flourish, she waved to Davy to take in the extraordinary scene of extensive and verdant growth that passed for a garden. 'Capability Brown would spin in his grave if he could see this lot. What do you say?' She looked round to see Davy's reaction. Nothing. Instead, she caught sight of him running at speed, trying to bring down some mouse rodent thing which had, up to that moment, been going carefree going about its business.

'Davy,' she shouted at the top of her voice, 'come here immediately, don't touch that thing, you've no idea where it's been.' Note to oneself; make sure all the dog's jabs are up to date.

'That's enough for one day. We can't sleep here tonight; there's no furniture coming until the renovation's complete. We are staying at the Harpsden Golf Club; it's the only place around that looks vaguely suitable. I hate the game myself, whacking a ball around with sticks, utter rubbish. Come on, Davy, look, the taxi is here.' She spent a few minutes locking doors and tussling with keys, trying to find the correct ones. 'Davy, Davy, where are you now?' She wandered over to the waiting car.

'Evening M'am. You said to come at six. Here I am pronto.'

'It's Your Ladyship. Now, where's Davy?'

'No one said anything about collecting two people. I'll have to review my charges.'

'It's not two people. Davy's my Peke. You haven't seen him, have you?'

'He's a grand little chap, been sitting on my knee for the last 10 minutes. He seems partial to these mints; he's had five at least. They're sugar-free mind,' the driver added, hoping that would make it okay.

'Oh, good God, man, don't you know they act as laxatives? Poor Davy.' Note to oneself: let no one feed anything to Davy but me.

They drove. 'Your bags are already at the Golf Club; they're expecting you, your Ladyship.'

'Good.' The rest of the journey was made in silence.

                                                                ~ ~ ~

Major Woods banged his gavel and spoke. 'I'm calling this Open Meeting to order.' He scanned down the Agenda. 'This brings us to the last item—Any Other Business.' A few members uttered their relief. 'Some of you may know we are expecting, any moment now, a distinguished visitor, Lady Wills of Henslow Manor. Although she's not a club member at present, it's just a formality.'

More disquiet ran through the audience. 'As always; it's not what you know, it's who you know.' someone said.

'Privilege gaining privilege only because she's a lady.' Came from another member.

'Okay, okay, please ladies and gentlemen.' The Major banged on the table. 'We're normally a democratic club which adheres to its rules and regulations, I know, but on this occasion, it was decided...'

The barracking continued, 'By whom?' Everybody looked at each other, shrugged or shook their heads.

'Can we have no more interruption please? As I was saying', Major Woods raised his voice, 'on this occasion I've decided as Club Captain and Committee

Chairman, sorry Chairperson, to forego the usual waiting time and selection procedures to allow for Lady Wills' membership to be expedited. There are two good reasons, and I'm sure once you hear them, you'll agree with me.

First, Lady Wills has just purchased a local stately home, which has been empty for several years and showing signs of decay. It needs substantial amounts of money spent on it, and I understand she's looking to restore it to its former glory, and more. She's a great believer in helping the local economy, and thus will bring much-needed work into the area.

In the interim, she'll be living here in the Club's Executive suite whilst the Manor's preliminary restoration works are undertaken. As only members can stay in the apartment, we have bestowed honorary membership whilst the paperwork for full membership is processed.

Second, Her Ladyship will pay £1000 per week plus direct expenses like her food, drink and so forth. Since the Club's funds are depleted, and we all know why.' He looked around the members for the recognition they knew what he was referring to, 'this will be a welcome financial injection. As an act of good faith, she, her ladyship, today deposited £10,000 into the Club's account.' That ought to shut them up, he thought.

'Any questions?' He paused. A hand went up. 'Yes, Mr Pryor?'

'As a former bank manager—'

'Yes, we know, get on with it.' Someone heckled.

'As a former bank manager,' he started again,

'and one with a more intimate knowledge of the workings of the local Constabulary than I care to know, I have become conscious of the workings of the criminal mind. The tricks they use these days are so sophisticated, and lulling one's victim into a false sense of security is not uncommon—'

'What are you trying to say?' Came from the floor. 'Ask your question.'

'If I had fewer interruptions, I'd finish sooner,' he rebuked. 'Now what I'm trying to say is, what do we know about this Lady Wills?'

'Good question, well asked' rang out across the Member's Lounge. Their remarks were interrupted by the clattering sound of the lounge double-doors swinging shut. All heads turned toward the doorway; there the Lady herself stood clasping Davy.

'Is no one going to answer?' She scanned the room. An awkward silence fell over the members.

'Your Ladyship,' Major Woods almost bent double as he grovelled.

'Enough of that. I'm here to stay. Can someone show me my accommodation? We're a little tired, driving, and all that.' She turned to leave the room. The Major hurdled the tables crossing the room to catch up with her. As he passed through the doors, he paused, turned and announced, 'The meeting's now over, thank you all for coming,' before he disappeared. The general level of noise rose considerably as everyone considered what they had just witnessed.

The Major caught up with her, 'Your Ladyship, I'm so sorry about that. We were just discussing—'

'Yes, I heard what you were discussing. No bother, we just need to freshen up. It's been a long and difficult day. Sorry, you are—'

'Major Woods, your Ladyship. We spoke on the phone. Please call me Graham, all my friends do.

'Major will do fine for the time being.'

'As you please. Now,—'

He told her about the Executive suite, its facilities, and how they don't allow pets, but on this occasion, they'll make an exception.

'And finally,' he concluded, 'My wife Margaret has put herself at your disposal to act as your local guide, an opener of doors, not literally of course, but Margaret knows everyone through her position of Chairperson of the Harpsden Ladies Guild, and she organises the Bridge Club. She'd be a companion just while you get yourself settled into the area.'

'So where is Margaret?'

'Well, she's not here at present, but I'll arrange for her to come to the Club say after breakfast tomorrow.'

'Splendid, I'll look forward to meeting her. Now, if you'll excuse us, we'd like to say goodnight.'

'Of course, M'Lady.' Major Woods was backing out of her front door, almost tugging at his forelocks. 'Goodnight, M'Lady.'

Marg knocked and waited. There was no reply. She tried again, this time a little harder.

'Come, it's unlocked,' she heard from the other side. Pushing open the door, Marg looked in. The room was empty. 'Just place the tray on the table; I'll be out in two secs.' The disembodied voice of Lady Wills went silent. Marg stood, feeling awkward.

'Oh, where's my breakfast? Who are you? Do you know where my breakfast is?'

'Sorry, I can't help you; I'm sure if you've ordered it, it'll be on its way. Actually, I didn't know they did room service.' Marg sounded a little surprised.

'They don't, well they didn't, but it's surprising what a cash incentive can achieve. Not just the kitchen porter, cash of the right amount you understand, seems to work with most people. By the way, who are you?'

'Margaret Woods, you met my husband last night, Graham.'

'Ahh, the Major. He's extremely agile, you know, for a man of his years. The Members Lounge didn't present any obstacle to him.'

Marg, though confused, let it pass.

'So you're here to be my guide—'

'And open doors.' Marg offered.

'Yes, I'm a little concerned. Everyone thinks I'm infirm or something. Your husband, too, said something about opening doors. I don't need help in that department as far as I know.'

'No, you misunderstand. I'm not here to actually open doors—'

'But I thought you said you were, and as I say, your husband said so last night also. Most strange.'

'Introductions. I'm here to help you with introductions, to introduce you to local dignitaries whom you may wish to meet.'

'I see. Do you have any?'

'Any—' Marg paused.

'Dignitaries I'd wish to meet.'

'Well, we have a couple of film stars who live nearby; a guitarist from a 1960's rock band, oh and the Chairman of the Hong Kong and Shanghai Bank.'

'Trade, not my sort of people.'

Marg was lost for words or knowing what to do next. Without thinking, she just blurted out, 'I like to play Bridge, pretty good at it. Do you play Lady Wills?'

'Diana.'

'Pardon?'

'It's my name, Diana. Truthfully, the Lady Wills thing is alright and, occasionally, jolly useful, but with friends, I do just prefer plain old Diana. Much easier, don't you think?'

Diana to her friends, and she's asked me to call her Diana. Well, that's rather good, Marg smiled. 'You're so right; everything has a place.'

'And a place for everything. My father, Lord Wills, was always saying it to the servants. We had this one chambermaid; she was such a scatterbrain, Father always had to remind her. I can hear him now, 'Rosy'. He was a bit deaf and tended to shout. 'Rosy, remember my gal, everything has a place and a place for everything. Learn that lesson, Rosy, and you'll go far.'

'And did she go far?'

'Well, from our house in Kensington, she got a job in Paddington, not too far, but for Rosy, well, she seemed happy enough.'

'Interesting.' Marg felt she'd entered a scene from

a Noel Coward play. 'Well, Diana,' it felt good calling Lady Wills Diana, 'do you play Bridge?'

'Well, yes, a little rusty. Three no trumps and all that. Why?'

'We play on a Tuesday morning and Thursday afternoon. It would be a wonderful opportunity to meet some of the local ladies. We have a friendly crowd.'

'Well, whatever you think. I'll leave it to you to organise.'

'What about today, now, anything particular you want to do or see?'

'The trouble is Margaret; you are comfortable with me calling you Margaret?'

'Oh, perfectly.'

'Good, as I was saying, the trouble is I'm new to the area and know no one or any place. I'm in your hands.'

'What about the house? Henslow Manor? Can we start by you showing it to me?'

'Splendid idea, now where's my breakfast?'

It wasn't long before Lady Wills was all set and ready to be shown around the local area. Marg had the Major's black Mercedes. He thought it more appropriate than Marg's Vauxhall Corsa, although the latter was only a few months old.

She could hear the Major now. *It doesn't have the same caché, Marg. Not that there's anything wrong with the Corsa, I just feel Lady Wills will expect something better.'*

Lady Wills chose to sit in the rear seat. Although Marg was more a friend than a chauffeur, Diana had to look after Davy. He sat curled up on her lap asleep, but now and then, an eye would open so he could check all was well with his mistress before closing it again.

'The nearest town is Harpsden, obviously, with the usual array of shops, plus High Street chains and a few specialist food and clothes shops. One of my favourites for morning coffee or lunch is Made by Bob. Although new, they've done a splendid job restoring the run down Corn Exchange into an avant-garde development.' Marg was feeling like a Thompson Tour Guide, but she found it interesting to see her hometown through fresh eyes.

The tour continued. 'Here is the Conservative Club. It's well attended, but mostly by the Young Farmers. I think more because the beer is cheap rather than for any political allegiances.'

Diana sat, appearing interested and now and then asked a question or made a comment. 'Although I like to go to town, I'm not a town person, really. I like the countryside and local villages. You know, far less hustle and bustle.'

Soon they were on the outskirts of Harpsden, heading toward Henslow on route to the Manor. Oxdenshire, being a rural county, was more conducive to Her Ladyship. It wasn't long before they were approaching the village.

'Here are your new neighbours. It's a pretty village with a welcoming pub; see over on the right.' Marg pointed to The Lamb Inn. 'The owner and landlord is Bob Critchley—'

'Bob, another Bob? I fear a certain lack of imagination when it comes to naming one's children.' Diana smiled. 'I tease.'

'Well, he's a pleasant chap, no Egon Ronay, but the food is wholesome, and he's welcoming. We come this way for Sunday lunch on occasion.'

'Why do I know his name? Critchley, Critchley, yes, wasn't it him or his public house on TV recently? I'm sure I recall hearing something.' She was still trying to recall.

'Ah well, I imagine you're referring to the minor incident we had a couple of weeks back. Yes, the whole media circus descended on The Lamb Inn following a goose attack.'

'Goose attack! Sounds frightfully scary.'

'Actually, see that lady walking up in front.' Marg flicked the indicator as she overtook a policeman on a push-bike before slowing the car for Diana to get a better look.

'Where?'

'Here, on the left, carrying her shopping.' Marg pointed. 'well, it was her geese that caused all the commotion.'

'Who is she?'

'Isobel Griggs, married to Colin Griggs. They own this farm.'

'That's not him standing in the field, is it?'

'Oh, Diana, no, that's his scarecrow. If you look beyond, you'll see their house.'

'Now you mention Griggs; I remember hearing that name on the news report as well.'

'Colin, oh, he's quite infamous in these parts.'

'Why? What did he do? Or shouldn't I ask?'

'Well, it said on the news report, it concerned—'

Marg hesitated, 'stockings.'

'Stockings! What do you mean stockings?' Diana was curious.

'Well, allegedly, he wears stockings.' Marg looked in the rear-view mirror to glimpse Diana's reaction.

'Why on earth was that on the news?' Daddy wore them all the time. He said it started in the War, 1942, or around then after the Americans brought nylons and chocolates over here. Around the house, he'd just wear his pants and these stockings. Apparently, he had circulation problems, varicose veins, and that sort of thing. He told Mummy that stockings, the nylon material next to his skin, felt awfully good and relieved his symptoms. I'm not sure the little bows on the tops or the suspender belt were essential, but he said they were in limited supply, and you had to take what you could get. You know, rationing. And, of course, without suspenders, they would just roll down his leg. I remember as a little girl just how funny that looked.'

'And if not at home?' Marg said, rather bemused.

'And if not at home, what, Margaret dear? Make yourself clear.'

'You say your Father wore them out also?'

'Well, of course, under his trousers, why wouldn't he? One of his favourite stories he'd recall at lunch was how he single-handedly introduced the wearing of stockings into the House of Lords. He said like him, they all wore them under their robes. I assume they all had circulation problems. They would compare the different makes and prices and where you could buy them. I remember how, after the War, Daddy would go to some shop near Euston Station. I was little then, but he'd often take me with him. They sold all sorts of lovely dresses too.'

Marg did a polite cough. 'I wasn't aware that stocking wearing was quite so widespread.'

'Doesn't the Major? He looks the type.'

Marg spluttered, 'Looks the type!'

'Are you alright dear? Ah, look here, it's my new home. Pull in the drive, the gates will open automatically.'

❧   ❧   ❧

'Has that Colin of yours been hearing any more voices? You should have seen his face; a real picture. I could hardly stop myself from laughing. He'd no idea I was behind that wall.'

'Kevin Glenn, one day those tricks of yours will come back to haunt you. You frighten folk half to death sneaking up on them like that. Mind you, that stuff about Lady Wills and Henslow Manor sure spurred him into action. So if you have any other useful snippets, feel free to pass them on.'

I will, Mrs G, I will. Don't forget to tell Colin I'm in The Lamb most nights—'

'And most lunchtimes, from what I hear.'

'Ah well, a little of what you like does you a power of good, so my old dad would say.'

'Didn't they bury him at 55 from liver failure?'

'That's as maybe, but Colin knows where to find me.'

'Right Kevin, I'll tell him. Must go now. Bye.' With that, Izzy set off out of the village, walking toward the farm. She'd gone a couple of hundred yards to where the pavement runs out when a black Mercedes passed her. *I know that car,* she thought. *I've seen it before, but not in these parts. Now, whose is it?* For the rest of the 10-minute walk back to the farm, she kept trying to place it. As she rounded the long bend, she could see the scarecrow across the field.

'You're standing all day watching the comings and goings. Have you seen that car before?' she shouted.

'Major Woods.'

'Crikey!' She dropped her shopping. Three oranges rolled into the road, 'What, who the flipping heck was that?'

'Sorry, Izzy, I didn't mean to make you jump, just trying to be helpful.'

'Oh, it's you, Ticker, strange I never heard you coming. You're unusually quiet on your bike, creeping up like that.'

'You were too busy talking to the scarecrow to hear me.'

'How'd you know it's Major Woods' car?'

'It passed me in the village just now, heading out this way. We haven't many black Mercedes round here, not local anyway. It's a policeman's job to notice these things, like you talking to scarecrows. Now we don't want that getting out, or the entire village will think the Griggs are—' he paused.

'More dappy than we actually are?'

'I was going to say eccentric; it's more polite.'

'So what do you think the Major's doing out here?'

'Ah, observation, observation, the secret of good policing. It wasn't him but her driving; Margaret, his wife. And what's more, she wasn't alone; a second woman holding a dog was with her.'

'You are good, so what did they have for breakfast?' She teased him.

'I'm good, but I know my limits. The second person is someone unknown to me, but guessing by the direction they were going in; it's the new owner of Henslow Manor, Lady Wills, I believe.'

'That's her?' Izzy looked toward the disappearing car. 'I hear she's spending a fortune on the place. We were only talking about her yesterday. Colin thinks it's an opportunity to sell her a few holes, you know, as part of the Griggs Hole Farming business. Our biggest problem is getting to meet her. She won't speak to the likes of us.'

'Well, you know she's friendly with Major Woods' wife, and I believe you had dealings with him in his role as chairman of the Golf Club. Maybe you can get him to introduce you.'

'Ticker, are you seriously suggesting that the Major would introduce Griggs Hole Farming to anyone, never mind someone like her? Pull the other one, it's got bells on.'

'Stranger things happen at sea. Nothing ventured, nothing gained, it always pays to ask.' PC Wright had run out of proverbs.

'As you say, nothing ventured, nothing gained.' They both laughed.

'I'll keep you posted.' With that, PC Wright rode off up the lane. In the silence, you could hear the sound of his wheel catching on the mudguard: tic, tic, tic with each revolution. *You'd think after 30 years, he'd get that fixed.* She picked up her oranges before heading off home.

'Colin, I'm back. Where are you?' She got no reply and continued putting her shopping away. *No one will ever know that these have been rolling around the road.* She placed the oranges in the fruit bowl. He appeared.

'Where have you been? You've been ages. I thought you were popping into the village for a few bits.'

'I'll have you know I've had an interesting conversation and I might have found a way to meet Lady Hoity Toity.'

'Wills. Don't forget she's a prospective customer. We don't want to mess this up.' Colin reminded her.

'You're telling me? Do I need to tell you again of—'

'Exactly, that's why we need to be more careful this time. Anyway, who've you been talking to?' He was curious.

'A friend of yours.' She was evasive.

'Who?'

'Someone you talk to, a dapper chap who hangs around all day keeping his eye on the World.'

'What, who? Come on, tell me.' He sounded agitated.

'The scarecrow, who did you think?' She chuckled out loud.

'Why didn't you just say so?'

'What, after what I said to you yesterday about talking to him?'

'So, what happened? Not that Kevin Glenn again?'

'No, not him, but I met him in the village. He asked me to remind you he frequents The Lamb Inn just in case you want to buy him the pint you owe him.'

'Does he think I need telling? Anyway, if it's not him, who was it?'

Izzy spent the next 10 minutes recounting her conversation with Ticker Wright blow by blow, but excluding the part about the oranges in the road in case it put him off eating them.

'You truly believe Major Woods would introduce us to her. Pigs might fly first.' Colin's expression changed from an optimistic grin to a look of incredulity.

'Well, I've been thinking, as I was putting the shopping away; this might sound a little crazy, but—'

He had the same idea. 'Why don't I join the Harpsden Golf Club?' Colin screwed up his face. 'That's not crazy; it's insanity!'

'So you don't think it's a good idea?' She sounded tentative.

'Not a cat in hell's chance. If I were to go anywhere near the place, the Major would throw a wobbly of such magnitude it would make Mount St Helens look like a damp squib.' He folded his arms across his chest.

A prolonged silence followed as they both pondered the situation.

Now Colin was tentative. 'What are you like playing cards?'

'We used to play Snap and Happy Families. Why do you ask?'

'If we can't get to the Major, then maybe we can get to his wife. Actually, if she and Lady Wills are chums, she's probably the better bet.'

'What's that to do with cards?' Izzy did not know what was coming next.

'You Izzy, my darling, are going to join the Harpsden and District Women's Bridge Club.' He looked at her expectantly.

'Snap and Happy Families, ' she repeated, 'Snap and Happy Families are a million miles away from Bridge. You might be Mr Blagger and able to convince the Lloyds Bank you were a sound investment or the Golf Club Committee to award you a hole contract, but I'm certainly not.'

'Excuse me, Isobel Griggs, I didn't blag Mr Pryor or the Golf Club Committee; I believed every word I said. I'm not some fly by night, giving it, what did Del Boy call it, all that chat! I'll have you know I'm from a long-standing, scrupulously honest—'

'Fourth generation Griggs, yeah, yeah.'

'Exactly. We have our pride.' He huffed.

'Okay, so how do you see this working, Mr Scrupulously Honest?'

He glared at her, 'Over and above knowing the rules of the game, cards are all about memory and Bridge especially, about listening and watching your partner.'

'But I haven't got a partner, so we're scuppered at the first hurdle. Any more bright ideas that don't involve superhuman feats on my part?'

'Just pay attention. The partner thing is not an issue. Once you're in the Club—'

'I'm certainly not getting pregnant at my age so that you can win a hole contract.'

'Now who's being flippant, you know what I

mean—the Bridge Club? They will sort you out a partner; you just need to get accepted.'

'And how, pray?'

'Remember how you taught me to use the mouse? You used a card game on the computer.'

'What, Solitaire?' Izzy threw her head back.

'Well, you can practise using that.'

'Colin, do you know anything about Bridge?'

'Well, sort of 'ish...'

'Nothing's what you're trying to say. However, unknown to you, you may have hit on a great idea, to find a solution to my Bridge playing skills, or lack of them!'

'What is it Izzy? What did I say?' He was getting quite excited about his achievement, but he'd no idea what he had done.

'The Internet brain box! Everything you want to know about anything, well almost, is on the Internet. It'll require some searching and study time, but with dedication, I guess, I could become passable at Bridge.'

CHAPTER 20

SOCIAL CLIMBING

After various Google searches and registering on several Bridge websites, Izzy eventually found 'omarshariff.com' with a whole range of tutorials and options for playing against the computer or live on-line with others. She got into it, to the point where Colin was felt somewhat neglected.

Izzy hardly let her eyes leave the screen. 'Have you fed the chickens yet, dear? And while you're at it, the geese and ducks, too.' She turned back to the computer and played her card.

Colin sloped off out of the back door, muttering, 'I suppose I'll have to get my tea as well.'

'Actually, Colin, I'm in the middle of a rubber, not sure how long we'll be. If you want to eat soonish, take something out of the freezer and pop it into the microwave.' She didn't even look up.

The back door slammed. *I hate frozen ready meals; they're like tasteless slop.* He looked enviously at the chicken's food. *No,* he thought, *a mouthful of raw corn can't be any better.*

Chores done, he came back into the kitchen. She hadn't moved, he stared hard in her direction. She didn't notice. The silence was broken by the freezer door being opened, followed by the sound of packets being moved around randomly, then grunts of disapproval and the dull thud of the door being shut. Still nothing; she was totally consumed.

'If I'd have known I'd become a computer widower, I'm not sure I'd have suggested you learning Bridge.'

Izzy made no response and pretended not to hear. He left.

The ping of the microwave announced his meal was ready. Colin wasn't around; she continued to play. A few more minutes passed, and still no Colin.

'It's ready, dear.' She tried to sound caring. 'It'll get cold.'

'I know, I heard.' He came back into the kitchen like a bear with a sore head.

'It'll taste awful if you don't eat it now.'

'Standing time.' He collected his meal and left.

'I'm doing this for you, remember?' she called after him. 'I'm doing rather well, actually; we won our Rubber.' He didn't hear.

The past week had been difficult for Colin, but Izzy was excited.

'I really think I've got the makings of an alright player, you know.'

'Well, the hours you've spent on the darn computer, no wonder.'

'Colin Griggs, I'm doing my bit toward getting this contract. What've you done toward it?' He looked sheepish and said no more.

'While you were doing nothing, Colin, I rang Julia Pryor earlier to find out about the HDWBC meetings. She says they're on a Tuesday morning or Thursday afternoon at the Guild's rooms. Apparently, you can just turn up as a visitor. You may or may not get a game, but at least you can meet some members and get a feel for the Club. You know, so you can see if you want to join.'

'To see if they want you more like.' He wished he'd never suggested Bridge.

'Come on, Colin, buck up. No gain without pain. Support me or—'

'Of course, I do.'

'We'll start by driving me into Harpsden. I need a new outfit.'

'Struth, are you playing cards or entering a fashion parade?' His moment of compliance disappeared. The look on his face gave away his true feelings. She saw.

'Sometimes, Colin Griggs, you drive me to distraction.'

'Well, it's better than driving you to dress shopping.'

'You're worse than a child; this is our business, our future, our joint,' she strongly emphasised joint, 'commitment. No more indifference, this petulant behaviour, or you're on your own.' By the time she'd finished, he was standing by the back door with the lorry keys in his hand.

'And another thing, Old Alfred Mac will have to go. I can't be seen riding around in an ancient lorry. We're climbing the social ladder, and I need to be seen to be doing so.'

'How can you say that about Alfred Mac? He's been servicing this family since before I was born. If he goes, that'll be the end of Griggs.'

'Okay, I might have been a bit hard, but I need a run-around. Something a bit more becoming of a lady.'

'You're going to play Bridge Izzy, not going to the Queen's Garden Party. Our £10,000 won't last long at this rate.'

They pulled out of the farmyard and headed off down the lane, and past the field with the scarecrow. Colin gave him an old-fashioned look. *Don't you dare ask me for a new outfit as well!*

'You've been a genuine treasure, Margaret, giving up so much of your precious time these last few days. Having driven up and down every highway and byway, I'm getting a real feel for the place. Such a lovely county. Now I need to get to know the people.'

'I really believe in the local community and am keen to use local tradespeople where possible on the Manor renovation project. In the past, what's worked well for me is getting recommendations. Looking at the local paper, there are so many adverts for carpenters, builders, decorators, electricians, but I do not know who's who and which ones are any good. So I've decided to hold a small gathering at the Manor in order to help me decide.'

'What, you're going to invite a whole load of tradespeople for drinks and canapés? And chat with them? Well, it's rather an unusual approach, but I don't see why it couldn't work.' Marg was trying to be supportive, but feeling quite the opposite.

'Do you take me for a complete nincompoop? No, I've no intention of inviting en masse a random bunch of tradespeople into my home. No, as I said, it's recommendations I go by so we can kill two birds with one stone.'

'How do you mean?' Marg was uncertain what Diana was alluding to.

'I can get to meet the local well-to-dos and at the same time get from them their personal recommendations. Then we can draw up a shortlist of prospective suppliers.'

'Ah, that makes more sense… So a party Diana, how super. Oh, what a great idea. Any inkling when?' Marg thought it a splendid opportunity to gain one-upmanship by organising a party with Lady Wills. 'Who are you going to invite, Diana?'

'Well, that's all down to you. Don't forget, I know no one around here. But I certainly hope to after next Saturday.'

'Next Saturday! We'll have our work cut out.'

'I know, Margaret, let's go to Bob's house for lunch. We can plan it while we eat.'

'I think you mean Made by Bob.'

At the restaurant, Marg thumbed through her Filofax of some 150 contacts. Although not fearful of computers, she preferred old-fashioned paper. It was less easy to delete things accidentally. Her Christmas list had been erased the last three years on the trot.

'I've organised Bridge for Tuesday morning, so

we'll be able to give out some invites then.'

'Let's limit the numbers to around 50; otherwise, there'll be too many, and I won't have a chance to talk to them all.'

'Sounds about right.' Marg was already thinking about who she was going to invite. 'It means I'll need to do some pruning of my list.'

'Now we'll have it at the Manor in the Entrance Hall and Drawing Room. The rest of the place is not serviceable. But of course, we'll need to bring everything, catering equipment, furniture, serving staff, glasses the lot. Any thoughts? Remember, I prefer to keep it local. Start the way I mean to go on.' Diana took another mouthful of soup.

'It will be a positive display of your intentions. I think the locals will be most appreciative. Now, where do we start at this short notice?' Marg flicked at the Filofax pages for inspiration.

Lady Wills was the first to come up with an idea. 'The Golf Club. They do catering all the time. Do you think they could manage this by next Saturday?'

'Mary, the Secretary, keeps the Events Diary; she'll know what's in the schedule. I'll ring her.' Marg took a bite of crusty baguette.

'Well, get on with it, Margaret. No time like the present.' Diana was a bit of an action woman. *Note to oneself: if you want something done, do it yourself.*

Marg thumbed the Filofax, looking for Mary's direct number. 'Ah, here we are,' she keyed the digits. 'I don't enjoy doing this in a restaurant. What will the other diners think?' She checked around to see if anyone was looking.

'Get on with it. Anyway, it isn't a restaurant; it's a Bistro, far more bohemian. I'm sure Bob won't mind.'

'Mary, it's me, Margaret. Yes, I'm fine, and you?'

Diana was making hurry along gestures.

'I'm ringing just to see what's in the Club's Events Diary for this coming Saturday.' She listened and repeated Mary's comments for Diana's benefit. 'It's on-line. I can access it via the Member's Login? Okay, but I'm not at home.' She listened again. 'Yes, I'm on my mobile. Isn't it what? Web-enabled? What's that? I've no idea. Can you just please tell me?' She put her hand over her mobile. 'Technology! Give me a pen and ink anytime.' She put the phone back to her ear. 'Okay, a wedding's booked for 200 guests. Thanks.' She pressed the "end call," key.

'Doesn't sound like the Golf Club can help? So who else, anyone more local? Think Margaret, think.' They both turned back to their lunches and cleared their bowls.

Diana had a brainwave. 'Bob, what about Bob?' 'Look, we've just had an excellent lunch. I take it yours was okay.'

'Yes, first-rate.'

'Then why not ask Made by Bob if they want to do it?' Without further ado, Diana was on her feet and across the floor to the kitchen before Marg had time to comment. Some five minutes later, she reappeared, shaking her head. 'Apparently, outside catering's in the business plan, but not for another year. They need to get established first. Pity. I suggested a cash incentive, but—'

'I've just had an idea,' interrupted Marg. 'You

mentioned Bob; what about Bob Critchley at The Lamb Inn? He's local and obliging. He fed and entertained the media circus with no warning. They just descended upon him.' She looked up at Diana for approval.

'Well, I guess desperate times call for desperate measures.'

'Diana, think positive. I'll call in to see him after I've dropped you back at the Golf Club. Is it about time for Davy's afternoon nap?'

'How do I look? Izzy turned and smiled at Colin.

The dreaded question, Colin thought to himself, *I knew it was coming.* 'That's the eighth outfit, Izzy. Can we get some perspective here? You're visiting a Bridge Club on a Tuesday morning, so don't look at evening wear or little black cocktail dresses.'

'What would you prefer me in? A twin set and pearls.'

'Just be you.'

'Oh, wellies and apron with a gilet on top! Yes, that'd impress them. They'd certainly remember me.' She gave him short shrift.

After much mind changing, clothes changing, and banter exchanges, the shopping trip drew to a satisfactory close—almost.

'Can we go home now?' Colin felt he'd earned his release.

'Not so fast; shoes. I need a new pair of shoes.'

'I'll tell you what, I'll find a cup of tea and meet you back at the lorry in say—'

'Sixty minutes.' She pre-empted him.

'Thirty.'

'Forty-five.'

'Thirty.' He held a pleading look.

She took pity. 'Get a local paper and see what's in the motoring ads. Do something useful with your time.'

He did what she said but the motoring ads ran over six pages. Colin got through two mugs of tea, a scone and a toasted teacake when he realised that his thirty-minute deadline had expired by a further thirty minutes. When he got back to the lorry, Izzy was sitting in the cab of Old Alfred Mac. His face appeared in the driver's door window. Even the glass and steel of the cab weren't sufficient to shield him from the intensity of her gaze. He opened the door, crawled into the driver's seat, thought about making an excuse, but thought better of it, given the look on her face. The sound of the engine was the only thing that broke the silence of the journey home. As they rounded the bend in the lane leading up to the farm, he wound down his window.

'Any bright ideas?' He called to the scarecrow. He listened. Silence. *Where are your friends when you need them?* He knew it was going to be a long evening.

She played on-line Bridge for over four hours. He microwaved his tea, and didn't dare object. He was in the front room in his favourite chair, wondering how he could get back into her good books. To break the silence, he turned on the telly; he turned it off again. He went and stood behind her, watching her play in a sort of supportive way, but got bored within a few minutes. Anyway, she resented his intrusion.

'I'm trying to concentrate here. Are all the animals fed and locked up?' Izzy didn't look up.

They were, he had already seen to them. He sat back in his chair. The paper bought that afternoon was nearby; he flicked through the pages. *Of course,* he thought, *I'll buy her a car.* He'd marked half a dozen possibilities earlier on. He re-read the adverts and using a pen and paper he drew a grid so that he could compare one against the other: age, colour, cc, MOT, tax, service history, price, mileage, fuel type, number of doors, extras. After completing his grid, he narrowed his choices to the three most likely candidates. He was sure she'd approve of his selection method and shortlist. *Right, let's ring to find out more.*

Colin dialled the number of his first choice. It rang once, twice.

'Yo.'

'Is that 819426?' Colin wanted to be sure.

'Yo.'

'You've got a car for sale? It's in the local paper.'

'Did. Sorry.' There was a click.

Colin listened to the dialling tone. *It looks like it wasn't just me who thought that was a good buy.* He dialled the next number.

'Hello, 844291, can I help you?'

'Yes, please, I've got the local paper here; you're selling a car.'

'Yes, that's correct.'

'Is it sold yet?'

'No, not yet.'

'Can you tell me anything about it?'

'Well, it's a car.' Colin waited for more.

'Anything else?'

'Have you read the advert?'

'Yes.'

'Well, there you are, then. You know all there is to know.'

'There's nothing else you'd like to add to make me want to buy it?'

'No, not really.'

'Tyres?'

'Yes, four, not counting the spare.'

'No, I mean their condition.'

'Well, we had new ones fitted about a month ago. I think. I'm not sure. 'Hold on, please.' Colin heard muffled voices. 'No, sorry, the wife said it was more like two months ago. Doesn't time fly!'

'Do you do many miles?' Colin would have preferred to hang up, but the thought of pacifying Izzy came to mind.

'Well, let me see. On Mondays, we go into town to Tesco's. Well, most Mondays, not every Monday. If it's a Bank Holiday, we don't bother. We usually go away on Bank Holidays to June's, that's my wife's sister. She lives in Scarborough. It's so nice there; we like it lots. We even talked about moving there a few years back.' The phone went silent. 'Yes, it was three years ago, according to May.'

'May?'

'Yes, May's my wife. Her parents were outdoorsy people and noticed the season's changing; that's why they called their daughters May and June.'

'Lucky they didn't have a brother.' Colin couldn't help himself.

'Sorry, no, she doesn't have a brother. She always said she'd have loved one so she could dress him up. That's always been one of her regrets, no brother.'

'I see. Do you drive to Scarborough?' Colin could have kicked himself as soon as he'd asked the question.

'We used to, but that was before they built the M1. It was a lovely journey through the countryside. Once they built the motorway, it was all lorries, road rage and speed cameras. It spoiled it for us—'

'But your car's just three years old according to the ad.'

'I know we've never driven to Scarborough in Matilda.'

'Matilda?'

'Yes, that's what we call this car. We started with Arthur back in 1950. Named him after May's Dad. Nice man, but he died in a road accident four years later; knocked off his bike. It was on a roundabout, and no one knew about roundabouts then. Anyway, Arthur was late home for tea, and instead of going left around the roundabout, he thought he'd save himself a bit of time and go right. Not one of his better decisions. Then we had Boris. He was a Mini, bright red, 1000cc—'

'Can I come and see it?' Colin interjected.

'Boris, no, he's long gone, probably one of those square cubes you see in a scrap yard, or they've made it into baked bean cans.'

'Not Boris, Matilda!' Colin wiped his brow.

'Don't you want me to answer your question, then?'

'What question?' Colin was losing the will to live.

'About how many miles we do. I've only told you about Monday. Now on Tuesday—'

Colin walked out to his front door with the phone in his hand and rang the doorbell. 'Look, sorry, someone at the door. Must answer it. Thanks' He put the phone down.

He went back to his grid and dialled the number for his third choice. Before it had time to ring, he heard a voice.

'Hello, have you rung about the car?'

'Yes,' He was taken by surprise.

'Well, it's still here on our drive. The chap who wanted it failed to show, so it's back for sale.'

Rather than risk losing another, Colin waded straight in. 'Can I come to see it, say tomorrow morning about ten?'

'Well, it's Saturday. Yes, I'll be here. What's your name?'

'Griggs, Colin Griggs.' Peals of laughter came from the phone. 'Oh Colin, take no notice of us; it's just something funny on the TV. Sorry about that. Right, we'll see you tomorrow. Ah, just before you go, my wife says, she has no problems driving it in her high heels. She thought you'd like to know.' More snorts and guffaws followed. Colin put the phone down a confused man. Pleased with himself and wanting to impress his wife, he cut out the ad from the paper, and taped it to a blank postcard. On it he wrote 'I hope you like it,' followed by three kisses. He put it into an envelope and wrote 'Izzy' on the outside. As he was going upstairs, he looked into the kitchen. She was still playing. 'Night,' he called. She didn't answer. He left the envelope on her pillow.

'Mr Critchley, nice to meet you. Thanks for seeing me at such short notice. Given our deadline, I thought it better we meet sooner rather than later.' Marg stretched out her hand in a greeting.

'My pleasure, Mrs Woods. I've seen you and the Major in for lunch, but it's always been so busy I've not had the chance to talk. So how can I help?' Bob took her hand and put on his best customer service smile.

'As I'm sure you are aware, Lady Wills has purchased Henslow Manor. I don't know if you know, but she's keen to promote local businesses and the local community. I've spent the last week driving her around the county, but now she wants to meet some residents.'

'Okay, that sounds nice; we couldn't be more local.'

Well, that's why I'm here. She's planning a party for a week today up at the Manor. Since the building's totally empty, we need to organise everything down to the last toothpick and roll of loo paper.'

'How many guests?'

'50'ish. As its such short notice, we'll invite more than as many will have prior engagements so won't be able to make it.'

'And what's she looking for?' Bob took out a pen.

'A bar with a range of drinks, including soft, you know orange, mineral water, tomato juice—oops, sorry, I guess you don't need me to tell you.' He gave her an old-fashioned look.

'And?'

'And food. Not a sit-down meal, just nibbles, buffet style. Plus some waiting staff, whatever you think for 50 people.'

'Well, let me see, three running the bar, two on the food counter and two in the kitchen. She has got a kitchen, hasn't she?'

'Not sure what's in it or what's working. I'll find out and let you know.'

'Two on the door as guests arrive and two more mingling with refills and collecting empties.' Bob started counting on his fingers, muttering and writing on a beer mat he found nearby.

'Well, that all sounds fine. You're the expert; I'm sure we can leave it for you to do a first-class job.' Marg shook his hand and left.

Bob went into overdrive. It was Saturday, and he needed to organise what he'd committed to. As usual, Lucy was working at Bates the Chemist, and wouldn't be back until after 5.00. He needed staff and quickly.

She's got some of her old school chums; I'm sure they'd give a hand. Bob racked his brain when he noticed Ann Bishop having a quiet lunch-time drink. She was talking to Kevin Glenn. *Maybe,* he thought, *Ann in the kitchen as no one would see her and Kevin on the door with a tray of drinks. He wouldn't have to move or say anything. Even he can do that, surely?* Bob saw the best in people when it suited him.

'Kevin,' he called across the bar, 'and you, Ann,

can you spare me a minute?'

'Look, I don't owe you anything. I told you before—'

'Whoa, whoa Kevin, it's not about that. I have a proposition for you both.'

Bob explained about the party and how he needed some extra temporary staff and given such short notice and how beggars can't be choosers.

'So it's not for our good looks, charm and wit you want us then?' Kevin pushed his thinning hair back; it made no difference.

'Kevin, all I need to know is that you'll do it, stay sober, wash behind your ears and put on a clean white shirt and black trousers. Oh, and no sneakers or wellies. We don't want Lady Wills to think we are a load of turnip heads.'

Kevin pulled himself up straight, tucked in his shirt, and wiped down his jacket. 'Of course I can do it. Anyway, what's in it for us?'

'And what about you, Ann?'

'You just want me in the kitchen? No waitressing? What about entertainment? I could knock out a few tunes on the old piano.'

'We all know that and very well too, may I say. But on Saturday, I just need you in the kitchen. £20 to you, Kevin, plus a clean slate, and £30 to you, Ann. Does that sound fair?' Bob had his first two staff signed up.

The rest of the day passed quickly as he made a list after list about all the different things he'd need— furniture, food, drinks, cutlery, crockery and where he might source it all from. By late afternoon, things were coming together. Favours being called in and friends and acquaintances pressurised into action. His throat was raw and his shoulders stiff from hours on the phone with the handset tucked into the crick of his neck to allow him to speak and write simultaneously.

'Lucy, have you got a minute?' She was home from work. 'We've got a party to cater.' Her dad went on, 'I've done most of the leg; I just need seven more waitresses and bar staff. Some of your old school chums might like to earn a few quid.' He looked hopefully at her.

'When and where, Dad?'

He explained, and within a few minutes, Lucy was busy texting her mates.

Colin and Izzy drove in Old Alfred Mac to view the prospective new car. Colin did all the usual stuff of kicking the tyres, looking under the bonnet and into the glove compartment. He even waggled the gear lever and turned on the windscreen wipers.

'All looks in order. Have you got the log-book and service history?' Colin rustled through the paperwork, checked the mileage on the speedo and enquired, 'MOT?'

'Unnecessary, there's another three months before the first one's due.'

'Well, Izzy, what do you think?'

'I like the colour; it'll go with my new jacket and skirt.' She sat in the driver's seat. 'I can reach the pedals and see out the windscreen. But it's low down after driving that lorry for all those years. I'm sure I'll get used to it.'

Soon, cash changed hands, and the convoy was ready to set off. Izzy in her new car lead the way, Colin in Old Alfred Mac followed behind. As Colin moved off, he had the window down and heard the ex-owner talking.

'I couldn't see any sign of a suspender belt. I wonder if he's changed to wearing tights?'

Soon Colin was out of earshot and none the wiser.

'Oh, Colin, thank you,' she gushed, 'my own car.' Standing by it, she took out a tissue and rubbed a minor blemish off the paintwork. It gleamed, she beamed, and he felt relieved to be back in her good books.

'Right, Bridge practice.' With that, Izzy was away into the kitchen and back on the computer. He knew that would be the last he'd see of her for several hours.

Her confidence and skill level grew with each new game. She was now well known on the website, and her playing name of Little Miss Muffet attracted quite a following.

By Monday night, they upgraded her skill level to 'advanced', and she was soon hoping to gain 'expert' status, but for now, she had to focus on the HDWBC meeting set for the following morning.

'Gosh, Colin, I'm getting quite jittery.' The usually cool, calm Izzy wasn't. 'All those ladies. What will they think of me? Izzy Griggs, farmer's wife, playing

Bridge.'

'Hey, there's no reason you shouldn't be playing Bridge. Anyway, you're not a farmer's wife, but a director and equity partner of Griggs Hole Farming Limited.'

'That sounds grand; let's hope that's how they see me.'

She left the room only to come back a few minutes later dressed in her new outfit, shoes and all.

'It feels special; I feel special. Do you know what Colin? I'm ready.' Slowing, pivoting as she spoke, he sensed her passion and determination.

He saw her with new eyes; this was the first time he had seen her like this. He liked it and felt proud of her.

'Izzy, my Izzy, I love you.' He took her into his arms, and looked deep into her chestnut brown eyes. The eyes he'd seen in that school girl all those years ago, the eyes he'd fallen in love with then and had remained so to this day. She lent in and squeezed him; they were one.

CHAPTER 21

PARTY ANIMAL

'Attention, please everyone.' Marg rapped the table with her knuckles. 'As always, we like to encourage new members and welcome any guests with open arms. Today we have a special guest whom I'm sure you're all hoping will become a member and a regular player at our bridge club. She is new to the area, but communities being what they are, I've no doubt you've all heard that Lady Wills has bought Henslow Manor. We'll she, sorry, her Ladyship, is here to get to know the area and the people who live in it. I've had the pleasure of driving Lady Wills around our beautiful county and felt it appropriate to bring her here today. Without further delay, can we have a heartfelt welcome for our esteemed guest, Lady Wills?' A round of applause rang out accompanied by various messages of greetings and calls of 'here, here.'

The noise abated, and Marg walked Lady Wills around the members, introducing each one individually. It was at that point that Marg realised they had a second guest that day.

'Mrs Griggs!' Marg tried to hide the surprise. 'Mrs Griggs, Isobel, isn't it? I didn't know you were here.

I'm so sorry, I should have introduced you—'

'Oh, no matter Mrs Woods, I came in while you were doing the introductions for Lady Wills. I didn't want to say anything; you were in full flow.'

'This is a surprise. You play Bridge, I had no idea.' *And that you scrub up so well*, she kept that thought to herself.

'Well, you know, in the winter, we have more time on the farm, so I practice with dummy hands—'

'Oh, and how is Colin?' a rather unfortunate non sequitur.

'Bridge is not his cup of tea.'

'Sorry, how forgetful of me.' Marg turned to Diana. 'This is Lady Wills.'

'My pleasure, your Ladyship, ' Izzy replied, offering her hand.

'Don't stand on ceremony, call me Diana.'

Marg shot a look between them; *that's what I call her. Only her friends call her Diana!*

'Actually, we saw you the other day walking out of Henslow as we drove past. What a coincidence we should meet here. Mrs Woods was telling me about your husband, Colin; he sounds interesting. A lot like my father. You must introduce me sometime.'

Izzy was feeling ecstatic. *All that Bridge playing has paid off, and I've only just got here.* She smiled inwardly. *Now steady, Izzy, don't blow it.*

'Well ladies, no time for chitter-chatter. Diana, would you partner me today? Julia, do you mind?' Marg almost pushed Julia out of her seat. 'Maybe you could partner with Isobel, put her through her paces; see if she's of a suitable standard for a club player.'

After much chattering back and forth, the room settled down to its first rubber. Izzy, paired with Julia; they made a formidable team as they quickly realised how the other thought and called.

Diana and Marg fared less well. Diana had gained her Bridge skills over the years in different countries and was apt to mix the styles and rules into some sort of bugger's muddle where her partner had little idea what suit she had or where she was long or short. Although Marg's reputation was under threat, she felt it was worth it for the reflected glory of being Lady Wills' new friend and confidant.

Around their table the forthcoming party was the principle topic of conversation. The arrangements, who was doing what, what had been agreed with Bob Critchley and, of course, the guest list. Marg had prepared personalised invites for Lady Wills and distributed them amongst the Club members. Everyone in the room got one, except for Izzy.

'Oh, that's alright.' She tried not to show her disappointment.

'Isobel, no. It's only because I didn't know you'd be here today. Your invite is at home with the rest waiting to be posted.' Marg lied so convincingly, even she believed it.

'Anyway, it's short notice. I'll need to look in the diary and to check with Colin whether we can make it.' Izzy lied convincingly, too.

'Oh, I hope you both can. Colin sounds like a real sport. I'm sure he and Daddy would have been great chums; so much in common.' Diana enthused.

Izzy looked quizzical. Diana saw. 'You know stocking wearing.' She said for clarification.

Izzy rolled her eyes back. *Oh, here we go again.*

'Just the other day, I was telling Margaret how Daddy wore stockings all the time. Ever since the War, until the day he died. He had circulation problems apparently, and the nylon against his skin would help the condition. He lived till he was over 90 and then died of pneumonia—poor sausage. So I guess they worked. So how is Colin's circulation?'

'It's fine,' Izzy held her breath, 'but I've a feeling it may get worse.' She felt herself getting tense. *You wait, Colin Griggs, till I get home.* She smiled and made light of it, but inside, she seethed. *Will this ever stop?*

The morning club meeting concluded with Izzy having ingratiated herself with Lady Wills, made a new friend in Margaret Woods who reciprocated more through obligation than desire, and a new Bridge partner in Julia Pryor, with whom she felt a warm connection.

Izzy sped through the lanes of Oxdenshire, feeling excited and pleased with her accomplishments on the one hand, puzzled and frustrated on the other. How was she going to resolve this stocking wearing thing? For Lord Wills, eccentric English behaviour wasn't out of place; in fact, it was expected, but for Colin Griggs, farmer and now businessman, it was a whole different story.

By the time she made it back to the farm, Colin had finished a toasted egg and bacon sandwich for lunch. He looked at her, trying to gauge her mood. She was confused by which emotion would predominate. Neither spoke; then they both spoke together.

'No, you first, I insist.' He was hoping for anything which might direct him toward her mood.

'I'm afraid,' she started, 'it's not good news for you.'

A look of dread came over his face. *What now,* he thought, he couldn't guess what was coming next.

'I need you to come shopping with me again.' She let out a huge smile and planted a kiss right on his lips. Inside, he felt a massive sense of relief.

'Of course, anything you say.' Shopping was the least problematic given all the scenarios he had played out in his head. 'Okay, so tell me all about it. Shopping for what? Come on, Izzy, and don't spare the details.'

'We've a personal invite from Lady Wills, or should I say, Diana, to her house party up at the Manor on Saturday. What do you say to that?'

'You clever old stick. That makes all my microwave dinners worth it.'

They both clasped each other's hands and jumped up and down together in a celebratory dance.

'You should have seen Margaret Woods' face after Lady Wills said to me, call me Diana. It was a real picture.'

'So does that mean that both the Major and Margaret are our sworn enemies?'

'No, no, quite the opposite. Margaret's need to be

accepted by Her Ladyship means that she's prepared to pay the price.'

'The price?'

'Yes, to be seen to be friends with us. The Major will do whatever she says, and better still, I'm partnered with Julia Pryor at Bridge. We won, and so she and Steve are also our best new friends. Colin, it's all working out; our plan is coming good.'

To say he was relieved, pleased, and excited was an understatement. 'So it's that little cocktail dress we saw the other day, I guess.' Colin was trying to compliment her, but his actual view of her in that dress came through.

'You know as well as I do. I haven't a cat in hell's chance of pulling that off. No, I need something more befitting a woman of my age and figure. I think this might mean a trip to London.'

He looked astonished. 'London! All the way to London! Surely Harpsden will have something in your size, style and colour. What's that new place just opened off the High Street? One of those dress agency places. You know, second hand.'

'Seconds Out, I think you'll find. And I thought it was all going so well.' She stared hard. 'Why would I go dressed to the biggest social event of the year, or in fact forever in Henslow, in a second-hand dress, and one probably that's been donated by one of the other guests? Can you imagine the gossip? How would she feel seeing me wearing it, and how would I feel? I'd just want the ground to open up and swallow me. No Colin. No, no, no. Get it!'

He got the message. 'Do you think I'd be of help? Haven't you got a girlfriend who'd go with you? What about Ann?' He said hopefully.

'Ann! Did I hear you right? Ann. Do you mean Ann Bishop? Have you looked at her recently? She's a lovely lady, but her dress sense. A black bin liner with neck and armholes would be a definite improvement in her usual attire…' Izzy tilted her head. 'What goes on in your head, Colin?'

'That's a no then. What about someone younger with more dress sense? Bob's daughter at the pub; she was extremely helpful to me.'

Izzy wasn't sure how to take that. 'Lucy. She'd have me wearing a pelmet for a skirt and a top so transparent I could use it to sieve fruit. No, it must be someone else, someone more my age, someone with taste.'

After a few more false starts, Izzy arrived at her preferred choice. 'I'll phone her right now.'

Colin, none the wiser, left her to it.

Julia answered. 'You must have read my mind. I was just saying to Steve how I'll have to go to town to find something. Tomorrow would be great. If we meet at the station, we can get the 10.00. Perfect.' They put the phone down. Izzy was delighted, and Colin was off the hook. He wanted to give Julia a big kiss.

'Colin, Bob Critchley here… Yes, fine, and you? Look, Colin, I've a favour. For this party at the Manor, I've located a whole load of furniture but need to get it collected and delivered. Any chance of using your lorry? I reckon we'd do it in one trip... Okay? Yup. Friday after lunch-time session? See you then.' Bob hung up and ticked off another item from his 'to-do list. It was all coming together. Even Lucy had got her friends to sign up for some waitressing. *Just the cash and carry Friday morning, and we're all set.* Bob was feeling pleased with how it was all going.

Lady Wills and Marg spent the last few days organising a cleaning company to get the Manor into some sort of serviceable shape. Davy had spent his time running in and out, dragging anything and everything back home in a desperate attempt to undo their good work.

'Davy!' *Note to oneself: never get another dog.* 'Margaret, what are we going to do with Davy?' She sounded exasperated.

'Maybe Stewart Ballard, the head groundsman at the Golf Club, could take him out. He walks the course most days; Davy would be well and truly exercised.'

'Yes, maybe. Have a word, please. Anyway, enough of that for now. How's the guest list coming?'

'I've handed out 90 invites, and so far, we have had 37 confirmed and 8 who can't make it. The rest we're waiting to hear from.'

Diana was trying not to let herself worry unnecessarily. 'Given this late hour, I don't think we'll hear from many more. It'll only be on the night we'll know. I hope that Critchley chap can cope.'

❧ ❧ ❧

By the Saturday evening of the party, the village was buzzing with the excitement. The Manor had seen more action in the last few days than it had done for many years. Bob was fretting, Marg was lording over everybody, and Lady Wills watched with curious interest while Davy slept.

The ladies retired back to the golf club to change, leaving Bob to complete the preparations. Bob's lists were well-thumbed, and nearly all the items ticked off to his own personal satisfaction. Even Kevin Glenn had made an effort, and provided he didn't speak, Bob believed he'd get away with using him as a waiter, greeting the guests with their first drink.

The bell on the Manor's Coach House Tower clock struck seven. Bob called his staff together.

'Right. We have just one hour before the guests arrive. You all know what you're doing and what you're responsible for.' He was feeling quite the Maitre d'. 'We want a slick, smooth operation. Lady Wills will arrive first and wants to do a quick inspection; after all, it's her house and party. She's entrusted me with the food and the bar. I'm putting my faith in you. Any questions?' He was hoping it was rhetorical. It wasn't. Kevin had a question.

'Kevin, what's wrong?'

'There's only one of me.'

'Some people might think that's a blessing.' The others laughed.

'No, I mean, shouldn't two waiters meet the guests with drinks?'

Bob thought for a few minutes. 'Can anyone fill in?' Everyone shook their heads. 'Okay, I'll see what I can do. Go back to your posts.' Bob was on his mobile straight away. Everyone he called was out or busy. He was stressing. 'Lucy, any ideas?'

'Not at this short notice. Basically, all my friends will be going out tonight. Oh, there is... no, sorry?' Her voice trailed off.

'Bob, we need some sort of dumb waiter. What about Griggsy? He's close by?' Kevin offered.

'Colin's on the guest list, Kev, so he's no good.'

'Well, I'm blowed! How'd he manage that?' Kevin thought hard. 'There is someone close to him who could do the job really well.'

'Who's that?'

'You'll think me a bit daft.' Kevin felt his cheeks go red.

'Depends on what you're going to say. Out with it, man.' Bob needed to get on.

'Colin's scarecrow. There I told you, you'd think I'm daft.'

'Scarecrow!' He wasn't expecting that. 'Have you lost your mind?'

'He just needs to stand here,' Kevin pointed to a space beside the main door, 'with a drinks tray propped on his arm. Me and him could do a double act. No one would notice. They'll help themselves to drinks, so what's the difference?'

'I'm not sure we have any choice. I'll ring Colin to say you're on your way. Go on, skedaddle! We've little time.'

Kevin was away on his mission. Bob was on his mobile. Colin and Izzy were too busy with their own preparations to answer the phone. Bob left a hurried message about borrowing the scarecrow and hung up.

Within a quarter-hour, Kevin was back with the scarecrow. He propped him up against the radiator and tied his jacket tails around the pipe for support. He then made a crook in its arm to get a silver tray to stay in place.

'I reckon I can get Bob to pay me twice using you. I've saved him from some embarrassment. What's the World coming to now! I'm talking to a scarecrow.' Kevin laughed to himself.

The sound of tyres on the gravel signalled Lady Wills' arrival, along with Major and Marg Woods. First through the front door was Davy, scampering and sliding across the polished wooden floors. Lady Wills led the Major and his wife. Kevin and the scarecrow were in place, with trays of sweet and dry sherry. Lady Wills, engrossed in taking in the unfolding scene, never noticed the scarecrow. Bob was hovering in the Grand Hall, watching for her reaction, while checking out his staff. The noise of more cars arriving filled the air. The guests were now coming in droves, and the sound of conversation replaced the noise of cars. Bob's stress levels increased; he was counting. She said 50 but the numbers had reached 58 already, and it wasn't eight-o'clock yet. He had allowed for extras, especially drinks, but the food was another matter.

The main staircase flowed into The Grand Hall. Lady Wills positioned herself on the third step up.

'I say, Major, would you be so kind as to quieten

the guests? I wish to say a few words.'

In his best military voice, he brought those assembled to silence.

'It is with great pleasure I see so many here tonight...' Lady Wills did her thankyous and told everyone about her plans and how she was looking forward to meeting and talking to everyone individually. 'And finally...' A marked sense of relief filled the room, 'I want to...' cut off in mid-flow as Colin and Izzy stumbled through the front door.

'Sorry we're late, but we've been robbed!' Colin's outburst silenced the room.

Everyone turned to see the commotion. Colin was out of breath, dishevelled, with clods of mud clinging to his shoes. Izzy looked the part in her Armani suit. The sight brought a variety of responses. Not the usual attire for the Griggs, nor were they seen as part of the "Harpsden set".

'Ah, Isobel, and Colin too, I presume.' Lady Wills raised her voice; the silence returned. 'So nice to see you, but please explain.'

'It's nothing, really.' Izzy was trying to make light of it. 'Just Colin has this attachment to, now this is going to sound daft—'

'Carry on, I'm curious. We're all curious.' Diana spoke for everyone.

'… in the field near the lane leading to the village, we've had a scarecrow there for more years than I care to remember.'

'Yes, I've seen him as we've driven past.'

'Well, he's become a sort of friend. Everyone talks to

him, even the local children. He's well-known hereabouts.'

Kevin was feeling uncomfortable.

'As we drove out tonight, Colin noticed he wasn't anywhere to be seen. After the Police helicopter incident of a few weeks back, where he'd been blown over, Colin thought he'd fallen flat on his face again. He stopped the car and peered into the field, but it was too dark to see. So he got the torch. You know, one of those megalite rechargeable jobs, with a five-mile beam. Nothing can hide from them. So he scanned the area and realised that the scarecrow was gone. Vanished, without a trace.'

Kevin coughed, hoping no one heard.

'You say gone, without a trace. But Colin, who would steal a scarecrow? There must be an explanation.' Lady Wills was trying to make him feel better. 'Can you think of anyone who would want to steal him?'

He shrugged his shoulders.

'You wait until the morning; he'll turn up somewhere. Now help yourself to a drink, both of you.' Diana made light of the situation.

They were both still standing at the entrance. Colin turned to Kevin, and Izzy turned toward the second waiter.

'Here you are, Colin. This will make things seem better.'

Kevin passed him a dry sherry. Izzy reached for her drink from the scarecrow's tray. Without looking up, she just picked up a glass, turning while she did, and walked toward the gathered guests. She never noticed.

Bob sidled up to Kevin. They spoke conspiratorially. 'That was a close one. How did she not notice? I thought you'd asked the Griggs if you could take him. Anyway, the bulk of the guests are here. Lady W will take everyone into the drawing-room real soon.' Bob continued in a low voice, 'I want you to slide our friend here out of the front door and into your car with minimum fuss and with no one seeing. If you can get him planted back in his field in his usual spot unnoticed, there's an extra tenner in it for you. Comprehendo?' Bob took a furtive look before leaving. No one seemed to be looking in their direction.

Kevin went on full alert, scanning the guests, paying special attention to Lady Wills and the Griggs. He waited. A few minutes passed. The flow of the arriving guests abated. *Okay*, he thought, *this is it! I just need to lose the tray and untie his jacket, and we'll be out of here in the blink of an eye.* Again, he surveyed the room of guests. The doors to the Drawing Room opened, and people moved through. *Now's my chance.* He had the scarecrow untied and under his arm in a trice. Making a last check around the Grand Hall, they were both out of the front door.

Bob noticed the vacant space but never saw them leave. *Excellent*, he thought. *Another crisis averted.*

Kevin headed down the drive at full tilt with the scarecrow propped up in the front passenger seat.

Jimmy Flanagan, as ace reporter, hung around the entrance of Henslow Manor, watching the arriving guests hoping to get a tit-bit or two he might use. *Okay, not crime reporting,* he thought, *but gossip is a good read.*

A vehicle careering down the drive drew his attention. Watching the fast-moving lights through the trees, poised, with camera in hand, Jimmy waited for it to reach the large stone pillars which marked the entrance to the estate.

Kevin glanced over at the passenger seat, 'Just hold tight, scarecrow; we'll have you back in the field in a jiffy. Poor old Colin won't know what's happened — oh, it's been stolen. He'll look a right chump, but that's not unusual for him.' The scarecrow never said a word and Kevin believed he'd got away with it.

Suddenly, the whole car lit up in a single blinding flash. Jimmy, hidden in the undergrowth on the opposite side of the road, pressed the camera's shutter. Kevin never saw the ambush. Confusion turned to panic, and he hit the accelerator pedal to the floor while yanking the steering wheel hard. The car's back end flipped on the gravel, spilling it from the drive onto the Henslow Road. In his adrenalin rush, Kevin let out a 'whoop', and within seconds the car had disappeared down the steep hill toward Griggs Farm.

Jimmy reviewed the picture. He was still standing in the bushes, and the light from the LCD screen lit up his face in an eerily haunting sort of way. *Wow, he thought, 'what are you two up to?* Now he was in a quandary. *Should I go to the Manor to view the party, or do I follow the fleeing vehicle?* He was drawn to the manor.

The free bar had seen a brisk trade for the last hour, with everyone sedately but constantly quaffing alcohol. The food had yet to appear. Lady Wills moved systematically around Marg's friends and acquaintances. She met a substantial number of people and was acquainted with far more names and other personal details than she'd ever recall.

Diana leaned over to Margaret. 'I think it's time we had something to eat. Can you be a dear and get Mr Critchley to do the honours?'

Marg slid away from the group to find Bob. 'She's ready for the food now. Can you get your staff to bring it from the kitchen?'

Bob scurried off.

Bob hoped she wouldn't disappoint him. 'Ann, are we ready to go?'

'Have been for the last half hour, Bob. Where's your daughter and her friends? I thought they were going to be waitresses.' Ann wiped her brow. 'Gosh, those ovens are hot.'

'So did I!' Bob looked about. 'The last I saw of them was around eight as they headed toward the scullery. Something about finding somewhere quiet to change. I'll round them up.'

Bob went out through the back door of the kitchen, looking for the girls.

'Ain't you ready yet?' Lucy was trying to get the other three to speed up. 'Dad will look for us soon. They'll want their food.'

Activity in the scullery moved at a pace. The door from the kitchen opened, and Bob entered. 'Right now, ladies—' He got no further. His jaw fell to the floor. Speechless, he just stared. They all noticed.

'Dad, what's up?' Lucy broke his trance.

'What's up? What's up? I don't know where to start. This is Henslow, not the Reeperbahn. You can't serve food dressed like that! What's Lady Wills going to say! In fact, what's anyone going to say? Look at you, all of you, you don't seem to realise most of the guests here are close to, if not already retired. This is a sedate party. Not a fancy dress night at the Pink Kitten Club.' His gast was well and truly flabbered. 'I distinctly remember saying to you, get four outfits suitable for waitressing. You know, a white blouse, black skirt with something for a pinny.'

'Oh, Dad, have you seen the stuff in Harpsden High Street? Most of its suitable for old maids. Basically, we wanted something trendier, something to make us look and feel good.' Lucy defended her purchasing decision.

'So where did these,' he paused, searching for the right words, 'these tart's outfits come from?'

'We're not tarts; they're rather well-fitting, snug, with little or no spare material.'

'So where did they come from?' Bob persisted.

'Ann Summers in Union Street.' Lucy sounded matter of fact. 'Apparently, French maids wear outfits like these. They're black with a pinny; I can't see what the problem is.'

'What about the four-inch stilettos and the bright red lipstick? And what's on your legs?' Bob thought perhaps he shouldn't have asked.

'Well, we needed something. Long pearly white legs in stilettos and short skirts don't look right somehow, so I got some stockings from where I work.' Lucy was straight faced.

'So stockings mean suspenders, no doubt!'

'Well, of course; otherwise, they'd roll down!

Don't you know anything, Dad?'

'What about the false eyelashes and the heavy mascara?'

'Okay, I guess we got kinda of carried away,' she looked to the rest for support, 'but I'm sure everyone will like the look. You'll see.'

Lucy and her three friends left the scullery and headed for the kitchen, leaving Bob verging on the edge of shock. All he could hear was the click-clack of high heels on the quarry tiles intermixed with the shrieks of laughter and the odd 'shhh'.

All four traipsed into the kitchen and took up a tray of canapés before heading for the drawing-room. No one spoke; Ann just watched in astonishment. Bob came in via the opposite door as the last girl left, mouthing something like, 'We've got to stop them,' but it was too late.

The drawing-room reverberated to the cheerful chatter and laughter of 70 plus guests who, at Lady Wills' expense, proceeded to get sozzled—nothing outrageous or untoward, just mellow, plus a little.

As the room was full and everyone was deep in conversation, the waitresses' entrance went unnoticed. They split up, heading for each corner of the room, distributing their lite-bites as directed. Toing and froing, click-clacking as they went, it became apparent that more and more of the guests noticed their apparel. Or more correctly, male guests took note. Chap after chap discretely nudged the fellow beside him, casting his eye toward some disappearing long stockinged leg as each girl moved around the room. Desperate not to alert their wives for fear of consequences, each snatched a sly, virtually imperceptible glance, but they didn't hide it for long.

Although no words were spoken, the ladies' elbows thrust harder and more frequently into the ribs of the by standing men as they observed each glance. Comments like 'eyes front' and 'you're old enough to be her father' were clearly audible. The parade of black nylon clad legs in four-inch stilettos kept on coming. It was only a matter of time until Lady Wills cottoned on.

'I say, Margaret, those young waitress gals…'

'Where? I hadn't noticed.' Marg was trying to play it down.

'What? Are you blind? Look over there.' Diana wasn't so cautious.

The Major came to life. 'They remind me of my time in North Africa. Fine gals there; you know, with the heat, they needed little clothing. Well, for a young hot-blooded man who'd been at sea for months, it was a sight to behold.'

'We're neither at sea, nor are they, young man!' Marg sounded quite rattled.

'I say, Major, these outfits are, well… just are—' Lady Wills was lost for words.

'Eye-catching, your Ladyship.' He rolled his moustache between his fingers as he contemplated the view.

'I was thinking more scandalous. Youngsters these days seem to think nothing of parading in the streets half-naked. You just watch them on a Friday night. Even in the depths of winter, hardly a stitch on, with their bits on display for anyone and everyone to see.' Though taken aback, Diana was seemingly accepting of the situation. The rest of the guests looked at her for a lead. Nonplussed, no one else made an overt fuss.

Bob Critchley peered into the drawing-room to see how his waitresses had gone down with the guests, and in particular with Lady Wills. He was relieved to see only a subdued commotion at their attire and pleased to see how busy they were. His bigger worry was the catering and the amount of food being consumed.

Jimmy Flanagan decided to visit the manor. After hiking up the long drive, he was now in sight of the building. The place was in near darkness, apart from the entrance hall and drawing-room. Gravitating toward the light, he got close to the windows for an uninterrupted view of the party. As usual, his camera was at the ready.

His eyes adjusted to the light to reveal an unexpected sight; a dog scurrying around the great hall, confused and excited. He wanted to be the centre of attention. Running between legs, he knocked a waitress off balance. Having lost her footing, she fell. In a hasty yet gentlemanly way, the Major lunged forward to steady her. Although he aiming for her waist, between her falling and bending, with an intention of stopping her from hurting herself, he placed his outstretched hand firmly on her buttocks. The momentum and twisting caused her already short skirt to ride up to reveal the full length of her stockings with suspenders, and the Major's

319

hand clasped to a pert cheek. Jimmy caught it all on camera.

He wasn't the only one to see. The dog's yelp plus Marg's scream alerted the entire room, who turned to see the commotion. The girl regained her balance, but various cries went up from around the room. 'Well held, Major!' and 'I see you got to the bottom of the problem.' 'Lookout Margaret; it'll be your turn next.' Major Woods tried to regain his composure. 'Only doing what any gentleman would do.' He spoke to no one and everyone. This brought more cheering and jibes. 'Was it necessary to leave your hand there so long?' And 'You dirty old man, you should be ashamed of yourself.'

The moment passed, and everyone appeared to be getting back to enjoying the party. In fact, they were all discussing the accident in hushed tones and threw the odd sly glance the Major's way.

❧ ❧ ❧

At the time incident Lady Wills was being introduced to Colin, as he stood with Izzy, Julia, and Steve Pryor.

'Colin, so nice to meet you finally; I've heard a lot about you and the accident. Poor thing; are you better now?' Lady Wills held out her hand.

Before he had time to take it or answer, a piercing scream filled the room, and all heads turned to see a show of stocking on a shapely leg.

'Oh, that reminds me, Colin, how is your circulation?' Lady Wills continued, 'I hear you're much like my father in that department.'

Colin's furrowed forehead said it all. 'That department? I'm sorry, I don't follow.'

'Yes, you know, don't go all shy on me now. Stockings, didn't your wife tell you? My father wore them all the time. It started during the War after the Americans arrived in Britain. He told Mother it was for his circulation; something about the nylon next to his skin.' She paused, 'You look unsure: did I get the wrong end of the stick?'

Colin muttered something, but it made little sense, and by which time, all the eyes had turned to the Major, so she never heard his response.

'I say, Major, there's spirit in the old dog yet,' Lady Wills added to the comments flying around the room. 'What do you say, Steve? You've known the Major for a good few years.'

'He's a proper gentleman, your Ladyship—'

'Diana, please.'

'I'm sure it was a complete accident. Anyway, walking around half-naked, it's not too surprising she got her—' Steve searched for a polite word, 'posterior felt.'

'You're right there, but mind you, she has a pleasing posterior.' Letting the comment lie, Lady Wills left the group to talk to more guests, leaving Colin, Izzy, Julia and Steve to ponder what they had just witnessed and what she'd said.

'Look, Colin. I've heard all this gossip and seen it on TV and in the newspapers. Go on, no one is listening, is it true?' Steve was trying to coax him.

'Is what true?'

'You know what Lady Wills was saying.'

'About her Father? How would I know? I never knew the chap?'

'No, Colin, about you.'

The question hung in the air. Colin was trying to think of some retort to get himself off the hook. Steve was hanging on his every word and had no intention of letting the moment pass. Colin took a deep breath. *If I shout out so everyone can hear, I might get rid of this elephant for once and for all.* Izzy sensed he was about to do something foolish and, in a split second, stamped on his foot. What came out was a loud howl and not the embarrassing revelation he'd intended.

Hopping in pain, he quizzed her. 'What was that for?'

'There's a time and place for everything, and now is neither the time nor place for stocking confessions.' Izzy looked daggers. 'We're just moving into society circles, and I don't want you putting the kybosh on it.'

'You were saying Colin.' Steve was still waiting for an answer.

'Oh, nothing; just you should never believe what you read in newspapers. Reporters put fiction writers to shame. If they don't know the truth, they make it up, and what is the truth gets blown out of all proportions? You should know better than anyone. Take your supposed attempted murder of me and look at how that was reported.'

Steve could only agree. He let the stocking subject go... nearly. 'But that young waitress wears those stockings well,' he was thinking to himself without realising that he'd made the remark out loud. Colin nodded in agreement, but Julia was close to stamping on Steve's foot. She didn't; instead, she looked daggers.

'Drink anyone?' Steve headed for the bar to extricate himself from his predicament.

'What is it with men and stockings?' Julia let the question hang. Colin didn't pick up the mantle; Izzy just mused with her, nodding in agreement. At that moment, a tray of lite-bites came in their direction, carried by one waitress. In unison, all three heads turned to watch her stocking-clad legs move across the room, added to by the familiar click-clack of her stilettos.

With everyone focussed on the disappearing legs, nobody noticed Lady Wills sidle up to Colin. 'Right Colin, we need to talk.'

'Your Ladyship!' He pulled back in surprise.

'Diana, please.'

'Sorry, Diana, what can I do for you?'

'I understand you have a hole business.'

'Err, well yes; Griggs Hole Farming.'

'Unusual, but as you know, I am planning extensive renovations. I believe I'll need your services. Now you'll soon find out my approach to getting the best job done is to use local people and work closely with them. That way, we can fully understand each other. You will know what I want, and I'll know what you can deliver. No nasty surprises doing it this way. How do you feel about that?'

'All sounds fine to me, your Ladyship... I mean Diana.'

'Right, good; I'd like to come and see your hole farm in the next few days. I'm quite free at present. How about Monday, early, say nine? Does that sound alright to you?'

He turned to Izzy. She'd been eavesdropping; she nodded. 'Yes, sounds fine. You know where to find us?'

'We've been driving up and down the lane daily for the last couple of weeks. I've seen your farm and him.'

'Him?' Colin echoed her.

'Yes, the scarecrow.'

'Oh, him! Yes, I think everyone knows him.'

'So I'll see you at nine. Will your animals mind Davy?'

'Davy, who's Davy?' Colin was clueless.

'Davy is my little Peke, the one that ran through that poor girl's legs. Luckily, the Major was there to save her.'

'Indeed lucky,' he shook his head, 'he was fortunate.' He looked wistful. Both Izzy and Diana looked at him in a rather old-fashioned way.

'I think we'd better be going, Diana. It's been a super evening, and so nice to meet you. On behalf of Colin and myself, I'd like to welcome you to Henslow. We look forward to doing business with you. Goodnight.' Izzy turned to Colin; they both smiled at Lady Wills.

'Well, thank you, Isobel and you Colin; until Monday morning.'

Soon the evening drew to a close, with no more incidents. Bob Critchley sighed, relieved it was all over. Ann popped the last sausage roll into her mouth, and the four waitresses phoned for a taxi to take them clubbing in Harpsden, dressed in their French maids' outfits. After all, it was only10.30 on a Saturday night.

Major Woods, Marg and Lady Wills, with Davy, took a taxi back to the golf club for a snifter.

'Well done, Margaret. I think that was a great success. A good turnout and plenty of hospitality. I trust you have the guest list. Maybe sometime next week we can go through it.' As she spoke, Diana viewed the night through the taxi window.

'Look there, Margaret, in the field.' The deep black shadow of the scarecrow against the night sky was clearly visible. 'I thought Colin said it'd been stolen. What was all that fuss about? Obviously, the man's mistaken. Did you see it, Major? How extraordinary! I'll be interested in hearing what he has to say on Monday. Most extraordinary.'

CHAPTER 22

EVERYTHING'S IN THE DETAIL

'Hey, it looks like we'll get an order. She's coming here; it's just what we wanted. See, all that Bridge playing, my new clothes, and the car hasn't been in vain.' Izzy, thrilled by the prospect of Dian's visit, danced around the kitchen like a four-year-old. 'She's coming here!'

She caught sight of her reflection. 'You know what? I'm going to have to go into Harpsden tomorrow for something to wear. Nothing too expensive, just a skirt and blouse to make me look professional like we're a proper business.' She bubbled over at the prospect of more new clothes. 'Of course, now I've got my car, I can take myself.'

I guess every cloud, Colin daren't speak his thought.

In more of an effort to make themselves look like an actual business, Izzy cleaned and polished the dining room table. They had stripped the room of domestic clutter and replaced it with business apparel. The bookshelves now contained box files, albeit they were empty, and she had brought the computer in from the kitchen. A pile of A4 pads with pens and pencils and a tray of coffee cups, milk, sugar and a plate of biscuits lay in the table centre. The dining room now looked more like a Board Room.

'Everything's in the detail,' Izzy whisked her duster over the table for the umpteenth time. 'We will sit her here,' she pointed to the head of the table, 'with you on her right. I'll sit opposite. She needs to feel welcomed and respected without feeling crowded and pressurised. The seating arrangements will assure her we are listening to her needs as a customer and not just forcing our ideas onto her.' She was animated.

'Colin, say something. I need you to be on top form, to have the answers to her questions, to sound authoritative, decisive and in control. She'll be here any minute. When she does, I'll answer the door, and as she comes into the room, be sure to stand and step forward to greet her.' Izzy scanned the room once more just to make everything was just so.

At the sound of a vehicle pulling into the yard, Colin took up his place; Izzy hovered in the doorway. They heard a door slamming, followed by the rat-a-tat-tat of their knocker. Izzy counted in her head to 20, straightened her blouse and skirt again, put a smile on her face and opened the front door, speaking as she did.

'Your Ladyship, Diana, good morning to you and...' she took in the sight, 'what on earth are you doing here?'

'Well, that's a great welcome; I guess you were expecting someone else. Here.' Bruce, the DHL driver, thrust a large reinforced envelope into her hand, the sort that photographs come in. 'Sign here please, Mrs G. How's your Colin? Saw him on the news again; he's a lad. Say hi to him.' Before she had time to answer, Bruce turned and left. As the DHL van sped off, Lady Wills' car came into view.

Izzy had no time to open the delivery before Diana was out of the taxi and heading up the steps with Davy tucked under her arm.

'Diana, good morning. How lovely to see you. Do come in.' They shook hands. 'We're in here.' Izzy directed her into the dining room as was.

'Your Ladyship,' Colin noticed her frown, 'sorry, Diana, I hope we find you well.' He shook her hand 'Please,' he held out a chair.

'Good morning to you both. I can see you're busy, and my needs are simple, so I suggest we get straight to the point.'

'Coffee?' enquired Izzy.

'Thank you, white without sugar, please dear.'

'What about Davy? Would he like a drink?'

'No, he's fine. Thank you all the same.'

Diana gave them a synopsis of her plans for the Manor, particularly her needs in the garden. She described the way she visualised a series of feature ponds running down the long walk, forming a continuous chain of points of interest. And how each pond would be stocked with different fish, goldfish, carp etc., and varieties of water plants to suit each fish type's habitat.

Colin and Izzy took copious notes. Uppermost in both their minds was the need to get the contract right. No more repeats of their last hole fiasco. This was a significant chance, in fact, their only chance of making the hole business work, of redeeming their reputation, and of getting a prestigious customer whose name alone would guarantee future orders.

Over the next hour, they talked, discussed,

questioned and summarised; sketches were made, site visits organised, timescales worked out. As they talked, Izzy and Colin kept throwing each other glances, confirming they understood her needs. They could sense this was an order for the taking, and although pricing hadn't been agreed, Diana's budget of £15,000 for the ponds made them attentive, excited, and extremely focused.

'So Colin, you're clear about what you have to do and what I'm looking for?' Diana needed reassurance.

'The site visit should fill in any missing gaps. I need to finalise the plans and prepare a quote. Have you your diary at hand? We might as well make a date now.' He was assertive, but not pushy.

'Well, how about tomorrow at,' she hesitated, 'isn't it Bridge tomorrow, Izzy?'

'Let's see, Tuesday, yes, in the morning.'

'Good, will I see you there?' From looking at Izzy, she turned to Colin. 'And after lunch, say 2.30 at the Manor. How does that sound?'

Once again, Izzy and Colin shared glances to checking their respective reactions. 'We look forward to it,' they chimed in unison. There were smiles all round. The sound of a vehicle drawing up interrupted the moment.

'Ah good, my taxi's returned.' Diana collected up her belongings, including Davy, and all three headed for the front door. As they watched Her Ladyship get into the rear of the taxi, with her back turned, they sneaked a quick celebratory cuddle. The driver closed her door, and she wound down the window.

'Colin, just one last thing; could you provide a testimonial or reference from a previous job? I find personal recommendations so reassuring and reliable.' The taxi started moving; Diana closed the window, waving as she did.

From happy, smiling faces, their expressions changed to sheer disbelief. If Diana had looked in the rear-view mirror, she would have seen them horror-struck, rooted to the spot, and nauseous with knotted stomachs.

'What are we going to do? Our only previous job was with the Golf Club. If she talks to him, we can kiss this contract goodbye.' Colin's complexion was ashen; Izzy was no better.

'Well, at least I'm talking to his wife. She'll be at Bridge tomorrow; maybe I can get her to put in a good word for us.' They both turned to go back into the house.

'Straws come to mind.' He shuffled his feet; he felt too troubled to lift them.

The large manila envelope delivered by DHL stood propped up on the hall stand; neither noticed. Colin's dropped shoulders suggesting he had all but given up. Back on the Boardroom table, their notes and sketches lay scattered. Scooping up the lot, he unceremoniously dumped them into the wastepaper bin, to Izzy's dismay.

'Colin, what the flipping heck—'

'There's no point. We're just kidding ourselves. The Major won't say anything good about us. Why would he? Look at the problems we've caused him, never mind the expense. It's hopeless, Izzy, just hopeless.' His head hung in his hands.

'I thought you were my hero, my rock, not some wimp who'd fall at the first hurdle. Nothing's easy. Think how far we've come since the Golf Course contract. Look at what we've both had endured. Don't buckle Colin, think!' She was standing over him. He reached out his arm and held her around the waist.

'I know you're right, but after the excitement of the meeting and seeing some light at the end of the tunnel, to be hit by this when you least expect it, I just feel like I've been punched, winded, deflated.' He pulled her toward him for a cuddle. 'I know you're right; we need to work out what we can do. A strategy; how we will make ourselves indispensable to Diana, so countering the Major's reference.' He slid his hand down from Izzy's waist to her bum and gave her a playful squeeze.

'Colin, I thought you were too upset.'

'If it's good enough for him, then it's good enough for me,' he joked. She smiled.

'What's that I can feel?' He slid his palm over her buttocks and thighs. 'Are you wearing stockings, Izzy?' His voice was tentative but hopeful. She squirmed.

'Oh, that reminds me, Bruce was here earlier. You remember, the DHL delivery driver who congratulated you on wearing stockings.'

'How could I forget?'

'He brought a large brown envelope.' She wriggled free before disappearing to retrieve it. 'I wonder what it is. It's got a cardboard stiffener and on the outside says 'DO NOT BEND'.' Fishing inside, she pulled out a large photograph.

'And,' he said excitedly.

Her mouth fell open as she stared at the image.

'Come on, show me. What is it?' Holding the top and bottom edges, she slowly rotated it for him to see.

'What is it? I'll tell you what it is; it's a guarantee of our £15,000 contract. It's a lifeline. It's more luck than we could ever have asked for. The Major is about to write us a glowing reference.' She was back on top of the world. Colin stared at the image.

The Bridge Club turnout included Izzy in yet another new outfit. From the outset, the chatter in the room was about Lady Wills' party: who had been there, who wore what, who'd drunk too much, the waitress' outfits, amongst other topics. The room was buzzing.

'Right, ladies; let's not forget why we're here. Silence now; there'll be plenty of time during coffee to catch up on all the gossip. Organise yourselves into fours. Let play commence.' Marg, paired with Diana, sat down at her table. Izzy and Julia made up the foursome. Cards dealt, the bidding began; Diana was on the dealer's left.

'Two Clubs.'

'Two hearts' came from Izzy.

'Two spades' was Marg's bid.

'Three hearts, ' added Julia.

'My hand is useless; no-bid.' Diana offered.

'Three no trumps,' Izzy called. 'So Diana, did you enjoy your party?' she continued.

Marg threw her a disapproving glance. 'Come ladies, can we concentrate on the cards?' She sounded testy.

Izzy wasn't sure if it was Marg's commitment to Bridge or her dislike of her and Diana's friendship, which seemed to be on a par with her own.

Although Marg wasn't involved with the Golf Club farce, she'd been subject to the Major's rants about that unforgettable day. Too, she saw Diana as her friend. After all, she'd just spent the last few weeks driving her around the area, introduced her to Bridge Club, and she'd organised a hugely successful party, yet Izzy was quite a Bridge master. *I'll have to keep my eye on her,* Marg thought.

Play continued; the atmosphere relaxed, and degenerated into more of a coffee morning with cards as an excuse. Marg, despite her firmness, was complicit in letting the conversation flow.

Diana peered over the top of her cards. 'One thing I meant to ask you yesterday, Isobel, was about your scarecrow. What happened on Saturday evening?'

Izzy looked rather embarrassed.

'I remember you and Colin arriving in a bit of a commotion, saying something about the scarecrow being stolen, yet as we passed the lower field a couple of hours later, there he was, for all to see.'

Marg nodded in agreement. *I'm interested to hear this excuse.*

'We're like you, Diana, confused. I'm certain he was missing as we left for the party, but by the time we returned home, he was back in his usual place, albeit rather wonky, and facing the wrong way. Later we found out he smelt of drink. It's as if he'd been down the pub for a few beers and was now the worse for wear.' She felt rather stupid; it was only a scarecrow, after all.

'I take it neither of you has seen yesterday's Harpsden Evening Post.' Julia was rooting in her shopping bag. 'Here, take a look.' She unfolded the paper. On the front page was a picture of a speeding car leaving the Henslow Manor Estate with two people aboard. The caption read 'New underclass serves the toffs!' The conversation around the table stopped. All four women exchanged glances as they tried to make sense of the picture. Izzy was the first to speak.

'There's no doubt who the passenger is, but what I don't understand is what he's doing in a car driven by Kevin Glenn and why are they leaving the Manor at speed.' Izzy felt relieved that her story about the scarecrow's theft was confirmed but confused as to why.

Diana was also confused, but clearly, the car was leaving her estate and the driver she recognised as the waiter on the door. In the blur of the moment she'd seen, there were two, but never noticed who the second one was. Someone obviously aimed the caption at her. Marg, too, felt guilty given she'd organised the catering, which reflected on her and how well she'd done.

While the others contemplated the picture, Izzy read the rest of the article; it said nothing but speculated about what might have been. Noticing the by-line, *so Jimmy Flanagan,* she thought, *you were hanging around the Manor Saturday night. Thank you so much.* She smiled to herself. As she saw it, the picture that arrived by DHL and now this one on the paper's front page put Marg and the Major on a back foot while obligating Diana to her and Colin.

'I think it's time for coffee, ladies.' Marg stood first, closely followed by Izzy.

'Can you spare me a minute, Margaret?' Izzy guided her away from the rest of the members. 'Whilst we're discussing photographs and newspapers, this has come into my possession.' She handed Marg a copy of the picture received via DHL. 'As Diana will seek a reference from the Major about Griggs Hole Farming and our ability to complete a contract, I was hoping we can rely on him to say the right thing.' Izzy watched Marg's expression change from quizzical to outright horror as she took in the picture. It clearly showed the Major grasping the thong-clad cheeks of a young lady's buttock.

'You wouldn't! You daren't! He's a pillar of the community. This could ruin him!' Marg's narrowed eyes and her facial contortion suggested she might burst. Izzy said nothing. Marg thought more about the situation and realised she had little option. She spoke through gritted teeth, 'Okay, I'll do my best.' Ungraciously thrusting the picture into her handbag, she turned on her heels and headed for coffee.

Izzy was left to reflect on what she'd done. She felt guilty, but in her mind, it was unjustified as they'd done nothing wrong at the Golf Club. *It was more of a lack of understanding about rabbits and their burrowing instincts, which created the disaster. And anyway, why should our future business prospects be blighted by over-zealous rabbits?*

The game concluded in near silence. Julia,

untouched by events, nor party to the various conversations, was oblivious to what was going on; she and Izzy won at Bridge.

'Are you coming with Colin this afternoon, Isobel?' Diana's inquiry broke the uneasy peace.

'No, this is his area of expertise; I do more the backroom stuff. It's a team effort.' She sounded reassuring. 'As soon as he finishes his drawings and costings, we'll get the quote to you. I know you're keen to get started.' Izzy glanced in Marg's direction.

Over a farm lunch, Izzy explained to Colin all the machinations of the morning. He, too, felt uncomfortable about what they'd done, but the feeling was short-lived. As he left for his meeting with Lady Wills, he had an extra spring in his step.

Izzy came out to wave him off. 'Don't forget Colin, this is important; no mess-ups this time. Always be professional, courteous, yet warm. People buy from people. Lady Wills is no different.'

With the sounds of her advice ringing in his ears, he set off. 'Come on, old chap,' Old Alfred Mac spluttered into life. 'That hill up to the Manor is a steep incline. I know you've got the power to get up there.' He pulled out of the yard and turned toward Turville, Henslow Manor and a new future. The knot in his stomach tightened as he drove through the large stone pillars into the estate. The drive was wooded on both sides until it came within a hundred yards of the house.

From here on, it was rolling lawns with assorted flower beds, stone sculptures, and steps leading to the different levels. At one time, it must have been magnificent, but now it was semi-derelict, forlorn, overgrown and in need of copious amounts of money and TLC.

The heavy rumble of the diesel engine had not gone unnoticed. Davy came scampering across the lawn to meet him, not as a friend but in his self-appointed role of the guard dog. By the time Colin had killed the engine and climbed down from the cab, Lady Wills had arrived on the scene also.

'Good afternoon Diana.' *Be professional, courteous, but warm, don't blow it,* he repeated to himself.

'Good afternoon Colin, I see you're right on time; excellent.' She was a bit of a stickler for punctuality. 'We'll start by taking a stroll down the Long Walk so you can see for yourself what's needed and where.'

With clipboard in hand, he took detailed notes and made many sketches. *Detail, it's all in the detail,* he repeated to himself. His knotted stomach freed as he felt more in control, more at ease, and more comfortable about what he was doing. He was enjoying himself.

While the pair were deep in conversation, Davy ran here about investigating all the while. In the long grass, there was a great commotion as he disturbed a rabbit. First, the rabbit and then Davy ran hell for leather passed Lady Wills and Colin. Diana chastised the dog, but Colin froze, a stark reminder of his last contact. All his fears and doubts came rushing back. He reminded himself to *dig deep and remember Izzy's advice. Where would I be without her?*

'Did you hear me, Colin?'

'Err, sorry your Ladyship, I mean Diana. Something distracted me for a second. Could you repeat that, please?'

'I said, do you think we ought to have one large pond or a series of, say, six smaller ones meandering down the Long Walk?' She sounded pithy.

'Well, let me prepare drawings covering both options, with costings so that you can make a better-informed decision. There are benefits and drawbacks to both. It's a big decision as it will impact the whole garden layout and so shouldn't be made without due consideration.' He felt he'd rescued the situation.

'Yes, you are right. Best not make such a significant decision until we have better information.' Her voice sounded much softer.

He could breathe again. 'I'll need half an hour to measure up here and make some sketches'

'Sketches!' Her voice showed some surprise. 'Oh, I thought you might use one of those digital cameras. Much quicker and far more accurate. Well, you know what you're doing. You're the expert, after all.'

That hit him like a punch in the ribs. She had a demure manner, but she was no fool. *I need to recover from that.*

'No, you misunderstand me; the sketches are conceptual drawings, you know, artists' impressions, of the potential finished project, and as clever as digital technology is, they haven't photographed thoughts yet.' His answer was delivered in a light-hearted, almost flippant style. He waited for her response. She just smiled and walked on.

'Let me know when you're finished. I'll be in the house.' She turned on her heels and set off back toward the Manor with Davy in hot pursuit.

He continued on his own measuring and drawing, making notes and recording until he had filled several sheets of his clipboard. Satisfied he had captured enough data, he set off back toward the Manor. *Before I finish here,* he thought, *I must check again to understand what she is trying to achieve.* He reached the front door. It was wide open, with many tradespeople coming and going. The house refurbishment had started in earnest. The large entrance hall showed no signs of the party. Instead, scaffolding towers were erected; dust sheets lain and a host of decorating supplies filled any free space.

'She does nothing by halves,' He said out loud, but to no one in particular. 'I need to make sure I get this right.'

'Ah Colin, there you are,' her ladyship spotted him amongst the paraphernalia. 'have you got all you need?'

'I believe so, thanks. I need some time now to sort it all out. Just to be clear, you are looking to me to provide six holes suitable for ornate ponds to be placed at intervals down the Long Walk?'

'Yes, that's it. I think six would be a good number. Any less, and they will lose impact as a feature, and any more would be too fussy. So yes, six I think will be just right.'

'And the idea of a single long pond, is that still on the cards?'

'No, on consideration, I think not. The six ponds will give a lot more scope for experimenting with different habitats and fish stocks.' Diana waited expectantly.

'Right, I'll be off now, your Ladyship. I'll get the quote to you by Friday.' He took her hand, shook it, turned and left. His stride was long and purposeful, reflecting his determination.

     ‽   ‽   ‽

Izzy busied herself in Colin's absence. He'd been gone two hours and his return wasn't soon enough for her.

'Well, how did it go?' She couldn't contain her excitement. 'What was Diana like? Do you think we'll get the business? Colin, tell me something.'

The sound of Old Alfred Mac's engine drowned out her questions. He closed it down and jumped from the cab.

'Hi darling, I think that went pretty well. She's spending a lot of money on the place. It's crawling with all sorts of tradespeople. You wouldn't recognise it at the party. She doesn't hang around. Any chance of a cuppa?' He sounded cheerful and headed for the kitchen with her in tow.

'Right, it's quote time. I promised we'd have it to her by the end of the week.' He rubbed his hands, readying himself for the task.

CHAPTER 23

A KISS FROM HENRY

'Marg, have you seen the back seat of the Mercedes? It's covered in dog hairs. It's just not good enough. That dog of Diana's shed fur like it was going out of fashion.' Graham stormed out of the kitchen.

The phone started ringing. Marg picked it up.

'Margaret dear, it's me, Diana. Glad I caught you. I've been meaning to ring you for a few days now. I've not truly thanked you for all the sterling work you did over the last month; all that driving and organising. It was so kind of you, more than kind, it was beyond the call of duty. Anyway, what I'm trying to say that I would like to repay your kindness and take you and the Major out to dinner. What day would suit you?'

'Oh Diana, that's sweet, but there's no need to, you know. It's been all my pleasure.'

'Margaret, come now, you've been at my beck and call, I insist, though I need to ask one more thing. Be a dear and book the restaurant if you'd be so kind. I don't know where the best places are to eat around here. Any ideas?'

'Well, our favourite is the Greedy Goose, an excellent gastro pub off the Harpsden Road. I'll call them and see what availability they have. It's popular, but they'll fit us in. Don, the owner, is a member of the Golf Club. I'll check with the Major, but I'll try for this coming Friday at eight.'

'7.30, if you don't mind. I prefer not to eat too late.'

'Sure, I'll confirm and let you know. Bye now.' Marg hung up the phone. 'Did you hear Graham?' There was nothing. 'Graham,' she called again; still nothing. *He's never around when you want him,* she thought and set about the house to find him.

He was in the garage, busy vacuum cleaning the back seat of the Mercedes. The noise made him oblivious to her calls.

'Graham, I've been calling you for the last five minutes.' Still no response. 'Graham' she was louder this time. The car's insulation muted the sound inside, and the noise of the vacuum further blotted out her cry's. She resorted to a poke in the ribs.

He was almost bent double when he received the unexpected prod. His reflex action was to stand abruptly and twist toward the source. As his head and torso were stretching into the back seat of a car, he had little room to carry out either, with any success. Instead, the outcome was less predictable, and the consequences more severe. The simultaneous actions of standing and turning resulted in him striking his half-turned head into the roof of the car with sufficient force to knock him off balance. Falling forward, rather than landing on the back seat, he ended up in the foot well. Wedged between the front and rear seats, he groaned. To add to this cacophony, the vacuum was still running. From a deep melodious drone, it switched to a high-pitched squeal as the nozzle resolutely tried to suck the side of his neck into the depth of its workings.

'Graham, are you alright! Sorry dear, I didn't mean to startle you. I just wanted to know if you were free on Friday night for dinner with Lady Wills.' Marg was caught between a caring wife and the need to know his answer.

The unexpected turn of events, the continuing screaming of the vacuum in his ear, coupled with his ungainly position, meant checking his diary was the last thing on his mind. The response that followed bore no resemblance to a coherent reply or, in fact, any intelligible answer of any sort. He vigorously shook his free leg and arm, but with his face pressed into the sumptuous seating material, his words were lost.

She was unsure what to do, but knew she must do something. Without thinking, she bent down, taking hold of both his feet, and pulled for all she was worth. Being all of 5 foot 2 inches and 8 stone, that wasn't a lot... fortunately. He was wedged tight.

The onslaught on his feet, with no prior warning, exacerbated rather than eased the situation. He didn't move, he just gesticulated wildly, shouted and became more firmly wedged. The screech of the vacuum cleaner penetrated her consciousness. She ran to the wall switch and turned it off. In the ensuing silence, she could make out his mumbles.

'Slide the front seats forward.'

She leapt first into the passenger side and shuffled her bum whilst holding up the locking mechanism till the seat had travelled its full distance. She then ran around to the driver's seat and repeated her actions. The extra few inches were sufficient for him to extricate himself.

'Oh, I'm so sorry. I never meant you to end up being hurt!' She smothered him with sympathy. 'I was trying to get your attention.'

'I'm Okay. Don't fuss. No bones broken.' He brushed himself down and straightened his clothes. 'Well, at least I cleaned up all those dog hairs.' He turned back toward the open rear car door and gathered up the vacuum. 'I think a cup of tea is in order, or something stronger.' He looked at his watch. 'It's after 6.00; I think something stronger wins.' He headed back into the house. She joined him.

'Glass of wine or a peg, dear?'

'Peg please, with plenty of water.'

As Graham was getting undressed for bed, she noticed his neck. 'What's that?'

He had his jumper half off, with his arms raised above his head, so the now inverted jumper blocked his vision.

'Look, Marg, I can't see a damn thing from in here. What are you on about?'

'Your neck; it looks like you've got a large love bite.' She sounded accusatory.

'Don't be ridiculous; where would I get a love bite from?'

'Exactly where, or more importantly, from whom?' She marched up to him to get a closer look. 'It's as plain as the nose on your face. I've not seen one for years, but I know a love bite when I see one.'

He was struggling to get the jumper off. The more he wriggled, the more difficult it became. 'Can you help me? This bloody jumper seems to have a mind of its own.'

'If you think I'm going to help you, you've another thought coming. Get her to help you. Your fancy woman, the harlot!' With that, Marg stormed from the bedroom.

Graham was still struggling with the jumper and the turn of events. 'What fancy woman. Marg, I've no idea what you're on about, and you don't either.' He bent himself double with his arms outstretched and head close to the floor to free himself. Stabbing with his right foot, he stood on the jumper before he gave a hefty yank. An 'ouch' followed, but he was free. Without hesitation, he headed into the bathroom and the large mirror over the sink. To his utter surprise, there it was.

'What the heck!?' He pulled at his skin and turned his head in a variety of poses for a better look. *It sure looks like one, but it can't be! I haven't been with another woman since I got married over 40 years ago, well, except in my head, but no way that would cause a love bite. The mind is powerful and can play many tricks, but manifest a mark like this is beyond even its capability.* 'Of course,' he said to himself. 'Of course! Well, if she thinks I can see another woman, I'll let her stew in it.' He set about cleaning his teeth. Smiling inwardly, he brushed with abandonment until he heard the sounds of her back in the bedroom.

'If you think I'm sharing a bed with you tonight, you've another think coming. How could you? Why would you?' Her welling tears made it difficult to understand her.

Returning to the bedroom, he was met with a loud sniff; she was now in full flow. Tears were streaming down her cheeks. He walked over to cuddle her; she recoiled at his touch.

'Get off me.' She wriggled free.

'Marg darling, see sense; I've not been with anyone else. There is no one else who could come close to you.' He didn't sound sincere. The lightness of the tone was inappropriate for the seriousness of the situation.

'And you're not even sorry.' She did another large sniff.

'Okay, I cannot lie.'

'You mean there is someone else?'

'Was.'

'Was; I suppose now you've been found out you're going to break it off with her and tell me how sorry you are, how it was a fling that meant nothing —'

He cut her off, 'it's a him, not her.'

'Oh, my God! And that's supposed to make me feel better!?' The tears gushed down her cheeks. 'A him! Graham, how could you? Do I know him? How long has it been going on? What's his name? Graham, don't make it worse for yourself; tell me everything.' She stood toe to toe with him, lifting herself as high as she could.

'Henry.' He was quite calm. 'And yes, you know him.' He sounded matter-of-fact.

'Henry!' she screeched. 'Henry? Henry who?'

'I don't know his second name, my love. I only know him as Henry.'

'I don't know any Henrys'. You said I knew him. What are you talking about?'

He reached out, taking a firm grip of her hand. She tried to struggle free, but he held it tight. 'Come on, follow me.' With that, he marched her out of the bedroom, down the stairs, they turned and stopped by the under stair cupboard door.

'Are you ready for this?'

'What? Why have you brought me here? Stop messing around. You won't get round me like this. We need to talk.' She could feel her blood boiling; her face turned puce.

He let go of her hand. Bending forward, he opened the door. 'Here, meet Henry.' She looked into the cupboard. There he was; his tubby red body, bright white eyes, ear to ear grin, all topped with a dome-shaped black hat staring back at her. It was the vacuum cleaner he'd been using earlier. 'This afternoon, when I got stuck in the back seat, remember how I fell onto the vacuum. The nozzle was sucking at my neck. There is no other woman or man. My love bite is only an over amorous cleaner. Satisfied now?'

She didn't know what to do or say. 'I'm so sorry—' she hesitated. She was relieved, angry, confused all at the same time. 'Why did I think—' again she faltered? 'Graham, I don't know what to say. I've been a bit silly. Of course, you'd never cheat on me, nor I on you. I should have known all along there was a perfectly reasonable explanation. Please forgive me. I am so sorry.' The sincerity in her voice convinced him. He smiled at her before leading her back up to the bedroom.

∾ ∾ ∾

'I'm looking forward to this.' Marg continued with her make-up. 'It'll be nice to see Diana socially; being her PA was insightful, but tonight we're her guests.'

Graham grunted in agreement. He was busy with his cut-throat razor, removing some stubborn bristles from below his bottom lip.

'Graham, you do realise she has an ulterior motive for inviting us.'

'What! I can't hear you properly. He had the tap running. 'Marg, I'll be finished in a minute. Can it wait?' He emerged from the en-suite, patting his cheeks and neck with a towel—it was peppered with blood spots.

'Why don't you use your electric shaver? The laundry service must think Sweeney Todd lives here.' He either didn't hear or chose to ignore her remarks.

'What were you saying about some motive?'

Marg raised her eyebrows. *It's a waste of time*, she thought; he *never listens to me*. 'Diana, she'll use the occasion to get your opinion on Griggs Hole Farming for her ornate garden ponds. She prefers to work on recommendations, remember? And since the Golf Club is their only customer, she'll value what you have to say.'

'Who's idea was that?' He couldn't believe what he was hearing. 'If I had my way, that Griggs man would never work again. He's caused me no end of trouble, never mind the cost, the pounds, shillings and pence—'

'We stopped using shillings when we went decimal in 1971.'

'I know that. Look, Marg, you know what I mean, and there's the cost to my reputation, to my standing in the community. I'm a laughingstock. Why would I recommend him? To my worst enemy perhaps, but not to the likes of Lady Wills. Such a refined person, a genuine aristocrat, a pleasure to know and an honour to have her befriend us. She trusts us. Why would I put that in jeopardy and definitely not for the likes of Colin Griggs?' His face crinkled as if he'd just eaten a lemon. 'A nice enough chap, I suppose, for a farmer, but under no circumstance would I give him a reference. I don't want to hear any more about it. Tonight I want to enjoy the food and the company and not have to be reminded of that, that, that incident.' He was close to shouting.

'You're definite about that? I couldn't persuade you to change your mind?' Marg wouldn't let the topic drop.

'Didn't I make myself clear?' He strode across the bedroom and threw open the wardrobe door. 'Under no circumstances.' He rooted through his suits, pushing them back and forth on the rail but not focussing on a particular one. He muttered. She couldn't make out what he was saying but knew she had to approach the subject again. She opened the bedside cabinet drawer and took out a large envelope. He appeared next to her, holding a beige summer suit.

'You can't wear—' she stopped herself. The look

of thunder on his face changed her mind.

'What's that?' He was abrupt.

'What darling?' She was trying to defuse the situation.

'That! In your hand; that envelope.'

'It's why you'll give Colin Griggs a glowing reference.' Tentatively, she held it out for him.

The deep furrows on his forehead told her he did not know what she was on about. He snatched it from her. She jumped up, hurrying to the bathroom to avoid the fall-out. As the door closed, he opened the envelope. The picture was backside foremost. Written on it was 'To Colin & Izzy. Sorry for all the problems I caused you. I hope this helps to make up for what I did. Jimmy'. He flipped it over.

'What have I done to deserve this?' He fell silent and just stared at the picture. After a few minutes, she became curious and concerned. Venturing forth from her sanctuary, she saw Graham sitting on the bed. He was static, not even looking up as she approached. She put her arms around his shoulders.

'You don't have to lie; just be economic with the truth. Diana knows there was a problem with the course opening, and in fairness, Colin worked hard. Yes, he was let down by rabbits—' Marg's consolatory words failed. At the mention of the 'R' word, he visibly flinched.

'I didn't mean to molest that girl. I was just trying to save her from falling over, from hurting herself.'

'I know, Graham, but the photo shows something quite different. Your hand is grasping her bare buttocks. Anyone seeing it would draw the same conclusion.'

'No more. Yes, I'll do it, I suppose.' He sounded defeated.

❧   ❧   ❧

'Ah, Lady Wills lovely to see you,' Graham kissed her on each cheek, 'sit here, my dear.' He pulled out a chair. Marg sat next to her while Graham sat opposite. The evening progressed with the usual chitchat about the weather, the journey, how nice the Greedy Goose was, menu suggestions and the like.

'Graham, you are looking formal. It's Friday night, and this is a thank-you meal for all the kindness shown to me by you both and, in particular, Margaret. Come on, relax. Lose the jacket and loosen your tie. Better still, take it off altogether.'

'No, that's okay, your Ladyship.' He shuffled in his seat. 'I like to dress for dinner. Army tradition, you know.'

'See, there you go again. It's Diana. How many more times must I remind you? Go on now, I insist; remove the jacket and tie.'

He was feeling bullied and felt he had little option. First, the jacket went and then, without further thought, he loosened his tie and undid his collar button.

'Better now, Diana?' He pulled at the unbuttoned collar to reveal his neck.

'Well, it's a start.' She smiled at him and stared. From where Marg was sitting, she couldn't see his neck and the 'love bite', but Diana had an uninterrupted view. She said nothing but couldn't help wondering about how he got it; after all, he always seemed so respectable.

'I hear the refurbishment is well underway.' Graham continued with his polite conversation.

'Well, I'm so glad you brought that up. Yes, we're a week into it now. I'm extremely pleased with how it's progressing. The party Margaret organised was such a triumph; meeting all those locals, I gathered so many tradesmen's details, all with great recommendations. It's been a real bonus. I feel so confident now that the project will be an enormous success.' Diana was upbeat about how it was all going.

Her enthusiasm sent a chill down Graham's back. *How can I lie about that Griggs fellow?* He broke out in a cold sweat.

'Are you okay, Major?' Diana noticed.

'Yes, sure, fine. It's rather warm in here, that's all.' He wiped his brow with his napkin. Pouring himself a glass of water, he drank deeply. 'So you take great store in personal recommendations, then?' He knew she did, but wanted to stall her, asking about the inevitable. He didn't find lying easy, nor did others find his lies convincing.

'It's the only way. People won't recommend it unless they are truly pleased with the outcome. After all, it reflects on them.' Diana looked directly into his eyes.

Ouch, that hurt. The Major recoiled. More beads of sweat ran down his brow. 'How do you mean Diana?' His voice was hesitant.

'Graham, you didn't get to where you are today by accepting the word of fools. You used your initiative, your guile, and your perceptiveness to sort the wheat from the chaff. Looking someone in the eye gives a true insight into their honesty and integrity. Likewise, listening to them enthuse about their refurbishment, or extension, or whatever, is an accurate reflection of how pleased they are with the result and so with those who did the work. Making a recommendation shows how capable you are of making good decisions, of not being duped, of being an excellent judge of character. All traits we like others to know we have or aspire to.'

He could feel the question getting closer. Marg, too, felt uneasy for him.

'Surely it's not the only thing you take into consideration when deciding about whom to choose?' Marg said, desperately trying to get him off the hook; the way he was now, he couldn't lie his way out of a paper bag.

The stress fired his imagination. An idea came to him out of the blue. *Of course,* he thought, *Stewart Ballard. Get Stewart to oversee Griggs, and he'd ensure they do the work to a high standard to meet Diana's needs. That way, neither I nor my reputation will be at the mercy of some incompetent nincompoop.* Now he couldn't wait for Diana to ask for the reference; instead, he pre-empted her.

'So Diana, Margaret was telling me you want a reference for Colin Griggs and his Hole Farming business.'

His turnabout surprised Marg. She shot him a look of disbelief. *What's he playing at? Inviting Diana to ask, I hope he's a suitable answer.* She kept her thoughts quiet.

'Well, yes, now you come to mention it. I know

you used him for the Golf Club refurbishment, and from what I understand, there were a few issues.'

'You have excellent sources. Yes, we used him, and yes, we had an issue or two, but in fairness, they were not down to him. I mean, give credit where credit's due. He's not a golfer and does not know the game.'

As Marg listened, her mouth fell wider and wider open. *He hates him, and now he's making excuses for him. I wonder what he's up to?* She continued to listen in amazement. It showed.

'Margaret dear, are you alright?' There was genuine concern in Diana's voice, 'You look sort of,' she hesitated, 'sort of peculiar. Don't take that the wrong way. It's just I've not seen you look like that before.'

Marg coughed to cover up her incredulity.

'No, nothing, just something went down the wrong way.' She smiled to show all was well.

'Graham, you were saying.' Diana turned back to him.

'Yes, Colin Griggs, his family has farmed here for over 100 years. Good people, all told. Farming is now a commercial activity, and the smaller farms are shutting up shop. Colin is trying to branch out, which is admirable, but he's still finding his feet. He's not afraid of hard work and seems determined to make a success of things, but has had bad luck along the way.' Graham was feeling relieved he'd not lied, nor had he put Colin down, nor had he played his trump card... yet.

'So you would recommend him?' Diana couldn't have been more direct. The directness caught him off guard.

'Well... err... yes, I suppose so.'

'Suppose so?'

'No, I mean, yes, it depends.'

'Now, Major, which one is it? You're not usually so indecisive.'

No one spoke. The noise of cutlery on crockery broke the silence.

'Yes, I would, but—'

'But?' Diana was curious about the 'but'.

'I would be happier if Colin worked alongside Mr Ballard, Stewart, our Head Groundsman at the Golf Club. They've worked together in the past and know each other from way back. I believe they were at school together.'

'Well, if you feel it's necessary.'

'As I said earlier, Colin is finding his way in his new business, and I believe you deserve the best. Stewart working alongside him would ensure that.' Graham sounded relieved.

'But the cost; Colin included nothing in his quote for an additional resource.'

'No, no, you misunderstand me; I'm offering Stewart for free, paid for by the Golf Club.'

'Does that mean you are that worried about Colin's ability? And you'd only recommend him under those circumstances?'

No, I'm worried he'll cock up and ruin my reputation, so I'm prepared to loan Stewart for free. He struggled not to verbalise his thoughts. 'Of course not, Diana, it's because I value your friendship above all else and want to make your time here a memorable one for all the right reasons.' *Thinking on your feet is what the army taught me.*

'Oh, that's so sweet of you. He's such a dear Margaret. You're so lucky to have him.' She patted her hand.

'Yes, I think so too. Always full of surprises is our Graham.'

CHAPTER 24

REACH FOR THE SKY

Saturday morning arrived like any other day. Colin and Izzy completed their usual farm chores. The postman and paperboy had been and gone. Nothing special there, yet there was an atmosphere of anticipation.

'Look, Izzy, how many more times? She'll ring when she's ready. All she said was, I want to get started as soon as possible, so I will let you know immediately I've made my decision. Hopefully, that will be over the weekend.'

'What about ringing her just to check if she has any queries with the quote? You know, just trying to be helpful, so she thinks it's part of the process: customer care and all that.'

'Diana's not a fool; she'll see through that…' the sound of the phone ringing cut him off in mid-sentence. Izzy was closest and picked it up. She was about to speak, but was beaten to it.

'Is Colin there?'

The gruff male voice confused her. 'Who's calling, please?'

'Major Woods.' He sounded curt.

'Oh, good morning, Major. I'll just find him for

you.' She pretended to search for him. She held her hand over the mouthpiece and spoke in hushed tones. 'Colin, it's Major Woods for you.'

'What does he want?'

She shrugged and passed him the phone. 'He doesn't sound too happy.'

'Major, Colin, how can I help?'

'How low will you stoop?' There was venom in his voice. 'They would never tolerate that type of behaviour in the Army. Spineless skulduggery. It's despicable, if I may say so.'

Colin was reeling but daren't interrupt him.

'You've got your reference. But I've told Lady Wills it's subject to you having Stewart Ballard working with you on the contract. I will not let you make a fool of me again. I'll have Stewart call you after the weekend to sort out the detail. Oh, and by the way, Lady Wills thinks I'm providing him for free. Don't disillusion her, but I'm not! You're going to have to pay the Club for his time.' There was a click, followed by silence.

'And what did he say?' Izzy couldn't hide her curiosity.

'I'm not sure. The Major has given Diana a reference, but it was provisional upon me working alongside Stewart Ballard. He wasn't happy, but I guess nobody enjoys being blackmailed! Mind you, I'm not happy about doing it myself; needs must and all that.'

She stopped hearing him after the mention of Stewart's name. It all seemed so long ago that he kissed her in the bunker. Without warning, all the memories came flooding back. She could feel his warm embrace, the softness of his lips on hers, the smell of him, so close not even a shaft of light could come between them. She was lost, gone from the kitchen, and was now back on the golf course on that fateful night.

'Are you listening to me?' There was no response. 'Izzy, what's wrong?' He took hold of her upper arms and shook her gently. 'Tell me, what's wrong?'

'Nothing, nothing.' The memories left as fast as they'd come, and she was back in the room. 'Sorry, I was just thinking.'

'Thinking what?'

'Oh, nothing really, err.' She hesitated. 'Well, umm, about how the Major must have felt on seeing the photograph.' She lied, just a small white one, but a lie, after all. 'No, I agree with you, blackmail is not nice.'

'Well, it's done now and anyway, it's not blackmail; more a little arm twisting.' He felt better after that. 'So if she's got a good reference, then I guess that's that!' He broke into song 'We're in the money, we're in the money!' He let go of her upper arms and took hold of her as if ballroom dancing leading her off around the kitchen, singing loudly.

She let herself be led; she was not with Colin but with her thoughts. Her reaction at the mention of Stewart's name confused Izzy. It was over 40 years ago, and apart from the 'kiss', there had been no contact, no secret assignations, no hoping she might accidentally bump into him. No real thoughts at all, but deep down, she still had feelings. Feelings she couldn't escape from, feelings she enjoyed. *No, it's just a schoolgirl fantasy; come on, get a grip*, she told herself.

Colin's singing had ceased as they had come to a halt outside the dining room, now office. The hall phone burst into life.

'I'll get it.' He was nearest. 'Hello, Griggs Hole Farming.'

Izzy overheard, but not clearly enough to know what was being said.

'No, that's great.' He paused. 'No, not a problem, I understand. No, sure, that's fine. Yes, he did, actually. No, I fully understand. Well, thank you, Diana. Be assured, Griggs Hole Farming will provide you with a first-rate quality service. Thanks again. Bye.'

Colin turned back to face Izzy. She stretched up to her full height and planted a long, wet kiss on his lips. 'Well done, you!' She hugged him tightly, burying her head in his chest. Although they often showed each other affection, this was more than she usually showed. Colin put it down to her exuberance following the phone call. She put it down to her guilt.

They were still in the embrace. 'I need to ring Stewart as soon as. We've got to get a plan sorted pronto. Do you have his number?'

He mentioned the 'S' word. Without thinking, she went on the defensive. 'Why would I have his number?'

'Because you're responsible for all the office stuff, remember?'

❧   ❧   ❧

Monday morning, nine o'clock sharp, Stewart swung his 4X4 into the Griggs's farmyard. Izzy saw him approaching the back door from the kitchen window. She was drawn to his demeanour. He was almost skipping by the time he reached for the door handle. Hesitant, she reminded herself to stay professional, as all that was a long time ago.

Stewart didn't bother to knock and walked straight in. Colin was in his office. He looked around before scooping Little Miss Muffet into his arms. Izzy protested, but his huge arms were too powerful for her.

'Let me go!' She thumped him on his chest and struggled some more. 'Colin's in the next room. What do you think you're doing?' As quickly as he'd scooped her up, he let her go.

'It's just a bit of fun. No harm done. You know how I feel about you so I thought I'd cheer up your Monday morning.' His casual manner confused her. He was playing with her emotions. 'Come on, Izzy. Give a chap a break. You so could have been Mrs Ballard. You only needed to say yes.'

'That was a long time ago. Anyway, you never asked me; not really.'

'I did, remember. That school trip to Henslow Village Church when we walked down the aisle together and Derek, whatever his name was—'

'Bolton'

'Yes, him. See, you do remember when he married us.'

'But we were 14. That didn't count.'

Stewart dropped onto one knee and fixed his gaze on her large brown eyes. 'Isobel Murfett, would you do me—' his proposal was foiled. Out of the corner of his eye, he caught sight of Colin coming down the hall. They saw each other at the same time.

'Ah Stewart, I heard you pull up. Is everything alright?'

'Yes, sure, just dropped my car keys as I came in and kicked them under the table. Anyway, you and I are working together again. I think the Major's afraid you'll blow up Henslow Manor! Understandable after your last job.' He chuckled openly, 'Just a bit of leg-pulling, Colin.'

'Thanks for the vote of confidence.'

'Take no notice of me; you did an okay job. You were just let down by your workers. No more rabbits this time, promise!'

'Yes, promise. I've learned my lesson. Lady Wills needs holes of substance. Six all told. Each one around 15 feet by 12 and about 5 foot deep. They're part of a water feature in the Manor gardens.'

'So what do you want me to do?'

Both men huddled around the table, with Colin's drawing and the copious notes he'd made on his site visit.

Izzy left them to it. More confused than ever, she kept pulling herself back to the fact that she was Mrs Griggs, for better or for worse. *Damn that man*, she thought. *Damn him.*

Several cups of coffee later, they'd hatched a plan.

'Okay, first we need a JCB, a forklift truck and to get fibreglass matting and barrels of resin. If we take the holes from the lower field near the road, we can get them onto the back of Old Alfred Mac and transport them up to the Manor and hey presto, the job's done.' Colin clapped his hands in a self-congratulatory way. He puffed out his chest, stood, and walked purposefully over to the kitchen sink. He surveyed the scene out of the window like some conquering War Lord.

'This is my Trafalgar. You're witnessing history being made. Colin Griggs, a former farmer, now a successful business entrepreneur, will no longer be looked down upon but looked up to. The man who came back from the brink. We'll hold our heads high as pillars of the community, a force to be reckoned with. Henslow, here we come.'

'Steady on, Colin! I think you've had too much caffeine; we're talking about supplying half a dozen holes. Not climbing Everest single-handed, blindfold!' Stewart wanted to bring him back to earth.

'I can feel it. My gut tells me I'm onto a winner here. This feels right. Careful planning, attention to detail, a methodical approach, your support and expertise; what could go wrong? With success like Lady Wills under our belt, there'll be no stopping us. Griggs Hole Farming is destined for greatness.'

'That's all well and good, but don't forget the feathers you've ruffled along the way, Major Woods, dare I say? Nor that people's memories aren't as short as yours appears to be.'

'But you can't make an omelette—'

'—without breaking eggs. That's as maybe, but that doesn't change the past. All I'm saying is to be cautious. You need friends, not enemies. This job is far from complete. If I knew what could go wrong, I'd stop it before it started! If you see what I mean? Anyway, I've got to go back to the Golf Club now. I've still got a day job waiting for me. See you same time tomorrow. I'll meet you in the lower field.' The sound of his engine leaving brought Izzy to the upstairs window. She was just in time to see his truck disappearing down the lane. Still confused, she felt excited and guilty all at the same time.

Colin busied himself for the rest of the day, ordering supplies, hiring equipment and reconnoitring the lower field to find the best location to take the holes from. The spring in his step and gaiety in his whistle, demonstrated to anyone watching he was ecstatic. Even the scarecrow, who stood solemnly keeping watch over the fields, couldn't fail to notice his mood.

'Well, scarecrow, I bet you didn't think you'd see the day when yours truly would be back. A new business in the making. A customer who is the most prestigious in the County and being assisted by Stewart Ballard, no less, the Head Groundsman for the Harpsden Golf Club.'

Over the next couple of weeks, Colin, with Stewart's guidance, crafted six holes as per the drawings and captured each in fibreglass moulded containers, ready to be transported up to the Manor. They stacked each hole inside the other for delivery on the back of Old Alfred Mac.

'Marg, have you seen my St Andrews Golf cufflinks?' Graham continued to push various items around the dressing table to discover their hiding place. In the shower with the water running she heard nothing. 'Why can't anybody leave anything alone?' He muttered to no one in particular. 'You put something down for five minutes, and it's gone!' He went on shuffling all and sundry, but to no avail.

'Marg,' he was shouting now, 'where are my cufflinks?' She appeared in the doorway to the en-suite, with her head swathed in a towel.

'Sorry, did you want something?'

By now, he was bent down on all fours with his face pressed hard to the floor, trying to look under the dressing table to see if they'd fallen down the back. Dressed only in his socks and his shirt, the sight greeting her was unexpected.

'Graham!' There was a genuine surprise in her voice. 'Lucky it's only me and not the cleaner! Would you mind? There are certain things a lady shouldn't be exposed to, and I think that's one of them.'

He stayed put. 'We've been married for goodness knows how long. There's not much you haven't seen before. Anyway, my cufflinks have gone walkabout.' Without moving his head off the floor, he switched his gaze to the bathroom door where she was standing in her birthday suit, apart from the towel on her head. 'Pot, kettle, black, springs to mind!'

She spun on her heels and disappeared. 'I thought you were a gentleman,' came from somewhere in the en-suite. He caught sight of himself in the wall of mirrors that made up the wardrobe doors. *I see what she means.* He pulled his shirt over his backside. *I guess I'll have to find them another time.* He got back on his feet and continued dressing.

'So why are we going to see Diana?' He spoke loud for her to hear.

'At Bridge, she invited us to see how the Manor refurbishment is going. Apparently, the house is well underway, and the garden landscaping starts today. We're just going for coffee at around eleven'ish. Then I thought we could take her back to the Golf Club for lunch. Nothing special, just a quick bite.'

'Some of us have work to do.'

'Don't fret; you'll have all afternoon. I'll drive her back to the Manor and come back for you around five.'

It wasn't long before they left the Turville Road, swinging the Mercedes into the Manor gates leading to the long drive up to the house. As soon as the car came to rest, Davy was out there in full voice, letting anyone in earshot know they had visitors. Lady Wills appeared.

'Davy, stop, that's enough. Go on, shoo. Margaret, Major, how nice to see you. Never mind him; his bark's worse than his bite. Here let me.' She opened the door for Marg before giving her a hug and a kiss like greeting a long-lost friend. Diana came around to his door. He held out his hand. He still felt uncomfortable about this 'French-style' of greeting. *Ever since we joined the EU, things have never been the same*.

'Drive okay?' She inquired, making small talk.

'Yes, fine, only takes 20 minutes, and apart from that steep right-hand bend, I'll never get used to it; it seems to spring from nowhere.' He felt he'd made enough small talk and thought best he shut up. By now, the ladies were walking arm in arm, engrossed in paint colours, fabrics, wallpapers and lampshades. The only one left listening to him was Davy. He was none too interested, judging by the way he kept chasing anything kicked up as they walked.

The party reached the Grand Hallway. Suitable oohs and ah's were made whilst Diana gesticulated this way and that.

'Gosh, it's made such a difference. So much lighter, and it looks bigger, too.' Marg had years of practice at being shown around friends' houses; she knew what to say and the right degree of enthusiasm to sound convincing. 'Don't you think so, Graham?'

'Yes, Major, you've not said much; what's your opinion?' Diana had her head cocked to one side, attentively listening as if waiting for him to issue forth some nugget of wisdom. He strode toward the Grand Staircase, where he climbed the first couple of steps before looking around, surveying all before him. The delay in his reply sought to increase the expectation of an enlightening pronouncement, some insight into colour schemes, harmony and balance or tonal qualities, or some revelation on the true nature and role of man's relationship with his living environment.

He played for time while frantically trying to think of something to say rather than *nice!* He knew *nice* wouldn't be enough, and that *nice* would end up with him in Mrs Woods' bad books, or worse, he knew *nice* would be a sad let-down for Her Ladyship. He needed a comment to reflect all she had done, to make her feel great about her choices and the money she'd spent, about her design skills, her tastes.

A bead of sweat formed on his brow, then

another, and another. The longer he said nothing, the more pressure he felt under. His neck veins visible throbbed. The ladies were too far away to see, but he could feel it. He faced them and opened his mouth. He took a deep breath. The air in his lungs was gathering momentum; he was committed to speaking.

The telephone in the hall broke the silence. *Saved by the bell.* He sighed. The hall devoid of furniture meant there was nothing to absorb the sound, and the ringing reverberated around the space. It broke the spell. Lady Wills grabbed up the receiver. Graham was off the hook which showed.

'Lady Wills.' She answered and listened but was obstructed from saying any more. She replaced the receiver, looking bewildered.

Marg broke the silence. 'Everything alright, Diana?'

'No, yes, fine.' Unusual for her, she sounded confused. 'It was Isobel Griggs. If I heard her correctly, they've got some issue with their delivery and will come later this afternoon instead.'

'Delivery?' Marg was curious.

'Yes, the holes they're supplying.' Diana was vague as she tried to recall Isobel's words. She had spoken so fast.

'Did she say anything else?'

'No, not really. Anyway, it's not a problem. An hour or two won't matter. Back to the matter at hand. Right, Graham, you were saying.'

He felt as if a bolt of thunder had hit him. 'Yes, well, I was going to say, erm, what I'm… erm—'

'Well?' Diana sounded impatient.

'Well, how nice it's looking. Yes, a truly splendid job.' As soon as he'd said the 'n' word, he knew he was in trouble.

There was silence from both ladies. In unison, they turned. They took each other's arm and disappeared through the drawing-room door, shutting it smartly behind them. Graham and Davy were left on the outside. Davy ran to the door and scratched at it. It re-opened enough to let him pass, but was closed again purposefully. Graham remained standing on the stairs, lost as to know what to do next. From the noises above him, it was clear the refurbishment work was still in full swing on the upper floors. He ventured up the rest of the flight to look, but a host of ladders, trestles, tins and an army of people, all busying away, carrying out their respective jobs and trades, barred his way. He watched for a short while before descending the stairs. As he stood on the bottom step, the drawing-room door opened. The ladies emerged, still engaged in conversation. They made their way toward the front door, ignoring him. He stood, rooted. As they passed, Marg, in a loud, direct voice, called out, 'Lunch.' Not a suggestion, nor a question, but a command. The Major clicked his heels and followed dutifully.

'Right Colin, back the lorry in through the gate. Careful now; you'll need to come in at a bit of an angle to avoid those big ruts. Now nice and slow, easy does it.' Colin inched Old Alfred Mac through the gate until the flatbed was alongside the stack of six holes. Stewart jumped into the cab of the forklift and fired up the engine.

'Can you guide me? It's difficult to see where you're going with the forks fully laden.' Stewart revved the engine and moved forward. Soon the lorry was loaded and made secure. The noise of the forklift truck was replaced by the banging and clanking of the diesel lorry now nearing its 300 thousandth mile, according to the odometer. Stewart was looking sceptical. 'Will it make it?' The banging just seemed to get louder and more ominous.

'300,000, it's not run in yet. Old Alfred Mac will see me out!' He inched the lorry forward to avoid disturbing the finely balanced load.

'You take it slow, Colin, and I'll follow behind with my truck. We don't want some silly bugger trying to overtake; especially not on that tight right-hander.'

Stewart saw Colin onto the road and waited until the lorry was out of sight before walking back to his truck and climbing into the driver's seat. As he selected first, a car from nowhere hurtled past, heading straight for Colin, the lorry, and the six substantial holes.

Idiot, thought Stewart. He squinted at the fast disappearing rear end, trying to see who it was. He glanced out of the corner of his eye to see the scarecrow. 'I bet you know who that was! But I bet you won't tell me.' Stewart was right; the scarecrow said nothing; instead, he just kept looking determinedly across the surrounding countryside.

Goodness knows what I'll find ahead. He let up the

clutch and squeezed the accelerator.

Up ahead, Old Alfred Mac was being pursued by some go-faster boy racer who seemed hell-bent on passing. Colin had nowhere to go. The lane up to the Manor was steep, narrow and near the hilltop quite bendy, including a tight right-hander. The lorry approached the bend, and by now, the impatient driver was looking for the smallest opportunity to over-take.

Colin felt under pressure to let him through. He kept the lorry over to the far left as possible, just about keeping his wheels on the tarmacadam. His speed had dropped to only 20, the right-hander was in sight. The driver sensed this could be his opportunity and knocked his car down a gear before pushing the accelerator to the floor. Unleashing the full potential of this highly tuned engine, the car jumped forward in a shower of pebbles, sticks and other detritus, scattering everything in its wake. Colin glimpsed him in his wing mirror. Then the car was alongside, parallel with the cab. The bend was upon them. Colin wrestled the wheel, first to the left to put some space between him and the car, and then hard right to negotiate the bend. The net effect was to dislodge the load of holes. They swayed gracefully, first right and then left, before shaking themselves loose from their binds.

With complete freedom, they descended from the rear of the lorry onto the sloping verge to be trapped firm by a scramble of fallen branches, briars, and saplings. The car sped up and turned with such force to cause its back end to whip across the road, narrowly missing the lorry's front bumper. Colin convinced he would collide with the swerving vehicle, stamped his full weight onto both the brake and clutch peddles simultaneously and brought the lorry to an abrupt halt. The engine stalled while the car shot over the brow of the hill.

Silence descended. For the next few seconds, Colin sat immobile, staring straight ahead, trying to make sense of what had happened. Imperceptibly, at first, the trees moved past him. Then with more certainty, though it took him a while to realise, the trees were stationary, and the lorry was rolling back over the road edge heading down the embankment. Now, the cab rose until the front wheels were head-height off the ground. All stopped moving, and everything was still again. Colin clung to the steering wheel to avoid falling back against the rear of the cab. He waited; nothing more happened. Disentangling himself, he sat back in the driver's seat at a rather precarious angle. Through the front windscreen, he now had an uninterrupted view of the treetops and sky. Knocking on the cab door drew his attention.

'Colin, Colin. Are you okay?' It was Stewart. 'What happened? Are you hurt? Shall I call an ambulance? Colin, answer me.' He was using a stick to knock with, as the cab was so far off the ground.

'Erm—I'm fine, just a bit disorientated.' He leant over and opened the driver's door. It wouldn't open; the weight kept it from swinging ajar.

'Looks like I'll have to climb out through the window.' He wound it down. 'What about the holes? Are they still there?'

Stewart wandered around to the back of the lorry. 'They're gone! All six.' He continued looking about. 'They've slipped off, and the lorry's rolled back into them. You're stuck in your own holes! Now that's something you don't see every day.' Stewart couldn't help but laugh. *Well, I thought I'd seen everything, but that takes the biscuit,* he mused. 'I say Colin; looks like you're in a hole lot of trouble.'

'Ha, ha.' Colin wasn't amused.

'Just hold on. I'll see what I can do.'

By now, Colin had one leg out of the window, and his foot was hunting around, trying to find the step used to get up into the cab. Within a couple of minutes, he was released from temporary captivity and around the back of the lorry, staring into the hole where the rear axle and wheels were wedged.

'Any ideas?' Colin stood, looking quite vacant.

'The good news is nothing appears to be damaged from what I can see, but it's going to be a bit of a job to get the lorry out without doing any. We need some sort of lifting gear. I'm not sure that just towing the lorry would work. The back end is well caught down the holes.'

'Reckon you're right there, Stewart. What about traffic? This lane is narrow, and we'll be stuck here for a bit.'

'I suppose we'd better call the local plod to get the road closed.' Stewart had his mobile out. 'Who is it around here?'

'Ticker Wright,' Colin offered, 'but he's only got his bike. Maybe you'd better phone Harpsden.'

'Harpsden Police Station, Desk Sergeant Walker,

who's calling?'

'Stewart, Stewart Ballard from the Golf Club.'

'How can I help?'

'We've got a problem here with a hole.'

'And I suppose you'd like the Police to look into it? Aren't you a bit old for pranks like that, Sir?'

'No, this is serious. There's a lorry stuck down the hole, and we need to winch it out.'

'A lorry, you say. Down a hole. Wouldn't be on the 13th green by any chance? Always unlucky for some.' Walker wasn't convinced that this wasn't a wind-up. 'Who's lorry is it?'

'Colin Griggs.'

'Griggs, Griggs, what's he doing driving his lorry around the Golf Course? I thought Woods had banned him from ever going near the place again.'

'No, it's not at the Golf Club.'

'But you just said it was.'

'No, I'm from the Golf Club; the hole is on the Turville Road out of Henslow, on the steep part where that sharp right-hand bend is.'

'So it's a pothole?' Walker was tentative.

'Not at 15 by 12, it's not! It's one of Colin's own holes. He was moving it, well, them, six altogether, to Henslow Manor for Lady Wills. They slipped off the back of the lorry as he took action to avoid colliding with a speeding car.'

'And—' The Desk Sargent was still somewhat dubious about the entire story.

'Well, he stalled before rolling back into his own holes. The lorry's still stuck there now. It'll take some time to get it out, and I'm worried about the other road users. So can you send a car?'

'Are you sure a set of skyhooks wouldn't be more appropriate?' Walker looked to the Heavens for guidance.

For Jimmy Flanagan, it was a slow news day. Birth, marriages and deaths weren't gripping for a young enthusiastic reporter. As no one was doing any of them today, he went looking for more engaging stories. His hunt took him to the Police Station. As he parked up, Billy Field jumped into his patrol car. They were still not on speaking terms. Billy sped off with sirens blaring. Jimmy followed at a discrete distance. He did not know where they were going, but thought that sirens blaring meant something.

It wasn't long before they left Harpsden and were heading out on the Henslow Road. The village came and went; Jimmy was getting more curious. As they passed Griggs Farm, he gave the scarecrow a nod. *See, nothing changes,* he said to himself. Beyond the farm, the road climbed as it headed up into the hills. He'd lost sight of the patrol car, but through his wound down the window, he could still hear the siren. It seemed to get closer or, at least, not going further away. There in front of him, Griggs lorry came into view. It was reared up on its back axle like a wild stallion. The sight mesmerised Jimmy and he nearly ran into Billy's patrol car. They exchanged glances, but Billy was too busy with Colin and Stewart to say anything.

'So gents, what have we here then?' Billy was trying not to laugh. 'No one injured, I trust'. He walked toward the back of the lorry. He saw the full extent of the problem. 'This puts a whole new twist on things.' Neither Colin nor Stewart reacted.

His walkie-talkie burst into life 'Tango Bravo Foxtrot'.

'Yes, Serg.'

'What's to report?'

'You wouldn't believe your eyes. Griggs has backed his lorry into a hole.'

'Don't tell me you're looking into it!'

Colin and Stewart looked at each other. 'I can see we're going to be the laughingstock of the village.'

The sound of laughter on the Police radio was clear for all to hear. 'So what next, Billy?'

'Not sure yet, Serg. I'll have a chat and report back.' The radio went quiet.

Jimmy used the time to shoot several photographs of the lorry and its predicament, as well as Colin and Stewart being interviewed by the Police. He was desperately trying to think of a headline to encapsulate the drama. I can see it now, 'Reach for the Sky' or 'Lorry on the up', or 'Bottom drops out of the hole business', or 'Griggs' are jinxed'. He continued to click away with his camera while muttering away to himself. As usual, his enthusiasm had taken over, and he was off in journalist cuckoo land, rather than paying attention to what was going on around him.

Billy was back in his car and off up the hill to set out some 'Road Closed Ahead' signs; Colin and Stewart discussed their options.

'Somehow, we've got to lift the rear axle to lower the front end onto the road. It cannot be towed as-is.' Colin looked perplexed. 'What about Harpsden Truck Recovery? They should be able to help. I've no idea of the number. Have you got it on your phone?'

Stewart busied himself pushing buttons, looking through his *recent* call log. 'I called them a few months back, but I do not know which of these is theirs.' He had a better idea and started dialling. 'Isobel, it's Stewart; we're in a spot of bother. Colin's backed his lorry into a hole… Yes, he's fine, but the lorry is rather precarious on its rear axle. We need the number for Harpsden Truck Recovery.' He listened for a few more seconds, then pressed the 'End Call' button and put the phone in his pocket.

'Well?' Colin looked at him expectantly. 'What's the number?'

'She's gone to find it, then text it to me. It'll take her a couple of minutes to Google it.'

'And in English—?'

'Come on, get with it.'

'So what's the plan?' Jimmy had finished taking pictures and was keen to get the rest of the story.

'You can see for yourself. We have this problem.' Stewart explained.

'Yeah, but how did the lorry get like this in the first place?'

Colin relayed the story of the speeding driver and how he tried to avoid the collision. Jimmy took copious notes as well as capturing it all on his smartphone.

The familiar phone tone of a text message

arriving interrupted them. Stewart fished his phone out of his pocket and opened the message. There was just a number, no other words, except on a line by itself a single X. Stewart smiled; his thoughts raced away. Is it just a simple sign-off, one friend to another or... He wasn't sure what to make of it? *If she had done two or three kisses, that would have been more obvious, but one…*

'Are you going to dial that number?' Colin's voice broke through his thoughts.

'Yes..., sorry, miles away.'

'And so is Harpsden! Get on with it. We need to get a move on here. Lady Wills is expecting her delivery today. I can't afford to mess this up.' There was a hint of panic in Colin's voice.

A realisation that the mess needed sorting replaced Stewart's thoughts of Izzy. He dialled. As his mobile was on speaker, the sound of a repeated ringing filled the air. After many rings, the dulcet tones of 'HTR' replaced the sounds of ringing.

'Sorry, who's that?' The phone was still on speaker.

'HTR, can I help?'

'I'm looking for Harpsden Truck Recovery. Have I got the right number?'

'That's what I said, HTR. How can I help?'

'We've got a lorry stuck down a hole and wondered if you can come and tow it out.'

'That's what we do. So where are you?'

'On the Turville Road out of Henslow, near the top of the hill on the sharp right-hand bend.' He spoke slowly and deliberately.

'Oh, yes, I know, but there are no holes there! I

thought you said you were stuck down a hole.' The disembodied voice sounded somewhat sceptical.

'Yes, we are, well, I mean the lorry is. The rear axle of the trailer. The front's standing up in the air.'

'Sounds like a pretty big hole. What happened, a landslip or something?'

'Or something is a better description.'

'What do you mean, or something?'

Stewart was getting exasperated. 'Look, can you just send out a recovery vehicle? It doesn't matter where it's stuck!'

'Oh, are you in the recovery business then, sir?'

'No, I'm not!' He sounded quite agitated. 'Just get a lorry out here,' he raised his voice and, as an afterthought, added, 'please.'

'I'll need to check availability. Paul's out on a job and not sure when he's due back.'

'Paul, Paul. Who's Paul?'

'My brother. He has the HGV license to drive the truck.'

'When do you think he can get here?'

'As I say, Paul's out, and I'm not sure when he'll be back. The diary says he's at a job near Oxden, so I don't expect him back for a while. At least a couple of hours.'

'And there's no one else?'

'No, I'm here by myself, so do you want Paul to come with the truck or not?'

'Not sure, we'll call you back.' Stewart hit the 'Call End' button. Silence returned; each man looked at the other.

'What now then?' Colin kicked at a few small

stones around the road as he wandered aimlessly about.

'Come on, it's not the end of the world.' Stewart went over to where he was standing and patted him on the back. 'Worse things happen at sea. It'll be alright, you see.'

Jimmy was feeling kind of awkward. He was a reporter, after all, and meant to observe situations, not take part.

'Maybe Billy Field will have some ideas. Ask him when he gets back.' Jimmy had no sooner finished speaking when the patrol car came over the brow of the hill. 'Here he is, now.'

Billy avoid the lorry and negotiated the bend, pulling his patrol car onto the verge beyond it. He left his blue flashing light going. 'So what developments? We need to get this road cleared as soon as. Is the breakdown truck on its way?'

'No, it's in Oxden.' Colin muttered at the ground.

'So what's Plan B?'

'There is no plan B.'

'Well, have you any idea when the tow truck's back from Oxden?'

'HTR were a bit vague.' Stewart joined in.

'I think some of that wouldn't go amiss around here, the way Colin's moping about.'

'What do you mean, Billy?' Jimmy couldn't help himself from asking.

'Those hormone things, they did my Mum a power of good. You ought to see her now, always on the go. Never stops like a new lease of life.'

'I think you mean HRT.' Jimmy couldn't disguise

his laughter; Billy looked somewhat embarrassed.

Before anyone had a chance to say anything else, they became conscious of a speeding car approaching from the village. Billy swung into action, standing in the carriageway centre, holding his arms aloft in a stop gesture. Jimmy could hardly believe his eyes.

'It must run in the family. These Fields must have some sort of death wish; first, John now—' his voice trailed off.

The car came to a halt, and the driver was out and running in Colin's direction. It was Izzy.

'Are you alright? Are you hurt? What happened?' By the time she had finished speaking, she'd reached him and flung her arms around him in a tight embrace.

'Hey, yes, I'm fine—no need to fuss. I'm more concerned we are going to miss the delivery times. Just when everything was going so right, this had to happen. It's such a bloody mess.'

'Less of that! It's just one of those things. Have you told Diana yet? She'll understand it's not your fault.' Izzy didn't wait for an answer; she got her mobile out. Diana was on speed dial, as was the vet. 'Diana, good morning.' She didn't listen for a response, but checked her watch. It was just before midday. 'It's Isobel Griggs. Just to let you know, Colin's had a spot of bother on his way to you with the hole delivery. Nothing too serious. I should make it sometime this afternoon. Thanks now. Bye.' The receptionist at Hardy's the vets looked at her handset in disbelief. She was trying to make sense of what had just happened. Izzy had cleared the phone down, not giving any chance for questions.

'That was rather abrupt, my love.'

'No, just a matter of fact.'

Colin wasn't so sure.

'So what's happening about the lorry, Colin?'

'Nothing at present. HTR is on a job in Oxden, and they don't know when they'll get here.'

'There must be someone else.' Izzy turned toward Billy Field. 'You know everyone around here; who else has a towing truck?'

Billy looked hard at the ground, seeking inspiration or maybe hoping for divine intervention. By now, Izzy was staring hard toward Stewart and Jimmy. 'Someone must have an idea.' The sound of her voice carried through the trees, but there were no responses, just more shuffling of feet.

'Are the holes damaged?' She was taking charge. 'Is the lorry damaged?' Everyone peered at both.

'As far as I can tell, all is okay.' It was left to Colin to answer.

'Right, so it's not a breakdown truck we want, more just a way of getting the lorry's front wheels onto the road.'

'I guess so. What have you got in mind?' Colin sounded cautious.

'Well, to get the front end down, we need to get the back end up. And without the availability of skyhooks—'

'That's what Sergeant Walker said. We need sky hooks.' No sooner had Stewart finished speaking when he wished he had never opened his mouth.

'I'm surprised at you.' She raised eyes to heaven before continuing. 'In the absence of skyhooks, we need to find a way to push it up from underneath.' She had everyone's attention now. 'Something we could inflate.'

'That sounds more improbable than sky hooks if you ask me!' She threw Billy a hard stare.

At the sound of the word inflate, Colin was hit by inspiration. 'Clive Beer! You're a genius, my love.' He gave her a big hug. 'Quick, give him a ring.'

'Clive Beer? What can he do for us?' She didn't understand.

'Remember how he lifted the VAT Inspector's car onto the shopping centre roof? Go on, ring him.'

'Okay, okay.' She put her phone on speaker. It answered.

Colin snatched it from her and piped up, 'Clive, Colin Griggs. It's been a while, I know, but I need your help again.' He filled him in on what had happened and how he could help. 'Right, great, see you in 20 minutes.' He hung up the phone.

'Can you ring Lady Wills again with an update? I want to keep on her good side.'

'You've got the phone; you do it.' She protested, unhappy with the way he had taken it earlier.

'Please, Izzy, it'll sound better coming from you.' He pushed the phone in her direction. Reluctantly, she took it and pressed the speed dial again. It rang several times before being answered. Without hesitation, she launched into a summary of what was happening without a by or leave, assuming that Lady Wills knew the background to the situation.

❧ ❧ ❧

The tour of the Manor refurbishment had finished. Lunch at the golf club was next on the agenda. Both women sat in the rear of the Mercedes. Graham, as impromptu chauffeur, minus the obligatory hat, closed the car doors behind them before taking to the wheel. The car sped off down the drive, passing through the Estate gates, turning left onto the Turville Road and down the hill toward Henslow. He sped up and just as speedily applied the brakes. The 'Road Ahead Closed' sign barred his way. The car stopped abruptly, but his passengers maintained their forward momentum to be thwarted by their seat belts.

'Graham, what do you think you're doing?' Marg sounded both startled and annoyed. He said nothing, only pointing toward the road sign.

'Well, what does that mean? I know nothing about this.' Diana was quite affronted. 'Nobody told me they were going to close my road. Was there anything when you came up earlier?'

'Where were you when the Spanish held their inquisition?' Graham coughed to cover his comment.

'Sorry, did you say something?' Marg heard him, but his mutterings went unnoticed by Diana. He opened the driver's door and went up onto the roadside verge to get a better look. Impatiently, Diana opened the rear window and called to him.

'Well?' He stood on tiptoe with his handheld to his brow, much like a visor, to get a better look.

'Well,' she repeated herself, determined to get a

response. 'What can you see?'

There was a pause.

At last, he spoke, 'It's difficult to say. I guess it's on that tight bend. I can make out several people milling around and what looks like a lorry standing upright on its back wheels.' His voice drifted away as he strained to make out what was going on.

'Major, be a splendid chap and walk down there. We need to know if we should turn around or if they are going to clear the road soon.' Diana's tone changed markedly.

It crossed his mind to comment, but decided a quiet life was more preferable. He jumped off the verge and strode down the hill and out of sight.

'Men are so fickle.' And without further reference to the incident, both women fell back into deep conversation.

As he neared the corner, he became perplexed. There was indeed a lorry standing up on its rear axle, but emerging from around the tailgate area was a castle turret in bright red. By now, he was close enough to see who was who and could make out Stewart Ballard standing to one side watching the whole proceedings.

'Stewart.' He called out in a loud whisper. No one had noticed him. The Major kept walking. 'Stewart.' He tried again, this time with more success. Stewart heard his name and looked about. It took a couple of seconds before he realised the direction from which it was coming. He nodded in acknowledgement and set off up the hill to meet the Major.

'What's going on?' Graham was still whispering.

'Colin Griggs and his holes—he's only gone and slipped down one of them. Now the lorry is trapped there until we can get it lifted out.'

Judging by the long furrows on Graham's forehead, he'd not grasped the situation. Stewart saw he was still confused and led him closer to the rear of the lorry to explain what needed doing. Colin and Clive were in the hole, wrestling with the unfolding bouncy castle. It was being brought to life by the notorious Hammer Koshi 400 compressor. The familiar sound of the engine haunted Graham, taking him back to that fateful Saturday of the opening of the refurbished Golf Course. He turned pale.

Neither Izzy nor Colin noticed the Major. She was on her mobile trying to get some commitment from HTR and alternately trying to get through to Lady Wills to update her on the delivery progress. Colin's preoccupation with the unfolding castle, the desire not to damage the holes and the over-riding need to get the holes delivered ASAP had his full attention.

Billy was keeping well out of it. He walked near his patrol car, radioing in updates to the great amusement of Desk Sergeant Walker.

On the other hand, Jimmy was everywhere, either taking pictures or asking questions, looking for the sound bite that would make his story a front-page success. He was now in the hole with Colin and Clive, his smartphone in his hand and the camera around his neck. *This is live-action reporting,* he thought. The Hammer Koshi was at full revs, making such noise to drown out any comments, but Jimmy didn't notice or seem to care. The excitement of the moment had overtaken him. The two men were pulling and heaving at the castle's thick plastic material, trying to manoeuvre it under the lorry.

Old Alfred Mac was steadfast. The pressure was building. The red turret standing proud seemed to be the only destination for the pumped air. It was now twice as large as it was designed to be and still growing. All eyes were on the hole and where the two men working.

Diana and Marg, fed up with the waiting and not knowing, left the car to find Graham. Davy, of course, wanted to follow and was out of the car and running as fast as his short legs would carry him. Diana called out in a vain attempt to bring him to heel. Whether it was his preoccupation with his mission or the screaming sounds of the Hammer Koshi, he never responded nor deviated from his chosen path.

Davy made it to the back of the lorry on the side where the turret was looming large. On route, he passed between the Major's legs as if to say, I'm here. Graham knew if Davy was present, then Diana wasn't far behind. As quick as a flash, he thought retrieving Davy for her would put him back into her good books. Without hesitation or consideration for his own safety, he was off in hot pursuit. Running bent double, as he was tried to scoop up Davy at the same time as catching up with him, he never had the time nor opportunity to notice the overstressed turret looming large.

The peace and tranquillity of this favoured part of the county of Oxdenshire being ripped apart by Hammer Koshi's sound returned to quiet in an instant.

An almighty explosion replaced the compressor's scream as the turret's fabric capitulated to the burden of the mounting air pressure. In a rush for stasis, the pressure wave lifted the Major and Davy clean off their feet, depositing them onto the bonnet of the nearby patrol car. The boom of the explosion rolled through the trees and off into the surrounding countryside. The sudden drop in air pressure caused the Hammer Koshi to shut down automatically.

The unexpected turn of events caused all those present to fall silent. Routed to the spot, each unconsciously checked themselves to ensure life and limb were intact; all except for the Major. With Davy grasped firmly to his chest, he slowly descended from his landing spot in his state of unconsciousness. Inevitably, they were drawn toward the waiting ground to form an unmoving crumpled heap of dog and man.

A whimper from Davy broke the silence. All heads turned in his direction. Lady Wills broke into a sprint; her status and demeanour laid aside, the wellbeing of her beloved Davy took precedence. Marg, too, had an adrenalin rush and was off and running. Both ladies covered a distance separating them from their loved ones with equal vigour, arriving together at the patrol car. Diana was the first to speak.

'My poor Davy—diddums, are you alright? Is my little diddums hurt? Come to Mummy.' With that, Diana prised Davy from the arms of Graham, raising the dog to her heaving ample bosom, as she filled her lungs, following her 100-meter dash.

Marg, crouched at Graham's head, patted his face

and called his name to bring him back to full consciousness. 'Graham, it's me, Marg. Speak to me! Are you alright? Is anything hurt? Don't move; just stay still.' She was panicking; he remained inactive.

'Please, anyone, help,' her voice sounded desperate. He groaned, she sobbed, and Davy yelped as Diana squeezed him tight to her chest. Everyone else was in that dazed place of disorientation—an aimless and confused state where it takes one's senses and brain a few moments to catch up with and process what's happened following an unexpected and sudden event.

PC Billy Field was the first of the rest to move. After a cursory glance at the bonnet for any signs of damage, he was on his radio requesting an ambulance and back-up. Jimmy appeared from around the blind side of the lorry. His camera, in video mode, was still running, once again making a complete visual and audio record of the unfolding events. The explosion's force had shredded the turret into thousands of pieces that were now falling back to earth, reminiscent of a ticker-tape parade in New York City. Stewart had, without thinking, thrown his arms around Izzy in a protective gesture to shield her from the force of the explosion. They were now locked in an embrace and, although they were doing nothing inappropriate, they held it for longer than necessary.

In the hole where the rear of the lorry was held fast, where Clive and Colin had wrestled with the bouncy castle, the pressure wave had its biggest impact. Both men, who only seconds earlier had been crouched down tugging at the material, took on the semblance of bowling balls. They came to rest deep in the undergrowth, held fast by a web of thorn-bearing aggressive brambles. The latter had made short work of their clothes, shredding the material with great efficiency, leaving them looking like rag dolls, but worse. Where the thorns had found flesh, they had not discriminated but sought to shred it also. Rivulets of blood formed body-wide, giving them the appearance of creatures from some horror movie.

Conscious but bewildered, disorientated and in a great deal of pain, Colin and Clive tried to extract themselves from their prickly prison. Each gesture was met with more pain. The brambles kept their hold and showed no signs of releasing their captors. The briar's tenacity was met with cries of distress as both men suffered further lacerations brought on by their attempt to free themselves. Their cries and blaspheming now filled the air, permeating the surrounding area. It wasn't long before everyone else, except for the Major, was aware of their plight, pain, and need to be released from their extremely distressing ordeal.

'That's my Colin!' Izzy pushed herself away from Stewart's clutches and ran screaming as she did. 'I'm coming, my love, I'm coming!'

The others watched before taking her lead. As a policeman, Billy had first aid training, but this was well beyond the course's remit—even if he could get to the two men. He was now back at the boot of his patrol car, looking at the Aladdin's cave of equipment to see if anything was suitable for the task at hand. Rummaging, he found a baton, heavy-duty pliers and a pair of Kevlar gloves. He took up his tunic from the back seat where his standard-issue riot gear lay, doing up all the buttons to give himself maximum protection. On top, he wore his fluorescent yellow, high-visibility jacket and topped the lot off with a helmet complete with a full-face visor. Finally, he grabbed his riot shield and slipped it over his left arm and held it tight. He was ready for battle. His size 12 steel toe-capped, impact-resistant, leather upper, rubber-soled police boots made quick work of the brambles. Those that didn't succumb to his kicking were hacked clear with the baton or swept aside by his shielded arm. Those that resisted were cut into pieces by the pliers. His frenzied attack soon pushed a path through to where the two men lay. Clive was closest.

'Just stay still; try not to move,' Billy said reassuringly. 'I'll have you free in a few minutes.'

'That's easy for you to say.' The pain in Clive's voice was clear. 'Those bastards are everywhere, quite literally. It's like being attacked by a hoard of marauding hedgehogs.'

Izzy waded in to help and was paying the price. 'Spare the chat, blast…, just get, ouch…, them, buggers, out.'

'Mrs Griggs, stop right there; you'll make matters worse.' Billy sounded stern. 'You've no protective clothing. Look at your legs already!'

Little droplets of blood were dotted around her shins where the thorns had done their worse.

'I'm made of sterner stuff; nothing that a bit of Dettol won't clean off. Here, give me those pliers.' Snatching them from Billy's hand, she set to cutting away at everything between her and her goal. As she cut,

Billy cleared the pieces. Soon Clive could stand. Motionless, he was trying to gather his senses and to come to terms with his freedom. Many of the thorns had snapped off and were embedded in the remnants of his clothing. They could continue with their task of protecting the bush, unaware of the futility of the exercise. He was all too aware of them and wanted relief. Pulling at his clothing in a desperate attempt to gain some, and in no time he was left with nothing but his boxers and socks.

It was late Autumn and none too warm. The wisdom of stripping down to his underwear crossed his mind and especially the part of taking off his shoes. Each step to freedom was as painful as his captivity. To escape further pain, he was on his tiptoes, lifting his legs high like a prancing horse. He increased the speed of each stride whilst spreading his arms wide for balance. The road surface was a welcome relief. *Free at last!*

Jimmy couldn't resist taking a picture or two of his plight before finding him a blanket from the Patrol Car's boot. Clive's ordeal was over for the present.

Colin fared no better. Billy and Izzy were busy releasing him, but he too was a victim of the thorn's ferocity and persistence. He followed Clive and was down to his boxers, but wisely kept his boots on. The three processed back toward the road, Billy led, still swinging away from his shield and striking out with his baton. Colin was in the middle, keen to avoid anything that resembled a briar and Izzy followed up the rear as a sweeper, collecting abandoned clothing items.

As they reached the road, the ambulance

screeched to a halt, lights and sirens still going. The two medics, who were used to scenes of disaster and devastation, sat dumbfounded in their cab. They turned toward each other and shrugged in a mutual realisation that they hadn't quite seen it all until now! Duty took over, and questions would have to wait.

Billy attempted to orchestrate proceedings, but he could hear little and make himself understood even less through his helmet. The two men swathed in blood and shivering climbed into the rear of the ambulance. The medics had the Major onto a stretcher and locked into position for travelling. Both Marg and Izzy wanted to go with them. The lack of space meant they had to follow. With Diana and Davy in tow, Marg started the walk back to the Mercedes. Reflecting on what had happened, they drove in silence, apart from Davy, who wriggled and whimpered now and then. Izzy followed in her car, leaving Stewart in charge.

CHAPTER 25

INTENSIVE CARE UNIT

It's usual for small town A&E departments to deal with small-time accidents and emergencies—a finger cut here or a marble lodged there. And in most hospitals, the mid-week early afternoon shift is, in general, free of drama, pain, suffering or high emotion. Knowing this, Nurse Tanya had opted for this rota slot. She was in for a shock.

The Ambulance Control Centre for the whole county is based in Oxden. Although Billy radioed in coherent reports of the unfolding events on the Turville Road, by the time they were filtered through the Police Station, and the Oxden Control Centre, before reaching Harpsden A&E Department, a certain amount of selective hearing and misinterpretation had taken their toll. At the A&E reception desk, the computer printer rattled into life; what Tanya read told her a different story.

'Exploding castle endangers lives of an unspecified number of bystanders. One man reported knocked unconscious by a flying dog—the extent of additional injuries unknown. Two further men, semi-naked and covered in blood, believed to have suffered extensive lacerations to the torso and limbs. No head injuries reported. Trauma expected. X-ray and surgical teams on standby.'

'So much for a quiet shift.' She re-read the report. 'I guess plan for the worst, and anything less will be a bonus.' She scanned the roster to see who else was around before dialling for help.

Jimmy felt he'd seen more than enough to get a front-page worthy story. His challenge now was to make tonight's paper, albeit the late edition.

'Facts and details', he repeated the phrase like a mantra. This time he was determined to win the praise of his Editor, and accurate facts with minutia were the way to do it.

He'd laid out his laptop, notebook, smartphone, and camera like an offering to the God of News. He sat at his desk determined to make this story count, the one that was going to make him a successful investigative journalist, the one his Editor couldn't ignore or ridicule. Secrets of a reporter's success are who, what, why, where, when and how. He grabbed a clean sheet of paper and scribbled the names of all those present. He flicked on his smartphone recorder app and played through the recording. As he listened, he uploaded his pictures and video from his camera and watched them as a slideshow on his laptop. The who, where, and when was easy. The what, why, and how were more testing. From arriving on the scene, he was cognisant of what had happened but prior would take more detective work. Time was against him.

This was a big story, but my Editor has deadlines. Presses have to roll, the ink needs to dry, and bundles of newspapers need distributing to shops and sellers.

Without the latter, my efforts are wasted, but the acts of printing and distributing news undermines the quality and currency of the reporting. Everything is a compromise. Frustrated, he started his article. Pressure; he wrote furiously; rather than capitulate, he rose to it.

This is what real journalism is like, he told himself. He reviewed his notes, skipped forward and back on the smartphone and identified the more telling pictures. The story was coming together in his head at least, but Tempus fugit.

Head down, he paid little attention to the surrounding hubbub; he was on a mission. The time had come for him to turn all his materials, thoughts, jottings, and ideas into a coherent story. It is not just a story, but the story that would elevate him to his actual goal. This would be pivotal to his career. All those hours sat around maternity ward waiting rooms or hovering around graveyards getting soaked whilst some total stranger was being committed to the earth, or worse, watching all those couples find true love and everlasting happiness, vowing their troths, whilst he noted down names, times, places, weights or whatever. That would soon be history. Nothing more than a stepping stone on his chosen career path, a means to an end.

The reality of reporting an involved and unfolding story to captivate the imagination of his readers was new to him and a far cry from what he normally wrote. He knew he would have to convince his editor of it's worth, and pay some attention to the truth, all in an ever decreasing amount of time. He typed, he reviewed, he amended, and corrected. Keeping one eye on the computer screen and the other on the office wall clock—the relentless second hand counting down to the copy deadline—Jimmy felt the pressure. Time was never right in his mind. Either time moved too fast in the morning when he was late, or too slow in the afternoon when he wanted to finish. Now it was pushing at his back to type faster, think quicker, and deliver sooner.

        ❧   ❧   ❧

'Look at him, Clive.' Colin spoke in hushed tones. 'Do you think he's badly hurt?' Both men stared at the Major. He hadn't moved since he was strapped to the stretcher.

'He's been out cold for ages now.'

'The paramedics don't seem too concerned.' Clive was more interested in his own condition. 'Look at me!' The blood streaks on his skin had dried. 'Colin, I'm thinking you're jinxed.' He turned back to examine his own wounds again.

The sound of the ambulance siren masked the sounds of the Major. If anyone had been paying close attention to him, they would have seen his lips moving. Not enough to make himself heard, but sufficient to realise he was trying to say something. The paramedic, Colin, and Clive remained oblivious to his utterings.

'So what happened then, guys?' The paramedic sounded cheerful. 'Looks like you two've been dragged through a hedge backwards several times. I've not seen nothing like it in all my years on the job.'

'A bit of a problem with a bouncy castle.'

'Oh, I see.' The paramedic clearly didn't. 'Were there any children hurt?'

'Children? What do you mean, children?' Clive was confused.

'Well, it is, or was, a bouncy castle, and it's unusual for children to bounce on them. Is it?'

'Yes, normally, but we had a lorry on it.'

'No room for children then, I guess? Just as well, given what happened, otherwise you could have been looking at a much larger disaster.' The paramedic gave a nervous snigger. 'Actually, what did happen?'

Colin and Clive regaled the story for the next ten minutes, each filling in for the other with copious details, descriptions and more than a hint of embellishment. All three were talking ten to the dozen, asking and answering questions. As they were telling the story, Colin got to thinking about what had happened and how it wasn't a joke but a serious situation and, as far as he knew, remained unresolved. Panic gripped him.

Jumping up, he ran for the rear exit door, shouting something about a hole delivery and how he had no time for hospitals, but he needed to find Izzy urgently. At that moment, the ambulance pulled in to its bay by the entrance to A&E and stopped abruptly. Colin, unprepared, was knocked off balance, falling heavily. The Major was yet again the recipient of his foolhardiness. This time Colin brought his full weight to bear on the Major's abdominal area. Like anyone having a heavyweight dropped onto their stomach when in the prone position, the result is an involuntary and uncontrolled desire to sit up without hesitation and at speed. The Major did just that. Unfortunately, Colin's head was in line with the trajectory of the semi-conscious

Major. Their heads collided. Colin took a powerful hit square on the right temple and crashed to the floor, wedged against the back door. On the way down, he bounced his left cheek off assorted medical paraphernalia. A pool of blood emerged from around his head. Both men were now out cold.

Like most accidents, it was all over in a split second. One minute Colin was off in a rant, the next he was lying in a heap on the floor, bleeding. It rooted the paramedic and Clive to the spot in disbelief, whilst the Major returned to that dark foreboding place—his unconscious. He'd split open the bridge of his nose and looked for all the World like a defeated boxer who had just completed in a title fight.

Outside the ambulance, they heard the commotion. In an instant, Nurse Tanya had the rear door open. She screamed as a naked leg followed by a second tumbled into view. The weight of the falling legs pulled the rest of Colin out and onto the tarmac. Bloody and semi-naked, he landed at her feet. Instinctively, she jumped clear as he came to rest. The paramedic appeared at the door. 'Don't just leave him there, get a stretcher!'

It took Tanya a little while to catch on to what had just happened. Two colleagues ran out of the hospital with a trolley, and all four picked him up together. As they turned him over, she realised who it was.

'It's Mr Griggs. Colin, isn't it?' She looked around for confirmation.

'Yeah, that's him. Not the luckiest chap around.'

'You're telling me. I had him in a few weeks ago; concussion then. Now it looks like he's had a severe beating and his body... All those cuts!'

'There are two more like him in the ambulance. Blew up a lorry with a bouncy castle or some such nonsense—and the other one got hit by a flying dog. Mind you, Colin here just gave him one hell of a thwack as they crashed heads.'

Making sense of what was going on was of lesser importance to getting Colin into X-ray and the Major in for triage. Never mind poor Clive, whose cuts were stinging like crazy with all the antiseptic being rubbed all over him.

'Mr Griggs,' Paul from HTR had arrived with the tow-truck, 'What's been going on here?' He killed the engine and jumped down from the cab. Stewart held out his hand.

'No, I'm Stewart Ballard. Mr Griggs had to go to the hospital. It's a long story.'

The two men surveyed the scene and discussed their options. Soon Paul had manoeuvred his truck into position and fixed a rope to the towing point on Old Alfred Mac. He extended the winch arm, lifting the lorry up and forward with relative ease before lowering its front end back onto the road. With all its wheels back on terra firma, Stewart assessed the damage done to the holes and the lorry itself.

'Will it start?' Paul was keen to get away and onto the next job. After a couple of tries, Stewart fired up the engine. He slipped it into gear and lifted the clutch. The lorry inched forward sufficiently to clear the road edge and give full access to the pile of holes.

'Before you go, can you winch this lot up onto the back of the lorry?' Stewart had his wallet out and was brandishing a couple of twenty-pound notes. It wasn't long before the two men had the load secured and Paul left.

Stewart turned the lorry into Henslow Manor drive and parked up near the rear of the house. He pocketed the keys and set off, walking back down the drive to retrieve his own 4X4.

A little late, but no actual harm was done, Colin. Lady Wills should be none the wiser. The thought left his mind as Stewart set a steady walking pace. He withdrew his phone from his pocket and chose the 'message' app. From his 'Favourites' he selected 'Little Miss Muffet'. `'Just to let you know, I delivered the load of holes to Lady W. I've parked the lorry at the Manor. The keys are with me and I'll drop by the hospital to let you have them.'` He hesitated over the number of x's to add to the end of the message. He plumped for one and pressed 'send'.

As he reached his truck, he saw Billy with his tape measure and notebook.

'Guess we ought to be prepared; you never know there might be a Court case. At some time I'll need to take a statement.' Billy continued measuring.

Without further ado, Stewart jumped into his truck.

'I hope he's alright. If it wasn't for his brave actions, my poor Davy might be no more.'

'That's my Graham; selfless to the last.'

The Mercedes sped through the countryside.

'You seem remarkably calm, my dear.'

'He's a War veteran; he did several tours of duty. I know he's faced greater dangers. Anyway, the paramedics are looking after him now. I'm sure he's in safe hands. You wait, by the time we see him, he'll be sitting up in bed drinking tea and chatting to the nurses as if nothing has happened.' Marg sounded calm, but like anyone, where there's uncertainty, there's anxiety deep inside.

'Now you mentioned tea, we've neither had lunch. You must be famished. I know I am.' Diana patted her stomach. 'Is there anywhere we can stop to get a sandwich before the hospital? I don't fancy an NHS one.'

'No, I know what you mean. You can't be sure where the sliced meat comes from. I often wonder what they do with all those bits they cut out in operations.' Marg curled up her nose at the thought.

'We'll definitely keep away from any pies,' Diana continued to stroke Davy, 'and you're not getting any either.'

'Quick, quick, stop now, Margaret, here on the left.'

Marg brought the Mercedes to an immediate halt in the bus layby.

'What is it, Diana? Are you okay? Is it Davy?'

'No, no dear, nothing like that. Look just behind us, there.' In the rear-view mirror, Marg could see Diana waving her arms in a vague direction.

'Can't you see? 'Fresh4Lunch', it's a sandwich shop.'

'Diana,' she sounded quite exasperated, 'I thought something was wrong!' She looked into the rear-view mirror again. This time all she could see were large silver letters spelling out 'Leyland', accompanied by the persistent honking of a horn.

'Hold still, we're going to have to move.' She slipped the automatic car into drive and pulled forward, turning onto a service road.

'What would you like?'

'Oh, anything for me. I'm not fussy.'

'Ham, cheese?' Marg was hoping for some guidance.

'Well, ham if it's cut off the bone—none of that processed stuff.'

'So cheese then.'

'Yes, that would be nice, but make sure it's Mature Cheddar or Double Gloucester or, I know, a Wensleydale. No, on second thoughts, I fancy a Brie—an English one, of course. See if they've got some grapes, too.'

Marg wished she'd never asked. 'And what bread?'

'Oh, any will do.'

Marg sighed a sense of relief.

'As long as it baked today and not out of a packet.'

By now, Marg was out of the car.

'One more thing,' Diana called after her, 'no spread, you know, margarine. Just a little butter, the slightly salted variety, made from goat's milk if they've got it.'

Marg smiled through gritted teeth and disappeared inside the shop.

Izzy tried her best to keep pace with the ambulance. It was easy in the countryside, but once they reached traffic in Harpsden, her sense of law-abiding kicked in. She jumped one red light in its wake but felt so guilty that she slowed to the pace of everyday road users.

Over the last few years, congestion in Harpsden meant it was quicker to walk much of the time. *This place needs a bypass.* Frustration replaced her anxiety as the traffic closed in around her. *Why didn't I slip-streaming the ambulance while I had the chance?*

He'll be alright. They're only scratches, she kept telling herself. *But the holes! What's going to happen to the holes? Stewart, of course, Stewart. But what if he can't? Lady Wills will think we're a right shambles and cancel the order, and then what?* She could feel her shoulders tightening up.

Izzy, get a grip! This is not like you. The thoughts kept racing around her head. Each new one compounding the disaster, she convinced herself was coming. Coming from deep within her handbag the sound of a new text message. It pulled back to reality. *I wonder who that is.* Which turned into, *I bet, that's the hospital with news of Colin.* Followed by, *I wouldn't be surprised if that's Lady Wills cancelling the order.*

With the traffic queued, she leant over and scrabbled around in the passenger foot-well for her handbag. Having decided that the message had to be read now, whatever, she yanked on the bag handle, trying to pull it up onto the seat. It caught around the seat's adjusting lever. The more she pulled, the more entangled it became, and the more frustrated she felt. The traffic moved; she didn't. The driver behind let her know his displeasure.

'Oh, shut up! Don't you know there's a crisis going on in here?' Of course, he couldn't hear nor see and doubtless didn't care. He just wanted to get on with his journey. In her haste, she ripped through the trapped handle and free the bag, but did so with such force to fling its contents around the inside of the car. She now had to find somewhere to pull over. Up ahead was a left turn into a residential street. Taking it, she stopped. The phone went again, another text. The sound-enabled her to track down its whereabouts to behind the passenger seat. She read the first message and deleted it. 'I want no more free minutes!' The next message was displayed. 'Would like to find out how things are progressing with the business. Can we arrange a conference call over the next few days? Thanks. Sarah.' Izzy's heart sank. *It was all going so well; what have we done to deserve this? All I need now is Sarah Weaver. Of all the times she could have picked, why now?* Her mind was off again. *I bet she knows, but she seems so nice.* Izzy slumped back in her seat; tears welled up in her eyes, one made its way down her cheek. A persistent knock on the window interrupted her thoughts.

'Yes!' she was short.

'My drive.'

'What?' She sounded almost aggressive.

'My drive.'

'What about your drive?' It hadn't twigged.

'I can't get out.'

She looked around her. 'Sorry!' She stabbed at the gear lever and moved off. She was wondering what to do next. Her phone went a third time as Stewart's text arrived. She read it once, then again. Then again, just to make sure.

'I could kiss you, our saviour!' She puckered her lips and kissed the phone instead. She had gone from the depths of despair to unbridled elation in a heartbeat. With a newfound purpose, she let up the clutch and set off. 'Colin, I'm coming!'

Her change of fortune continued; the road she'd turned into led to the hospital visitor car park. *All things come in threes,* crossed her mind. True to form, the first line of parked cars yielded a parking space. Although it was in sight of the A&E entrance, it was too far away to see what was happening. She set off at a brisk pace. The kerfuffle around the ambulance bay had drawn to a close by the time she neared it. She did not know what had just happened and was still on cloud nine.

The receptionist greeted her with a pleasant smile. Behaviour begets behaviour. She was beaming, and the receptionist reflected her mood.

'Colin Griggs, please.' The girl scanned her list of names. Izzy could see she was struggling to find him and helpfully said, 'I think he's just been admitted.' The girl flipped over her sheet of paper, paused, scanned the list of names before flipping it back.

'No one here with that name. Are you sure you're in the right place?' To be helpful, she added, 'This is A&E.'

'Well, he had an accident, and the ambulance brought him here, so I guess it was an emergency. That sounds like A&E to me.'

The receptionist didn't appreciate the sarcasm and gave her a withering look. 'Was he admitted recently?'

'Today, within the last hour. Can I see him?'

'What was wrong with him?'

'An accident with a bouncy castle and a lorry.' She couldn't believe what she had just said. Even to her, it sounded far-fetched. Yet she was there and saw it all.

'Oh, why didn't you say? You need the ICU.'

'ICU?'

'Yes, the Intensive Care Unit. Down the corridor, second door on the right.' The receptionist was making helpful directional gestures as she spoke.

'Why is he in the IUC or whatever you call it? He's only got a few scratches, albeit all over him, but—'

'No, he's unconscious. When the nurse opened the ambulance doors, he fell out onto the ground.' She sounded matter of fact.

'What do you mean, fell out unconscious?' Panic was setting in; Izzy could feel it rising from her stomach. 'Where is he now? I must see him.'

'ICU, down the corridor, second door on the right.' By the time receptionist finished talking, Izzy was out of earshot. She burst in through the double doors into the ICU. The corridor's glare was replaced by a sea of darkness except for four islands of light, each picking out a bed surrounded by clusters of machines, all twinkling away in virtual silence except for the bleeping rhythms of the heart rate monitors. The nurses' station, positioned centrally, had a good view of the patients. Two of the beds were empty. Around the two remaining beds, several people were working. Izzy headed for the activity.

'Sorry.' From the gloom, a nurse appeared and blocked her progress. 'Only medical staff in here. Can I help you?'

'That's my husband; what's happened to him? Why is he in here?' She tried to push past.

'Please, madam.'

'Don't madam me! Just let me see him.'

'I can't do that just now. Who are you?'

'Mrs Griggs.' Izzy was looking beyond the nurse, trying to see what was happening.

'Well, Colin's in excellent hands. Now come with me.' The nurse placed a hand on her shoulder and turned her away from the beds and toward the station. 'Sit here, please. We have some questions we need to ask you.'

'Is he going to be all right? What happened? When I saw him last, he had severe scratching. This is intensive care! Why is he here?'

'We're not sure what happened, but during the ambulance journey, someone knocked your husband unconscious and fell heavily, causing extensive bruising to his head, neck, and torso. There was another man involved. A Major Graham Woods, I believe. We are trying to establish what happened, but I think there was a fight. The Major too is unconscious and bleeding profusely from a cut to the bridge of his nose.'

In that instant, Izzy felt her future fly out of the window. 'No, he wouldn't; he's not that stupid. Why would he hit the Major?' Although she was talking, she was actually thinking out loud. 'Why would he do that?'

'We don't know what happened, but it seems like the Major hit your husband.'

That bit of news didn't make it any clearer what might have happened, but at least it would be better for

Colin if it was the Major who started it.

'What about Clive? He must have seen everything.'

The nurse looked quizzical. 'Clive?' she repeated.

'Yes, Clive Beer. The bouncy castle also blew him up and he went in the ambulance.'

'We've not got a Clive in here. Try A&E.'

Drawn between staying with Colin and the need to find out what happened—both Colin's health and their future were at stake; the anguish showed on her face.

'You can't do anything here right now, but he is stable.' Said the nurse.

That decided for her, and Izzy set off back to A&E.

'What's this?' The Editor brandished several sheets of paper a few inches from Jimmy's face.

'It's my scoop. Yeah, I just happened to be near the Police Station earlier today when I saw a patrol car shoot off all sirens blaring, so I followed it.'

'So you followed it. Good, that's using your initiative. And—'

'Well, you have my piece; it's all in there.'

'I know. I've read it, well, most of it, and very good it is too.'

'So?'

'So, what time is it?'

Jimmy looked at the office wall clock. '6.30.'

'Well, at least you've got that right.'

'What do you mean?'

'Deadlines; my life is driven by deadlines. They may mean nothing to you, and quite clearly they don't, but to me, they govern my every move.'

'I know, it had it on your desk before the copy deadline.'

'I grant you two minutes to six is not 6 o'clock, but this is a major story, worthy of the front page and an inside double spread.'

'Gosh, thanks.' Jimmy straightened up in his seat.

'It impacts every other story in the issue and would involve reworking the whole paper. That's not a five-minute job. This isn't Fleet Street, and I'm not Rupert Murdoch. A rework like that takes hours.' He stared hard at Jimmy. What's more annoying is it's well written and would have contributed significantly. What were you thinking? Why didn't you let me know what was going on? A simple phone call from the scene would have done. I could have held the front page.' The Editor was animated, tutting, muttering and gesticulating. After a few more rants, he started walking back toward his office. Calm was descending, but without warning, he spun around on his heels. 'Why didn't you tell me?' His eyes had the look of a madman. Jimmy flinched.

'Why!' he barked again.

'Cos I thought you'd—,' Jimmy's voice reduced to a mumble.

'What! Speak up.' The Editor glared at him.

'Cos I thought you'd tell me to come back, and I'd miss my opportunity to be a proper reporter.' Jimmy cast his eyes to the floor.

'Well, it didn't need me to screw up your opportunity. You did that perfectly well for yourself.'

The words rang in Jimmy's ears; he returned to

his desk, reflecting on what had just happened. As he re-read his piece, he recalled the words the Editor had used to describe it. It gave some solace. Eventually, he plucked up enough courage to go down to the loading bay and find a copy of the Evening Post. Ever hopeful, he scanned the front page; nothing. Page 2, nothing, page 3, still nothing. Now despondent, page 5 proved more fruitful even if it was only a three-inch column headed Lorry in Accident on Henslow Hill. His 1,500 words with pictures ended up as 60 words and, of course, none of them included his name.

The loading bay led onto the street, and the street led to the Railway Arms public house. Jimmy ordered a large whisky and took himself off to the far end of the bar. He sat, staring at his drink. He'd never drank whisky but felt this would be a good time to start.

Okay, be positive. At least he liked the story; more than liked it. It wasn't what I did, but rather what I didn't do that was the problem. He picked up the glass and sniffed its contents. He grimaced and put the glass back down. His disappointment and frustration ebbed to be replaced by a new resolve to rescue the story and get the recognition he deserved. He checked his watch; it was just after seven. He jumped down from the barstool.

Right, I guess the Griggs will be home by now. He looked at his watch again. *20 minutes to drive out to the farm, half-hour interview, then back to the Golf Club to see what has happened to the Major. A plan; excellent.* He picked up the whisky glass again and brought it to his lips. As the liquid moved down the glass toward his mouth, he got a whiff and changed his mind. *So maybe I'm not cut out to be a whisky drinker.* He left the glass with its contents intact and headed off to find his car.

They ate as they drove. Marg felt she ought to be in more of a hurry, but Diana was treating it like a day out. They had shared many a sandwich during their time touring the County, but that wasn't today.

'Good choice Margaret. Even Davy thinks so, and you know how fussy he is.'

Marg let the comment pass. Her focus was now on Graham. She pushed the accelerator down in response to her own thoughts but only arrived at the junction quicker, forcing her to brake harder. They stopped with a jolt.

'You know what my father always said: more haste, less speed.' Came from the back of the car.

There are times, Diana, when I could strangle you and your father. She kept that to herself. 'I guess he never drove in Harpsden traffic.'

'No, of course not, dear. We lived in Chelsea, and anyway, we had Stanley.'

'Stanley? Who's Stanley?'

'Daddy's driver. Took him everywhere, any time of day or night. Right until he died.'

'Who, Stanley?'

'No, Daddy, of course.'

'Oh, silly me.'

'You weren't to know. I didn't know you then.'

'No, quite.' Marg decided not to pursue Stanley any further. She had more pressing things on her mind.

They pulled into the hospital visitor car park and

found a space. She went into 'caring wife' mode and forgot her passenger. Marg was out of the car and running and had made it halfway across the car park before she realised she was alone.

'Oh, my God! Diana!' she shrieked at the top of her voice. 'I'm coming,' and with that, she sprinted back toward her car. As she got closer, she peered into the rear, expecting to see Diana staring back at her, but saw nothing. She pressed her key fob twice to unlock all the doors, throwing open the rear near-side as she did so. The seat was empty.

Straddled across the back of the front seats, Diana was trying to crawl over to make good her escape.

'Diana, please forgive me.'

'Just get me out of here!' Diana didn't sound forgiving.

'It's the child locks; I forgot they were on. You never know with grandchildren what they'll get up to.'

'Right now, I don't care about grandchildren. Just get me out!' She tumbled into the front, sending Davy flying as he had been sitting on her back, watching the antics of his mistress with curious interest.

As dignified as one can in a situation like this, Diana climbed out, straightening her clothes and hair. Soon she was looking her immaculate self and none the worse for her ordeal.

She spoke as if nothing had happened. 'Right now, the Major. Let's find out how he is. Come on Margaret, pronto.' Diana set off in full flight with Davy tucked under her arm and Marg running behind to keep up. They reached A&E reception together.

'Yes, can I help?'

'I'm Mrs Woods; I'm here to find out how my husband, Major Woods, is.'

'Sorry, we have no Major Woods here.' Marg looked quizzical.

'Look for yourself.' The nurse showed her a page of names, and Graham wasn't amongst them.

'So where is he?'

'Are you sure he came to this hospital? To the A&E Department?'

'Well, he was taken away unconscious in the ambulance, so I assumed they'd brought him here. Where else might they take him?'

'Unconscious, you say. He wasn't one of the men playing on the bouncy castle by any chance?'

'He was connected with the bouncy castle incident; yes, why?'

'Well, he's in Intensive Care then. Apparently, he was involved in a fight and knocked another man unconscious.' Marg shot Diana a look of horror mixed with bewilderment.

'So where is Intensive Care?' The urgency in Marg's voice was telling.

'Just down the corridor, second door on the right.' Before the nurse had finished, both women were gone.

'Excuse me..., Mrs Woods.' She called after them, 'please come back here. Mrs Woods.' The nurse's repeated calls went unheeded. She had no choice but to run after them. 'Dogs,' she sounded breathless, 'no dogs in here, sorry.'

Diana had forgotten she was clasping Davy. 'Keys

Margaret, give me the keys, and I'll wait in the car.'

Soon, Marg disappeared through a set of double doors, leaving the corridor's bright lights for a sea of tranquil darkness. Her eyes took a few seconds to adjust as she made her way to the nurse's station.

'I'm Mrs Woods. I believe my husband's here.' She was rather hesitant, 'because he's been fighting.' She raised the pitch of her voice as if asking a question.

'Yes, he's here in bed 4. We're not sure what happened. He came to us unconscious and bleeding profusely from a cut on the bridge of his nose. The paramedic said something about your husband and a Mr Griggs fighting in the ambulance.'

'And where is Mr Griggs?' She wasn't sure she wanted to know.

'Here, in bed 3.' The nurse pointed to a pool of light next to Graham's bed.

'Are they alright? What's going to happen next? What can I do?' Her calmness evaporated.

'Mrs Woods, just take a deep breath. They're fine. Neither is in any immediate danger. We need to dress the wounds and determine their treatments. They'll be going to x-ray shortly, but for now, we just need to make sure their breathing's stable and blood pressure's okay.'

'Have you seen Mr Griggs' wife, Isobel? Is she around anywhere?' Marg asked.

The nurse thought for a second. 'Yes, she was here some time ago. She went to find a Clive Beer; I think she said. He was also in the ambulance.'

The opening and closing of the double doors disturbed the half-light of the ICU.

'Ah, here are the porters to take both patients to x-ray. If you take a seat in the waiting room, we'll come and find you when he's out. He'll be going onto Ward 4a, it says here…, in around half an hour.'

Marg left to find Izzy. Heading toward A&E, she noticed Stewart at the reception desk.

'Stewart, am I glad to see you! The Major and that Griggs fellow are in Intensive Care following a fight. They've just gone to x-ray. Nobody seems to know what happened. Isobel Griggs is here somewhere looking for Clive Beer. I've not seen her yet, but I have Lady Wills in my car with Davy. Of course, he cannot come in here, and she can't leave him in the car alone.' She drew her breath. Stewart looked around and spotted Izzy sitting in the far corner of the waiting area. She was alone.

'Look there is Izzy, erm, I mean Mrs Griggs.' He pointed in her direction. She hadn't seen them. 'There's no sign of Clive. Maybe he's in a cubicle.' They set off to see her.

'Izzy.' The room was busy, but not crowded. Still, she never heard. 'Izzy.' By now, Stewart was closer; she looked up, their eyes met. He had an urge to take her into his arms and to tell her everything would be alright, but with Marg right behind, he could do none of it. Izzy felt no such inhibitions and jumped up, throwing herself at him with such force she almost knocked him off his feet.

'Our Saviour! How can I thank you enough?' He regained his balance, tactfully removing her arms. She resisted. Marg saw but said nothing, only feeling a sense of confusion. She wasn't sure what she'd just witnessed or why it had happened.

'Margaret, how nice to see you.' Izzy hadn't noticed her up to that point and now felt self-conscious. 'I've found Clive. He's in for an assessment at present. We've not talked, so I do not know how come they're both in Intensive Care.'

'They've gone for x-rays now. The porters took them up there.' Marg informed her.

'X-ray, what happened to them? My poor Colin.' Izzy struggled to hold back her tears.

'I guess that's what they're trying to find out. The nurse in the ICU said go to the waiting room. She expects to have some news in half an hour. They're being moved to Ward 4a.'

'So not back to Intensive Care. Well, that must be good news, surely!' Izzy looked at both of them for confirmation. Across at the reception desk, she noticed Lady Wills. 'There Margaret, look.' She pointed in her direction without making it too obvious.

'Diana, cooee.' She didn't hear. 'I must go.' Marg hurried off.

'But what about your husband?' Izzy inquired, but by now, she was out of ear shoot. She looked at Stewart, who just shrugged. 'Look, she's coming back.'

'Diana is so considerate. She's sending Davy back to Henslow Manor by taxi; so one minor problem solved.' Marg looked at her watch. 'Gosh, look, it's been half an hour. We should go to the ICU waiting room.' Marg turned on her heels to leave.

'What about Clive whatever his name is…,' Diana stopped Marg in her tracks. 'We can't leave him, he's got no clothes, car or naything.'

'Does Clive's wife know he's here?' Marg looked at all three.

Izzy and Stewart shrugged in unison and said, 'I've not told her.'

'I've Clive's mobile number, but no idea where he lives.' Izzy continued, 'His clothes, nor Colin's for that matter, aren't wearable—full of thorns.'

'Are they letting Clive go home?' Stewart asked. This time, Marg and Izzy shrugged. 'So we don't know then?'

'I think that's a fair assessment.' Izzy rolled her eyes to heaven. 'Stewart, would you be so kind and wait here with Lady Wills for him to appear, we'll go to the ICU for news of Colin and the Major.'

❧   ❧   ❧

'She said half an hour, and that was over an hour ago.' Marg continued to pace up and down the waiting room.

'I'm sure they'll be alright. You know what these places are like, well-meaning but—'

'I don't actually, Isobel, we normally go private!' There was a cutting edge to her tone. 'And anyway, we wouldn't be here at all if it weren't for your husband. A ludicrous idea; Hole Farming. Look where it's got us. My poor Graham, he's a quivering wreck after the Golf Club fiasco, and now he's ended up in Intensive Care.'

The mood in the room changed. Izzy fought off her compulsion to defend Colin, biting her tongue instead.

'What's more, he never meant to grab that girl's bottom. He was trying to save her from getting hurt.'

Marg's anger flared.

'Be fair; that was nothing to do with Colin.' Izzy felt that was one comment too far.

'Maybe, but you used the picture to blackmail him into giving a good reference; despicable, absolutely despicable!' She locked Izzy in a hard stare.

In the nick of time, the waiting room door opened. 'Mrs Griggs, Mrs Woods. Just to let you know, both your husbands are going to Ward 4a. The nurses need to settle them in, then you can go up there after 6 o'clock. Visiting times are from 6 to 8 pm. We try to stick to them as we don't want to upset the ward's routine. Here, this should help.' The nurse held out a copy of the Welcome to Henslow Hospital—a Guide for Patients.

'You take it, Isobel. The Major won't be in here long enough to need it.' Marg glanced at her watch and left.

The nurse smiled at Izzy. 'Everything alright?'

'Oh, I think she's on edge. You know how it is when you don't know what's going on. You always imagine the worse. I'm sure she'll be fine. Just gone for some fresh air, I expect.' Izzy took the booklet and read it. She had another hour to kill.

'Thanks, Nurse...' Izzy looked up, hesitant.

'Tanya.' The nurse pointed to her name badge.

'Yes, of course, Tanya, you've been most helpful again. Aren't you the nurse who came to our farm?'

Nurse Tanya smiled at Izzy.

Izzy set off to A&E to find Stewart. She needed a friend, and he was just the person.

He hadn't moved from where she left him.

'What news of Clive?' Izzy took him by surprise.

419

'Izzy, I didn't see you there. Well, from what I can gather, they're going to keep him in overnight with so many lacerations and potential for tetanus.' His voice trailed off as he could see the moisture gathering in her eyes. 'Izzy, what is it? Why are you?' He didn't have time to finish before she was in a full flood of tears.

'She blames us for everything; it's not fair. Colin is a good man, he tries hard.' For the second time today, she threw her arms around Stewart. This time he didn't resist and hugged her back.

'There, there. It'll be okay. You just wait and see.' Somewhat confused, 'She is?' Stewart enquired.

'Margaret Woods, who else?' Izzy sobbed into his jacket.

'Okay.' *Marg may have a point*, he thought, but he kept that to himself.

'She just stormed out; I do not know where she is. I assume she'll be back for visiting time. We cannot see them until then.' It was difficult for him to understand her given her face was buried in his jacket.

He took a surreptitious look at his watch. 'Not long now,' he said, trying to comfort her. 'At least they're on a ward and not in Intensive Care. That must mean things aren't so bad after all.' He was trying to make her feel better.

They stood locked in the embrace for a good few minutes. She eventually relaxed her grip.

'Better now?' Stewart looked down to see the runs of mascara down her cheeks, and her lipstick smudged around her mouth.

He fished out a handkerchief. 'Here, take this.'

She wiped her face.

'You need to go to the ladies. There's a mirror in there.'

'I must look a state.' She stood on tiptoe and kissed him on the cheek. 'Our Saviour!' She left.

'Are you with Mr Beer?' A nurse was standing by his side.

'Err, yes, I suppose so.'

'Well, we're keeping him in tonight. Ward 4a. You can see him after six.' The nurse disappeared as quickly as she came.

'Oh, okay. Thanks.'

Stewart sat down and picked up a discarded local evening paper and flicked through it. He'd just got to the Sports section as Izzy returned.

'That's better. More like the Izzy, I know. Nothing in here about the lorry. Happen, the reporter missed the deadline.'

'That's the early edition; you need the late one. Won't be here for a while.'

He returned to the Sports pages, and she sat in contemplative silence, reflecting on the day's events.

'What do you think is going to happen? I mean, if the Major punched Colin, then that's assault.'

'Provoked, though.' Stewart didn't look up.

'Well, maybe a little, but it was Diana's dog and Clive's castle.'

'Come on; we'll have a bit more of an idea when we see them. It's nearly six. Let's go.'

The wards were well signposted; they walked in silence. There were plenty of other people milling around, most of whom seemed to know where they were going.

'It's been 41 years since I spent a night in the hospital. The last time was when I had my tonsils out at 18.' Stewart said.

'I didn't know that.'

'Well, you were too busy with Colin to notice me.' He looked wistfully at her.

&ro;   &ro;   &ro;

'Here we are, then. Don't forget the hand-wipe.' The outside of the ward doors were covered in reminders. The six beds of Ward 4a were in the side unit, and it seemed the six o'clock rule was fluid—three of the patients already had visitors. The other three, laying side by side, looked like something from the Lost City of the Pharaohs. A row of freshly wrapped mummies greeted the visitors. Without their name boards, it was difficult to tell who was who.

'Colin, it's me, Izzy.' She qualified herself just in case he couldn't see. 'How are you? Can you talk? Can you hear me?' There was no reaction to her presence. 'What's wrong with him, Stewart?'

'I'll chat to Clive and see if he can tell us what happened.' He was in the next bed but one, with the Major in the middle.

'Clive, it's me, Stewart. Look at you, what happened in the ambulance?' Stewart could see Clive's eyes moving behind the bandages. 'How come you're mummified also?'

'Cos I had so many thorns all over me, especially my scalp. There's a lot of skin damage. They're concerned

'Yeah, it's all safe in her car. I'll let Caroline know and get your stuff brought in.' Stewart moved closer to Clive. 'So what happened with the Major and Colin? I heard the Major took a swing at him.'

Before Clive had time to answer, Marg with Diana arrived at the Major's bedside.

Diana spoke, 'Oh, look at him, poor chap. All of them, Margaret, this is terrible.'

She had no choice but to agree with her, but did so through gritted teeth. *There's only one poor chap in here*, she thought, *and that's my Graham.* At that moment, he stirred and let out a low groan.

'Graham, it's me, Marg. Are you okay?' There was silence. She took hold of his hand. 'Squeeze if you can hear me.' He duly obliged. 'Thank goodness for that.' She placed her mouth near his ear. 'Colin Griggs is in the next bed.' She kept her voice down, hoping no one else could hear. He still had hold of her hand. At the news, he squeezed it with alarming force. She jumped back in surprise, and of course, everyone noticed. 'Oh, he's feeling delicate; I must have hit a sore spot.'

Izzy, too, was trying to get a reaction from Colin. He was conscious, but his hearing was impaired following his fall in the ambulance, and the swathe of bandages covering his head.

'Colin, what happened?' Her whisper was loud enough for all but Graham to hear. 'Did you fight with the Major? Everyone seems to think so, and that he threw the first punch.'

Marg and Diana gave the appearance of tending to Graham, but they were both hanging on her every word. Colin stalled his reply as he tried to make sense of what had happened before sharing it with anybody. Despite his groggy state, he knew it was important to get it right.

'Izzy, I know what it may seem, but it's not like that.' The Major cut him short.

'Griggs!' he called through muffled bandages. 'Griggs,' he tried again.

'Shhhh, Graham, everyone's listening.'

'I don't care. You just wait till I get my hands on him.' With that, the Major tried to lift himself off the bed. He was too weak and fell back. 'I haven't finished with you yet. In fact, I've not even started!'

Diana intervened, 'Now, Major, don't be too hard on the poor chap. He's a sick man too. Despite everything, they delivered my holes today as promised.'

'Holes, holes. The only good hole will be the one they bury him in!'

'Graham, how could you? Say you're sorry.' Looking around her, Marg continued, 'I think it's the drugs he's on. The Major's not like that really, you know.'

'That bloody man almost killed me! I've every right to be angry.'

'He's not responsible for all the things that have happened.'

'Maybe not directly, but in one way or another, he is.'

Marg wanted to put a positive spin on events. 'It

was you who saved Davy.'

'And we're ever so grateful. If he were here now, I'm sure he'd give you one of his big licks as a thank you.' Diana patted Graham's hand.

'Yes, well, that's as maybe, but he wouldn't have needed saving if Griggs hadn't backed his lorry down those ridiculous holes.'

'It wasn't on purpose,' Izzy piped up, 'some young lad forced him off the road. He did it to avoid an accident, actually.'

'Well, what about the Golf Club? Did he do that to avoid an accident?' The Major's anger radiated from him.

Colin listened to these rants and felt more despondent with each new accusation.

'I've been a respected member of this community for more years than I care to remember. Captain and Chairman of the Golf Club, a distinguished and decorated military career, a committed supporter of my wife and her extensive charity undertakings, a pillar, a rock, until—' He ran out of steam exhausted.

'Yes, yes, my love.' Marg wanted to appease him.

'If that bloody man thinks he can ruin me, then he's another thought coming. As soon as I'm out of here, I'll be onto Companies House to get him banned as a Director. He's not competent to organise a… a ...' he lost his train of thought. 'Whatever, never mind; run a business.'

'Sush dear, everyone can hear. I know you're angry, but just wait until the morning; you'll feel different then.' Marg smiled at the room.

'Different, different. Why will I feel different? Will

the divine hand of providence make it all right? Will the Golf Club greens be useable again? Will my head stop throbbing? Will my reputation be untarnished? I don't think so!'

'Blood pressure, think of your blood pressure. You don't want to go making yourself more ill.' Marg's concern was genuine.

'But I am sick, sick of that man in my life.'

'You know you don't mean it.' Marg turned toward Diana. 'I'm sure it's just the medication. He's normally so understanding.'

'Well, he does not understand right now.' Diana paused. 'Did I make the right decision to use Colin?' She waited for confirmation. 'After all, it was the Major who recommended him to me.'

'See Griggs, now what have you done? You've besmirched my good name.' Graham tensed his whole body, trying to lift himself off the bed.

Izzy kept schtum so as not to give the Major any further reason to attack her Colin. Stewart and Clive were trying to avoid being drawn into the fracas, keeping any thoughts to themselves, while Diana remained uncertain of what she had done. The room went quiet.

'Here they are, Julia, all together.' Mr Pryor appeared at the entrance to the ward. 'That'll make visiting easier.' Steve was feeling full of the joys of summer. 'Well, gents, I heard you had a spot of bother today. Mind you, going by your looks, I would say it was rather a big spot! What on earth happened?'

Nobody offered a response; they all looked at each other.

'Your Ladyship, Marg, Mrs Griggs, Stewart, tell me what happened?'

Marg broke the silence.

'It was nice of you to come, Steve, but as you can see, all three aren't ready for visitors. Maybe tomorrow.'

'But everyone down at the Golf Club's asking. The phone's ringing off the hook. I thought I'd better come up to find out.' Steve insisted.

'Well, you can tell everybody there are no bones broken. In a few days, they'll all be right as rain.' Marg thought that was sufficient without going into detail.

Graham growled, 'Why did you do it, Steve?'

'Sorry, Major, I don't quite understand. I can't hear you through your bandages?'

'Oh, take no notice of him; it's his medication.'

'Marg, will you stop saying that, I know exactly what I'm saying. Steve, if it wasn't for you giving Griggs that business loan, we would never be in this state.' Graham sounded aggressive.

Colin winced.

Steve shot a look in Graham's direction. The dressings meant he could not make sense of any reaction. Izzy hid her face, trying to become invisible. Lady Wills looked at the floor, moving uncomfortably in her chair, while Marg just raised her eyebrows.

'This is not a suitable moment, I take it.' Steve looked at each in turn.

Julia shrugged and gaped at Marg, hoping for some clarification.

Graham would not let it go. 'Well, what have you got to say for yourself?'

'I'm sorry, Major, but it's neither the time nor the place to discuss such matters. Anyway, the relationship between the bank and its customers is private. The code of conduct still binds me.' Steve hoped that would shut him up.

'I'm your captain, Chairman, and you're retired. Your loyalty is to me.'

'I think we'd better go, Julia. Obviously, this isn't a good time.'

Stewart got on his feet. 'Actually, Steve, I'll come with you. I assume you're going back to the Club?' He was out the door in a flash.

'Er, well, if you're going that way, a lift would be most welcome.' Lady Wills moved toward the door.

'Diana, please don't bother Steve; I'll run you home. It's the least I can do.'

'Margaret, you have plenty to do here. I wouldn't presume, but thank you.' Diana stood. 'Goodnight gentlemen, Major. I'm glad to see you're on the mend.'

The room emptied, and the Major continued his verbal attack. 'Griggs. I know you can hear me. From now on, I'm going to make your life hell!'

'Graham, please,' Marg attempted to diffuse the situation, 'you wait dear, everything will look better tomorrow.'

Colin felt he needed to defend himself. 'Major,' came a muffled response, 'please try to see it from my point of view.'

'The only thing I want to see is you leaving

Henslow in your knackered old lorry, heading away from here. I don't care where you go as long as you're out of my life.' It hurt him to shout, be he felt it was worth it.

'Izzy,' Colin turned to her, 'what are we going to do?' He sounded beaten.

She looked lost, unsure, and confused.

'I wish I could find a hole to crawl in and disappear.' Colin pulled the bedcovers over his head.

'Oh, Colin, things aren't that bad. Don't take a tunnel view on life; there's always tomorrow.' She felt she should bolster his spirits. The room fell silent for a few minutes, apart from Clive's snoring.

'Did I hear you right, Izzy? Did you say tunnel?' Colin re-emerged from the covers.

'Yes. Why?'

'That's got me thinking.'

'Colin, what now?' She didn't like it when he thought.

'I'm not sure, but maybe I've been thinking too small.'

'Too small; too small in what way?'

'About holes, of course.'

Izzy looked puzzled. 'What do you mean?'

'Our hole business; you get nowhere unless you think big.'

She looked to see if anyone was listening. Marg was busy trying to feed Graham a drink of water; no one else was around.

'And?' she said it in a loud whisper.

'I've got an idea...' Colin bid her closer. 'You know, on the Harpsden road leading out of the village, where it always floods, I heard they want to build a culvert to drain away the excess water.'

'Colin, you talk in riddles. I think it's the bang on the head.'

'No, listen, Izzy. The culvert will run under the road to drain into the fields. That means they'll have to direct the water through a tunnel to get it to the other side.'

'So—' she was none the wiser.

'That's where Griggs Hole Farming comes in.'

'A tunnel, but we're hole farmers.' *Though I have my doubts.* 'You just said so yourself.'

'Yeah, but don't you see? A tunnel's only a hole on its side.'

Believing it was his medication or the accident, she let him be. If she could have seen behind his bandages, she would have witnessed him beaming at his new idea. In his mind he was somewhere else.

… to be continued…

Read on for an extract of Book II
of The Hole Trilogy

A Tunnel is Only a Hole on its Side

CHAPTER 1

A PERSONAL THANKYOU

Unable to sleep, Colin wondered if it was the cold or the anxiety he felt in the pit of his stomach. He tossed and turned while Izzy slept beside him. He judged by her deep, rhythmic breathing that she was in a far better place than him. The clock had moved on fifteen minutes since he'd last looked: five o'clock; dead on. The distant bells of Henslow Church confirmed it. *Why us? Why now?* He couldn't answer himself, but neither would the thoughts let him alone.

Pulling the covers over his head challenged the cold—it was bitter in their bedroom—but it did nothing to drive away his angst. *I can't disturb her; that's not fair. But she is my wife, and she is great in a crisis.* He leaned over to shake her. Watching her sleep, he couldn't bring himself to do it. The conversation played out in his head. *Okay, creep downstairs, jot down my ideas, and come back with a cuppa. She'll never know.* He had a plan; action took over from thought. First one foot, trailed by the second, emerged from the covers. Before his body had time to follow, his feet re-joined him back in bed.

'My, it's cold out there!' Shocked, he blurted out the words. Realising this, he shushed himself: *Don't wake her. Are you a man or a mouse?* He was back in his head. Hesitating before answering, he dwelt on his response.

Colin, get a grip; slippers and socks are by the bed, and your dressing gown is on the back of the door. Quickly and quietly gather them up, then head for the landing. His thoughts and actions were in sync. Making his way downstairs, he remembered that the third from the top produced a loud squeak. Stepping over it, he stumbled past the next two treads. In the dark, he'd misjudged the distance. He struggled to maintain his balance and ricocheted off the walls like a pinball in an arcade machine. The bottom step came quicker than expected, but at least he was down in one piece. Gathering himself, he listened for signs of movement from Izzy, but he heard nothing.

Passing the coat stand, he grabbed a scarf, a matching bobble hat, and fingerless mittens. The central heating wouldn't come on for a couple of hours. It was so damn cold. The relentless north-easterly wind made it feel like Siberia. *Poor buggers,* he thought, *they live with this most of the time.* Slipping into the sanctuary of the kitchen, he dressed for warmth. The Rayburn offered some solace, but against the pernicious gusts growling around the window and door, it was all but useless.

He pulled the table and chair as close to the cast-iron structure as he could. With a pen at the ready and tea in hand, he settled into the task. Henslow church bell rang six times: the kitchen clock confirmed it. He'd made several notes, nothing of any significance, more like headings. What he needed were incisive questions if he was going to sort this out. He wished Izzy was here; after all, it was she who started him off on this path of uncertainty.

She must have sensed his needs; her head popped around the door.

'Are you in there?' She yawned as she spoke: 'I wondered where you were.' Entering the room, she rubbed her eyes against the bright light. 'How long have you been here?'

He realised he'd nearly gotten away with it. 'Only a few minutes, dear.' He lied. She didn't like it when he couldn't sleep.

'Tea? I'm making one for myself.' She pulled a chair out from under the table. 'What are you doing?'

He didn't know if it was his wife or mother speaking. Either way, he felt better knowing she was there. 'It's what you said at teatime, you know, about the bypass coming through our farm…'

'Colin, is that what's got you up? For goodness' sake, it's only a rumour I heard in the village. You know what they're like. Take no notice.' She cringed at the thought, 'Porridge and toast?'

How do women do that? From devastating news to breakfast needs in the same breath without batting an eyelid. He didn't ask her the question. 'Yeah, great. Thanks.' He continued with his deliberations.

❧ ❧ ❧

Watching dawn break was a pleasure Izzy enjoyed, especially on a cold, frosty February morning. Their farm took the brunt of any bad weather; the metre-thick stone walls proved more than a match. She felt reassured knowing the house had stood for a couple of hundred years. The weight of hoar frost bent double the various trees, shrubs, and saplings scattered around the yard. They glistened white. Devoid of foliage, the water vapour crystal-covered branches formed magnificent structures. The tendril-like twigs, enclosed in a thick coating, lost their individuality as species while assuming a uniformity of colour. *Nature, despite the efforts of man,* she mused, *accomplishes extraordinary feats.*

'Have you seen outside?' Lost in his deliberations, he didn't answer. She tried again. 'Have you looked out this morning?'

'What? No, sorry. What did you say?' Despite it being Saturday, he had no time for trivia. Given the potentially devastating news of them losing their farm and livelihood to a new road, took his focus.

The view from the window captivated her. 'Oh nothing, love, just looking at the hoar. I wondered if you'd seen it.'

'What? A whore?' He lifted his head to confirm what he'd heard.

'I'm talking about the hoar frost. Anyway, that's a horrible expression. If any girl must do that for money, I feel sorry for her. It must be dreadful—all those stinky men groping and slobbering. Now you've ruined it for me. I was thinking how amazing Mother Nature is til you filled my head with disgusting thoughts.' The sound of post being pushed through the letterbox interrupted her. 'Oh, I wonder what exciting offers we'll be unable to resist today.' Scurrying out to the hall, she returned. 'Here…' She plonked a stack of letters in front of him.

Too engrossed to notice, he slapped his pen on the table and flopped back in his chair. 'I stopped traditional farming because of paperwork, and now my hole-farming business is under threat from road building.' He shook his head. 'What does one have to do…?

While he talked, she sorted the post; most went to recycling. One caught her eye. 'I think you'll want to see this.' Izzy pushed the envelope towards him.

The handwritten address, with its large, expressive curls, suggested confidence, creativity, and attention-seeking in the writer. It worked. Colin took it for a closer inspection. He recognised the handwriting.

'It's from Lady Wills.' He didn't disguise his anticipation.

Izzy leaned in. 'Go on then, open it.' She was just as keen.

Picking up his knife, he licked off the residual Marmite before placing the tip in the envelope's seal. An incisive movement revealed the contents. He laid the letter, accompanied by two inserts, on the table. Each had their draw: Izzy's eyes landed on the gold-embossed writing of an invitation; Colin's on the cheque for £15,000 for the holes he had supplied her. Broad grins filled their faces.

'Go on, tell me! What does she say?'

Colin flicked open the folded sheet. He turned towards the light and cleared his throat.

'*Dear Colin and Isobel…*' he read aloud.

'Isobel? That sounds a bit formal. I wonder why she calls me Isobel?' said Izzy.

'It's just the way she is. Now shush. Let me finish.' With that, he flexed his arm, holding the letter high so as not to cast a shadow across it.

'*Dear Colin and Isobel,*

I know the recent past has been difficult: starting a new business; the various accidents befalling Colin; the incident with the geese; Mr. Pryor; the Major; stockings; and so on, but throughout this time, you have shown dedication and commitment to your business and, more importantly, to your customers; namely, me.

I want to thank you personally for your efforts and show you my appreciation by extending the hand of friendship. Accordingly, I invite you both to my house-warming party. Your contributions have been significant in getting the magnificent gardens back to their former glorious state, with the added feature of a series of ornate ponds that now adorn the Long Walk. Please find herewith a cheque for the same. I'm planning to incorporate the ponds into the party with a torchlight parade, so everyone will get the opportunity to wonder at your achievements.

I do hope you accept my invitation. As you will notice from the enclosed invite, it is a fancy dress "Come as you are" party. A prize will be awarded to the couple whose outfit most closely resembles their picture. See the invite for details.

For now, yours sincerely.
Diana.'

'Oh, Colin, fancy that; a personal thank you, extending the hand of friendship, and featuring your holes in a torchlight parade. When's the party?' Reaching across him, Izzy grabbed the invite. 'April, that's…' she counted on her fingers, 'about eight weeks. I'm not sure I can wait.'

She moved into the light. 'Have you seen it?' Holding her arms outstretched, she ran her fingers over the embossed writing. The cream card featured an ink drawing of the manor; subtly done, it had sufficient depth to be recognisable but not so much as to overwhelm the writing. Diana herself had handwritten their names. 'Look, it's the same writing as the envelope.' Izzy placed them side by side to check. 'Such a distinctive hand. She's a woman of class.'

Her eyes widened. Darting across the words, she read them again and again. Her lips curled; a smile grew to fill her face. In her mind, she was far away, not in the kitchen of the old farmhouse, but walking gracefully, elegantly down the Long Walk of Henslow Manor. She imagined all the other partygoers admiring, pointing, and commenting on Colin's holes.

Contemplating the text, she chewed her lip. She didn't want him to speak, to break the spell. Then she realised. 'Oh my gosh! It's a come as you are party: pictures, prizes. Colin, you know what that means?' She waited. An answer wasn't forthcoming: 'We need pictures of us now, dressed like this. Where's the camera?'

The puzzled look on Colin's face told her he'd not been listening.

She insisted, 'The invite… it's a fancy dress party with the theme of coming as you are. That means you should come dressed in the clothes you're wearing when you get the invite. And she's asked for a picture to be sent with the RSVP to prove it.'

Colin looked up at her and said, 'What me? In my blue-striped winceyette PJs, with knitted bobble hat and matching scarf? Izzy!' He shivered, emphasising how he felt.

'Look here,' she said, running her fingers over the text again. 'It clearly says, "Come as you are". It's just a bit of fun. Everyone's in the same boat. Can you imagine our old bank manager, Steve Pryor, in his pyjamas with his fat belly?'

'I'd rather not, thank you.' He surveyed his own substantial stomach and sighed. 'Do we have to?'

With her mouth slack and her eyes wide, she stared. 'Colin, you aren't serious?'

Her gaze followed his but didn't stop at his paunch. Instead, she was drawn to the fly of his pyjama trousers. 'You'll have to wear underpants. You can't walk around Henslow Manor like that.' Colin's manhood was clearly visible.

'You shouldn't be looking.' He blushed as an automatic response.

'We've been married for forty years, there's not much left to shock me.' Playfully, she grabbed at his masculinity.

'Izzy, no… Not now. I'm busy. Anyway, we're in the kitchen; that sort of thing remains in the bedroom.' He brushed her hand away.

'I'm only teasing. We still need a picture. Have you seen the camera?'

Colin wasn't listening. He'd gone back to his notes.

'Colin? Camera? Have you seen it?' She rested her hand on his shoulder.

'Umm… yes… no. I don't know.' He didn't look up.

'Is it in Old Alfred Mac?' asked Izzy.

'What?' He was still refusing to take part in the conversation. Rather, he doodled.

'What? You know what? The camera! You took it with you to get some pictures of the ponds in the Long Walk, remember? Did you take it out of the lorry?'

'Look, I'm trying to concentrate. Can you be quiet for a minute?'

'Did you leave the camera in Old Alfred Mac?'

Colin was drawn back to the pressing subject at hand. 'What about the route? Exactly how close is it coming to our farm?'

'I don't know; it was just gossip. Now where's the camera?' She was getting fed up with the sound of her own voice.

He, too, fed up with hearing the same question, pushed back his chair. The legs scraped across the kitchen flagstones. Their noisy protest drowned out his mutterings. In his haste to retrieve the camera, he slammed the back door. His movement triggered the security lights in the yard, and she saw he'd nothing on his feet. The cold of the frozen ground got to him. Up on tiptoes, his gait reminded her of a praying mantis. Making steady progress, it faltered when he trod on something obscured by detritus. An interlude for toe-rubbing, accompanied by a stream of expletives, followed. Soothed, he resumed his journey towards the lorry cab.

She used his absence to make herself more presentable: she ran a comb through her hair, removed her gilet, donned a cardigan, and a pair of shoes more becoming than her faded pink lamb's wool slippers.

He was back. 'Here!' He thrust the camera at her.

'Look, Colin, I don't like the bypass idea any more than you do, but I'm just the messenger. Anyway, you were the one who went out with nothing on your feet. You can't blame me for that.' She took the camera.

'Go on then, take your ruddy picture. I need to get on.' He held a false smile; the grin was so wide it hurt.

'I can't take it yet; the camera's cold.' She held it up for him to see. The lens was misty after coming from the unheated lorry cab into the warmth of the kitchen. 'Give it a few minutes.'

Dropping his smile, he flopped back into his chair. The fly on his pyjama bottoms gaped. There was nothing to see. She thought, *it must be cold out there*. It crossed her mind to warm him up but given his foul mood and how he had reacted earlier, she thought better of it.

'Okay, it's ready now.' She waved the camera under his nose. He grunted in response. 'Come on, Colin, the sooner we do this, the sooner you can get on.'

Reluctantly, he stood. Pushing back his chair, his actions were accompanied by the screech of the flagstones.

'Do you have to?' *He's like a petulant child*.

'What?'

'You know very well what? Come over here.' Izzy had the camera positioned on top of the refrigerator with the timer set. 'Stand there!' She pointed towards the sink. 'And smile.' She depressed the shutter-release button before darting back to join him. The ten-second timer counted down.

'Are you sure it's…?' The flash interrupted him.

'You ruined that. We'll have to do it again.'

'You think so?' He wasn't convinced.

She showed him the image on the review screen. 'Is this how you want Henslow to see you?' The camera had caught him in mid-sentence; he looked more like a goldfish than her Colin. He said nothing; she set up the camera again.

'Right, ten seconds.' In a trice, she was back by his side. 'Smile.' They waited.

'It's funny, you think ten seconds is such a…' Once again, the flash interrupted him.

'Oh, for pity's sake, Colin! Just shut up and wait. Ten seconds is ten seconds. Try counting elephants. Okay, here we go again.'

'One elephant, two elephants…'

'No. Not out loud, you…' She was thwarted by the flash. 'Look what you've made me do! Count in your head.'

After repeated attempts, she was successful.

Casually reviewing the image she said, 'It's no David Bailey, but it'll do.'

Colin took the camera. He studied the screen.

'Are you sure you're happy with this?'

'Yeah, it's not great, but it's recognisable as us, and Diana can see what we're wearing. Why?'

'Before emailing it, you need to study it more closely.'

She snatched the camera back. 'What do you mean?' Her intense scrutiny produced a result. 'Ooh! We can't send that! It's pornographic!' She flushed bright red.

'I thought after forty years of marriage nothing could shock you.' He couldn't help smiling to himself. She fired up the computer. 'I'll upload the image and crop it from the waist down. No one will know.'

ABOUT THE AUTHOR

James is a full-time fiction author. Prior, he spent 35 years in the IT industry and wrote on a wide range of non-fiction IT subjects, including many hundreds of training manuals. He has authored fourteen fiction books to date.

Born 1952 in Oxfordshire, UK, James draws on his local knowledge to provide inspiration and settings for his characters and locations for his plots.

He turned his attention to writing fiction during the summer of 2009. Writing with unbridled passion was new to him. The excitement of not knowing where a story was going but having an evolving host of characters spurred him on. Writing for the inner child in all of us, **The Hole Opportunity** was the first product of his imagination. **A Tunnel is Only a Hole on its Side**, book II of the Hole Trilogy was published in 2013. Book III of the Hole Trilogy — **Marmite Makes a Sandwich, Dynamite Makes a Hole**, was released in 2021.

The book, **The Unexpected Consequences of Iron Overload** was explicitly written to raise awareness of Haemochromatosis — a genetic condition he inherited.

More recently, James is focused on the importance of values in child development. To this end, he's written an eight-book series **Billy Growing Up** for children and parents.

Websites: www.jamesminter.com
E-Mail: james@jamesminter.com
Amazon Author Page: amazon.com/author/jamesminter
Goodreads: www.goodreads.com/james_minter
X (Twitter): @james_minter
Facebook: www.facebook.com/author.james.minter

OTHER WORKS BY JAMES MINTER

A Tunnel is Only a Hole on its Side, Book II of the Hole Trilogy

Book II and sequel to the well-received *The Hole Opportunity*, sees Colin striving to build on his business success by turning his attention to supplying even larger holes.

The town of Harpsden is to get a bypass; the proposed route cuts directly across the golf course. After much local objection led by the Golf Club Captain, Major Woods, a compromise route is drawn up involving a half-mile tunnel section under the fairways. The contract for the tunnel is, in Colin's eyes, a perfect way to grow his hole business since a tunnel is only a hole on its side!

With no love lost between the Major and Colin, the ensuing debacle spawns a host of hilarious situations, scrapes and misunderstandings including the resurgence of stocking wearing but this time not by Colin.

Marmite Makes a Sandwich, Dynamite Makes a Hole, Book III of the Hole Trilogy

In an utterly shocking twist to the national news cycle, not one, not two, but fifteen never-before-seen drawings by Constable have been unearthed. The art world is in a frenzy, but so is George, the boss of a south London gang notorious for their...uh...fondness for bank robberies.

Now, George isn't one to appreciate fine art. But what he does appreciate is an opportunity to make some quick cash. He thinks to himself, "Why tussle with city security when you can have a countryside jaunt?" Thus, an audacious plan is hatched.

A quick internet search leads George to Griggs Hole Farming. Here, he stumbles upon Colin, a man with an unusual set of skills. Colin, it turns out, is an expert hole-maker. No, not a burglar, not a digger—just a guy who makes really, really good holes. George reckons that this is just the kind of talent he needs to sneak into the local Lloyds bank.

But Colin's in a pickle. His commitment to the local community which he's been a part of for decades pulls at his heartstrings. Yet, the pressure applied to his wife, Izzy, leaves Colin with no choice.

And then, there's the matter of the stockings. If you thought bank heists and stockings were a cliché, think again. Because this time, it isn't just Colin squeezing into a pair of tights. Seems like the entire gang's going for a new fashion statement.

Billy Growing Up,
An Eight Book Series for 7 to 9-year-olds.

Billy and his friends are at that unique stage where childhood meets young adulthood. They're trying to figure out a world that's brimming with opportunities, but also comes with its fair share of contradictions and challenges. Every step they take towards becoming responsible adults is influenced by the values they pick up along the way.

In their younger years, kids often look to their parents as their primary role models. But something shifts around the age of eight. Suddenly, there's this urge to explore, a desire for independence, and a new-found ability to interpret feelings and experiences on their own terms. It's like they're carving out their very own place in the world.

That's where the "Billy" series steps in, aligning with the idea of Values-based Education (VbE) introduced by Dr. Neil Hawkes. The heart of VbE? It's all about setting kids up for a successful life by helping them embrace positive values, not just for the moment but for the long haul. The Billy books tap into the age-old power of storytelling, contrasting not-so-great choices with their brighter counterparts. It's all about showing kids the big picture when it comes to values.

For parents, guardians, and educators (especially those diving into PSHE Key Stage 2), these books are gold. They tackle the real issues young folks are dealing with but do so with a gentle, story-driven touch. By setting challenges and solutions within relatable tales, it offers kids a fresh way to see things. Plus, these books are great conversation starters, making those tricky talks between adults and kids a bit easier.

The Unexpected Consequences
of Iron Overload

A Paranormal, Romantic, Humorous, Thriller written to raise awareness of the life-threatening condition – Haemochromatosis.

Iron Overload, or as the pros call it, Genetic Haemochromatosis (GH), isn't just some medical jargon—it's been my companion all my life. It might not be the talk of the town or the star of the evening news, but as we all age (like fine wine, I'd say), its effects become more pronounced in the general population.

Now, why did I write this book? To shine a spotlight on GH and give a standing ovation to the Haemochromatosis Society. And I thought, why not add a dash of humour to the mix? After all, laughter is that wonderful elixir that's not just free but comes without any "Terms & Conditions" (and absolutely zero side effects!). So, I've woven together a thrilling paranormal spoof with a side of romance. I like to think of it as a full-course meal for the soul!

Get ready for a delightful ride of quintessential British humour—think awkward moments, hilarious misunderstandings, and all sorts of comic shenanigans. It's a hearty chuckle with an underlying earnest note. Cheers to that!

Printed by Amazon Italia Logistica S.r.l.
Torrazza Piemonte (TO), Italy

52799882R00261